DE[

Dunk Hoffnung has tasted success on the football field after his team, the Bad Bay Hackers, competed at the very highest level of Blood Bowl. But Dunk soon reconsiders his playing career after half of the team are killed in a match against the Chaos All Stars. Never being one to admit defeat, the Hackers Coach insists that the team must get back on the horse, so they find themselves heading to the mist-shrouded land of Albion to compete in the Albion Cup. Can the Hackers beat the odds and win or will the pressures and distractions of fame get in their way?

A BLOOD BOWL NOVEL

DEAD BALL

Matt Forbeck

Dedicated to my brother Mark and my sisters Kim and Jody, for a childhood filled with sports and fights

Special Thanks to Marc Gascoigne, Jervis Johnson, Lindsey Priestley, and (most especially) Christian Dunn

A BLACK LIBRARY PUBLICATION

First published in Great Britain in 2005 by
BL Publishing,
Games Workshop Ltd.,
Willow Road, Nottingham,
NG7 2WS, UK.

10 9 8 7 6 5 4 3 2 1

Cover illustration by Max Bertolini.

A CIP record for this book is available from the British Library.

ISBN 13: 978 184416 201 7
ISBN 10: 1 84416 201 X

Distributed in the US by Simon & Schuster
1230 Avenue of the Americas, New York, NY 10020, US.

Printed and bound in Great Britain by
Bookmarque, Surrey, UK.

See the Black Library on the Internet at
www.blacklibrary.com

Find out more about the world of Blood Bowl at
www.specialist-games.com/bloodbowl

'Hi there, sports fans, and welcome to the Blood
Bowl for tonight's contest. You join us here with
a capacity crowd, packed with members of every
race from across the known world, all howling like
banshees in anticipation of tonight's game. Oh, and
yes there are some banshees... Well, kick-off is in
about two pages' time, so we've just got time to
go over to your commentator for tonight, Jim
Johnson, for a recap on the rules of the game
before battle commences. Good evening, Jim!'

'Thank you, Bob! Well, good evening and boy, are
you folks in for some great sporting entertain-
ment. First of all though, for those of you at
home who are unfamiliar with the rules, here's
how the game is played.

'Blood Bowl is an epic conflict between two
teams of heavily armed and quite insane warriors.
Players pass, throw and run with the ball,
attempting to get it to the other end of the field,
the end zone. Of course, the other team must try
and stop them, and recover the ball for their side.
If a team gets the ball over the line into the
opponents' end zone it's called a touchdown; the
team that scored the most touchdowns by the end
of the match wins the game. Of course, it's not
always as simple as that...'

# CHAPTER ONE

THE LAST THING that went through Henrik Karl-mann's head was the spike on the front of the football.

Dunkel 'Dunk' Hoffnung, star thrower for the Bad Bay Hackers, stood close enough to Henrik to catch the lineman when he fell. The ball juddered from Henrik's forehead on its long, sharp tip. His dead eyes were crossed, still trying to focus on the thing that had killed him, his arms caught halfway up to where they would have been needed to save his life.

'And Karlmann's down!' Bob Bifford's voice echoed through the stadium via the Preternatural Announcement system, magically audible over the near-deafening roar of the crowd. 'Ooh, Jim, that's going to leave a mark!'

'More like a marker, Bob – over his grave!'

'That's already three in the kill column for the Chaos All-Stars today, Jim. Do you think they could break their team record?'

'To do that, they'd have to top their TPK from the Chaos Cup playoffs against the Stunted Stoutfellows. The Hackers are a bit tougher than halflings at least.'

'I always thought it should be TOK for Total Opponent Kill, Jim.'

'Well, Harry "The Hammer" Kehry coined the phrase back in 2482, and he never could spell. When he said 'Total 'Ponent Kill', would you argue with him?'

'Not unless I wanted to end up like poor Karlmann there. Let's hope the Hackers have a generous funeral insurance plan. It looks like they're going to get a lot of use out of it.'

Dunk's silvery eyes took one look up at Chthton – the octopus-armed beast that had thrown the bullet-like ball at his friend – and snarled. In one swift move, he snatched the ball from his fallen friend's forehead and tucked it under his arm, taking care not to stab himself on its bloodied spikes. With the slavering, tentacled beast in the all-black helmet and jersey bearing down on him, Dunk had no time to get rid of the ball by passing it downfield. First, he had to scramble clear.

Dunk jinked to the left then broke right, but the Chaos-tainted Chthton spread his tentacles wide. One of them wrapped around Dunk's arm as he tried to dash past, its wet, puckered cups adhering to Dunk's shoulder pad and holding fast.

Dunk heard the fluid from Chthton's tentacle flowing down his armour, sizzling as it went. Where it dripped off the shoulder pad onto his bare bicep, it burned like a red-hot brand. The second-year thrower howled in pain and pulled on the hard-stuck tentacle like an ox hauling a plough.

Chthton snorted something green and wet as he pulled back against Dunk, and the young Hacker felt his forward progress grind to a halt. He looked back at the warped creature and growled in pain, anger, and frustration. If he didn't break free of Chthton soon – if the creature managed to tackle him – this game might be his last.

A thin hand shot out and hacked down at the tentacle, cutting it in half. As Chthton fell backward, blood spurting from the maimed stump of its arm, Dunk stared at his saviour.

Gigia Mardretti stood nearly as tall as Dunk's six feet. Long, black hair cascaded from beneath her golden helmet, on the side of which a green, block H was emblazoned, overlaid with three crossed swords that followed the lines of the letter. Blood ran down her arm where it had sliced through the overstretched tentacle. She bore a satisfied little grin on her ruby-painted lips.

The blade embedded in the edge of Gigia's gloves was illegal in Blood Bowl. In this sport, the players – and their armour, and maybe the ball – were supposed to be the weapons. Using anything else in the course of a match broke the rules.

Not that anyone paid much attention to the rules, including the referees. Perhaps especially the refs, who seemed to have taken their dangerous jobs just so they could solicit large bribes. Some sold themselves to both sides, their loyalties swapping back and forth faster than they could pocket their money.

'Thanks!' Dunk said as he spun to face back toward the All-Stars' end of the field. Henrik had fallen deep in the Hacker's territory, and now Dunk stared down eighty yards of Chaos-infested Astrogranite standing between him and the goal line.

A pair of All-Star blitzers came stampeding down the field toward Dunk as he cut right, looking for some daylight. None of his team-mates were open downfield, so he sprinted to the right, hoping to find some blockers or at least keep out of the blitzers' grasp until he could get rid of the ball.

'Would you look at that human run?' Bob's voice thundered over the PA. 'He looks like a halfling being told mealtime's almost over!'

'You'd run for your life too if the All-Stars had the kind of grudge against you that they have for poor Hoffnung,' said Jim. 'Don't you remember what happened when they met in the Chaos Cup finals last year?'

'How could I ever forget? It's not often you see someone kill the opposing team's captain in the middle of halftime. Not to say that players don't try it all the time, but to succeed, that's something else.'

'Especially against a mutant minotaur like Schlitz 'Malty' Likker. That bull had a six-pack of horns that could open most players up like a keg of ale. What was Hoffnung's defence again?'

Dunk tried to shut out the blather coming over the PA. None of that mattered now. The Hackers had lost that game, and it had been over six months ago. In the world of Blood Bowl, that was a dozen lifetimes past – maybe more if you added in how many players the Hackers had lost just today.

Lars Englehard stepped up between Dunk and the two All-Stars on his tail. The lineman lowered his shoulders and took out both of them at once. It wasn't until Dunk heard Lars start to scream that he wondered if the All-Stars weren't really after the ball anyway.

'I think Hoffnung said that Malty was "possessed by a daemon," Bob said with a laugh. Jim joined in.

'I think half the All-Stars on the field today might meet that criteria. And what about Nurgle's Rotters?'

'Too true, Jim. If we start removing players for any kind of possession, we won't have many teams left!'

As Dunk stiff-armed a goat-headed blitzer wearing a carved-up All-Stars' helmet, he thought perhaps that wouldn't be such a bad idea. The game was lethal enough without adding daemons from hellish realms of Chaos into the mix.

The goat-man's horns sprang forward and clamped around Dunk's forearm like the jaws of a tiger. His vambrace there protected his flesh from being torn away, but when he tried to pull his arm free he discovered he was caught. The goat-headed creature bleated in low, guttural glee as it raked at Dunk's face with its arms, which ended in cloven hooves.

Dunk swung his free arm around and stabbed the spiked ball up under the goat-man's chin with desperate strength. The horns fell slack as the All-Star went silent and slid off Dunk's hand.

'Now that's a turnabout for you,' Bob said. 'Hoffnung gets free, and the Hackers chalk up their first kill for the day.'

'That ball's getting a lot of action out there today, Bob. I'm glad to see they brought "Ol' Spikey" back for the *Spike! Magazine* playoffs. Believe it or not, some people complain that a ball like that makes the games too deadly.'

Bob scoffed at Jim. 'That's like saying you can have too much Bloodweiser after the game. Wait, I didn't think we were talking about what happened to you last night. I don't think I've ever seen an ogre that tipsy.'

'That's not fair,' Jim said. 'Vampires like you can't get drunk.'

'Right,' Bob said sadly. 'Now *that's* unfair.'

'Such is unlife.'

Free from the goat-man, Dunk scrambled back to his left, saw two more All-Stars blocking that way, and dropped back to his right again. Then he saw what he wanted: an open Hacker downfield.

Percival Smythe stood near the end zone in his green and gold uniform, sweeping his arms up and down in the universal signal for 'I'm wide open!'

Dunk cocked back his arm and hurled the ball down the length of the field. It flew in a perfect spiral, the spikes spinning around its sides like a set of lethal wheels. Dunk wondered, not for the first time, how anyone could catch a pass like that without getting killed, but thankfully that was Percy's problem, not his.

'Oh, that's a beautiful pass!' Bob's voice said. 'And not an All-Star within 10 yards of Smythe!'

'Yeah,' Jim said, 'but do you see Mackey?'

Dunk glared down the field and wondered what the announcers were talking about. Mackey Maus was the All-Stars' new team captain, the one who'd taken over after Likker's death, but he wasn't anywhere near Percy. No one was.

The crowd, scores of thousands strong, roared as the ball sailed into Percy's grasp. The noise drowned out anything else, so he didn't hear the footfalls of the player who came up behind him and slammed him into the Astrogranite.

'Hackers score!' Bob's voice said, his magically enhanced voice ringing out over din.

Dunk would have cheered, but he found that he couldn't breathe. The player on top of him had driven the air from his lungs. He tried to push himself up on his arms, and something hit him hard in the back of the head. If not for his helmet, the blow would have caved in his skull. As it was, he felt the metal protecting his cranium dent in and dig into his scalp. Stars danced before his eyes.

'Enjoy those cheers,' Dunk's attacker shouted, 'until I tear off your ears!'

A long, sharp talon reached under Dunk's neck and slashed at his throat. He felt something give and then wetness. Adrenaline coursed through Dunk's veins, despite the fact he thought it was too late. He had to be dead already, but his body just didn't know it.

In one desperate move, Dunk wrenched his body around. As he did, his helmet came off, and he realised that it was its leather strap he'd felt giving way. The cut on his neck burned, but the hope that it was only superficial surged in his heart.

The creature atop Dunk managed to maintain its position, even while the young thrower squirmed beneath him. It glared down at him from behind a greasy-furred, rat-like snout poking out through the open face of its jet-black helmet. Its ebony eyes glittered with madness as glowing, green spittle dripped from its long, narrow muzzle filled with short, sharp teeth. Dunk recognised the spitting-mad beastman instantly: Mackey, the Chaos-mutated skaven who'd been taking cheap shots at him all day.

Throughout it all, Dunk had tried to tell himself it was nothing personal. Death and dismemberment was all part of the game. Maybe it wasn't legal by the rules, but people expected it. The fans, the coaches, the players, they all expected it.

Even the referees expected it. They didn't haul the killers off and throw them in jail. They just hit them with a penalty.

But when a blood-parched, mutant skaven sat on top of Dunk and drooled something green and vis-cous on to his face, where it stung and burned like fire, he had his doubts.

'Don't let them get to you, son.' Dunk's agent, a rotund halfling by the name of Slick Fullbelly, had said the same thing to him over and over. 'It's their job to try to put you down, just as it's yours to do the same to them. The trick is to do unto others *before* they do unto you. It's nothing personal, for you or them. Remember that.'

'This one's for Schlitzy,' Mackey said as he raked down with his long, filth-caked claws. 'Say hi to him for me in hell!'

Faster than he could think, Dunk's hands snapped up and caught Mackey by the wrists. He held the skaven's arms out away from him, the tips of his talons only inches from Dunk's face.

The crowd booed, hissing at the All-Star. It was one thing to kill someone while the ball was in play. Watching mayhem like that happen was a good part of why most of the fans showed up to the games. The chance to be spattered with warm blood proved too much for them to pass up.

After a score, though, it was time for the gridiron warriors to return to their respective corners, to lick their wounds until it was time to face each other again. To violate that understanding was more than just breaking the rules. Players chewed up the rulebook and spat it out during every game.

To try to kill someone during one of these few down moments, though, was known as a dead ball foul. Few fans would tolerate this worst kind of cheating. Not even the best-bribed referees could afford to ignore so flagrant a foul.

So the crowd cheered when Dunk sat up hard and bashed his forehead into Mackey's sneering mouth. He felt teeth snap and flesh shred in the skaven's mouth, and when he drew back, blood, mucous, and the creature's glowing saliva coated his own forehead.

Dunk tried to shove Mackey off, but the skaven snapped down at him instead, trying to savage him with its broken front teeth. To keep himself from the creature's reach, Dunk fell back again. When his head hit the Astrogranite, though, he knew he had nowhere else left to go.

Panicked, Dunk pressed up against Mackey again, trying to throw him off, but the skaven, mad with pain, refused to relent for a moment. He used his weight to press down against Dunk's arms, lowering his snapping, bloodied snout inch by inch toward Dunk's exposed neck.

Dunk tried to swing his legs up and throw the skaven over his head, but Mackey's legs clamped around his waist like iron bands. Those jaws of his kept getting lower and lower.

Mackey had Dunk's arms pressed hard against his chest now. The Hacker thrower tried to butt the skaven with his head again, but he couldn't get the momentum to do more than annoy the insane beast.

Mackey chortled at this, coughing and snorting up blood and mucous that dripped through his shattered teeth. He shoved his snout down at Dunk's neck, but the thrower managed to deflect the skaven's nose with his chin. Quick as a snake, Mackey forced his sopping-wet snout past Dunk's cheek and began to pry the Hacker's chin up with the end of his pointed nose.

'Stop it!' Dunk said, unable to think of anything else to do. Where were the referees when you needed them? Probably they didn't want to get involved in the middle of a mortal combat like this. It was one thing to give out a penalty to someone who committed a foul. It was something else entirely to risk your life trying to get between two trained and armoured Blood Bowl players.

Mackey responded by snuffling its nostrils against the underside of Dunk's jawline.

'Hey!' Dunk shouted. 'Not on a first date!'

'Your blood.' Mackey growled softly into Dunk's ear. 'It smells delicious.'

At times like this, Dunk sometimes wished he was a praying man. He'd seen enough of the fickleness of the gods to know that using your last breath calling on them was a waste. Still, nothing else more useful came to mind either.

Dunk tried to think of something pithy, some last words that would sting his killer or at least give the world a reason to remember him. The jagged touch of the creature's teeth pressing down over his jugular vein, though, forced everything but blind panic from his head.

Dunk gritted his teeth and closed his eyes. As he did, he found images of Spinne Schönheit whirling through his mind. The beautiful catcher for the Reikland Reavers had only been dating him for a few months, but he already knew that he loved her with all his heart, that he wanted to marry her, to have kids, to grow old. Now none of that would happen – growing old, most of all.

Dunk felt Mackey spread his teeth, readying himself for the bite that would end Dunk's life. He felt the skaven's acidic drool burn its way around his throat as if preparing the way for the mortal wound.

His eyes still closed, Dunk felt Mackey's face draw back, and he stiffened for the final blow. Instead, he heard a sickening snap and felt Mackey's grip on him fall slack.

Dunk peeled one eye open and then the other to find a massive creature towering over him. He stood over eight feet tall and massed at least four hundred pounds, twice the size of Dunk. Polished tusks jutted from his lower jaw, and a golden ring the size of a bracelet hung like a doorknocker from the septum of his broken nose.

The ogre peered down at Dunk, Mackey's head in one hand and his body in the other, hot blood pouring from them both.

The crowd went nuts. The cheers were so loud Dunk wondered if his ears might bleed.

'Dunkel okay?' the ogre said, concern furrowing his massive brow as he let the separate parts of what had once been Mackey drop to the Astrogranite.

'I am now, big guy,' Dunk said as he took the ogre's hand and let the creature haul him to his feet. 'Thanks, M'Grash.'

As Dunk wiped Mackey's blood, snot, and spit from himself, a tall, thin orc in a black-and-white striped shirt ran up and threw something at M'Grash: a sack of sand wrapped in a long, yellow ribbon of cloth. It fluttered to the ground after bouncing off the ogre's chest.

'I don't believe it!' Bob's voice said over the PA. 'They're going to call a penalty on K'Thragsh!'

The crowd's cheers turned to boos. Dunk started to shout something at the referee, but the official just waved him off. Then the orc stood to face the announcer's box and crossed his arms in an X over his head. Then he pointed to M'Grash.

'Holy Nuffle's battered balls!' Bob said. 'It's a dead ball foul on M'Grash!'

'What's the penalty going to be?' asked Jim.

The ref pulled back his hand and then stabbed his finger to point out over the top rows of the stadium.

'He's kicking M'Grash K'Thragsh out of the game!'

'Oh, the crowd doesn't like this, Jim.'

Dunk put his hand on M'Grash's arm and felt the ogre flex his muscles. They were like steel.

The ref started to back-pedal as he watched M'Grash glare at him with his saucer-sized eyes. He put up his hands and flinched when the ogre snorted. The crowd went wild.

'Give! Him! To! Us!' the fans chanted. 'Give! Him! To! Us!'

The ref turned and sprinted away down the field.

'M'Grash,' Dunk said, trying to hold on to the ogre's arm. 'Don't do–'

Before he could finish, though, M'Grash tore free and lumbered after the fleeing ref with a stride twice as long as his prey's.

Dunk threw up his hands and decided to watch and enjoy the chase. 'They've already kicked him out of the game,' he said. 'What else can they do to him?'

CHAPTER TWO

CHAPTER TWO

'CAN YOU GET that through that thick excuse for a head you keep stitched on top of your shoulders?'

Dunk had rarely seen Captain Pegleg Haken, the head coach of the Hackers, so mad. The ex-pirate had the hook that stabbed from his left sleeve linked through M'Grash's nose ring and had pulled the ogre's face down to his so he could scream right into it.

'Sorry, coach,' M'Grash said, whimpering like a kicked puppy.

Dunk knew the ogre could kill Pegleg in an instant, just as he'd torn Mackey apart out on the field, but he also knew he wouldn't. To M'Grash, Pegleg stood at the right hand of Nuffle, the sacred god of Blood Bowl that most of the game's players and many of its fans worshipped. From the way most of the other players in the locker room pressed against the walls, trying to stay as far away from Pegleg's wrath as possible, Dunk guessed that M'Grash wasn't the only one who felt that way.

'Sorry isn't going to cut it!' Pegleg said. He gave the ogre's nose ring a last tweak and let it go from his hook. Then he turned to glare at the rest of the players. Sweat ran down his reddened face, and his eyes blazed with fury.

'What in Nuffle's name is wrong with the lot of you?' Pegleg asked. 'It's only halftime, and we've lost five players!' He shot a murderous look at the ogre. 'Besides M'Grash, we'll need funerals after the game for four of them!'

'Coach,' Dunk said, interrupting Pegleg's rant. He instantly regretted it. The temperature in the room seemed to drop from hot and bothered to ice-cold mean in the space of a second. No one moved, apparently frozen in place. Pegleg might have stopped shouting, but Dunk couldn't hear anyone else breathing, not even himself.

He glanced over at his agent, Slick Fullbelly, who stood hiding in the room's far corner. At only three feet tall, the rotund halfling seemed to be trying to hide under his unruly mop of curly dark hair. None of the other players' agents dared to come into the locker room for fear of incurring Pegleg's wrath. The coach considered most agents vermin and would as soon stab one as talk to him, but he tolerated Slick, who always walked around like he owned the place.

Pegleg turned to stare at Dunk; his eyes wide and amazed as if the young thrower had just had a second head sprout from his nose. 'Yes, Mr. Hoffnung?' he said with a formal smile that showed a gold tooth in the centre of his rotted teeth.

A shiver ran down Dunk's spine. Ever since the Blood Bowl finals last season, Pegleg had called him by his first name as a sign of the respect he'd worked so hard to earn.

Slick stared at Dunk in horror and mouthed a single word to him: 'Run.'

Dunk ignored the halfling's advice, even though a part of him wanted nothing more than to run screaming into the relative safety of the playing field. Instead, he met Pegleg's steely glare and spoke, taking care to not let his voice crack.

'Coach, they're killing us out there, literally. Maybe we should—' Dunk stopped here to swallow. 'Maybe we should call it a day.'

When Dunk stopped talking, the room fell silent. No one else breathed a word. For a moment, Dunk wondered if some horrible magic had frozen them all in place, including him. He thought of trying to test it, but he couldn't manage to convince his body of the promise the idea held.

Pegleg reached up with his hook and inserted it into his ear, where he screwed it around two or three times before taking it back out. 'Would you care to clarify that? I don't think I could have heard you properly.'

Dunk looked down at Pegleg's hook and saw blood smeared on it.

'Maybe.' He took a deep breath, 'Maybe we should forfeit.' He held up his hands as he heard everyone in the room gasp – everyone but Pegleg, who stood watching him like a statue.

'Coach, we've lost five players. That brings us down to eleven. If we lose another, we won't have enough left to field a team.'

'What, Mr. Hoffnung, is your point?' Pegleg reached up and wiped the stone-sharpened tip of his hook clean on his tricorn hat as he spoke. The blood left a dark red streak along the bright yellow crown.

'If we lose another player, we'll have to forfeit anyway, right? Since we've already lost five players in one half, I don't doubt–' Dunk cut himself short as he realised some of the other players, the ones not too terrified of Pegleg, were laughing. 'What?' he asked, flushing with anger. 'We're going to lose this match. Let's call it quits before another of us has to die.'

The rest of the players started to snigger, and soon the locker room shook with laughter. Pegleg had to sit down to hold his belly with his hook and wipe the tears from his face with his good hand.

'What?' Dunk asked. 'Are you all so jaded you don't care if one more of us dies before we lose the game?'

Rhett Cavre, a hard-muscled, dark-skinned man standing next to Pegleg, spoke. 'Dunk, you don't need eleven players to keep playing.' Cavre had been on the team longer than anyone and had become a legend on the Blood Bowl pitch. He also worked as the team's assistant coach and, when travelling by sea, Captain Haken's first mate. Dunk knew Cavre took the game as seriously as anyone, but he couldn't believe his own ears.

'You don't? But if we don't have at least eleven, they won't let us on the field, right? Remember that game in Kislev? We could barely get six of us on the field, and they made us forfeit the game.'

'That's because the rest of us were too hung over to move,' Percy said from a far corner of the room. Maybe the catcher was still riding high from his touchdown reception. Most days he'd have been too cautious to say something like that in Pegleg's presence.

'Damn that Bloodweiser they serve there,' Slick said, turning toward Pegleg to keep him from turning and plunging his hook into Percy's chest. 'They call it by the same name, but it's not. They've been brewing that stuff in the same cauldrons for a thousand years, and it's strong enough to bring an ogre to his knees.'

M'Grash let loose a whimper at the thought of the hangover he'd endured that day. It had taken three men to pull his head out of the bog.

'Blüdvar, the Kislevites call it. Translates into "Blood War", I think.'

Slick's voice trailed off as he noticed Pegleg looming over him like the shadow of death, his eyes trying to burn holes down through the halfling's head, straight to his furry, unshod toes.

'Anyway, son,' Slick said, scurrying toward Dunk to get out of range of Pegleg's hook, 'you only need eleven players to *start* the game.'

Dunk stared at the halfling for a moment, and then glanced over at Pegleg. The captain wore a grim look on his face that Dunk could not read.

'But, coach,' Dunk said, 'how many people are we willing to lose before we – well, before we give up?'

Pegleg hobbled over on his good leg and the wooden stump that sprouted from the bottom of his right knee. Standing as tall as Dunk, he stared deep into the young thrower's eyes. His were the blue of the open sea, filled with the wisdom of his years but deep and hidden all the same. Although his voice was rough and low, it carried throughout the room as if he spoke over the stadium's PA system.

'This is the nature of the game, Dunk. Some teams play to score points. Others play to kill.'

'What about us?'

'We play to win.'

Dunk swallowed hard, and then nodded, never taking his eyes from Pegleg's.

A tiny snotling, a goblin-like creature only half the size of Slick, poked his head into the locker room and said, 'One minute until the second half.' His high-pitched voice sounded like that of a child with a bad cold, but no one laughed.

The snotling peered around the room at the Hackers' sombre faces. 'You always have such rousing halftime speeches?' he said.

Pegleg snatched off his hat and hurled it at the little, green-skinned creature. It sailed toward him, spinning like a disc, and smacked into him with a non-hat-like *thunk*. The snotling let out a little 'Eep!' and dropped to the ground unconscious.

'I've hit my limit today for stupid questions,' the coach roared as he spun around to glare at each of his players in turn. 'The next person to ask one will think the snotling got off easy. Now let's get out there and win this damned game!'

Dunk charged past the coach and led the way out on to the field.

* * *

IN THE MIDDLE of the second half, Dunk threw another touchdown pass to Otto Waltheim, one of the Hackers' best catchers. The score put the Hackers ahead of the All-Stars, three to nothing, but after the catch an All-Star with an octopus for a head knocked Otto into the stands.

Dunk and the other Hackers could do no more than watch as the fans grabbed Otto and passed him up to the top edge of the stadium and pitched him over. The same thing had happened to Dunk in last year's *Spike! Magazine* tournament, and he'd survived only by the sheer luck of tearing through a series of awnings before landing on a food vendor's cart. By the way the crowd roared again soon after they tossed poor Otto over the edge, Dunk guessed his team-mate hadn't been so fortunate.

As Dunk and the remaining Hackers lined up to kick the ball, he allowed himself a quick headcount. Only ten Hackers were left. There were three catchers: Gigia Mardretti, Percival Smythe, and Simon Sherwood; three blitzers: Andreas Waltheim, Milo Hoffstetter, and Rhett Cavre; and three linemen: Kai Albrecht, Karsten Klemmer, and Guillermo Reyes. Dunk, the only thrower left, made ten. M'Grash was the only player left on the sideline, and he'd been banned from the game.

Milo kicked the ball, and the rest of the team raced down the field to take it away from the All-Stars. As Dunk sprinted along next to Guillermo, he smelled something dark and pungent that made him want to cough. Downfield, he spied a plume of smoke coming from the area where the ball had landed.

'What are those Chaos cultists burning down there?' Dunk asked Guillermo, but the big, bearded Estalian just shrugged his shoulders.

'Smells like oil,' Guillermo said. Then a loud buzzing noise, like the sound of a hive of angry, giant bees, came from the same direction. 'Sounds like mayhem.'

With all the players still between him and the ball, Dunk couldn't see what was going on. Kick-offs often ended up in pile-ups of players that sometimes had to be pried apart before the game could continue.

Then the screaming started, and the crowd went wild.

'Did you see that, Bob?' Jim's voice rang out over the loudspeakers. 'I think I saw an arm come flying out of that scrum down there.'

'It could have been a leg – or a tentacle. It's hard to tell from here. Let's take a look at the Jumboball image at the end of the field, brought to us by Wolf Sports, the top name in Cabalvision broadcasting. And I'm not just saying that because they sign our cheques!'

'No, the network's Censer Wizards make sure of that. Nothing like the threat of being roasted over a crucible filled with red-hot coals to motivate an on-air personality, eh?'

Dunk shaded his eyes to glance up at the twenty-foot-tall crystal ball mounted over the rim of the stadium's west end. It hadn't been there last year, but he'd heard that Wolf Sports had installed it to show the fans in the stadium what they were missing at home.

The Jumboball didn't produce any sound, but the screams still threatened to pierce Dunk's ears as he and Guillermo stampeded toward the pile. In the Jumboball, Dunk saw a close-up image of the stack of players piled over the ball. The players in the pile would normally all be jabbing and stabbing at each other, trying to inflict an injury that a referee wouldn't be able to see. Now, though, smoke and a reddish mist that could only be blood obscured most of the view. On the edges of the pile, Dunk saw the Hacker players trying to break free while the All-Stars pulled them back into the pink smoke.

The buzzing from inside the pile grew to a roar as Dunk charged into the fray. Then a dwarf in Chaos All-Stars armour burst from the smoke, madness pirouetting in his wide, ice-blue eyes. These were the only things that showed clearly under the splattered blood and gore that coated the front of the dwarf's armour and his face and bushy beard in a thick layer of red.

Something horrible growled in the dwarf's hands, the like of which Dunk had never seen before. It stretched from the Chaos-tainted creature's hands the length of a sword, but its handle roared like a dragon and belched black smoke into the air. The edge of the sword's blade bore three-inch long serrations shaped like a manticore's teeth, and they carried bits of bone and gristle caught between them.

The dwarf cranked something on the weapon's handle, and the serrations began to move. They started slow but soon spun around the edge of the blade so fast they became a blur of crimson and steel.

'Nuffle's holy gridiron!' Bob's voice said over the PA. 'It's Gimlet the Lost, and he's got a chainsaw!'

Somewhere, Dunk heard a whistle as a referee called the play dead, but he knew it wouldn't matter. From the look in Gimlet's eyes, he wasn't going to let anything stop him until he ran out of fuel, and the chainsaw – if that's what that thing was – seemed fully loaded.

Dunk gave Guillermo a shove and pointed for the lineman to circle to Gimlet's right. Without looking to see if Guillermo complied, Dunk veered left, hoping to catch Gimlet in a pincer move. He hoped this might confuse the blood-drenched dwarf, but if it didn't at least it would mean he could only attack one of them at a time.

Gimlet swung his chainsaw in a wide circle, trying to gore both of the Hackers as they came at him. The blade missed Dunk, but it caught Guillermo on the side of the helmet and sent him sprawling. Gimlet followed up on the attack, raising the chainsaw over his head as he stomped after the downed lineman.

With Gimlet's back to him, Dunk charged at the All-Star and tried to tackle him. He wrapped his arms around the dwarf, but he could not bring him down. It was like trying to tackle a rock. His grasp kept the dwarf's arms trapped close to his body, but Gimlet kept marching forward, step-by-step, dragging Dunk along behind him like an overlong cloak, until he stood over Guillermo's body.

Dunk peered over Gimlet's shoulder to see that the dwarf's first blow had cracked open the lineman's helmet and spilled out the contents like a rotten egg.

Gimlet cackled with mad glee and began to bring his hands up, angling his wrists so that the chainsaw pointed back over his shoulder, straight toward Dunk's own helmet.

As the chainsaw's buzzing blade came lower and lower, the sound almost drowning out the shouts from the crowd, Dunk squeezed Gimlet harder and harder, trying to force the dwarf's hands back down. All he managed to do was slow the blade's inexorable progress. He had to try something else, fast.

Dunk wrapped his leg around to plant his foot in front of Gimlet's legs. The dwarf snorted, perhaps thinking Dunk only meant to try to squeeze him with his legs as well. Gimlet leaned forward harder, pushing the chainsaw back behind him as he did so. The whizzing blade met, screeching and sparking against Dunk's helmet.

Dunk let go with his arms, keeping his foot steady where it was. Freed from the Hacker's arms, Gimlet brought his blade back down in front of him and let out a wild laugh. As he tried to step forward, though, his feet met Dunk's booted foot, and he tripped.

Gimlet landed on his chainsaw face first. The blade screeched right through his exposed face and then his breastplate, digging its way through his hot, gurgling corpse.

The machine was still running when the referee came over and shut it off. The scene played over and over again in glorious crimson colour on the Jum boball high above them.

'Did you see that move, Jim? And the way that chainsaw parted Gimlet's armour? Amazing!'

'It sure is, Bob! It looks like Dunk Hoffnung, one of last year's most promising rookies, is taking charge of this game.'

'It's about – wait! What's this?'

Dunk looked up to see what the announcers were chatting about, and he saw a yellow penalty flag flutter over the Astrogranite and land at a bloodied player's feet. Then he looked down at the artificial turf before him. The flag sat right there.

'They've called a penalty against Hoffnung! Can you believe it?'

'Well, Jim, it's clear whose gold is lining the ref's pockets today. What's the call?'

'Illegal use of a weapon! The ref is accusing Hoffnung of using that chainsaw to kill Gimlet!'

'You can't do this!' Dunk screamed into the ref's face. He pointed down at Gimlet. 'It's his chainsaw. He killed all those people!'

The tall, thin elf sneered back at the Hacker. 'So you say. You see it your way, and I'll see it mine. But only mine counts.'

Rage threatened to explode Dunk's head from the inside. A red veil dropped down over his eyes, and the next thing he knew he found himself chasing the ref back up the field.

The crowd loved it.

CHAPTER THREE

DUNK NEVER CAUGHT up with the referee. The dark elf ran with the grace of a gazelle – which probably explained how he'd survived so long as a referee – and Dunk's armour and injuries slowed him down. He kept pace with the ref until they reached the Hackers' end zone, on the opposite end of the field from all the carnage, but as he crossed the goal line his rage lost its battle with his legs, which refused to run any more.

Dunk bent over and grabbed his thighs as he tried to suck more air into his lungs. As he did so, the crowd booed. The fans had tasted plenty of blood today, but it had only made them hungry for more. To Dunk, it seemed they wanted the referee dead as much as he did.

'The crowd is not happy about this!' Jim said.

'No, Jim, they're not. I haven't seen a referee show such a blatant disregard for the rules and for any sense of fair play since the Athelorn Avengers played the Dwarf Giants.'

'Bob, that was only last week!'

Dunk raised his head and stared up at the Jumboball. Images of Gimlet's death flashed through it. Then he saw the referee racing away from him, thumbing his nose first at Dunk and then the crowd.

The sequence played through again, although more wobbly this time, and Dunk – enough air in his lungs at last – stood up to glare at the ref. He considered chasing after the corrupt dark elf again, but the way his vision had been shaking he didn't think he was up for it. As he stared at the ref, though, he realised there was nothing wrong with his vision.

'I think the fans have a plan for revenge here, Bob,' Jim's voice said.

'Sure,' Bob said, 'but do you think they've really thought this through?'

'They wouldn't be Blood Bowl fans if they had. Look at that Jumboball shake! The fans up there in the cheap seats are going to get more than nosebleeds if they keep that up!'

Dunk peered up at the far end zone and saw the Jumboball juddering like – well, like the spiked football had in Henrik's head. A sense of dread filled him, but before he could give it voice, the wooden stand that held the boulder-sized crystal gave way with a crack he could hear clear across the stadium.

The ball hung there in the air for a moment before spilling forward onto the people standing in the seats beneath it.

The crowd howled in pain and fear as the ball began to roll down the inside of the stadium's bowl, crushing both the slower fans and the stands from which they sought to scramble. It picked up speed as it went, and it reached the Astrogranite in mere, bloody seconds, busting through the low restraining wall meant to keep the fans from making easy grabs at unwary players.

When the Jumboball entered the All-Stars' end zone, the players still stuck in the remnants of the pile-up around the ball realised something was wrong. Dunk saw Gigia stand up and try to pull a wounded Milo out of the massive thing's rolling path, but he was too injured to do more than slow her down. Andreas tried to pitch in to help, but he only doomed himself as well. The red-stained crystal smashed all three Hackers beneath its rolling bulk.

A number of the All-Stars went down too, as the Jumboball didn't take sides in this, the first game it had ever entered. It just kept rolling along, oblivious to the destruction it left in its wake.

Dunk peered past the ball, forgetting the treacherous referee in the face of this new threat. He saw Cavre and Simon racing away from the ball, running north, toward the Hackers' dugout. With any luck, they would be safe.

In the centre of the field, Karsten and Guillermo sprinted toward Dunk at top speed. If they were hoping to outrun the monstrous crystal ball, it seemed they were doomed to lose. The two linemen realised this and turned right, heading toward the All-Stars' dugout.

Dunk breathed a sigh of relief and started for the Hackers' dugout himself. First he headed north, planning to hug the edge of the field to keep as far from the Jumboball's path as he could.

To Dunk's amazement, the Jumboball veered off to the left, forging a new path that would intercept Karsten and Guillermo long before they made it to the relative safety of the All-Stars' dugout. Dunk was sure that any Hackers who literally landed in their foes' laps were in for a savage beating, but at least they'd survive that. Probably.

Dunk shouted a warning to Karsten and Guillermo, but the roar of the crowd at the Jumboball's abrupt change of course drowned out any hope of his friends hearing him. Despite this, the two Hackers glanced back to see where the Jumboball was and found it hot on their tail. Guillermo shoved Karsten to the left and took off to the right himself, splitting them so that the Jumboball would pass between them and roll right into the All-Stars' dugout.

This dugout, like the Hackers', featured a set of steps that led down into the ground. Tall players standing on the broad floor could look out over the field at about eye level. Others could achieve the same effect by climbing a few steps.

A concrete roof angled back to protect the occupants of the dugout from the fans in the stands behind it. Riots seemed to break out in just about every game, and when they did the players could dive right into their dugouts to avoid thrown beer steins, rotten tomatoes, and even rusty knives.

Dunk wondered if the roof would be enough to stop the Jumboball. Or would the massive sphere crush the structure and everyone in it? As much as he hated to see people die, a part of him felt that if any team deserved such carnage it was the Chaos All-Stars.

The Jumboball ground to a halt before it reached the dugout. It hesitated there for a moment and then veered left.

'Wow! Have you ever seen anything like that, Bob? Talk about playing on an unlevel field.'

'Uh, no. Never! It seems like that rogue Jumboball has a mind of its own.'

Dunk wondered for a moment if he was seeing things. Then he spotted a familiar face in the All-Stars' dugout: Schlechter Zauberer.

Dunk had last seen the middle-aged wizard at last year's Chaos Bowl, in the middle of the same game at which he'd killed the bull-headed Likker. He wore the same midnight-blue robes with bluish-white piping that highlighted their edges, and the same polished silver skullcap that glinted in the midday sun. He waved a wand that resembled the blackened thigh-bone of some large bird, and the Jumboball followed his gestures.

Although Dunk had almost made it to the safety of the Hackers' dugout, he saw only one course of action. He sprinted across the gridiron to rip Zauberer's wispy white beard off his receding chin.

'Dunk!' Pegleg called after him. 'Get back here, damn your meaty legs!'

The thrower ignored his coach's pleas, pretending he couldn't hear them over the crowd. It wasn't hard to do.

As Dunk neared the All-Stars' dugout, a pair of benchwarmers leapt from the dugout and charged at him. The first, a twisted lizardman bearing two massive tails, threw back its head and hissed a challenge at Dunk. A pair of eyeballs twisted on the end of its long, sinuous tongue as it slipped in and out of its toothy maw.

The second creature worried Dunk more. The stone-skinned troll stood twice as tall as the Hacker and bore spike-knuckled fists, each as large as Dunk's head. It bellowed at the thrower as it lumbered toward him, smashing holes in the Astrogranite for emphasis.

The crowd cheered. Dunk glanced to his left to see Karsten's flattened remains come slipping off the backside of the Jumboball, which had just run him over. The ball came to a halt, then backed up, running over Karsten again and heading straight for Dunk.

Dunk looked back toward the All-Stars' dugout and saw that the lizardman and troll were coming at him like a pair of runaway battlewagons. He turned and ran in the other direction. Zauberer would have to wait.

For a moment, Dunk thought he had a chance. Despite the troll's long strides, he could outrun him in a fair race. The lizardman, though, wasn't going to give Dunk a chance. The lizardman couldn't run any faster than Dunk, but he was fresh off the bench. Dunk's legs felt like he wore lead anklets that became heavier with every step.

And then there was the Jumboball.

'This is amazing, Bob,' Jim's voice said. 'Hoffnung seemed to be hunting for an epic death with his charge into the All-Stars' dugout, but at the last moment he lost his nerve.'

'It's one thing to die,' said Bob. 'As a vampire, I know all about it. It's something else to be torn to pieces and eaten. Chaos trolls like Krader there have been known to do that.'

'That's if Sseth Skinshucker doesn't get a hold of Dunk first. As we know from last year's Blood Bowl qualifying rounds, Sseth doesn't like to share.'

'I've never seen anyone swallow a halfling whole like that before. I understand it took him the better part of the week to digest poor Puddin Fatfellow.'

'True, although I hear the Greenfield Grasshuggers took longer than that to select a new captain!'

These words spurred Dunk on toward the All-Stars' end zone. As he leaped over the pile of dead bodies near where Gimlet fell, he heard a low rumbling noise under the maddening roar of the crowd. He glanced over his shoulder and saw the Jumboball bounce along over the corpses only a dozen feet behind him. Sseth and Krader had veered off to the south to give it room to pass, but they still kept pace.

'Ooh! It looks like the jaunty Jumboball is going to win that footrace instead, Jim.'

'It could be – but wait! We have a new entrant into the fray!'

Dunk snapped his head around to see what Bob could mean. As he did, he saw M'Grash come stampeding in from the Hackers' dugout and hurl himself into the Jumboball's spinning side.

Despite the ogre's size, the Jumboball stood more than twice his height. This didn't faze him for a moment. He lowered his shoulder and smashed his spiked spaulder flat into the massive crystal. A loud crack rolled through the stadium like instant thunder, and the ball's path skewed south.

Sseth leapt out of the way on his powerful haunches. To Dunk it looked like the lizardman's tail propelled him out of the way. The troll, however, wasn't so fortunate. Krader roared in protest before the Jumboball rolled over him, crushing him behind it as it smashed into the south stands.

Dunk skidded to a halt then ran back around to where M'Grash stood, holding his bruised shoulder. 'What did you think you were doing?' the thrower shouted. 'You could have been killed!'

To Dunk's surprise, the ogre blushed. 'Me sorry, Dunkel,' he said, lowering his eyes. 'Didn't want Dunkel to die.'

Dunk's heart fell. M'Grash had the brains – and the moral framework, sadly – of a two-year-old. He hadn't considered the risk to his own skin. He'd only known he had to save his friend's life.

Dunk clapped M'Grash on the arm. 'It's all right, M'Grash. Actually, it's better than that.' He leaned over to peer up into the ogre's weepy eyes. 'Thanks.'

'Mean it?' M'Grash said as he wiped his eyes, a half-proud smile spreading across his face.

The thrower nodded. 'Damn right. If not for you, I'd be– '

Dunk had to stop talking when Sseth's tail knocked him clear past the ogre to land face first atop the pile of chainsaw-savaged cadavers.

'Wow!' said Bob. 'You don't see cheap shots like that every – wait! Yes, I guess you do!'

'Too true, Bob,' said Jim, 'but that was a classic of the genre. The Cabalvision networks will be playing that one on the highlight feeds all week long.'

Dunk pushed himself to his knees, his battered back painfully protesting. He looked down and saw a body in a green and gold uniform beneath him. He had to squint, but it looked like Kai. Just three feet to his left, he spotted Percy's severed head staring out at him through his intact helmet.

To Dunk, this had long since stopped being a game.

He stood up and cheered as he saw M'Grash grab Sseth by his long, green-scaled tail. The ogre leaned back and started to spin around, swinging the lizard-man around by his extra appendage. After a half-dozen rotations, M'Grash let go and hurled Sseth right over the Jumboball and into the south stands.

'So, Jim, what do you think the chances are of Skin-shucker making it out of there alive?'

'If the Gobbo was here, he'd lay six to one odds, Bob. Ooh! It looks like the fans might be putting Skinshucker's last name to the test. That's gotta hurt! I haven't seen that many scales ripped off someone since my wife's last trip to the spa!'

Before Dunk could run over to M'Grash to congrat-ulate him, a sound like the bellow of a wounded dragon came from behind the Jumboball. The gigan-tic crystal dislodged from where it had come to rest against the crushed restraining wall separating the field from the stands. As it rolled to the right, Krader appeared from behind it, pushing himself up from where he'd fallen.

As Dunk watched, the troll's battered skin and broken bones reknit themselves together. The crowd gasped, then cheered with delight.

'With their regenerating powers, Bob, it's hard to keep a good troll down.'

'Or a bad one for that matter, Jim!'

Dunk looked down at his feet and spotted the end of the chainsaw sticking out through Gimlet's armoured corpse. It would certainly make a better weapon than the thrower's bare fists.

Dunk flipped Gimlet over and dragged the chainsaw out of his corpse. He'd never seen anything like this before, some strange amalgam of sorcery and alchemy, he guessed. Still, if a creature like Gimlet could run it, then perhaps Dunk could too.

He fumbled with the contraption for a moment until his hands found the proper grip on it. How had Gimlet turned the thing on? Dunk had been too far down the field to see the chainsaw start up.

'It looks like Hoffnung has decided turnabout is fair play, Bob.'

'Too bad no one engraved a set of instructions on the side of that thing!'

Dunk cursed and glared up at the announcers' box, high above the stadium's north flank. It was bad enough he couldn't figure out the damned thing without disembodied voices mocking him in front of thousands of people.

Then an odd thought struck Dunk. He turned the chainsaw over on its side. There, just under the left handle, someone had scratched a set of instructions: 'Grab left handle. Pull chain with right.'

Dunk looked at the serrated chain running along the outside of the blade. He couldn't imagine anyone would want to grab that to get the thing going. Not even a Chaos worshipper like Gimlet could be that willing to risk his fingers every time.

'Try the T-grip,' Guillermo said.

Dunk almost leapt from his armour at the sound of the Hacker's voice behind him. He swung the chainsaw around to smack the man but managed to recognise him in time. 'Where in the Chaos Wastes did you come from?' he said.

Guillermo tossed a thumb back at the stands. 'Been hiding in the crowd.'

Dunk scowled as he looked for this 'T-grip' Guillermo had mentioned. 'They didn't pass you up over the edge?'

'Too busy watching the show.'

Guillermo tapped a fist-long wooden dowel dangling from the right side of the chainsaw's handle. Like most of the rest of the machine, it was stained with fresh blood. Dunk reached down and grabbed it with his right hand. Bracing the chainsaw in his left hand, he hauled back on the T-grip with all his might, and the smoke-belching beast roared to life.

Dunk nodded his thanks to Guillermo over the machine's deafening roar and turned to see Krader and M'Grash pummelling each other to death. The ogre seemed to be getting the worse of it, which was no surprise. The troll had a couple of feet of height on him and countless pounds. Worse yet, Dunk could see every wound M'Grash inflicted on the troll was already healing. The same couldn't be said for the half-dozen gashes Dunk spotted in the ogre's hide.

'Let's finish this!' Dunk said, charging forward with the chainsaw buzzing in his hands.

As he approached the massive combatants, though, he saw the Jumboball start to move again.

'Gee, Jim,' Bob's voice said, 'that hardly seems fair.'

CHAPTER FOUR

THE CROWD ROARED at Bob's joke as Dunk turned to face the twenty-foot-tall crystal ball rolling toward him. Then he did the only thing he could think of, and charged straight at it.

Dunk knew that if he tried to run the ball would outpace him before he could reach safety. It would have done so before if M'Grash hadn't stopped it, and the ogre was too busy to lend a hand right now. So he ran straight at the thing, hoping it wouldn't build up too much speed before he reached it.

As Dunk neared the Jumboball, he dived to the right. He misjudged the ball's size, though, and it clipped his shoulder as it rolled by him, sending him sprawling to the ground.

Dunk wrestled with the chainsaw as he fell, refusing to share Gimlet's horrible fate. He landed on his back, holding the machine over him in his outstretched arms, its vicious teeth whirring only inches from his face.

'I think Hoffnung's taken too many blows to the head today, Bob,' Jim said.

'Lots of people have underestimated the Hoffnung brothers before. Remember how Dunk's younger brother Dirk pulled out that win in last year's Blood Bowl final?'

'Are you kidding? That was the best Blood Bowl I've seen since the glory days of Griff Oberwald. Somewhere in a dark corner of hell, Reavers' founder D. D. Griswell is still smiling about it!'

Dunk scrambled to his feet and saw that the Jumboball hadn't got far. It had stopped rolling away and stood hesitating only a few feet away from the Hackers' thrower. As it started toward Dunk again, he launched himself forward and stabbed the chainsaw's roaring blade into it.

Where the blade met the crystal, it chipped off large chunks of it, and the ball slowed to a stop once again. Sensing the advantage, Dunk jammed the chainsaw forward, taking larger and larger pieces out of the thing. A moment later, though, the sphere pressed forward harder, and Dunk had to dodge out of the way once again.

Dunk spun around as the ball passed him. He spotted a pair of large cracks running through the thing. The first came from when M'Grash had smashed into it, and the second sprung from the deep gouges he'd managed to carve into it. These same divots didn't keep the Jumboball from still rolling along the Astrogranite in fine form though.

Beyond the glassy sphere, now smeared with layers of blood, Dunk saw Krader beating M'Grash into the Astrogranite. The ogre had fought valiantly, but he looked like he might fall over exhausted at any moment. Dunk had to do something to help him now, or he might never get another chance.

Dunk ran around to the other side of the sphere. It wobbled there for a moment as if unsure which way to go. Dunk jabbed at it with the chainsaw again, and huge hunks of crystal spun away from it. The ball leaned toward him once again.

Dunk ran straight for the battle between the ogre and the troll. Krader had knocked M'Grash to his knees, and he was about to finish the bleeding, battered ogre off. He had his back to Dunk and didn't hear the chainsaw over the crowd until it was too late.

Dunk shoved the tip of the chainsaw straight into the troll's back and fought to hold it steady as it bucked against the creature's rocky hide. At first, he thought the creature didn't feel the whirring teeth biting into its skin, but then Dunk realised that M'Grash had wrapped his fists around Krader's arms and was holding him down.

Krader pulled back his head and screamed. Dunk's ears rang so hard he thought he might never hear again. At the moment, though, that was the least of his problems.

In his pain-fuelled rage, Krader backhanded Dunk, who went sailing off to the west. As he wondered whether his jaw might be broken, the thrower looked up to see the Jumboball roll right into Krader and knock him flat.

The crowd went nuts.

'Now that's the kind of turnaround I like to see in a Blood Bowl game, Bob. This is fantastic! I wonder how we can top this next week?'

'Careful what you wish for, Jim. I wouldn't be surprised to see the rogue Jumboball become a regular event!'

The Jumboball tried to slow down before it smashed into Krader, but it failed. The troll reached up to stop it too, but he only ended up being able to put up his arms to keep it from crushing his upper body, even as it pulverised his legs.

M'Grash summoned up some hidden reserve of energy and sprang at the Jumboball. At first, Dunk thought the ogre might try to attack it with his bare hands, but he soon realised that M'Grash just wanted to hold the thing in place.

'Hit it, Dunk!' Guillermo shouted from behind.

The thrower didn't need another prompt. He launched himself forward and slammed the chainsaw into the Jumboball, searching for a weak spot, digging at the cracks that had already formed. Under his assault, those cracks widened into seams and then to gaps.

'So, Bob, how much do you think one of those babies costs?'

'I don't know, Jim, but I'm glad it's not coming out of *my* pay cheque.'

'No!' Krader shouted. 'Stop! Please!'

For a moment, Dunk considered showing the troll mercy, but before he could even haul back on the chainsaw, Krader lashed out with his arms and knocked M'Grash's feet from under him. The ogre went down like a brick wall in an earthquake.

'I'll kill you!' Krader said. 'I'll kill you all!'

He reached for Dunk then, but the thrower ignored him. The Jumboball, he saw, was rolling towards him once again.

Dunk took three steps back and looked up at the monstrous sphere. His arms felt like wet logs, and his fingers wanted nothing more than to let the sputtering machine in his hands fall from their numbed grip.

The chainsaw coughed twice and then went dead.

Dunk grabbed at the T-grip and pulled. Something in the machine whirred around, but the chainsaw failed to leap to life.

As the ball rolled closer, Dunk tried the T-grip again and again.

'Run!' Guillermo shouted.

Dunk didn't bother to glance back at the lineman. This had to work. It *had* to. He pulled the T-grip again, and the machine choked and rumbled again, then let loose a hungry roar.

The Jumboball loomed over Dunk now, the midday Estalian sun gleaming off its gore-spattered surface. The thrower hefted the smoking, coughing chainsaw behind him and then pitched it right into the sphere's path.

The sphere rolled over the still-whirring chainsaw, its teeth scoring huge gashes in its underside. As the crystal fragmented along the bottom, Krader came crawling around from its far side, his legs starting to heal even as he dragged himself along by his boulder-like hands and powerful arms.

'I'm going to pick my teeth with your bones!' the troll snarled, blood spluttering from between its broken teeth. 'I'm going to use your hide to wipe my–'

The chainsaw's fuel tank exploded under the Jumboball, which smothered the blast. The resultant shock sent thousands of cracks through the sphere and shattered the already cracked crystal into billions of shards. For a moment, the shards hung there in the air, nothing holding them together any longer but memories. Then they cascaded downward like water from a burst skin, driving themselves into the hapless troll below. The tremendous weight of the countless razor-sharp shards shredded Krader's flesh into a bloody stew.

Dunk lurched backward to avoid the falling remnants of the Jumboball. The crowd's cheers hit him with the force of a wave. He fell to his knees and wondered what might happen next.

'Well, Bob, that's one way to kill a troll I've never seen before!'

'True enough, Jim. I prefer to barbecue them myself, but to each his own!'

'I CAN'T BELIEVE that after all that we had to forfeit the game?' Back in the locker room, Dunk shook his head, his short-cropped black hair still dripping with sweat, as the apothecary the team had hired stitched up his wounds. The white-haired woman didn't believe in painkillers, but her needle was so sharp that Dunk barely felt it. He'd waited for the old Estalian mystic to help out some of the others first. He'd wanted her to take care of M'Grash too, but the ogre had threatened to smash her skull between his thumb and forefinger if she didn't minister to Dunk first.

'We only have five players left alive, son,' Slick said, his voice filled with a rare reverence. 'And you and M'Grash were kicked out of the game. Even Pegleg won't fight odds like those.'

'Weren't you the one telling me I should give up when we had eleven players left, Dunk?' said the coach, who stood nearby, watching over the apothecary's handiwork. 'Now there's only M'Grash, Cavre, Sherwood, Reyes, and you.'

Dunk let his head hang down. He focused on the stab and pull, stab and pull, of the old woman's needle and thread. It kept his mind off the grief.

'It is okay to mourn our lost, Mr. Hoffnung,' Cavre said from his spot on a bench across the room. Dunk raised his head to meet the man's gentle stare. 'Tonight, we number eleven less than this morning. This is much for even the hardest minds to comprehend.'

'It's like we've been through a war, innit?' said Simon in his clipped, Albion accent. His eyes bore a haunted look, rounded with deep, dark circles that reminded Dunk of the black paint many players wore under their eyes to cut down on glare during a game. Simon had washed off his black grease long ago, but the darkness remained.

'Ah, the shame,' Guillermo said, 'it is tremendous. Here, in my homeland, in front of my family and friends, to be humbled so.' He fell silent for a moment. 'I cannot wait until we leave.'

'Aren't we going to stick around for the rest of the tournament?' Dunk asked. 'The finals are next week. The Reavers still have a shot.'

'We don't really care about your brother and your girlfriend, now, do we?' Simon said. 'We have enough problems of our own.'

Slick stepped in front of Simon. 'There's no need to get personal about it,' he said sharply. 'If it wasn't for my boy there, we'd be down to the three players who managed to hide the best.'

Simon unfolded himself to his full height and glared down at the tiny Slick. 'I don't care for how you choose to talk to me.'

'Sure,' said Slick, 'now you can play the tough guy, when you're facing down someone less than half your size.'

Simon raised his foot high enough to stomp on Slick's head. A large man, Simon stood taller than Dunk, and far more than twice the halfling's height. He looked like he could squish the little agent like a cockroach. 'You watch your little tongue–' the catcher started.

He stopped when the even larger M'Grash grabbed him by the scruff of the neck and hauled him into the air like a helpless kitten. Simon's feet pedalled in the open air beneath them as he strove to pry the blitzer's massive hand from around his neck. M'Grash held the full-grown man out at a safe arm's length and shook his head at him.

'Put me down,' Simon snarled, his dark eyes blazing at the ogre as his face flushed to the colour of a watermelon's flesh. 'Put me down, or I'll – urk!'

The catcher's tirade came to an abrupt end as M'Grash squeezed off the last bits of air flowing through Simon's throat.

'Stand down!'

All heads snapped around to stare goggle-eyed at Pegleg, who stood atop one of the benches in front of the lockers, glaring down at the others. 'What in Nuffle's nine nastiest names do you lot think you're doing?' he said. 'It's not enough that we lost eleven players to the Chaos All-Stars today, is it? You have to go finish the job for them?'

The others hung their heads in shame. M'Grash let loose his grip on Simon, and the catcher came crashing to the floor. He missed crushing Slick by scant inches.

'I'm all right,' Simon said after a long, silent moment.

'For now,' Pegleg said. 'If I catch any of you fighting with each other again, I'll kick you off the team.'

The players looked at each other for a moment, none of them willing to risk their coach's wrath. Or so Dunk thought.

'You're joking,' Simon said as he stood up and brushed himself off. He looked around at the others. 'With only five of us left, you can't afford to lose any of us.' He smiled, and the sight of it felt like a knife in Dunk's belly. 'I'm the only catcher you've got.'

Pegleg leapt down from the bench and landed right in front of Simon. As he did, his hands moved quicker than Dunk could see. Pegleg's hook caught Simon around the back of his neck, and a short, gleaming knife appeared in the coach's other hand, pressed against Simon's throat. A line of blood appeared along its edge, right where it met the catcher's flesh.

'Coach!' Dunk started toward the ex-pirate, but Cavre's firm hand on his shoulder held him in his place.

The thrower couldn't let Pegleg murder Simon. No matter how much of a bastard he might be, the Albionman was a team-mate, and that had to mean something.

Pegleg ignored Dunk as he hissed into Simon's ear. 'I already have to replace eleven players after today, Mr. Sherwood. What's one more body dumped in the deep?'

Simon's flesh turned a ghostly pale. 'You – you mis-under– my apologies, Captain Haken. I was out of line.'

'That you were, Mr. Sherwood.' Pegleg removed his hook from the back of Simon's neck and pushed him away. The catcher fell back into M'Grash's arms, blood trickling from the shallow cut on his throat.

The coach glared down at Simon and then around at each of the others in the room, like a wild tiger who'd awakened to find himself in a cage full of fresh, poisoned meat. 'If you – any of you – cross that line again, the consequences will be swift and horrible.'

With that, Pegleg turned, his long green coat flaring out behind him, and fled the locker room.

'Well,' Simon said, 'that was a bit much, wasn't it?'

'Shut up,' Slick said, shaking his head at the catcher in disgust. 'You're lucky he didn't cut you right there.'

'From the team?'

'From life.'

Simon started toward the halfling, but Cavre stepped between them and put a hand on the catcher's chest. 'There's been enough blood shed here today, Mr. Sherwood.'

Simon opened his mouth to speak, then reconsidered and closed it. He nodded at the team captain's cool-headed wisdom and took a step back.

'So,' Dunk said, trying to fill the awkward silence. 'What happens now?'

Cavre answered, thankful for the change in subject. 'I suspect it's back to Bad Bay for us,' he said. 'We might stay here a bit to see if we can round up some new recruits, but the other teams snapped up most of the top prospects before the tournament began.'

Dunk nodded, remembering how he'd joined the team that way just over a year ago. He hadn't made the first cut then, although Simon and Guillermo had. That thought shocked Dunk. Of the Hackers still left standing at the end of today's game, only M'Grash and Cavre had been a part of the team for more than a year.

Pegleg had only offered Dunk a job after someone murdered the 'top prospects'. Dunk hadn't known then that he owed his job to M'Grash's amoral efforts to get him placed on the team. When he'd found out, he'd nearly choked.

Thankfully, Dunk had been able to clear all that up during the last Blood Bowl tournament, casting the blame on Kur Ritternacht, then the Hackers' starting thrower and Dunk's chief rival. Kur had killed enough others and had tried to destroy Dunk enough times that Dunk felt no guilt for that. Sadly, it seemed to be just another part of the game.

'Maybe we should go to Albion instead,' Simon said.

Everyone turned to gawk at the catcher. 'This isn't a chance for a quick vacation,' Slick said. 'We have to rebuild fast for any chance to play in the Dungeon Bowl tournament.'

'Will the Grey Wizards sponsor us again?' Dunk asked. 'After all, the only reason we got in last year was that cave-in that almost destroyed the Reikland Reavers.'

M'Grash had been behind that too, Dunk recalled. Fortunately, his brother Dirk and lover Spinne hadn't been killed. Otherwise, he might never have been able to forgive the ogre.

Dunk glanced over at the massive, morose creature. He'd never seen M'Grash so quiet, so depressed. The ogre's simple nature meant he probably felt the loss of their team-mates sharper than anyone else, Dunk guessed.

Cavre frowned. 'They've said as much, but this may change things. Wizards love their plans. They set schemes in motion that take years to bear fruit. They do their best to eliminate uncertainties.'

'And a team with just five players left, she qualifies as 'uncertain'?' Guillermo said.

Carve shrugged. 'It's hard enough to fathom the mind of a single wizard. I won't hazard a guess at the thoughts of an entire college.'

'I wasn't talking about taking a holiday,' Simon said. 'Albion is a cold, dreary place. If I never went back, that would sit fine with me. I'm talking about going after the Far Albion Cup.'

Dunk's face went blank. He'd never heard of this cup before, but then he'd avoided anything to do with Blood Bowl until that incident with the 'chimera that wasn't anything at all like a dragon' last year, after which Slick had convinced him to forget about dragon slaying and give the game a try.

Dunk's agent saw his confusion written on his face. 'It's the Albionish equivalent of the Blood Bowl tournament, son,' Slick said. 'If you can call what they play over there by the same name.'

'It's not 'proper' Blood Bowl, for dead sure,' Simon said. 'But the teams play hard. I was a star player for the Notting Knights before I joined the Hackers.'

'Happens all the time,' Slick said to Dunk. 'Far Albion League players get full of themselves playing in their little league and decide to try their fate in the real league. Most of them get sent back home in a pine box.'

'We have some cracking players,' Simon said. 'But the Old World league pays far better. It drains away all the real talent.'

'So how'd you get in?' Slick asked.

Simon ignored the halfling. 'I wasn't talking about the Far Albion League though. I meant the Far Albion Cup, the league trophy. The actual cup from which the gods of Albion drank the blood of their slaughtered forebears. The great god Feefa himself handed it down from the Highlands to the founders of the Far Albion League.'

'The legends say that those who control the cup cannot lose,' Cavre said softly. Dunk couldn't remember ever seeing the unflappable man so impressed.

'Must have made for some dull tournaments,' Dunk said. 'Right? Once a team won the trophy once, who could beat them?'

'It's a travelling trophy,' Simon said. 'The winners have to give it up before the start of the tournament every year.'

'If we had the cup, Mr. Sherwood,' Cavre said, his eyes wide and distant, 'we'd never have to suffer through a game like this again.'

'Do we even know where this thing is?' Dunk said. 'This all sounds a bit too easy: Steal the cup and never lose again? What are we waiting for?'

'You confuse 'straightforward' with 'easy,' Mr. Hoffnung.' Cavre nodded at Simon to continue.

The catcher cleared his throat. 'Sadly the Far Albion Cup was lost.'

'What happened to it?'

'It was stolen – over 500 years ago.'

'And where do you think you're going to find that?' Slick snorted. 'Everyone but Nuffle himself has been hunting for that old trophy for centuries. They all failed. What makes you think you'll be any different?'

'When I was with the Knights, our team wizard was Olson Merlin.'

An unsettling silence fell over the room. Slick, Cavre, and Guillermo stood with their mouths gaping wide. Even M'Grash stopped picking his nose for a moment, withdrawing a chipped, mucous-coated nail from a nostril large enough to engulf Slick's head.

'Who?' Dunk said.

'The immortal wizard of Albion,' Simon said, smiling. 'It's said he's cursed to wander this earth forever – or until he finds the cup and drinks his own blood from its gold-lined bowl.'

'Now that's what I call an incentive clause,' Slick said.

CHAPTER FIVE

MOST NIGHTS DURING the *Spike! Magazine* Tournament, Blood Bowl fans in Magritta packed the wharf-side tavern known as Bad Water to the rafters. When Dunk and Slick entered the place, though, just after the game after theirs had started, the place was half empty. The bartender, a sun-worn dwarf with a long, damp beard, waved the pair over from behind a thick, wooden bar that bore the scars of countless fights.

'Well met, Sparky,' Slick said to the bartender. 'Get us a round of Killer Genuine Drafts, would you?'

'Got a special on Poor's Silver Bullets,' Sparky said. He narrowed his eyes at his two new customers. Thanks to a narrow shelf that ran the length of the bar's interior, about three feet off the ground, his eyes met Dunk's at the same height. 'Neither of you werewolves, are you?'

'No!' Dunk said, startled at the implications. His head snapped about so he could glance at the other patrons, and he wondered how many of them might transform into a wolf as night fell.

Slick smirked. 'You get a lot of that sort around here, do you?'

'Just enough that it pays to ask.' Sparky used the end of his beard to wipe up some of the spilled beer on the bar in front him.

'What happens?' Dunk asked.

Sparky cursed as his tangled beard caught on something white and jagged sticking out of the bar. He reached under the bar and brought out a long pair of rusty pliers. 'Ever seen a man try to tear through his belly and rip out his own stomach?'

Dunk shook his head as Sparky yanked at the white thing with his pliers. After a moment of wiggling back and forth, it popped free. Sparky smiled and held the thing up to the light: a long, jagged tooth over two inches long. Blood coated the part of it that had been shoved into the bar.

'I thought Kurtz left something behind.' Sparky wiped the thing clean with his beard, and then stuffed it into a pocket on his shirt.

'Kurtz?' Slick asked. 'The starting blitzer for the Orland Raiders?'

Sparky nodded. 'He's a big fan of your Hackers, he is. Had a hundred gold on you in the game. When Dunkel got kicked out of the game, he had a fit. Threatened to kill every All-Stars fan in the bar.'

Dunk smiled. 'Too bad he lost then.'

Sparky stuck the end of his beard into his mouth and started sucking on it. 'Oh, he didn't lose,' he said around the blood- and beer-soaked hair. 'You should have seen the other guys. Took our cleaning crew three buckets of clean water to mop it all up.'

Slick looked at Dunk, then said, 'We'll take a couple of Killers, Sparky.'

The dwarf shrugged and went to pull a pair of pints for them. 'Suit yourselves.'

A crystal ball hung in one corner of the ceiling over the bar. Bob and Jim's voices blared out of it, but Dunk ignored them, concentrating on the images instead. Slick remained quiet while waiting for the beers to arrive, for which Dunk gave thanks.

'Dirk and Spinne look good,' Slick said as Sparky slid a pair of commemorative steins in front of Dunk. The thrower tossed Sparky a coin for the drinks, which the dwarf tucked somewhere into his snarled mess of a beard.

'They always do.' Dunk didn't feel much like talking, but he knew that Slick could never stay silent for long. 'Who are they playing again?'

'The Evil Gitz,' Slick said. 'A goblin team from the Badlands.'

'They don't look like much.'

Slick smiled and sipped his beer. 'They're not.'

'How'd they make it to the playoffs then?'

'Same as always. They play dirtier than anyone else around. This time around, I hear they managed to find mostly halfling teams to play.'

'Ah,' Dirk nodded. 'So that's what happened to the Tinytown Titans. I saw the funeral procession last Tuesday: sixteen little coffins headed for the cemetery.'

'It's getting awful crowded up there, son,' Slick said. 'The game's more violent than ever, these days.'

'I wouldn't know. I've only been at it for a year. Fatal is still fatal, as far as I can see.'

Slick pursed his lips for a moment before taking another belt of his beer. 'Ever think about giving it all up?'

Dunk stared at Slick as if he'd just sworn off food. He peered around the top and sides of the halfling's head and said, 'Did you get hit by a flying body part during the game? You practically begged me to give Blood Bowl a crack, and now you want me to walk away?'

Slick stuck up a short, thin finger. 'I never said that, son. I only inquired as to your own feelings on the matter. After all, you've seen a lot of death in your short time in the league. I just want to know where you stand.'

'Why?' Dunk said, leaning closer to Slick. 'You worried I'm going to quit and leave my salary behind – along with your cut?'

Slick scowled and pressed a hand to his chest. 'That hurts, son. That really hurts. You think just because I'm half your size my heart doesn't beat as fast? Do you think I don't care?'

'I think you're an agent, Slogo. You didn't get the name 'Slick' for your way with the lady halflings.'

Dunk took a long pull from his beer too. When he finished he saw Slick staring at him aghast. 'Hey,' Dunk said in awe, 'you're serious.' He leaned forward to apologise, but Slick pulled back.

'No,' Slick said, putting his hands in front of him. 'I deserve it I suppose. I've put a lot of effort into farming that image, so I shouldn't be surprised when even my closest friends buy into it too.'

'What are we buying here?' a high-pitched crackle of a voice said off to Dunk's left. It could only belong to one person, and the thought made the thrower groan out loud.

Slick and Dunk turned as one to see a pale, greasy creature with wide, bloodshot, baggy eyes and a large, wart-coated nose over a wide, repulsive smile that showed a mouth of blackened and broken teeth. His oily hair hung in long, dirty locks over his face and broad, bald pate, except where he'd drawn it back into a greasy ponytail that looked like a fire hunting for a match.

'Gunther the Gobbo,' Dunk said, ignoring the hand Gunther stretched out in greeting. 'You're looking well.'

'Thanks, lad!' the Gobbo said. 'I'm glad someone's finally noticed how I'm trying to better myself.'

Dunk grasped the edge of the bar to keep himself steady, as the odour of Gunther's breath threatened to knock him over. The thrower picked up his stein and did his best to breathe through his beer until the vertigo passed.

'We were having a private conversation,' Slick said, glaring at Gunther with open disdain. 'No one around here is interested in doing any kind of business with you.'

'So you say, so you say.' Gunther grinned, and Dunk feared that several of the Gobbo's teeth might decide it was better to dive from his polluted mouth than remain there a moment longer. 'But you're involved in Blood Bowl, and Blood Bowl is my business. Sooner or later, everyone thinks they have a sure thing in a game, and that's when they come to place their bets with me.'

'There's no such thing as a sure thing,' Dunk said. 'Didn't the Black Jerseys teach you that?'

Gunther's smile fell into his face. 'Kid, you're not suggesting I had anything to do with that horrible group of game-fixing players, are you?' He spoke louder than ever, his voice warbling with nervous energy.

'No,' Slick said, trying to wedge himself in between Gunther and Dunk. 'He's not *suggesting* anything.'

Gunther stared into Dunk's eyes as the thrower remembered how the notorious bookie had tried to draft him into that 'meta-team' of Blood Bowl players who worked with him to force the maximum profit from the multitude of fans who wagered on the big games. He'd managed to avoid that until the Game Wizards from the Wolf Sports Cabalvision force had put an end to the Black Jerseys' reign.

The Gobbo let his eyes fall to the ground. 'All right then,' he said, his voice tinged with regret. 'I thought businessmen like ourselves could let the past stay in the past.'

Slick gasped. 'You're starting them back up again, aren't you? I'm surprised any respectable player would come within ten feet of you of his own accord. What will you call your group of crooks this time? The Black Benchwarmers?'

Gunther scoffed, bringing up a hunk of dark phlegm that landed on the bar. Sparky reached over and wiped it up with the end of his beard. 'Poor's Light for you, Mr. Gobbo?' the dwarf said.

'Make mine a Bloodweiser,' Gunther said. 'Got to support the sponsors of my pre-game show on the Extraordinary Spellcasters Prognosticated News Network, after all.'

'I thought you were with Wolf Sports,' Dunk said. 'Get fired?'

Gunther's greasy smile returned. 'Let's just say I saw a better future with ESPNN.'

'So you've reformed entirely,' Slick said, shaking his head.

Gunther sniggered. 'You and your lad here have nothing to fear from me,' he said. 'I've given up buying players.' He leaned in and whispered, 'It's far more economical to purchase referees instead.'

Dunk nearly spit out his beer. 'Wait,' he said. 'What happened in the game today. You didn't–'

'*I* didn't do anything,' Gunther said, wearing his mock innocence like a halfling's dress. It didn't do anything to really cover him and looked horribly inappropriate. 'Those were some really awful calls though.' He patted Dunk on the shoulder with a slimy paw.

Dunk shrugged off the hand. He wanted nothing more than to tear off the Gobbo's head and hurl it across the room. He clenched his fists instead and spat out, 'We lost eleven good players today.'

Gunther shook his head, unaware of Dunk's designs on it. 'That's why it's called *Blood* Bowl, right? At least your finest players made it through. It's survival of the fittest at its best!'

'I ought to kill you right here,' Dunk said.

'Hey, kid, don't take it personally. It's just business after all.' Despite his jovial manner, Gunther started to back away. Then he stepped forward again and whispered, 'Be sure to tell Pegleg that, for the right price, things could start to go the Hackers' way again.'

Dunk gritted his teeth and brought up his hands to lunge at Gunther, but before he could Slick leapt from the top of his barstool and thrust his fingers into the bookie's watery eyes.

Stunned, Dunk froze where he stood and watched as Gunther screamed out in pain. Slick landed on the bookie's chest and started to hammer at him with his little fists, giving everything he had in his murderous rage.

Sadly, it wasn't much. The blows bounced off the Gobbo's corpulent head and shoulders like rain on a helmet.

'Get off!' Gunther squeaked, shoving Slick away from him and catapulting the halfling over the bar.

Dunk thrust himself up and backward and reached out with both hands, catching Slick between them. He hauled his little friend back in and cradled him in his arms like a child, protecting him as he crashed down behind the bar.

Everyone in the bar had turned to watch the fight. As Dunk and Slick disappeared behind the bar, the onlookers all gasped and fell silent. When Dunk sprang back to his feet, holding Slick up in his hands like a prized trophy, the rest of the patrons cheered at the top of their lungs – all but Gunther, who skulked out of the bar as fast as his podgy legs would carry him.

As Dunk set Slick down on the bar, the halfling scooped up his stein and sent it flying after the bookie. It shattered on the doorframe just as Gunther raced through it.

Once Gunther left, Slick turned around and dusted himself off. As he did, he looked down at Dunk and said, 'Do you still think the league's no more dangerous than normal, son?'

Dunk shrugged. 'How could it get much worse?'

A GENTLE RAIN fell on Magritta the next day as Dunk, Slick, Cavre, M'Grash, Simon, Guillermo, and Pegleg stood by the graves of their fallen friends. Thunder rolled in the distance, but Dunk never saw any lightning to go with it. Three other groups of players huddled together at other points in the cemetery, each of them mourning their own losses.

One of them, a group from the Oldheim Ogres, sang a dirge that reminded Dunk of nothing more than whale songs. Slow and mysterious, it moved him, although he could not understand a word of it.

M'Grash, on the other hand, wept like a battered child. Some claimed that being raised by human parents had stripped the ogre of the savagery that was his birthright. The way the Oldheimers wailed for their lost compatriot, though, Dunk wondered if all ogres were like his friend under their ferocious facades.

A band of Norscans from the Thorvald Thunderers cheered off to the west. From the slurring of their songs, Dunk guessed they'd been there since daybreak, toasting their friend's toasted remains atop a burnt-out pyre that had stayed lit throughout the night.

Off in the distance, Dunk spotted a trio of lovely, pale women dressed in black corsets. They didn't seem to be part of any entourage of mourners, instead watching each of the ceremonies intently. The thrower nudged Slick and nodded at the blanched beauties.

'Them?' Cavre said softly. 'They're recruiters for the Deathmasques, an all-undead team. That blonde one in the middle is their coach, Rann Ice.'

Slick scowled. 'It used to be those bloodsuckers would at least wait until nightfall before coming around, looking for fresh kills. Damn Sun Protection Fetishes. SPFs like those have ruined the traditional night games.'

'I thought this was hallowed ground,' Simon said. 'Don't their sort have to stay far away from here?'

Everyone looked to Pegleg. The coach hadn't said a word since they'd entered the cemetery. He'd taken off his yellow tricorn then and let the rain mat down his normally curly locks, but not a word had crossed his lips. He'd just walked from one grave to another, spending a few minutes staring down at each as if he could engrave some additional words on the gravestones with invisible beams from his eyes.

After a moment, Pegleg detected the silence, and his head snapped up. 'What, me hearties? What is it?'

Without a word, Cavre pointed at the three vampires standing to the east. Pegleg's face flushed as he spotted them, but it faded just as quickly. 'What? Do I look like a priest?'

'Isn't this hallowed ground?' Simon asked.

Pegleg sucked in his lips for a moment, then shook his head. 'No. These poor souls didn't rate such treatment.' He stabbed his hook toward a hill to the north, a grassy patch of land that looked down over the city below and the sheltered bay beyond.

'Don't you – doesn't the team have enough money to pay for it?' Guillermo asked.

Slick slapped him on the back of the leg, and the Estalian realised he'd made a terrible gaffe. He started to apologise to Pegleg, but the coach raised a hand to cut him off.

'Only the greatest players are buried on the Hill of Fame, which is hallowed by priests of a dozen denominations. You can't buy your way into it. You have to earn it.' Pegleg glared down at the eleven gravesites before them. 'None of these fine people were granted that honour.'

'So now these teams of undead can recruit our friends at will?' Dunk said with a visible shudder.

Cavre spoke up. 'They only want the best players, Mr. Hoffnung. Players who cannot survive a match don't meet their needs.'

Dunk cocked his head, confused. 'If they're not recruiting, then why are they here?'

A white smile cracked Cavre's dark-skinned face. 'They are recruiting, Mr. Hoffnung. They're looking for the better players – those who survived: us.'

A silent terror fell over the Hackers. Dunk wondered how powerful the vampires were and if he and his friends could manage to leave the cemetery alive. Before he could say anything though, a mighty roar erupted from the west, and he looked over to see the Norscans come stampeding across the cemetery toward them.

A moment later, the Norscans veered around the Hackers and headed straight for the three pale ladies. Just as the Thunderers reached the vampiresses, though, they faded to mist and disappeared. For a moment, Dunk thought the Norscans might turn on each other for lack of a clear foe, but then another cheer went up as the man who carried the keg of ale finally caught up with the others.

The Hackers turned to each other and smiled. Although they'd lost nearly a dozen of their number, they somehow managed to find room in their hearts for a hint of laughter. Dunk felt a good deal better because of it.

'On that note,' Pegleg said, drawing attention from the Thunderers and back to himself again, 'I have some good news and some bad news.'

The Hackers each composed themselves and readied themselves for their coach's revelations. He cleared his throat hard before he began, covering his mouth with his hook.

'The Grey Wizards have pulled their sponsorship of us.' Pegleg waited a moment for that to sink in. 'We are no longer invited to play in the Dungeonbowl Tournament. Instead, they will return to using the Reikland Reavers as their representatives.'

Dunk frowned. In one way, not having to play in the Dungeonbowl was a relief. So soon after losing eleven players, he found the arena held few thrills for him. He didn't know when he'd be ready to return, but not so soon he'd hoped. It seemed his wishes had come true.

On the other hand, he didn't want the Reavers to take the Hackers' place. That meant Dirk and Spinne would be at risk again. They survived their game last night – won it, even. Even though he'd seen them risk death week after week for the past year, he worried about them now in a way he hadn't considered before.

'Is it back to Bad Bay for us then?' asked Slick.

Dunk grimaced. Even though they wouldn't play in the Dungeonbowl, it didn't mean they wouldn't have a full slate of games before them. As soon as Pegleg managed to line up enough recruits to fill the team out again, they'd be at it, playing in local or regional games until the Chaos Cup came around. That was six months off though. At least the Hackers would have a chance to practice with their new team-mates and ease back into the game with a few patsy matches before facing their next tournament.

Pegleg shook his head and allowed a shadow of a smile to spread across his face. 'That's the good news, Mr. Fullbelly. Instead of crawling back home to lick our wounds, we're going to take the kind of bold, decisive move that defines champions, both in the game of Blood Bowl as well as life.'

The bottom of Dunk's stomach fell out. Even as Pegleg spoke, the thrower knew what his coach was going to say. As much as he dreaded it, he couldn't turn away.

'We're going to Albion, my Hacker dogs!' A mad light of greed danced in Pegleg's eyes. 'There, we'll find the Far Albion Cup and bring it back to dominate the Blood Bowl League – or die trying!'

CHAPTER SIX

'SO YOU'RE DEAD for sure,' Dirk said, raising his voice to be heard over the noise in the Bad Water. The other patrons cheered as Khorne's Killers scored another touchdown against the Chaos All-Stars. The Killers' team captain, Baron Von Blitzkrieg, celebrated by ripping the second, vestigial head off one of the All-Stars' linemen and spiking it in the end zone.

Dunk scowled at his brother. Although Dirk had been playing Blood Bowl for a few more years than he – under the assumed last name Heldmann – Dunk was still the elder. It galled him that his little brother – who stood an inch taller than him – liked lording this difference over him so much. But that was the point, Dunk supposed.

'We're going to Albion,' Dunk said. 'We'll wander around there for a while looking for a trophy that no one's seen for over five hundred years. We'll come back in time for the Chaos Cup.'

'You'd better,' said Spinne. Sitting next to Dunk, her arms wrapped around him, she gave a squeeze tight enough to make sure he knew better than to argue with her.

Dunk smiled as he looked deep into Spinne's grey-blue eyes. He pulled an arm free from her grasp and used it to brush a few stray strands of her strawberry blonde hair from her eyes. Most of it still hung in a long braid that hung behind her, but it had been a long day.

After Pegleg announced the Hackers' plans, Dunk had gone looking for his lover. He'd tried the Reavers' camp first but had been told she'd left for a run. He'd caught up with her on a beach on the western shores of the bay, and they'd spent the rest of the day frolicking in the surf and sun.

Dunk had told Spinne right away that he'd be leaving the next morning, and she'd only nodded silently. They'd never said another word about it – until they met Dunk's brother Dirk on his way for a drink at the Bad Water. He'd insisted they join him and fill him in. Dunk hadn't seen a good way around it, despite the fact he knew it would break the spell of denial Spinne and he had spun around themselves.

'It sounds like madness to me,' Dirk said. 'Making an open-sea voyage in Captain Haken's rickety old boat, across the Sea of Claws, so you can wander around that hapless excuse for an island nation. And what if you do find the Far Albion Cup? How are you going to get it out of the country if everybody there wants it just as bad as you do?'

'One step at a time,' Dunk said. 'It can't be any more dangerous than playing a match of Blood Bowl.'

Dirk shook his head. 'I'll take my chances on the gridiron any day. Those Albionmen are just weird. They talk funny, they have strange, stuffy manners, and they dress like fops. They're all 'cheerio' and 'pip, pip,' and all the while they're looking to stab you in the back with a polished blade. I'd rather take a tour of the Troll Country. At least there you know when someone's trying to kill you.'

Dunk stared at his brother. 'What do you know about Albion culture? Just what you've seen on Cabalvision?'

Spinne snorted, then looked at Dunk, surprised. 'You don't know?' She goggled at Dirk, and then grinned. 'You never told him!'

Dirk blushed. 'There's never been, well…. I just haven't been able to….' He scowled. 'It never came up!'

'What?' Dunk said staring back and forth between his brother and his woman. Then it dawned on him, and he gaped at Dirk. 'You played in the Far Albion League!'

'No,' Dirk said, raising a finger. Then he dropped it. 'Well, yes, but not even for a full season.'

Spinne held Dunk's arm, enjoying Dirk's discomfort. 'Your brother tried out for the Reavers, but he didn't know much more about Blood Bowl than you did when you started.'

'Hey,' said Dirk, 'at least I was a fan. I knew how to play the damned game.'

'Not very well, it seems,' said Dunk.

'I – it's not as easy as it looks. *You* should know.'

Before Dunk could respond, Spinne cut in. 'After your brother got cut from the Reavers' tryouts, he jumped the first ship to Albion to try his luck there instead.'

Dirk threw up both his hands. 'It's my story, damn it. Let me tell it.'

Spinne nodded and gestured gracefully for Dirk to continue. 'Please. I'm sure it will be inspirational,' she said with a giggle.

Dirk ignored Spinne and focused his attention on Dunk. 'You know how our family never wanted me to play Blood Bowl.'

'Either of us.'

'But I was determined. Hells, there I was – fresh sprung from the life of an aristocrat – and I wasn't about to live like a peasant. But the only skills I had came from our tutor, Lehrer. Sadly, the things a noble child learns are meant to help him keep his wealth. They don't do a damn thing to help you get rich in the first place.

'Working a regular job is no way to get ahead in this world. Sure, I could have tried my hand as a guard or a mercenary, but the people who hire you are the ones with all the money. They keep you around to protect it, not share it.

'So, I figured I had two options. I could either become a Blood Bowl player or a dragon slayer. And what kind of idiot wants to go up against dragons?'

Dunk's face reddened at this as he remembered his own ill-fated stab at that career path. He'd thought it more honourable than playing Blood Bowl, despite the inherent dangers in challenging monsters the size of small castles. Slick had talked him out of that.

Sometimes Dunk wondered if he'd made the right choice. As a Blood Bowl player, he had plenty of money and more fame than he cared for, but he knew his parents would be as disappointed with him as they had been with Dirk. Still, being a live football player beat being a dead dragon slayer any day.

'When the Reavers turned me down, I thought I might head for the Grey Mountains and try my hand at hunting dragons instead. I'd heard one had been haunting the area around Dörfchen for years.'

'That's just a rumour,' Dunk said, clearing his throat. 'Trust me.'

Dirk looked at Spinne and shrugged before continuing.

'Anyway, one of the other hopefuls who got cut was an Albionman by the name of Nigel Priestly. 'It's a bad spot of luck,' he told me, 'but at least I can always fall back on the Far Albion League for another season.'

'I hadn't heard much about this before, but Nigel filled me in on it. He told me it was much easier to make a team there and that the Old World leagues sometimes used the FA League as a farm system, recruiting the best players to join them in the big time.

'It sounded better than dragons to me, so Nigel and I worked our way across the Sea of Claws on a vessel of fortune.'

'I heard you went drinking in the wrong pub and ran into a pirate ship's press gang,' Spinne said.

Dirk grinned. 'All part of the master plan. It was hard work, but since Nigel and I didn't have a gold piece between us it made good sense. Best of all, they grabbed us before we settled up with the bartender that night, so we got a free night's drinks out of it too.' He tapped his temple with a forefinger. 'Clever.'

Dunk shook his head. 'Only you could say that about that plan with a straight face.'

'You're just jealous. When we made it to Albion, it was just as Nigel had said, only much, much worse. The Albionmen are a weak-spirited sort, living on the scraps of dignity left over from some former empire they claim to have once been a large part of – the Far Albion Royal Consortium Empire. I'd never heard of it before, but they made sure to tell me all about it every chance they had.

'It's all long gone now, of course. As Nigel put it, they "live on in the fading echoes of their former glory." I don't know about that. All I can say for sure is that their taverns close too damn early for anyone to make a proper night of it and that their football teams suck.'

'It's probably because we take all of their top talent, right?' Dunk said.

'That and a true lack of a killer instinct. How many Albionmen do you see in the Blood Bowl League?'

'There's Simon Sherwood,' Dunk said.

'He's a catcher. Catchers don't count. I'm talking about *real* – ow!'

Dirk lurched to the side, rubbing the ribs into which Spinne had jabbed her elbow.

'Thrower,' Dunk said to his brother, 'meet your star catcher.'

Dirk flushed, but his face didn't turn as red as Spinne's.

'What's that supposed to mean?' she demanded. 'Catchers are just as tough as any other players.'

'Catchers are tall, lean people with the legs of a horse and the hands of a spider. They can't tackle to save their lives, and they fold like cheap chairs when you smash into them.'

Spinne raised her fist to punch Dirk again, but another hand snapped out to hold it back. The catcher snarled and pulled her arm around, dragging her attacker after it.

A gorgeous woman in an attractively cut version of a nobleman's clothes rolled over Spinne's shoulder and landed in Dirk's lap. She pulled her long auburn hair out of her deep, dark eyes and glared up at Spinne. 'Careful there, player!' she said through her ruby-painted lips. 'I was just trying to defend my man.'

'Lästiges Weibchen!' Spinne said. 'You're lucky I didn't throw you over the bar.'

Dunk nodded. 'It's pretty nasty back there. Take it from me. I hear they used to let the rats lick it clean, but they kept vomiting everything back up.'

Dirk started to say something, then thought better of it and planted a big kiss on Lästiges's full, pouty lips. Dunk and Spinne watched them for a long, uncomfortable moment. Then they picked up their beers and each took a long pull. Then Spinne let loose a loud, long belch.

Dirk and Lästiges broke their embrace and stared over at Spinne. She smiled at them with closed lips, then said, 'Excuse me.'

'Good to see you again, Lästiges,' Dirk said before the others could respond. 'I thought you'd be busy covering the game for Wolf Sports.'

Lästiges extricated herself from Dirk's arms and took an open chair between him and Dunk, across the table from Spinne. 'Normally, I would be, but I don't care much for those all-Chaos games. They're just too…'

'Chaotic?' Spinne said.

'Messy. Some of those mutant parts just aren't attached as well as they should be. I suppose that's what you should expect, they being so unnatural and all, but it's no fun working as a sidelines correspondent when you're getting splashed with hot ichor during every change of possession.'

'So you pulled some strings to get a night off to be with me?' Dirk said with a hungry grin.

'Don't I wish, darling.' Lästiges caressed Dirk's square chin with her well-manicured, crimson-tipped fingers. 'If I had that kind of pull with the network, I'd never work a Chaos game again. No,' she said looking at Dunk and then Spinne. 'I've been given a new assignment for which I must ship out in the morning.'

'That's just too bad,' Spinne said without a dash of sincerity. 'What are you on to next? Writing an exposé on the mating rituals of trolls? A hard-hitting investigation of what's rotten in Kislev? Or perhaps you're off to stir the ashes of Middenheim?'

Lästiges's Cabalvision reporter's smile dazzled Dunk with its falsity. 'I thought of following around a trollslayer until he finally found his doom, but then I thought "that's been done to, well, death." I could have charted the meteoric rise of great female catchers in the league, but then I realised there weren't any.'

Dunk put a hand on Spinne's arm to keep her in her seat. The reporter continued quickly before the catcher could throw off the restraint.

'Then my boss, Ruprect Murdark, he heard that one of the Blood Bowl league's premier teams was going to leave town with its collective tail between its legs and run off to the Far Albion League.'

Dunk took his hand from Spinne's arm, but before he could get up to protest he felt her hand pull him back into his seat.

'He thought that would make a great story,' Lästiges said. 'Since he owns the network, I could hardly disagree with him. Right then. In public.'

'You're probably right,' Dirk said. 'I can't imagine who would care about something like that. A bunch of major leaguers going to romp around in the minors? Who'd—'

Dirk stopped cold then stared at Dunk. 'Oh.'

'Welcome aboard,' Dunk said to Lästiges.

'Literally,' the reporter said, the same patently false smile on her perfect face. 'I've booked passage aboard the *Sea Chariot*.'

'On the Hackers' own ship?' Spinne said. 'Pegleg would never rent space out to outsiders.'

'He let Slick and I join him on the way to Magritta last year,' Dunk pointed out.

'You were a prospect. She,' Spinne pointed a long finger at Lästiges, 'she is a reporter.'

Lästiges let her smile drop. 'Look, dear,' she said. 'I'm not thrilled about this either, but Mr. Murdark is dead set on it. Reality shows are all the rage on Cabalvision these days, second only to Blood Bowl itself. A reality show about a Blood Bowl team? It's sure to be a smash hit!'

'Then why don't you want to go along?' Dunk asked. 'I mean, you're as aggressive a ladder-climber as I've ever seen. Don't you want to host a hit show?'

Lästiges reached over and grabbed Dirk's hand. 'Normally, yes, but your brother here has, well...'

Dunk couldn't believe the woman actually blushed. He'd thought nothing could embarrass the shameless story-hound.

'Altered my priorities,' Lästiges finished. 'I pushed for being assigned to follow the Reavers, but Mr. Murdark said he needed his top reporter on this job.'

'What happened to Cob Rostas?' Spinne asked. 'Or Mad Johnny? Or–'

'He chose me,' Lästiges said. 'I'll be leaving with the Hackers tomorrow morning.'

'Dirk was just telling us about his time in Albion,' Spinne said.

'Really, darling?' Lästiges turned to the startled Dirk. 'Don't let me interrupt.'

'Um, there's nothing much to tell, really,' he said. 'I spent a few months there playing for the Blighty Blighters before the Reavers figured out what a mistake they'd made and offered me a contract. I slipped out of the country like a thief in the night and never looked back.'

'Did you ever play for the Far Albion Cup?' Dunk asked.

Dirk nodded. 'Once. Turns out the 'cup' is just this battered tin replica of the real thing. It's been passed around from team to team so many times, you almost can't recognise it as a cup any more. Kind of disappointing, you ask me.'

'Sounds like you didn't care much for Albion, my sweet,' said Lästiges as she cuddled up next to him.

'It's nothing like home,' Dirk said. 'Most of the people there are so damned proper you'd think they hadn't figured out sex and violence yet. They pour a damn fine pint, but most of the time when I was over there I was just, well, bored.'

Spinne frowned as she put her hand on Dunk's. 'Let's hope your trip is just as uneventful.'

'Nuffle's 'nads!' Lästiges said. 'I hope not. I need the ratings!'

'So,' DUNK SAID, wrapping his arms around Spinne as they lay naked next to each other in the wide, feather-stuffed bed. 'What's next?'

'I was thinking about ringing for some room service,' Spinne said, a contented smile on her face. 'That always gives me an appetite. I hear they make a great paella here.'

'They should, for how expensive it is.'

Spinne gave Dunk a gentle poke in the ribs. 'You have regrets? Or are the Hackers not paying you enough?'

Dunk grinned. 'As a Blood Bowl player, I make more money than I've ever seen before in my life. I remember having less gold, though, and prices like that still shock me a bit.'

She spun over and lay on his chest. 'So, it's regrets then?'

'Not one.' Dunk's lips met hers in another passionate kiss. 'I just wondered what might happen next between us.'

The afterglow faded from Spinne's beautiful face. 'What do you mean?' she asked.

She sat up and moved to the edge of the bed. 'This is just one last fling, right?' She started to put her clothes back on. 'I've been down this road before. You're leaving town. You want to see other people.'

'Wait,' Dunk said, getting out of the bed and reaching for her. 'That's not it.'

'Ah,' Spinne said, turning her shoulder to him. 'It's the old 'it's not you, it's me' speech then.'

'No,' Dunk said. 'I want to be with you, I just—'

'What?' She spun to face him, her flashing eyes the colour of a stormy sea.

'Do you want to be with me?'

A tiny gasp worked its way past Spinne's soft, sweet lips. She stared at Dunk for a moment, and he saw tears welling up in her eyes. She looked like she might attack him right there. He braced himself for anything.

Still, he didn't expect the kiss. She wrapped her arms around him and kissed him so hard he fell backward onto the bed once again.

When they broke their embrace, Dunk looked up into Spinne's eyes once more. They were bright and happy.

'Is that a yes?' he asked.

She kissed him again, and they needed no more words.

* * *

LATE THAT NIGHT, as Spinne slept in his arms, Dunk lay awake and thought of the future. He'd never loved anyone as much as he loved this woman. In his younger days, he'd dallied with a few damsels, but most of them had been after his family's money. When that had disappeared, so had they – all except for Lady Helgreta Brecher, to whom he'd been betrothed.

While Dunk had liked Helgreta well enough, the thought of marrying her had given him many restless nights. He'd not been a good fiancé to her, but she'd stuck by him, even through his family's fall from grace. Her parents had demanded that she abandon her commitment to him, but she'd refused. It had been Dunk who'd had to dissolve their agreement.

Marrying Helgreta would have restored Dunk to some semblance of nobility in Altdorf, but at the cost of his self-respect. He'd only discovered after the fall of his family that he had any, and he wasn't about to sacrifice it so cavalierly again – even for a shot at getting his old life back.

Dunk had never wanted to play Blood Bowl. He'd shared his father's contempt for the game, and he'd joined in the family's scorning of Dirk when he left home to play. Still, so many good things had come to him since he'd let Slick talk him into trying out for the Reavers: wealth, fame, and now even love. He had a hard time imagining why he'd fought it for so long.

Then Dunk remembered the fallen on the gridiron. He'd lost many team-mates – friends, even – in the past year. Were all the gains in his life worth having to watch good men and women die?

As Dunk's eyes wandered about the room, his gaze drifted past the window, and he saw something there that made him leap from the bed. His movement thrust Spinne away from him, and he heard her sleeping form crash to the floor as he reached the window and threw open the sash.

'Ow!' Spinne said as she awoke. 'What in the Chaos Wastes?'

Dunk shoved his head out the window and glared all around. They were on the building's third floor. He couldn't have seen what he saw.

'What is it?' Spinne said, her voice filled with concern as she crept up behind him.

From down on the street below, a shout went up. Dunk looked down and saw a small group of Blood Bowl fans staring up at him and pointing and laughing. He waved down at them as he wondered how they could recognise him from this distance and in the dimness of a half moon.

Then he looked down at himself and saw that he was naked.

Dunk slammed the window shut and turned to find himself nose to nose with Spinne.

'Trying to give your fans a free show?' she asked.

Dunk blushed, first with embarrassment, then with frustration. 'I just – I thought – I saw something outside.'

Spinne peered around him at the half moon framed in the window, the silvery light spilling over her toned body and smooth skin. Then she reached up and put her arms around his neck. 'You had a bad dream,' she said.

'No.' Dunk shook his head. 'I saw it. It…'

Spinne stared up into his eyes. 'What?' she said. 'What was it? What could upset you so much you'd knock me clear out of bed?'

'Sorry about that,' Dunk said, caressing her thighs. 'Are you all right?'

'Are you?' she asked.

He hung his head sheepishly. 'It…' He drew a deep breath. 'I thought I saw Skragger.'

Saying the name somehow made it all seem even more real. As a star Blood Bowl player for the Orland Raiders, Skragger had held the record for most touchdowns in a year. When Dunk's brother Dirk had closed in on the record, Skragger had threatened to kill them both. He almost had.

Spinne's eyes grew wide. 'He's dead. We all saw him jump out of that window in Altdorf. We saw his body after he landed.'

'I know,' Dunk said, 'but…'

Spinne took Dunk's arm. 'Come back to bed. It's the middle of the night, and you're anxious about your trip.'

He let her pull him back into the bed. 'Are you hurt?' he asked as she pulled the sheets over them and settled down next to him.

Spinne winced a little as she curled into his arms. 'If I didn't love you so much…'

Dunk froze for a moment before his face broke into a wide, toothy grin. 'What did you just say?'

'Shh,' Spinne said, laying a finger across his lips before resting her head on his chest. 'Don't make a big deal out of it.'

Dunk gazed down at her face as she closed her eyes and melted into him. He'd never seen anything so beautiful. 'I love you too,' he said.

Spinne smiled.

 # CHAPTER SEVEN

DUNK VOMITED OVER the side of the *Sea Chariot* as the sea churned beneath the Hackers' ship. He watched as the remains of his breakfast splashed into the briny waters and swirled about. A school of sharks following in the ship's wake attacked it as if it was alive, devouring it in seconds.

'Dunk gonna die?' M'Grash said from behind, patting the thrower on the back.

Dunk peered back over his shoulder to see the honest concern etched on the ogre's massive face. The creature had lost most of his own meal half an hour earlier, and he looked a bit less green now than he had before. Dunk suspected that incident had attracted the sharks in the first place.

'I'm not that lucky,' Dunk said, reaching back to pat the back of M'Grash's kettle-sized hand.

'That's what you get for blowing off Nuffle's services before every game,' Simon said with self-righteous dignity.

The fact that he looked happy and healthy only made it worse.

'How are you not dying along with the rest of us landlubbers?' Dunk asked, thinking he might have to force some sort of misery on Simon just to even the score.

The Albionman patted his belly. 'Iron stomach,' he said. 'Runs in the family. I come from a long line of seamen.'

'Don't we all,' Slick cracked. He bore a steaming bowl of something in his hands.

'What's that supposed to mean?' Simon asked, his happy façade cracked.

'Never mind,' Slick said as he handed the bowl to Dunk.

The thrower tried to shove it away. 'I don't care if that's food from the fields of the gods,' he said. 'I'm not putting it in my belly just so it can launch itself straight out again.'

'Nonsense, son,' said Slick, pressing the bowl into Dunk's hands. 'Pegleg made this himself. A weak broth to help settle your stomach. It's a long way to Albion still, and you have to keep your strength up.'

Dunk accepted the bowl but couldn't bring himself to try the broth. It was so thin he could see through it to the bottom of the bowl, but it still seemed like too much. He bent over it and gave it a good, long sniff. Then he shoved the bowl back at Slick and went back to his spot on the railing.

The halfling shrugged. 'Suit yourself.' He took up the spoon and tasted the broth himself. 'Ah, now that's good stuff.'

Dunk tried to retch, but his stomach refused to produce anything from its emptiness. After a moment, he turned back and slumped down on the deck, his back to the railing. As he did, Guillermo dashed up next to him and blew his own breakfast into the rolling waters.

When Dunk could look up again, he saw Cavre waving at him from the bridge. The dark-skinned man looked at home there behind the wheel, as comfortable on a ship as he was on the gridiron.

'Only another day from here, Mr. Hoffnung,' he called.

Dunk groaned at the thought of the torture ahead of him. He'd felt fine for the first part of the trip, but they'd reached the open sea sometime last night. Between that and a squall that had stirred up the rough seas, his stomach seemed determined to crawl up his oesophagus and leap straight out from his mouth. If he could have, he would have let it.

'How's Pegleg?' Dunk asked.

Slick drained the last of the broth from the bowl and put it down on the rocking deck. 'Fine,' the halfling said. 'Good thing too, as he absolutely refuses to leave his cabin still.'

'Does he ever?' asked Simon.

'Not while we're at sea. You know how he is about studying game tapes.'

'Can't he get those on Daemonic Visual Display yet?' Dunk asked. 'Dirk was right. Those DVDs are amazing.'

Slick shook his head. 'These all come from Albion, and they don't use the same broadcast standards as we do in the Old World. Pegleg had to buy an Albion-made crystal ball just so he could watch the tapes.'

'Really?' said Simon, perking up even more than usual. 'I'll have to ask if he gets any Soaring Circus broadcasts on that cryssy. I haven't seen that show since I left home.'

'Does anyone else wonder why we haven't seen any other ships out here?' Dunk said as Guillermo slipped down next to him, wiping his mouth clean. 'Maybe it's because everyone smarter than us turned back. Here we are with an ex-pirate captain – who's afraid of water – and a crew of six others, three of whom are too sick to stand.'

'Don't you worry about it, son,' Slick said, patting the thrower on the shoulder. 'Cavre is an excellent sailor. Why, he could take this ship all the way around Albion and back home by himself.'

'Can't he save himself the trouble and start back now?'

'You'd miss fair Albion entirely?' Simon asked, staring out to the northwest. 'What a pity that would be.'

Dirk turned and saw nothing but rolling seas stretching to the horizon. He had to sit down again. 'The way you talk about the place, I thought you didn't miss it.'

Simon seemed to ponder this for a moment. 'I often like to say that Albion is a fine place to be *from*.' He smirked a little at this. 'Still, it's where I was born, and I still have many friends and family there. It's a land unlike any other, an island unto itself in more ways than mere geography. I shall enjoy my time there again, and I shall miss it when I leave.'

'And will you leave it again?' Guillermo asked. 'If this home of yours is so fantastic, I would think you would stay instead.'

Simon bowed his head before he spoke. 'Leave it I shall, I'm afraid, for leave it I must. Its pull increases as I draw near, I confess, but there are other matters drawing me away as well.'

With that, the Albionman turned and strode back across the deck toward the bridge where Cavre stood waving at him to lend a hand.

'Seems the nearer he gets, the more his mouth runs on about it,' Dunk said.

'Perhaps,' Slick said, 'he protests too much.'

'Now THIS IS more like it,' Dunk said as he hefted a massive glass of beer to join in a toast to the Hackers' arrival in Albion. He'd not had anything to eat in two days. Even when they'd finally made it to the shores of this distant land, his stomach had been too busy swirling around inside of him for him to attempt to put food in it.

The Albion beer, though, looked too good to pass up. He'd ordered a round of ale upon walking through the door of the nameless, whitewashed pub. It had taken the bartender half of forever to supply it, with Simon blathering all the while about how the pints here were hand-pulled in the old way – none of those magical taps so popular on the Continent, as he'd now taken to calling the Old World.

But the beer was here now, and a table full of food that Simon had ordered for the team was on its way. Dunk raised his glass and joined the others in saying, 'Cheers!'

When Dunk knocked back the beer, he almost choked. Although it looked just a bit darker than the Killer Genuine Draft he favoured back home, this stuff had far more flavour. So instead of the refreshing cold drink he expected, he got a mouthful of warm sludge.

Dunk glanced around. Slick, sitting on a high stool that brought him up to the height of the others – who sat on leather-upholstered benches around the low table that squatted between them – smacked his lips as he put lowered his drink and cradled it in his hands like a long-lost child perched safely on his lap. Simon put his pint down after draining half of it, a wide and satisfied smile on his face. Pegleg drained his entire glass and then smashed it on the floor.

Cavre put down his pint with great care, the liquid in the glass barely touched. M'Grash had popped back his first and second pints while waiting for the others to finish their toast. Now he nursed his third. Guillermo drained about half his pint, and then stopped dead, his eyes bulging. He turned and spat everything in his mouth onto the floor, gagging and coughing as if nearly drowned.

The others stared at him for a moment, none of them moving. Pegleg nodded at M'Grash and said, 'Give Mr. Reyes a hand, Mr. K'Thragsh, would you?'

The ogre nodded, then reached out and slapped Guillermo on the back with a meaty mitt. The blow knocked the Estalian from his feet and into a nearby table, where Guillermo made a poor first impression on a group of local dockworkers by smashing their table to pieces and spilling all their drinks in the process.

The angry dockworkers dragged Guillermo to his feet. One of them, a surly dwarf with a blue-tinged beard and a series of piercings along his right cheek-bone, smashed the top of his glass off on the back of his chair and jabbed it at the Estalian's face. An instant later, the same dockworker smashed into the far wall of the pub and slid down to the floor in a broken heap.

Dunk clapped M'Grash on the arm for taking out the primary threat so quickly. Then the other dock-workers – none of whom looked any more reasonable than the first – turned on the Hackers and snarled at them like a pack of hungry wolves.

'Now, gentlemen,' Slick said, spreading his arms open wide as he stood upon his stool. 'It was a simple accident followed by a misunderstanding. Can we buy you a round and call it even?'

One of the dockworkers – a balding, pot-bellied man burned a deep brown from constant exposure to the sun – stepped forward, a pair of short, sharp knives filling his hands. 'Ye killed the Runt,' he snarled. 'Ye won't be leaving the pub alive.'

Dunk nodded at the man, and then turned to M'Grash. 'Take care of them, would you, big guy?'

The dockworkers each took a step back as M'Grash stared out at them. Then the ogre looked down at Dunk, confused. 'Hurt them?' he said. 'Dunkel said hurting wrong.'

Dunk goggled at the ogre. In the previous season, Dunk had discovered that M'Grash had murdered people to help out his friends – Dunk included. The thrower had put a stop to that and had sat M'Grash down to explain to him in no uncertain terms that killing was wrong.

'Remember what I said about self-defence,' Dunk said. 'These people want to hurt us. Isn't protecting your friends why you knocked the Runt clear across the pub?'

'That wrong?'

Dunk grimaced at how eager the ogre was to please him. He'd worked hard to try to impart some sense of morality to the creature. He should have expected something like this to happen.

'No, M'Grash,' he said, patting the ogre on his elbow. 'There are exceptions to every–'

A pint of ale sailed through the air and smashed into the side of Dunk's head, coating him in beer and broken glass. He fell to the ground, dazed. A mighty roar from next to him nearly ruptured his eardrums. Still, he heard a stampede of footfalls rushing away from him and then the screams of souls in mortal fear of losing their lives. Many things smashed, and a chair flew over his head and crashed into the wall behind him before he could raise his head again.

'You'll be all right, son,' Slick said, standing at Dunk's side. 'M'Grash could take down the whole lot of them by himself.' A series of pounding noises punctuated the agent's words. 'Ouch. That has to hurt.'

When Dunk managed to stagger to his feet, he looked up to see the Hackers standing in the centre of a ruined room. Every set of tables and chairs lay in chunks on the floor; unconscious patrons sprawled across them, sleeping as if the bits of smashed furniture were more comfortable than any bed. In the opposite wall, three men hung slack from their necks with their heads shoved straight through the battered plaster.

'Any of the rest of you scurvy dogs care to try your luck?' Pegleg snarled, brandishing a bloodied hook before him.

The other patrons of the bar, who'd all stopped whatever they were doing to watch the fight, turned back to their drinks and restarted their conversations. All but one man, that was.

The man stepped up from a distant corner of the pub. He wore a royal blue cloak with a set of ram's horns embroidered in gold thread on his cowl. Underneath the cloak, he stood tall and broad, unbent by his years, at which Dunk could only guess from the wrinkles on his hands and the tip of his reddish-grey beard that jutted from the darkness under his hood.

The man strode forward with an athlete's grace. The others in the bar parted for him as he approached and closed behind him again as he passed. He walked straight for Dunk and Slick, ignoring the others. The other Hackers, sensing a threat, closed in around the stranger. M'Grash reached out to grab the man and hurl him out of the pub, but a gesture from Pegleg froze the ogre in his tracks.

When the man stopped in front of Dunk, the thrower could see his eyes glittering under the cowl. Blue and piercing, they seemed as if they could peer straight into Dunk's soul. The thrower felt a strong urge to ask the man what he saw there. Before he could, though, the man spoke, his words flavoured by a thick brogue.

'Faith, it's been a long time since We've seen a man who tried to face a foe with words 'stead of a fist.'

The man's lilting accent tickled Dunk's ear and threatened to make him smile. Instead, he stuck out his hand in greeting. 'The pleasure's mine.'

The man hesitated for a moment, then grasped Dunk's hand and shook it. He had a strong, rough-handed grip.

'You're with the Bad Bay Hackers,' the man said. 'Your name is Dunk Hoffnung. We've been expecting you.'

Dunk wondered if this man was some kind of mind reader. Then he realised that he was probably just a Blood Bowl fan who'd seen him on Cabalvision. Lästiges had made sure that their departure from the Old World was seen far and wide. It must have reached Albion as well.

'You don't speak like an Albionman,' Dunk asked. 'Can I ask your name?'

'Surely,' the man said, pulling back his cowl and revealing a wizened face under a full head of the same reddish-grey hair as his neatly trimmed beard. His eyes were the same grey as the overcast Albion sky, but they burned with knowledge and deep intent. The other thing Dunk noticed were the man's ears, the tops of which came to a sharp and elegant point.

'You're an elf,' Dunk said. As he did, he regretted his words, which sounded as profound as announcing that he was still actually breathing.

'Our name is Olsen Merlin,' the elf said. 'And we think we could be a great deal of help to each other, you and us.' He turned to look at the other Hackers staring down at him. 'And the rest of your friends, as well.'

Simon stepped forward and shook Olsen's hand. 'Mr. Merlin,' he said with a wide grin. 'I had the pleasure of playing on the Notting Knights a few years back. You were our team wizard.'

Olsen's face fell. 'Ah, sure 'twas, laddie, but we've put all that behind us now. There's nothing left in the game for us any more.'

'Why's that, sir?' Cavre asked. Dunk had never seen the man treat anyone with such reverence before, and the star blitzer was renowned for his respectful ways.

'Perhaps you've decided that the game that once sustained you has nothing left to offer you?' Pegleg asked. Olsen just shook his head.

'Or maybe you long to return to your homeland once more and leave Far Albion behind?' said Guillermo.

'Nay,' said Olsen. 'We bid good riddance to Hibernia when we left it centuries ago. Too damn many of the wee folk wandering around the place for our taste.' He eyed Slick carefully. 'You're a bit large for a fairy, aren't ye?'

'I'll have you know I'm a halfling born and proud of it,' Slick said, mustering every bit of indignity he could find. 'There's nothing the least bit "fairy" about me.'

Olsen reached down and patted Slick on the shoulder. 'No need to be so *dramatic* about it our wee friend.'

Dunk thought he saw steam escaping from his agent's beet-red ears.

'Did you decide to retire to a life of rest and riches?' Dunk asked, hoping both to distract the wizard and to get Slick's refocused on something that mattered much to him: gold.

Olsen shook his head. 'Nay. A team wizard can make a pretty penny, to be sure, but ye rarely have a steady contract, no damn benefits, and ye constantly have to worry about the other team trying to either bribe ye or assassinate ye. It's not a life fit for any self-respecting elf.'

'Friend?' M'Grash said, reaching out a monstrous hand to the downtrodden wizard.

The Hackers all froze. As Dunk knew, when M'Grash made a friend, the two were bonded for life. The ogre's brain held no room for two opinions about a soul. It branded each person it met with a label, and that stuck for pretty much ever.

'That's kind of ye, laddie,' Olsen said, patting the back of M'Grash's hand like that of a small child, despite the fact it was three times as wide as his own. 'But we've never been much of a friend to anyone, we fear.'

M'Grash's face fell so hard Dunk thought he might hear it bounce along the floor.

'Ah, cheer up, me grand ogre,' Olsen said, his eyes sparkling as he chucked M'Grash under the chin. 'We dinnae mean anything against your gentle soul. We're just too tired and crusty to think much on such things anymore.'

'So, why don't you just bugger off then?' asked Slick, who stood tall on his stool, glaring into the wizard's eyes.

'No!' the rest of the Hackers shouted in unison. According to Simon, Olsen alone had any hope of helping them find the Far Albion Cup, and they weren't about to let Slick run him off.

Cavre pulled out a chair for wizard, and Guillermo helped him into it. Pegleg cleared off the space on the table before Olsen with his hook, shoving the glasses there to shatter on the floor. Simon grabbed an unattended pint from the bar and placed it in front of the wizard, over the bartender's half-hearted protests.

Dunk placed himself between Slick and Olsen, hoping that the halfling wouldn't be willing to go through his meal ticket – Dunk – just to get at the wizard. M'Grash just sat down on a low bench against the wall, looked down at the bewildered elf, and flashed a toothy, too-innocent smile.

'Now that's what we call service, lads,' Olsen said. 'Good on ye.'

Then the wizard turned serious. 'Of course, we don't expect that you're being so kind for nothing. we may be old, lads, but we ain't that kind of fool.'

He leaned over the table as the others took their seats around him, each of them focusing every bit of their attention on his face. When he opened his lips to speak, they hung on his every word – even Slick.

'Aye,' Olsen said. 'You're here to learn all about the original Far Albion Cup, are ye not?'

The Hackers all nodded with excitement they could not contain. The wizard took a long pull on his pint, and then put it back down without bothering to wipe the foam from his moustache. He cleared his throat and then leaned forward again.

'Lend us your ears, lads. We've got a tale to spin.'

CHAPTER EIGHT

'A LONG TIME ago,' Olsen said, 'before any of ye were born, we played Blood Bowl like we meant it.'

Dunk glanced around and saw that every eye in the place was on Olsen, including those of the bartender and the other patrons. He got to his feet, his chair scraping out behind him loudly in the silence, and stared out at the others in the room. They all turned back to their own companions, and the bartender set to sweeping up the mess from the brawl once again.

'You were a Blood Bowl player?' Simon said. 'I thought you were just a wizard. I mean, not *just* a wizard – a wizard's a very fine thing to be, of course – but I never imagined that you played the game as well.'

'Aye,' Olsen said, giving Simon a hairy eye. 'As an elf, we've led a long, long life, and we've done many a thing, some great and some not so much so. But we did play Blood Bowl, we did.

'Our team was called the Eiremen.'

'Ire Men?' Guillermo asked. 'I, R, E?'

'No, lad. E, I, R, E. Eire. As in another name for our fair homeland, Hibernia.'

'This is good,' Guillermo said blushing. 'I thought you might all be angry all the… Um, never mind.'

'Never will, laddie.' Olsen clapped his hands together. 'So, where were we?'

'Just about to tell my audience everything!' a feminine voice said as its owner burst into the pub.

Lästiges stormed through the room, straight up to the Hackers' table. A small golden ball hovered in the air just in front of her. As she reached the table, it turned around, and Dunk spied a small, eye-sized hole in the thing, staring out at him and the rest of the Hackers.

'Ah, Miss Weibchen,' Pegleg said as he got to his feet and doffed his yellow, tricorn hat. 'A pleasure, I'm sure. I didn't think you'd catch up with us this quickly.'

'Captain Haken, Wolf Sports paid you good gold to reserve a berth for me on your ship, the *Sea Chariot*. Why did you set sail from Magritta without me?'

Dunk could see that Lästiges was furious with Pegleg but unwilling to admit it to anyone. A sparkle of light flashed on the golden camra ball with its floating daemon inside, recording everything it could see and hear through the ball's open end. Dunk wondered if Lästiges could shut the thing off or would have to live with it recording everything she did until she returned home. Then he asked himself which of either Wolf Sports or his brother Dirk must have been behind such a thing. Maybe both.

Pegleg cleared his throat and shot an apologetic look at Olsen, like a parent embarrassed by an obnoxious child. He stood to address Lästiges, doing his best to ignore the floating globe that zipped around her head, trying to find a good angle from which to film them both.

'My dear,' the pirate said, flashing her his best smile, which proved to be far more creepy than comforting. 'We would have waited for you, but we were on a tight schedule. If we were to meet our new friend here, I knew we'd have to be gone at high tide or we'd be lost for sure.'

Lästiges showed Pegleg a pouty frown. 'Because of you, captain, I have no images of you and your players aboard the Sea Chariot. That was supposed to be the starting scene of my report. What will I do without it?'

Pegleg patted Lästiges on the shoulder and said, 'Do not worry yourself with such trivial matters. When we return, you can record our trip then. Just use those images for our venturing forth as well. No one will be able to tell the difference.'

'Huh,' Lästiges said, narrowing her eyes at Pegleg. 'I suppose that *might* work.'

Before the reporter could press Pegleg again, Cavre stood up and said, 'May I ask how you got here so quickly after us, Miss Weibchen? I thought that you would have been delayed at least until the next high tide, putting you half a day behind us.'

A smile snaked across Lästiges's face. 'I've been here waiting for you for days. My employers at Wolf Sports have deep pockets,' she said. 'Very deep pockets. They paid to have me flown out here immediately once I'd realised you'd left without me.'

She looked around at the wreck of the room, including the sunlight shining in through the three holes in the far wall, from which the hapless patrons had finally been extracted while the Hackers spoke with Olsen. 'All I needed was to find you once you showed up. You and your team-mates didn't make that too difficult.'

'Well,' Pegleg said, pulling over an empty chair with his hook, 'now that you're here, why don't you make yourself comfortable?'

'We're not 'comfortable' with that,' Olsen said.

'And you are?' Lästiges wrinkled her nose at the wizard.

'Merlin,' he said, pointedly not extending his hand in greeting. 'Olsen Merlin.'

'Whatever.' Lästiges rolled her eyes at the wizard. 'Wolf Sports didn't send me here to follow some old coot of an elf who wants to cadge free drinks out of the tourists with stories born of his dementia.'

All of the Hackers winced at this, including Dunk, who half-feared – well, hoped maybe – that the reporter might disappear in a flash of smoke to be replaced by a warty frog. They all gaped in horror at Lästiges and then looked to Olsen to see if they might have to flee from his reaction to avoid any collateral damage.

The wizard stared coldly at Lästiges for a moment, and Dunk thought he saw his hands twitch beneath his cloak. The thrower prepared to grab Slick and throw them both behind M'Grash for safety.

Then Olsen drew forth a long, gnarled finger and pointed it directly at the reporter's nose. He opened his mouth to speak, and out came a deep, hearty chortle. 'You, you, you,' he said to Lästiges, punctuating every word with a stab of his finger as a smile curled on his lips. 'You have spunk. We like you.'

Tentatively, the Hackers joined in with Olsen, offering up half-hearted chuckles of relief – perhaps masking a bit of disappointment.

Dunk leaned over and whispered in Lästiges's ear. 'This wizard is going to help us find the Far Albion Cup. He's ancient and powerful. Don't make him mad.'

Lästiges's dark eyes twinkled as she glanced at Dunk. She turned to whisper in his ear. 'I think he's been mad since long before he met me.'

'And we've been able to hear people whispering about us since before any of you were born.'

Dunk and Lästiges, shame flushing their faces, looked up to see Olsen and the rest of the Hackers staring straight at them. Dunk cleared his throat.

'I was just trying to impress upon our friendly reporter here the reverence with which one should treat a person as important as yourself,' Dunk said.

'My deepest apologies,' Lästiges said. 'After spending years interviewing people who think they're something special, it's a pleasure to finally meet someone who really is.'

Olsen raised a hand to cut them off. 'Don't think we don't appreciate the obsequious utterances, lass, but we tire easily of such things. Besides which, we believe we have more pressing matters than massaging an old elf's battered ego.'

The wizard glanced up at the golden ball hovering over Lästiges's head. 'Is that camra on?' he asked, running a spit-slicked hand through his hair. 'We'd prefer to not have to repeat ourselves later.'

Lästiges's ruby-red lips spread in a hungry smile. 'I'm ready anytime you are – sir.'

Olsen grinned and then gestured for everyone to sit down and gather close. 'All right, then. Let us tell you the story of the Far Albion Cup.'

Lästiges, Slick, and all of the Hackers huddled tight around the wizard, each of them giving Olsen their undivided attention. Even M'Grash, who often had a hard time focusing on anything more complex than a meal, hung on the wizard's every word.

'Over five centuries past, the people of Albion caught Blood Bowl fever. We'd only just heard rumours of this most amazing of sports back then, and when Farley 'the Foot' McGintis returned from a tour of the Old World, he triggered off a national rage over the game.

'Farley had played in the NAF – the old Nuffle Amorical Football league – for a while, for the Champions of Death. He'd had a good run there until an opposing team's wizard resurrected the poor sod right in the middle of a kick-off return. They tore the poor lad to pieces.

'Of course, that's not always the end for the undead players of the Champions of Death. Farley wanted to play so badly he offered to kill himself again right there on the spot. Coach Tomolandry, the greatest necromancer to ever field a team, wanted to help Farley out, but they never were able to find all of Farley's parts to put him back together again. Seems that some vital pieces got thrown into the stands and disappeared. Rumour has it some bits appeared in a nearby rat-on-a-stick stand sometime in the second half.

'In any case, old Farley's career as a player was over. He packed up his things and caught the next boat back home to Albion. On the way, though, he realised that just because he couldn't play any more didn't mean he had to give up the game entirely. Those who can't do, coach.'

Pegleg harrumphed at this, but when everyone else at the table shot him a steely glare, he sealed his mouth once more.

'Within a week of his return, Farley had assembled enough players for four full teams. After that, it was just a matter of finding sponsors and venues. For that, he lined up Bo Berobsson, who had formerly been in charge of Big-Ass Ales – or B'Ass, as it came to be known. Bo got all the finances arranged while Farley taught the players and the coaches how to play the game.

'Now, Farley knew the rules as well as anyone else, but he didn't exactly teach us the right ones. Instead, he told us that football was a game in which you weren't allowed to use your hands. Also, when he figured out that kicking around a properly oblong pigskin didn't work all that well, he introduced a round ball with black and white panels into the game instead. Rather than carrying it into the end zone, you had to kick it through a big, white frame he called a goal.'

'Wait,' Lästiges said. 'You're telling me that this Farley changed the game all around? But why? Just to be different?'

Olsen tapped his nose twice, then pointed at the woman. 'Aye, that's what many thought at first when we figured out just what Farley had done, but it was too late then. We'd already played a dozen seasons of Albion Blood Bowl, and the people here loved it. There was no way for us to go back.

'Sure, some of the purists were appalled at Farley's lies, but as the 'father of the game' here in Albion, they couldn't touch him. They tried to change the rules to the proper set, the ones decreed by Nuffle so long ago, but they didn't take. We just played our variety of football here, and the Old Worlders played their way over there.'

'But why?' Lästiges said. 'Why did Farley do it?'

Olsen shook his head with a sad grimace. 'Ah, well, the injuries that poor Farley sustained in his playing days, they altered the man's makeup in some serious ways. If you'd seen him, you'd have no questions as to why he'd do something like that.

'Perhaps the old lad thought he might be able to play again himself someday, although he never did. Maybe he thought no one would listen to him as a coach of the proper game. It's hard to say. Still, he did what he did.'

Lästiges leaned forward, pressing the question. The golden ball closed in tight over her shoulder, as focused on the wizard's face as any of the other listeners.

'Why?' she asked.

Olsen let loose the sigh of a person who'd seen more than his share of tragedies in his centuries-long life. 'There's the rub of it, lassie. Not to put too fine a point on it, but poor Farley lost both his arms in his last game. He couldn't pick up the ball himself, so he made sure that no one else could either.'

Not waiting for a reaction from his listeners, Olsen pressed on with his tale. 'Of course, when Berobsson found out about Farley's deceit, you could have steamed a fish on the man's forehead. He decided he'd find out for himself just what the real game was like. This time, he refused to take anyone else's word for it. So he founded a team he dubbed the Albion Wanderers, and he took them off to tour the Old World and play against some of the NAF teams.

'Needless to say – but I'll say it anyway for your delightful camra there – the Wanderers were nearly eaten alive in their inaugural season. Literally. They lost three players to the Gouged Eye, and those damned orcs spit-roasted them right there on the sidelines, with Berobsson and the rest of the Wanderers powerless to stop them.'

Many of the players gasped in horror. Pegleg nodded knowingly. Dunk noticed that M'Grash licked his chops instead.

'When Berobsson came back, he pilloried Farley in every public venue he could find. He forced the man to buy his shares of Albion League Football, and he used the proceeds to found the Far Albion League, a proper,

Nuffle-would-be-proud group of football teams dedicated to bringing real football to the Isle of Albion.

'Despite Farley's best efforts, Berobsson's work led an exodus of fans and players away from his weaker variety of football to the real thing. Still, we have a strong contingent of Albionmen who, to this day, claim that ALF football is the real thing. They've gone so far as to even come up with their own god – a rough sort of chap by the name of Sawker.'

'Sucker?' Slick wondered aloud. When he realised others had heard him, he slapped his hand over his mouth and blushed.

Olsen clapped the halfling on the back with a smile, nearly knocking Slick off his high stool. 'Some say so, wee one, but Sawker's adherents take him dead seriously. We have a bit of a feud that goes on here between those who revere him and the right-minded souls who appeal to Nuffle instead.

'Fans of Sawker have felt the pinch hard in this past while. For decades now, we've had to worry about these hooligans rampaging through the streets after an ALF game, kicking over everything they can find. They refuse to use their hands, of course, which means the believers of Nuffle can usually take them in a straight fight, but against helpless, inanimate objects Sawker's devout do a great deal of pointless damage.'

'Can anything be done to stop them?' Lästiges asked in her best investigative reporter's voice. Dunk saw the corners of her mouth turn up in a measure of perverse pride.

'Aye, lass,' Olsen nodded. 'That's where the Far Albion Cup comes in. Thanks for your kind prompting to keep an old elf's mind on track.'

Dunk couldn't tell if Olsen meant to be sincere or not, but the elf pressed on before he could guess.

'When Farley started the ALF, he produced a cup to use as the league trophy. It was an amazing thing, made of a reddish metal rarer than gold and set with a fortune in emeralds and diamonds. Legend has it that Farley stole the cup from Tomolandry the Undying, but we've not been able to confirm that. Farley's long dead now, and no one else seems to know for sure.

'When Berobsson started the FAL, he took the cup from Farley and made it the league championship trophy. It lasted in that position for six years before it disappeared.'

'It was stolen?' Pegleg said, scratching his hook across the table, scarring its already abused surface.

'It didn't take itself out of the Notting Knights trophy case, now did it?' The wizard's irritation shone through, but Dunk couldn't tell if it was from frustration with the disappearance or with the question itself.

'Our apologies, lad,' the wizard said. Dunk had never heard anyone call Pegleg anything other than captain, coach, or sir. 'We've been searching for the damned thing for the past 500 years, and we don't seem any closer now than we were then. It's the most stubborn mystery we've ever encountered, and no one seems to have any notion how to resolve it.'

'So what's the big deal?' Slick asked.

All heads swivelled toward the halfling. Dunk couldn't believe his ears. It wasn't like his agent to not care about something as valuable as the Far Albion Cup.

Slick checked his nails for a moment before pretending to realise everyone was waiting for him to continue. He favoured Olsen with a condescending smile.

'I mean, a wizard like you would hardly spend his whole life searching for such a thing if we were only concerned about the jewels in it, right? You can get diamonds anywhere. All it takes is money, and if you're involved in Blood Bowl, you're probably swimming in that. You're after something you can't buy, aren't you?'

Dunk watched the wizard seethe, his mouth drawn into a tight, straight line, and his eyes narrowed almost to a single point. The thrower thought the wizard might summon up the ability to spit fire and fry Slick to a cinder right there atop his stool. He braced himself to move, although whether toward Slick or away he wasn't sure.

'You're a cunning wee one, you are, laddie,' Olsen said in a flat, reserved tone. He nodded as he continued. 'The Far Albion Cup isn't just a fancy beer stein. It has devilish powers that no one has ever been able to duplicate. Blood has been spilled over it. Bodies been buried for it. And now it's up to us lot to find it, before it's too late.'

'Too late for what?' Dunk asked.

The wizard swivelled in his chair to stare deep into Dunk's eyes. When he spoke, his voice rasped like the scraping of a stone lid being removed from a long-buried grave.

'Too late to save the world.'

 **CHAPTER NINE**

'You've lost the stitches on your balls,' Slick said. 'If
you're looking to save the world, I hope you've hunted
for better help. We're not heroes. We're football players.'

'You're not,' said Guillermo to the halfling.

'Good point,' Slick said, nodding forcefully. 'And neither is Pegleg or the lovely Lästiges over there. You've
got five players, a halfling, a twice-maimed ex-pirate,
and a hack of a lady reporter hurtling straight from up-
and-coming to washed-up has-been – sorry, never-was
– and you expect us to save the world?'

'All right,' Olsen said, ignoring Lästiges's protest at
Slick's evaluation of her career arc. 'Fine. Point granted.
Recovering the Far Albion Cup may not save the world,
but it will put a stop to the plotting of a fiendish coven
of cultists who plan to use it to cast all of Albion into
their master's hellish realm!'

The wizard climbed to his feet as he spoke, and he kept going. By the time he finished, stabbing his finger into the air as he did, he'd clambered atop the table in the middle of the group. The table shook beneath him as he gazed down at the others, realising how far he'd let his fervour carry him.

'*All* of Albion, Mr. Merlin?' Pegleg asked, giving the wizard the respect that Slick had neglected to supply.

The wizard bowed his head, and his shoulders slumped. 'Well, maybe not *all* of it. But a damned good chunk, mate!'

'Which chunk?' Slick said, squinting into Olsen's eyes.

'Uh, well…' The wizard lowered his eyes.

'Aren't you really doing this for your own reasons?' Slick asked. 'Legend has it that you can only die by drinking your own blood from the cup. Perhaps you tire of this life and want to use us to help you out the door?'

M'Grash stood up and cracked his knuckles at this, his head scraping against the ceiling of the pub, which hadn't often hosted an ogre before. 'Help now,' M'Grash said with a smile.

'Aye, lad,' Olsen said, reaching over to pat the ogre on the shoulder. 'We appreciate the offer, but we're afraid it would do us no good. You could pummel us into a pink paste–'

'I could!' M'Grash tried to jump for joy but smashed a dent in the ceiling's plaster instead.

Olsen put up his hands. 'Not that we're asking you to. Faith! We wish it would work. We've been killed many a time, to be sure, but the next morning we always wake up without a scratch on us.'

'So you can't be killed, then?' Lästiges said. 'Permanently, I mean.'

Olsen shook his head, a grim smile on his face.

'Does it hurt?' Dunk asked softly, without meaning to. Every face turned toward him, but he ignored all but Olsen's. 'Dying. Death. Does it hurt?'

Olsen nodded sagely. 'Aye, lad. Dying's never any fun. Being dead's not so bad, especially for one so ancient as us. It's getting to that point that's the trouble.'

'And that's where the Hackers come in,' Lästiges said, a smug grin parting her lips.

Before anyone could respond, Pegleg held up his hook for silence. Then he turned and spoke to the wizard.

'The question, it seems to me, Mr. Merlin, isn't why you want the Far Albion Cup. It's why should we bother to help you?'

Olsen smiled as he reached out and shook the ex-pirate's hook. 'Exactly right, lad. Got it one, you did. There's nothing we appreciate more than a mercenary point of view. You know where you stand with such people at every moment. It's not about saving the world or even lending a helping hand to a poor elf in need. It's all about the gold.'

'That's not quite–' Cavre started, but Pegleg cut him off.

'So?' the pirate said, a steely glint in his eyes.

The wizard glanced around, making sure everyone at the table was ready for what he had to say. 'If you lot agree to help, and if we – meaning all of us – manage to recover the Far Albion Cup, then we – meaning ourself – will agree to remand the cup entirely into your keeping once we have employed it in the way we desire most.'

A confused M'Grash looked at Dunk. 'What?'

'If we help him out, we get to keep the cup.'

'Ah,' the ogre nodded with a pleased expression. 'Good.'

'Mr. Merlin,' Pegleg said, doffing his yellow tricorn hat, 'I think we have a deal.'

'WHERE IS IT that we are again, please?' Guillermo asked.

Dunk was grateful that the Estalian had asked the question that he was sure had been burning in most of their minds for the past day. After leaving the pub, they'd gone with Olsen to hire enough horses to carry them all – except for M'Grash. None of the mounts Dunk had yet seen in Albion could have ever hoped to carry the ogre.

Walking seemed to suit M'Grash just fine though. He hadn't complained a whit since leaving town, just strolling along beside his friends' mounts, matching their walking speed with his long, smooth strides. It struck Dunk that M'Grash must have felt cramped for most of his life. Having been raised by humans gave the ogre the necessary civilization that allowed him to play on a human Blood Bowl team like the Hackers, but it also meant that the ogre had never been able to use his body to its fullest – except on the gridiron.

Walking next to Dunk most of the time must have felt to M'Grash like stumbling along with a slow child at his side. Now, able to stretch out and move at something closer to his own pace, the ogre wore a wide and toothy grin on his face.

'This is the Sure Wood,' Olsen said, gesturing at the tall, leafy trees all around them. As the Hackers had followed the wizard down the iffy and fading trail that led into the forsaken place, the branches had grown higher and thicker together until they almost blotted out the midday sun.

'Sherwood?' Slick said, looking over at Simon.

The Albionman shook his head and spelled out the place's name. 'My family does hail from the far side of the wood though. Our name is probably a corruption of the original.'

'A corruption of a corrupted place,' Guillermo said with a shiver.

'Does this make your family doubly damned,' Lästiges asked, her camra swivelling to aim at Simon, 'or do the two effects cancel each other out?'

'Doubly damned is nothing,' Olsen said. 'These woods are thrice-damned at the least.'

'You paint such a pretty picture,' Slick said to the wizard. The halfling bounced along astride a stalwart, russet-coloured pony that was the fattest such creature Dunk had ever seen. It wheezed as it rolled along, and the thrower feared it might fall over at any moment.

'This was once a clean, well-lit place, as such things go,' the wizard said. 'Upon a time, a clan of bright-leafed treemen called these woods home, and it was them from which the place took its name.'

'Were they 'friends sure and true'?' Dunk asked.

'Nay,' Olsen said. 'They were righteous bastards, always going on like they knew everything there was to know. They were never wrong – could never be wrong – and they let you know it.'

'Awful *sure* of themselves, weren't they?' Slick said, unable to suppress a snicker.

'Exactly. But that was the source of their downfall. When they finally encountered something for which they had no good explanation, they fell to pieces.'

'Literally?' Cavre said.

'Nay right away. The thing they were surest about was the fact they were immortal. When they started dying off, they couldn't figure out why. At first, they just chalked the first few deaths off to accidents. But they kept dying, one by one.

'When there were only a few left, they called us in to figure out what was happening to them. You'd never seen such a sorry lot in your lives. They'd pulled out most of their own leaves in worry, and those they had left had turned a bright red from the shame they felt straight down to their roots.'

'Did you ever figure out what happened to these legendary creatures?' Lästiges asked.

The wizard nodded. 'Root rot. It ate away at their nether regions until they were too fragile to stay upright any longer. Then, well, tim-beeerrr!'

'And that killed them?' Dunk asked. He looked up at the woods around them, which seemed to be growing darker and closer by the minute.

'Nay, lad.' Olsen peered out at the trail, which looked to be disappearing as they followed it. 'That just brought them down to where the cultists could get at them with their axes. They could have just waited for the rot to take them entirely, but that might have taken years, of course.

'Root rot's a horrible thing for a treeman, but when it gets to their knotty excuse for a brain, it's even more terrible. We found one once that the cultists had somehow missed. He'd been lying there in a gully for months, trapped and waiting for the rot that immobilised him to finally force his grip from life.

'The thing's voice was long gone, whittled down to a rasp from weeks of screaming for help that never came. We only stumbled upon him after following a trail of rot spoor that he had left behind as he wound his way into the gully. At first, we didn't even recognise him as a treeman, stretched across the old streambed like a fallen log. We were walking across him, using him like a bridge when he awoke.

'The nasty creature spun as we crossed over on him, sending us spiralling into the stream. He tried to tear us apart with what few limbs he had left but we'd fallen out of his reach. Soon enough, we figured out what had happened to him. He whispered a plea for us to finish him off. Those were his last words, lads. His last words.'

'So the cultists just took advantage of this rot to kill all the treemen?' Lästiges asked. 'How awful.'

'That's not the half of it, lass,' Olsen said. 'The cultists weren't just opportunists. Nay, they were *instigators*.'

'How do you mean?'

'They caused that root rot in the first place. It was all part of their master plan to make the Sure Wood theirs.'

'Or ours!' a voice shouted from somewhere in the darkness.

Guillermo let out a startled yip. Lästiges caught herself starting to scream. Dunk didn't even have time for that before he saw several piles on the leaf-strewn floor of the woods around them rise up and point swords and arrows in their direction.

At first, Dunk feared that a group of young treemen – Treelings? Saplings? – had ambushed them, ready to tear them to pieces in moments. Then he realised that such creatures wouldn't bother with weapons, instead using their own whip-like branches to flay the intruders to death.

These were men covered with sticks and leaves. They must have heard the Hackers troupe coming from a mile off and decided to set a trap for them. By burying themselves in the thick layer of rotting detritus on the forest's floor, they'd kept hidden until the Hackers were right on top of them.

Dunk cursed himself for not paying better attention to everything happening around him. Lehrer, his old teacher, would have smacked him on the back of the head for such a mistake, pointing out that it could cost him his life. Now it was time to find out if the old man had been right.

'Stand and deliver!' a leaf-swaddled man standing in front of Olsen's mount said. 'Make a false move, and we will knock your mounts from beneath you.'

'What scurvy fools–?' Pegleg started. Olsen cut him off with a curt wave of his long, thin fingers.

'Faith, we don't know how we get ourselves into these things, but,' he sighed, 'we know how to get us out.' The wizard pointed at the one who'd spoken, assuming him to be the leader of the group they faced.

'You. What god would you like to pray to before we strike you dead?'

The man stood silent for a moment, then threw back his head and laughed. He stood tall enough to look Olsen's horse in the face, and the sword he bore danced lightly in his hand as he spoke. 'You are a man of great bravado,' he said with a wide grin. 'I like that.' He gestured wide with his sword. 'Sadly, it will do you no good. Do I need to point out that we have you surrounded and outnumbered?'

Dunk noticed Cavre's head nodding as he finished tallying up the opposition. 'They have nineteen men on their side,' he said. 'We are but nine.'

A flash like a bolt of lightning filled the air, followed by painful crack of thunder. The blackened outline of the outlaw who'd been standing in Olsen's path stood there for a moment before crumbling into a steaming pile of ash.

'Right,' the wizard said. 'Now it's only two to one. Do those seem like fair odds, lads?'

'Robin!' a tubby man carrying a worn quarterstaff cried, shrugging off his mantle of leaves to reveal his shaven head. He gaped at the low pile of the robber's remains and shook, although with rage or fear Dunk could not tell.

'You killed him!' said a large man who stood nearly as tall as M'Grash. He stretched back his bowstring and pointed an arrow the size of a branch at Olsen's heart.

'And we'll do the same to the lot of you unless you let us pass,' Olsen growled. 'None dare threaten our life without tasting death themselves.'

'I thought you'd been killed a dozen times over,' Slick whispered from atop his pony. The halfling had his hands up in the air and bore a fake grin on his face as he watched the outlaws gape at the wizard's power.

'We never went down without a fight.' Olsen's hands crackled with power.

'Great,' Slick said. 'Let's follow the lead of the immortal who rises again the next day every time he's slain. He'll have a real incentive to get the rest of us out of here alive.'

'Hold it!' Dunk said, climbing down from his horse and stepping between the tall robber and Olsen. 'We don't have to do this. If we fight here, now, people are bound to die on both sides.'

'We think that's the point,' Olsen snarled.

'Perhaps we can see now why he had trouble finding others to help him in his quest,' Lästiges said into her camra. 'Did word of the wizard's ways scare off potential aid, or did all of his other protectors get killed on the job due to his abrasive manner?'

'Look,' Dunk said, desperation cracking his voice. He stretched his hand toward the tall man and asked, 'What's your name?'

'Wee Johnson,' the archer said, switching his aim from the wizard to the thrower. 'What of it?'

'Oh,' Slick said, slapping a hand over his face. 'You, son, need to find some better friends. Anyone who'd give someone a nickname like that?'

Wee Johnson adjusted his aim again and loosed his arrow. It zipped past Dunk's shoulder like a hurled log. The thrower turned just in time to see Slick get knocked back off his pony with a strangled cry.

Dunk leaped forward and socked the archer in the jaw, sending the tall man stumbling back. The thrower pressed his advantage and snatched Wee Johnson's bow from his hands. He smashed it into the man once, twice, knocking him to his knees.

Swift as a snake, Dunk slipped behind Wee Johnson and pulled his bow up under the tall man's jaw. He pressed it hard into the outlaw's throat and drove his knee into the man's spine. 'You son of a snotling!' Dunk hissed. 'That was my–'

'I'm okay!' Slick shouted, bouncing up behind his pony as if on springs. He pulled on a tear in the shoulder of his thick jacket. 'He just grazed me, son!'

Dunk froze, then looked down at Wee Johnson and realised that he'd almost killed the man in a blind rage, with his bare hands. Then he looked out at the other outlaws gaping at him, and he wondered if maybe he shouldn't have stopped.

The idea that he'd been ready to kill this man made Dunk ill. There had to be a better way out of this. He saw now that many of the outlaws had their bows trained on him. If he broke Wee Johnson's neck, as he'd been about to do, they'd fill him full of shafts before the tall man's body hit the ground.

Dunk glanced at the others. Most of them bore blades in their hands. M'Grash clenched his fists, forming them into hammers and staring at the heads of the outlaws as if they were nails.

'Hold it!' he said. 'Anybody else fires an arrow, and I'll snap Wee's neck.'

The tall man gurgled something at his fellows, and the bald man stepped forward, a hand raised in the air to ward the other outlaws off. 'Let's talk,' the man said. 'We don't want any trouble.'

'Ambushing people seems like a poor way to go about avoiding it,' Pegleg said, glaring at the outlaws all around them.

The bald man stared down at the pile of ashes. 'No one was supposed to get hurt,' he said. 'Robin there, he said no one would dare stand up to a gang like ours. "They'll trip over themselves to give us their money", he said.'

Dunk gaped at the man as he got a better look at him. He wore plain robes belted at the waist with a simple rope. A small religious icon carved from soapstone dangled from a string around his neck. 'You're a priest!'

The holy man nodded as he knelt down and made a small blessing over his friend's ashes. 'We like to say 'cleric.'' He rose and stood in front of Dunk, placing a hand on the bow still choking his friend. 'I'm called Brother Puck.'

Dunk let off some of the pressure on Wee Johnson's neck, and the archer swallowed deep gulps of air. The thrower had never had much luck with religious leaders, be they priests, brothers, or something more sinister. He remembered all too well the priest in Dörfchen who'd tried to trick him into feeding himself to the chimera living over their town.

'An outlaw priest?' Dunk spat into Robin's ashes, sending up another puff of steam. 'What were you thinking?'

Puck's eyes fell, and he pressed his hands together in a ritual of pleading. 'There aren't many in these parts who have the gold to spare for the gods, not to speak of the less fortunate. Our collection plate lay empty for many weeks. Robin – he was one of our church elders – he came up with the idea.'

'What idea?' Lästiges said from behind. The camra, which had been taking in the scene from high in the trees, floated down to focus tight on the cleric's face.

'Rob from the rich and give to the poor,' Brother Puck said, fat tears rolling down his pale, dirt-crusted face.

Slick tried to stifle a snort, but failed. Then Pegleg let loose half a cackle. Soon after, Lästiges giggled. Before Dunk knew it, every one of the Hackers beside him was bent double with laughter.

The outlaws surrounding the Hackers lowered their weapons, disarmed by this complete lack of respect for the basic principle upon which their merry band had been founded. Some of them shuffled their feet. One even started to laugh a bit himself before another of his compatriots smacked him in the back of the head.

'What?' Brother Puck said, confused.

'Son,' Slick said, wiping the tears from his eyes as he ambled toward the cleric, 'that has to be one of the stupidest things I've ever heard.'

 **CHAPTER TEN**

CRESTFALLEN, BROTHER PUCK stared at the halfling as if he'd just blasphemed his mother. Sensing that Wee Johnson was too entranced by Slick's bravado to be a threat, Dunk let loose the bow, releasing the man's throat. Still, he kept a tight grip on it with his other hand, just in case.

'Think about it, 'brother,'' Slick said.

'Wait,' the cleric said. 'Don't you dare start up with the old, 'if you rob from the rich, they're not rich any more, are they?' bit. Or 'if you give to the poor, do you then have to rob them too?' questions. The plan was a good one. We were comfortable with it. And it worked.'

Brother Puck looked down at the pile of ash that had once been Robin. 'At least it did until today.'

Slick shook his head, pity overtaking his smugness.

'No, son. It's just the futility of what you're trying to do.' He looked back at the others, who'd all stopped laughing now. 'The rich are rich for a reason. It's one thing to come into money. It's something else entirely to keep it.'

'He's right, mate,' Simon said, lowering his sword.

'You may take my word on this,' said Guillermo. 'We piss through gold like it was beer.'

'You see,' Slick said. 'You give money to people who have never had money before – like just about any Blood Bowl player – and they don't know what to do with it. It runs through their fingers like water. Soon enough, they don't have a copper left to their name. That's how we get players to come back again year after year.'

Wee Johnson, still on his knees, goggled at the halfling, who he still towered over. 'I thought all play-ers were rich. That's why Robin came up with the plan to get ahead of you after you left the pub and rob you.'

'Sure, they're rich,' Pegleg said, snorting. 'On payday. Maybe for a few days after. Most of them run through their cash before the next game rolls around.' He raised his eyebrows at his players. 'I've given out more than one payday advance in my time – for a vicious amount of interest, of course.'

'So if we give money to the poor, they'll just waste it?' Brother Puck looked as if he'd swallowed a hornet. 'I can't believe that.'

'Unless you teach them how to handle it,' Slick said. He swept his eyes over the assembled outlaws in their filth-stiff clothes. 'But I doubt any of you have those skills yourself.'

'I don't believe it,' Dunk said, surprising even himself as the words slipped from his mouth.

Slick nodded. 'Take yourself, son. What do you do with your money?'

'What do you mean?' Dunk didn't think he'd like where this was heading.

'What do you do with it? Do you spend it all every week?'

'Of course not. I spend a bit more than I should maybe, but I save a lot of it.'

'How?'

'I deposit at least half of each paysack in a bank backed by the Emperor.'

'Does that leave you enough to live on?'

Dunk nodded. 'More than enough.'

Slick turned to Simon. 'How much have you saved?'

'Saved?' The Albionman turned a bright pink.

'What about you, Guillermo?'

The Estalian shook his head.

'Cavre?' The dark-skinned man hesitated for a moment before dropping his eyes.

'What about Pegleg?' Dunk asked. 'Coach, you pay all of us. You have to know about handling money.'

The ex-pirate grimaced. 'I give just about every thin copper I must to my players. What I have left over goes back into the team's resources: the tents, the training camps, hiring an apothecary to stitch you dogs back together. Keeping a ship like the *Sea Chariot* isn't cheap either. Plus, there's Nuffle's tithe.'

Dunk gaped. 'You donate gold to the Blood Bowl god?'

Pegleg looked shocked. 'Of course, Mr. Hoffnung. How do you expect us to win a game if we set Nuffle against us from the start?'

Dunk stared at Pegleg for a moment, then at Brother Puck, then Slick. 'So that's how I manage to hold on to my money.' He turned his attention back to the cleric. 'See? There are far easier ways to part fools from their gold.' He threw down Wee Johnson's bow and backed away in disgust.

Brother Puck glared at Dunk for a moment. Then a window seemed to open in his head. He stepped toward Pegleg and the others, his arms spread wide. 'Friends,' he said. 'Can we impose upon your kindness for a moment?'

Dunk's friends glanced at each other for a moment, and then nodded at the cleric.

'I am a priest of the angry god of the Sure Wood. He has decreed that we should request a small donation from all who pass through his lands so that we may – in service to him, of course – maintain his wooded temple and alleviate the misery of the poor souls who nest beneath his boughs.' The cleric snatched a hat from the head of one of the other outlaws and turned it over and stretched it out toward the intruders. 'Can you find it in your hearts to help?'

Guillermo and Simon looked to each other. Simon spoke. 'It's like this, mate. As coach here told you, we don't have much to spare until we play another game, and that seems to be a fair ways off at this point.'

'You wouldn't want to anger the god of Sure Wood, would you?' Brother Puck asked, his face filled with concern. 'I ask only out of consideration for your own well being. Only this morning, I heard good Robin blaspheme our god, denying his existence, and well…' The cleric let his eyes fall and linger on the pile of ashes where Robin had last stood.

'Coach?' Guillermo said. 'Can you help us out?'

Pegleg sighed. 'I'm afraid I used most of the last of our cash to outfit this little expedition of ours. I don't have much left.'

'I must admit some admiration for brave souls like you,' Brother Puck said. 'To so blithely ignore the will of the gods, well, that's something few have the pluck to manage so well.'

'Mr. Merlin?'

'We'll have no truck with these dastards,' the wizard said. 'Faith! They're lucky we don't fry them all on the spot.

'Mr. Fullbelly?' Pegleg asked.

The halfling pursed his lips. 'I'd do it, but I'd end up expensing it back to the Hackers. Would you be good with that?'

'Ms. Weibchen?'

The reporter snorted. 'If the Hackers won't pay for it, I don't think Wolf Sports would be interested in covering it.'

'But if we did, they would?'

'Then you'd have already paid for it,' Lästiges said, smiling wide.

'Rhett?'

Cavre opened his mouth to speak, but before any words came out M'Grash broke in. 'Coach,' he said. 'Here!'

The ogre reached into his pocket with a ham-sized fist. When he pulled it out and opened it, three bags lay in his palm. 'This enough?' he asked.

Brother Puck's eyes lit up like lanterns on a moonless night. The other outlaws brightened too, standing up straight, their attention riveted on the ogre's open hand.

'Ah!' said Slick. 'A new way to avoid blowing your wealth: being too dumb to spend it.'

'Hold it!' Dunk said. 'M'Grash, put that money away.'

'But Dunkel,' the ogre said, crushed, his shoulders and face sagging with sadness. 'Just want to help.'

'I know, big guy.' Dunk rubbed his chin. 'And maybe there's a way.'

'Surely there is,' said Brother Puck. 'You make a dona- tion to the god of Sure Wood, and we all go away happy.'

Dunk shook his head. 'I have something more… equitable in mind.'

'THINK THEY WERE telling the truth, son, about where the cultists' hideout is?' Slick asked, back bouncing along atop his tubby pony.

'We paid them well enough for it,' Olsen grumbled back from his mount, positioned once again in the lead.

'You mean M'Grash paid them well enough for it.' Dunk stuck out his hand for a high-five from his large friend. Experience told him to roll with the blow when it came, and he did. Otherwise, he was sure he'd have been knocked clear from his saddle. 'Good job, big guy. You got us all out of there alive.'

'Not Robin,' M'Grash said, his voice choking just a bit.

Dunk smiled to himself. In many ways, the ogre was a large child – one who could rip your arms off in the middle of a tantrum. Still, the two had become good friends over the past year, and Dunk had come to admire M'Grash's honesty and loyalty and even his simplicity.

'As deaths go, it was a good one,' Dunk said. 'It was so quick, I'll bet he didn't feel a thing.'

Olsen turned around in his saddle and started to contradict the thrower, but Dunk cut him off with a steel-hard stare. The wizard shut his mouth for a moment, and then opened it again. 'We'd best be prepared for the worst with these cultists,' he said. 'They worship the Daemon Lord Nurgle, Prince of Pathlogy, Dark Duke of Disease, and Count of Corruption.'

'Sounds a real *sicko*,' Slick said with a grin.

'Joke all you like, our little friend,' Olsen said. 'See how well you laugh when your lungs fill with phlegm.'

'I think I can *hack* it.' The halfling chortled out loud.

Olsen reined his horse to a halt and turned to glare at Slick. 'This is a matter of the utmost seriousness, wee one. If you do not treat it as such, you may very well die – and threaten the lives of the rest of us in the process.'

'Come now, Merle,' Slick said, rolling his eyes. 'We're talking about a handful or two of tree-hugging wackos who've probably been chewing on the wrong kind of mushrooms found in this forest for the past twenty years. I saw how you toasted old Robin back there. With people like you and M'Grash on our side, how can these numbskulls pose a threat to us?'

'For such a wee person, you show a grand amount of ignorance,' Olsen said, his eyes blazing. 'I've seen such cultists control a horde of maggots once that stripped the flesh from a horse's bones in a matter of seconds. If they touch you, if they so much as breathe on you, you could find yourself bleeding from your ass and eyeballs in a matter of minutes. You'd consider yourself lucky if your innards didn't liquefy in the process, but you might beg for such a thing to happen to release you from other kinds of suffering they can inflict.

'Or is that not clear enough for you?'

'Like the blue sky.' The wizard's speech had snuffed the halfling's good mood.

'So,' Guillermo said, as they started around a wide bend in the trail, 'why is it that we are doing this again?'

'Stow that chatter, Mr. Reyes,' Pegleg said. 'We've set ourselves on this path, and we're not getting off it until–' The ex-pirate cut himself off for a moment, then continued in a low, awed voice. 'Whoa.'

Dunk looked up and saw a massive log blocking the way before them. The fallen tree had to over six feet across its middle – at least as tall as Dunk – and it stretched from one darkened part of the woods to another. The riders hauled their horses up short in front of the log and gazed up and over it, their mouths hanging open.

'Let's just go around it,' Simon said. 'It can't be that long.'

'We wouldn't recommend that, lad,' Olsen said. 'We smell a trap here. The cultists likely felled this rotting tree here to encourage intruders to wander off the path and into the danger beyond. Here, we are safe. There,' the wizards shuddered, 'wise men fear to tread.'

'I'll go,' M'Grash said brightly. 'No man here.'

'Belay that, Mr. K'Thragsh,' Cavre said. 'Even if you made it safely, the rest of us would still be stuck here.'

The ogre's face fell hard enough Dunk thought he heard it slam into the forest floor.

'We could jump the horses over it,' Dunk said. 'I used to make leaps taller than this back in Altdorf.'

'Even if you could teach us how to manage that, son, I don't think my pony here would manage it,' Slick said, still staring up at the log in awe.

'Couldn't our vaunted wizard do something about it?' Lästiges asked, her camra zipping around Olsen's head, looking for the best angle from which to capture his squirming.

'We could, lass. Aye, we could, but is that wise?' The wizard stroked his beard as he considered the log once again.

M'Grash stepped forward, squatted in front of the log, and shoved his maul-size hands under it. He grunted and groaned with all his might, snarling and growling at the fallen tree so loudly that Dunk thought any other attackers who might lay in ambush out there would have to be insane not to turn and run. Then again, they were talking about cultists who worshipped the evil god of rot.

'There's no way he can do that,' Lästiges whispered so that everyone could here. 'Can he?'

No one responded. Then, with a great roar from M'Grash, the log moved an inch. Encouraged, the ogre shoved his fingers in further beneath the log and redoubled his efforts. His biceps looked as big around at Dunk's waist, and the thrower feared the ogre might burst them with his heroic effort.

'Shouldn't we stop him?' Dunk asked. 'If he hurts himself, how can we haul him out of here?'

'Hush,' Slick said. 'Let him work.'

The tree must have lain there in the forest for years, perhaps decades. The soil of the forest floor had risen around it, almost as if the tree had cut into the land it had fallen on so long ago, like a sword through flesh. There it had stuck, probably forever, until the ogre came along.

M'Grash let loose a pealing howl that echoed throughout the forest. Dunk wondered if they could hear the ogre's cry back in the pub.

Then the tree came free of the earth. Dirt scattered everywhere, showering the riders with tiny pellets. The horses, already spooked by M'Grash's howling, scrambled backward, out of range of the log, which the ogre now stood holding over his head.

It turned out that the tree's top only extended a few yards to the left, and that now stabbed into the air. The right end, where the roots sat, still rested on the ground somewhere in the darkness beyond.

Dunk let out a cheer for his friend, and the others joined in. They let up only when the ogre shouted out, 'Hurry! It's heavy!'

The others stared at their companions, daring each other to go first. Dunk ignored them all and started down the path again, aiming to ride straight under the lifted log. Even on horseback, he saw there would be plenty of room for him under the ogre's outstretched arms. As he went, he reached down and slapped Slick's pony on the rump. The startled creature shot forward, moving under the tree ahead of the thrower, the halfling howling in dismay the whole while.

As Dunk passed under the tree to the left of the ogre, he heard a low, hollow voice say, 'Oi! Leave off, will ya!'

The thrower glanced up to see a set of glowing green eyes staring down at him from what he'd thought were a pair of knots in the bark of the tree. A rough stub of a branch stuck out beneath them, closer to M'Grash. Right over the ogre's head, between his hands, a horizontal crack that seemed like an old axe-wound moved like a set of lips.

Dunk's brain refused to understand this, and he stopped there under the tree to gape up at this strange face that had appeared in it.

'You there!' the tree said, snarling at Dunk. 'Tell this bloke to get his fingers out of me face!'

Lästiges screamed. The noise broke Dunk from his trance, and he spurred his horse forward just as M'Grash dropped the tree. The thing's branches brushed against his horse's tail as it fell down behind him.

Dunk brought his horse around next to Slick and his pony.

'I don't think I like this forest much,' Dunk said.

'Son, that's the smartest thing you've had to say all day.'

CHAPTER ELEVEN

M'GRASH SAT THERE between Dunk and the tree, staring at the thing in horror. 'What *is* it?' the ogre asked, panic slicing through his voice.

The branches on the side of the tree started to move, and M'Grash crab-walked backward until he sat next to Dunk's horse. As he did, the branches pressed themselves into the ground, and the tree lifted itself up on them.

'Agh,' the tree said, raspier this time. 'That bloody hurt.'

The tree slowly rolled away from Dunk, Slick, and M'Grash until it could get a proper look at them through its eyes, which glowed as if lit from within. 'You lot really know how to cock things up.'

The tree collapsed back to the forest floor with a thud that Dunk felt through the horse beneath him. It closed its eyes as it did, and for a moment the thrower wondered if he'd just imagined it all. Perhaps this was some kind of sorcerous illusion or a hallucination brought on by breathing the foul air of the Sure Wood. Or maybe he'd hit his head on the bottom of the tree as he'd raced under it. Or possibly it had even fallen on him and crushed him dead. The last seemed the most likely at the moment.

'It – it's a treeman,' Slick said in the sort of tone that priests reserved for direct conversations with their god. Dunk had never heard such reverence in Slick's voice, but he'd never seen a talking tree until today either.

'Yer bloody right it's a treeman,' the treeman said as it opened its eyes and glared at the halfling.

Slick leapt backward as if someone had stabbed him. 'Remarkable,' he said.

'Maybe we should go,' Dunk said, pulling on his horse's reins as he prepared to urge it to flee. 'The others will catch up when they can.'

'Right!' the treeman said. 'Fine! Wake up a poor, sleeping bloke and then race off into the woods like a gaggle of frightened geese. It's all I expect from yer kind of chaps.'

Dunk shook his head. 'What kind of chap?'

'Breathers,' the treeman said. 'Axe wielders. Fire users. Scum.'

'You're mean,' M'Grash said, standing up now.

'You'd be bloody mean too if you'd just spent the last year face down in a dried patch of mud!' The treeman roared so forcefully in its hollow voice that the wind ruffled Dunk's hair.

A little, gold globe zipped up over the treeman and focused on its face.

'What in the sap-burning hells is that?' the treeman said. Startled, it swatted at the globe with its branches. One of them caught the camra on its side and batted it away into the woods. A squeal of protest that could only have come from Lästiges sounded from the other side of the treeman.

'It's not important,' Dunk said. 'We didn't mean to bother you. We just wanted to get by.'

The treeman frowned. 'Just like that black-robed lot that's always trooping through here at all hours of the night.'

'He means the cultists,' Olsen shouted over the treeman.

'Of course I mean your bloody cultists! If you can call them proper cultists. Nothing like the mean bastards that used to run the Sure Wood with an iron axe. These just want to gather in their clearing to screw under the stars. Pfaugh!'

Before Dunk could stop him, Slick dismounted from his pony and sidled his way toward the treeman, stopping just out of reach of the thing's branches. Dunk didn't know how much protection this offered, as they'd already seen the thing move. He put his hand on the hilt of his sword, ready to draw it in the blink of an eye. Perhaps he could lop off a branch before the thing struck, giving Slick enough time to break free. Would such a creature bleed – or just leak sap?

'How long have you been there, old boy?' Slick said. Again, his tone stayed so respectful that Dunk wouldn't have recognised it as coming from Slick if he hadn't been there to see it.

'Your bloody cultists, I–' The treeman cut itself off. It grimaced, and then continued on. 'They were chopping down some of my saplings for firewood. Can you bloody well believe it? This bloody place is full of dead and dying trees, and they have to go and cut down some tree barely past being a seedling, their branches almost as green as the bloody grass.'

The treeman fell silent then, until Slick prompted him again. 'What did you do?'

'I chased them out of there. That's what I bloody well did. I chased them out through the rain-soaked disaster of a forest. I almost had them too. If I'd have got them in my branches, I'd have turned them into fertiliser in just bare, bloody moments.'

'What happened?' Slick said.

Dunk flinched, anticipating another rant from the treeman, this worse than any of the rest. Instead, the creature cracked open its bark-lined mouth and said, it a voice soft but clear, 'I tripped.'

Slick didn't respond. Everyone else remained silent. Dunk could hear M'Grash breathing loudly next to him, the ogre enthralled by the treeman's tale. Eventually, the treeman continued on.

'I bloody tripped, and I fell face down in the muddy path. I–' Dunk saw a line of sap pour out of the treeman's eyes and roll down its bark. 'I got stuck. I've been lying here ever since, afraid that they'd come back for me with saws and axes.'

'They didn't,' Slick said. 'We're friends.'

M'Grash started to say something to deny that, but Slick stopped him with a hand on his shoulder.

'You're safe now, old boy,' Slick said. 'You're safe.'

'Bloody, bloody hell,' the treeman said. 'You're a dead good lot, you are, to be sure. It's about bloody, damned time.'

'Do you need a hand up?' Slick asked.

The treeman shook for a moment, and then pushed itself up on its branches. It rose high enough into the air that Dunk could see Olsen, Lästiges, and the rest of the Hackers gaping up at it as it trembled there in the air.

'You,' the treeman rasped at M'Grash. 'Give an old, thick trunk a hand, would you now.'

M'Grash leapt to his feet and charged over to cradle the treeman's face in his arms.

'Not in my bloody eyes, you damned beast!' the treeman shouted.

M'Grash yelped and leapt back. As he did, the tree-man crashed to the earth again. The ogre turned to Dunk and held up a hand that bore a long, red mark around its thumb.

'He bit me!' M'Grash said.

Dunk dismounted and reached out to examine the ogre's proffered palm. It looked as if someone had slammed it in a rough-hewn, oaken door. The thrower started plucking the splinters out of the whimpering ogre's hand.

'That's gratitude for you,' Dunk said.

'Gratitude!' the treeman said, forcing itself up on its branches again. 'A bloody ogre pokes me right through my bloody eye, and I'm supposed to get down on my roots and kiss his bloody feet? Do you know how long it takes for me to grow back one of those bloody things? Besides, *it bloody hurt!*'

'He's only trying to help you,' Dunk said, flicking one of the larger splinters at the treeman's face. 'Maybe you'd rather we just left you here instead.'

The treeman shuddered along its entire length at that thought. 'No, nay, no,' it said. 'You seem like good blokes. Give an old tree your leave. It's the months in the mud talking, that's all. I appreciate all you've done, I do. Give a weary log another chance.'

Dunk looked up into M'Grash's eyes, each larger than a fried egg, as he pulled the final splinter from his massive hand. 'What do you say, big guy?'

The ogre wiped his nose with a long, thick finger and nodded. 'I try again.' He stood and walked back over to the treeman. 'But no biting!'

'Just grab him a little lower if you can,' Slick said, pointing to a spot well below the treeman's face. M'Grash went straight for it and started to lift the tree-man up again.

'There,' Slick said, 'that's it. Now just work your way back along to his roots. Kind of walk your way under him with your hands.'

M'Grash did as the halfling suggested, and the tree-man's upper end rose into the air, step by step. Once it was vertical, the creature looked down at M'Grash – at nearly twice his size, it towered over him – and said, 'You have my thanks, my – Hey! Wait! No!'

M'Grash had given the treeman just a bit too much of a push at the end. The treeman tipped back over the other way, spinning its branches wildly, then flapping them like a flightless bird doing its level best to defy gravity.

It failed and came toppling back toward the earth.

The treeman wrapped its branches around the bare trunk of a nearby tree as it fell, stopping it from crashing to the ground.

'Sorry!' M'Grash said. 'Can I help again?'

'NO!' the treeman shouted. 'Stay back, you bloody-!' It sighed deeply as it gathered its strength. 'You've done enough, chap. I can manage it from here, cheers.'

Dunk led M'Grash back to where the others stood and watched as the treeman righted itself. It brought its wooden legs closer to the tree it held like a long-lost brother. Soon, it pushed back, on its own roots again. It wobbled a bit, unsteady on its own legs for the first time in months, but it stood.

'Ah,' the treeman said with a deep sigh. 'That's much better. My thanks to you, you tame beast you,' it said, patting M'Grash on the head with a leafy branch.

Then the treeman surveyed the people standing around it, its great, green eyes scanning them each in turn. If it looked for some sign that these visitors to its forest could not be trusted, it seemed to come up empty. Other than its own suspicious nature, it had no reason not to treat Dunk and his friends with the utmost kindness.

'Now sod off!' it said, pointing the intruders back in the direction from which they'd come.

Dunk and the others all stared up at the wooden creature towering over them and stood there in shock. When M'Grash turned to Dunk, the thrower saw tears welling up in the ogre's eyes. Something snapped in Dunk at that moment, and he stepped up and stabbed a finger at the treeman.

'You ungrateful bastard,' he said. 'We almost literally stumble upon you in the woods and lend you a hand, and you're nothing but spiteful. M'Grash here, he helps you up despite the fact you bit his hand, and you practically spit at him.'

'Right,' the treeman said. 'Let me correct that.'

The treeman made a horrible noise in the back of its throat and then leaned forward, spitting something brown and sticky at M'Grash's feet. The ogre took a step back, trying to pull his bare toes from the mess, but the sap stuck to his skin like glue.

'That's it!' Dunk said drawing his sword and stalking toward the treeman. 'You're going to start treating us right, right now.'

'Or else what?' the treeman said. It took a single step, and its long stride carried it right in front of Dunk.

The thrower craned back his neck and looked straight up at the treeman, meeting the angry gaze in the thing's glowing green eyes. The creature wanted to intimidate him, but he refused to let it. He reversed his grip on his sword and stabbed it down through the tangle of roots that passed for the treeman's feet.

The treeman laughed. 'You can't hurt me that way. It would be like trying to hurt a fleshy thing like you by cutting your hair.'

'M'Grash,' Dunk said, beckoning his friend over with his free hand. 'Knock him back down.'

The ogre stepped up from behind Dunk as the thrower stepped back and out of the way. The tree-man tried to walk away, probably thinking that its long legs would let it outrun the ogre, but it found that Dunk's sword had pinned its foot to the earth.

'Wait,' said the treeman. 'Let's be bloody reasonable about this.'

'Sure,' Dunk said. 'Give me a *reason* not to have M'Grash turn you into toothpicks.'

'I–' The treeman looked down at the ogre, horror growing on its bark-covered faced. 'I–' It cast its gaze wider, but Dunk met it with an impassive glare. The others showed it no sign of sympathy either.

'I know where the cultists are,' the treeman said, holding up its branches. 'I can lead you to them.'

Dunk raised a hand, and M'Grash stopped cold, his hands only inches from the treeman's roots. 'Seriously?' the thrower asked the treeman.

The creature nodded as best it could with its rigid trunk. It seemed more like a quick series of bows. 'For good friends like you blokes, I can point you right in their direction.'

Dunk waved M'Grash to commence the tooth-picking of the treeman.

'Ah, I mean, take you right to them, of course. I could do no less for the fine gentlemen – and lady – who showed me such kindness as you lot have.'

The treeman ended on a hopeful note, and Dunk repaid him by signalling for M'Grash to stop, just as the ogre wrapped his fingers around the treeman's trunk.

Dunk turned to glance back at the others. They all nodded.

'And you'll guide us back out of this accursed place,' Olsen added.

'Of course,' the treeman said. 'I could do no less for such good folk as yourselves. I'll be happy to escort you straight from the Sure Wood, and to do my best to ensure that you leave in at least as good a condition as that in which you so elegantly arrived.'

Pegleg nodded. 'I can see how this one survived the great purge of the treemen from this forest.'

'Now that's hardly–' The treeman made to move toward Pegleg but found M'Grash's grip ripping at its bark, so it stopped itself short instead. 'Fine, fine, fine. Whatever you like. I've made you an offer, and I thought we had an agreement. There's no need to get personal about it now. I'll be happy to fulfil my end of the bargain if you blokes are willing to fulfil yours.'

'And why should we trust him?' Lästiges asked, her camra zipping about to get a close-up of Pegleg's face.

Slick answered instead. 'It's the quickest and easiest way to get rid of us,' he said, the earlier awe he'd had for the creature no longer evident. 'We get what we want, we leave, and it gets what it wants.'

'Which is?' Simon asked.

'We *leave*, son,' Slick smirked at the Albionman still gaping up at the treeman. 'Try to pay attention.'

CHAPTER TWELVE

'WHAT ARE THEY doing?' Dunk whispered as he stared down at the mass of cultists in the hollow below. A massive bonfire burned in the centre of the place, and in its light Dunk could see dozens of naked bodies writhing among each other in strange rhythms he could not decipher.

'Why, Dunk Hoffnung,' Lästiges said. 'Don't tell me you've never witnessed an orgy before.'

Dunk blushed six shades of red. 'Um, sure I–' He shook his head. 'Wait, I mean, no.' He looked at the dark-haired woman out of the corner of his eye. 'Have you?'

Lästiges giggled and flashed a hungry smile. 'A lady never tells.'

'So what's holding you up?' Slick asked.

Lästiges backhanded the halfling, and he tumbled back from the crest of the hollow, down toward the trail that wound around it far below. If M'Grash hadn't whipped out a hand to catch Slick, Dunk might have found himself without an agent. The ogre cradled the halfling in his palm like a newborn child for a moment before placing him back along the crest, this time out of Lästiges's reach.

Satisfied that the only part of Slick hurt was his pride – of which, as an agent, he had little to harm – Dunk glanced over and saw the others watching the scene in the hollow below. Simon and Guillermo had cocked their heads all the way to the right, trying to get a better angle on some bit of the action. A knowing smile played across Cavre's face as he looked on. Pegleg wore a scowl as he squinted from the naked forms below to Olsen, who stood by his side, frowning and scratching his beard.

'Where's the cup?' Pegleg said, never one to be distracted from riches.

'Huh?' Olsen said, his mind leaping back from the hollow. 'Oh, yes.' He pointed at a tent hunkered down against the hollow's opposite side. 'My guess is that it's there. If we hurry, we might be able to get to it before they bring it out to use in their unholy ceremony.'

'Hrm,' the treeman rumbled behind them. 'That lot don't seem to be in much of a hurry, now, do they?' He tried to crank his head to the left, but the movement threatened to topple him over. 'You humans are a bloody messy sort.'

'How do treemen reproduce?' Lästiges asked. Her camra zipped up into the treeman's face, and he swatted it away with a leafy branch. Undaunted, it returned straight away, but this time it kept a respectful distance.

'Er…' The treeman's eyes turned a soft shade of red for a moment. 'It's all about pollination with us: blossoms, seeds, saplings – that sort of thing.' His eyes resumed their normal colour. 'This seems a bit more effort. Why do you bother with it all?'

A voracious grin split Lästiges's face, and Dunk blushed at just seeing it. 'That's not reproduction,' she said. 'It's sex, and it's incredible fun.'

A loud groan erupted from the base of the hollow, followed by two more similar noises. 'See?' Lästiges said, batting her eyes at the treeman.

The creature shook its branches. 'If you say so. Sounds bloody painful to me.'

The reporter reached out and caressed the treeman's bark. 'It's just the opposite.'

Olsen cut in, his voice and manner both fragile and edgy as he hissed at Lästiges. 'Can we put an end to the education of our treeman friend about human mating habits for–?'

'Edgar.'

The wizard craned his neck back to glare up at the treeman. 'What?' he spat.

'My name,' the treeman said. 'It's Edgar.'

Olsen stared at the creature for a moment, and then shook his head. 'All right, then, *Edgar*. We'd like to focus on our stated goal here for a moment, if that wouldn't trouble you over much.'

'Get on with it then,' Edgar said, unperturbed. If he'd heard the sarcasm in the wizard's voice, he gave no sign of it.

'I have a question I would like to ask,' Guillermo said. Beside him, Simon nodded along.

The wizard sighed through his nose. 'And?'

'I thought these people were supposed to be some kind of plague spreaders.' The Estalian pointed to the active folk in the hollow as more groans escaped from their pile of writhing bodies.

'And?'

'Well, they don't look so unhealthy to me.'

'Faith save us.' Olsen winced, and Dunk had the impression he was counting to himself under his breath. When the wizard opened his eyes again, he fixed his gaze on Guillermo and said, 'Have you ever heard of venereal disease, lad?'

The Estalian frowned. Lästiges leaned over and whispered something in his ear. Guillermo flushed so red that Dunk feared the cultists might see him like a signal fire.

'Really?' Guillermo said, glancing down at the front of his pants.

Lästiges patted him on the back and said, 'Let's just say you're better off enjoying the performances down there from a distance. A *long* distance.'

'Is that quite enough?' Olsen asked, frustration lacing his voice.

Guillermo swallowed hard and nodded.

'I have a plan, Mr. Merlin,' Pegleg said. He'd doffed his yellow tricorn hat. 'Simple, but serviceable.'

The wizard nodded for the ex-pirate to continue.

'A few of us set up a distraction on the east side of the hollow.' Pegleg pointed to the right, which meant they had to be on the hollow's south side.

Dunk had turned around entirely during their time wandering in the Sure Wood, with no sun or stars to steer by.

'While the cultists investigate, we send our fastest runners into the tent to snatch the Far Albion Cup. We rendezvous back at the place where we found Edgar. Then we leave the wood with all due haste.'

'Who do you picture in each force?' Olsen asked.

'Mr. Reyes, Mr. Sherwood, and Mr. K'Thragsh will generate the distraction.' Pegleg stabbed his hook at each player in turn as he spoke. 'Dunk and Mr. Cavre, you two will go for the prize.'

'And what will the rest of you be doing while we're off risking our lives?' Simon asked, staring at Pegleg, Olsen, Lästiges, and Slick.

'Come now, Mr. Sherwood,' Pegleg said. 'Don't be a coward. This is a sound plan, and I've assigned the best people to each role. Would you rather Mr. Fullbelly here raced into the tent? Or myself?'

'We have a wizard with us,' Simon said.

'So we do.' Pegleg nodded. 'And if coaching Blood Bowl for so many years has taught me anything, it's that you leave your wizards in reserve until you need them – and you hope you never do.'

'What about me?' Edgar asked in a forlorn tone.

The coach stepped back and goggled up at the treeman. 'You'd care to help?'

'Sure,' Edgar rumbled. 'Why the bloody hell wouldn't I?'

Pegleg smirked as he twirled his moustache. 'You've fulfilled your "end of the bargain". You're free to go. We won't bother you again, Mr. Edgar.'

'But I'd–' Edgar fell silent for a moment. The others gazed up and him and waited. 'It's dead dull in this bloody forest since all the others have been gone.'

'You're bored?' Dunk said.

The treeman stabbed a branch at the thrower. 'That's it. That's it right in the heartwood. I'm bored. There's nothing like a full year face down in the bloody muck to make a body wish for a change.' He looked down at them all. 'You lot seem to be my best chance at that.'

'Are you certain, Mr. Edgar?' Pegleg said. Dunk could almost hear the gears whirring behind his coach's sparkling eyes. Or perhaps that was the ghostly sound of gold being scooped into a bag. 'If you come with us, I can guarantee you'll not be bored.'

The treeman's upper branches waved in a way that Dunk now understood to be his equivalent of nodding. 'It's either you bloody fools or those humping idiots down there.' He looked at them each in turn. 'You don't bother with all that sort of thing, do you?'

'Not often enough, honey,' Lästiges said with a dry chuckle. 'Not often enough.'

Not for the first time, Dunk wondered if this lady reporter had truly captured his brother's heart or just his loins. Perhaps Dirk wouldn't make such distinctions, but Dunk couldn't bring himself to not.

'Right then,' Pegleg said, scanning the faces of his players. Dunk could feel him sizing them each up, determining if they were all up for the jobs he had in mind for them. 'Let's go over this once again.'

Pegleg stepped forward and began to use his hook to scratch a diagram into the side of a nearby tree. Dunk had seen him do the same thing dozens of times before, although the coach usually used the wall of a locker room instead.

'Yowch!' Edgar howled. The treeman slapped the ex-pirate's arm away and stumbled backward. 'What in the bloody Chaos Wastes did you do that for?'

Pegleg took a step back. 'You can feel that?'

'I just *look* like a bloody tree! There's the "man" part of the word too. "Tree-*man*." The "man" part *hurts!*'

A silence fell over the hollow as Edgar bellowed down at Pegleg. None of the Hackers or their companions spoke a word. Then Dunk realised that the noises from the hollow had ceased too.

The thrower glanced down at the orgy and saw that its participants had frozen in their various, now-awkward positions, right in the middle of whatever pleasurable thing they'd been doing. One trio fell over onto each other, unable to maintain their balance any longer.

That seemed to break the spell Edgar's outburst had cast over the hollow. One of the cultists stood up and pointed at the towering forms of Edgar and M'Grash, just visible, Dunk guessed, on the fringe of the bonfire's light.

'Intruders!' the man shouted.

The people in the hollow scattered in a dozen different directions, each of them shouting for help or screaming for mercy. Some of them seemed to run in circles around the bonfire, gathering up scraps of clothing and wriggling into them as best they could. Many of the gatherers cared little whether the clothes were theirs or not, it seemed, as shown by one fat and hairy man who slipped into a corset in an instant.

Dunk later wondered at how easily the man had performed that task, but he put that detail out of his head as something he'd rather not contemplate for long.

'I think we have our distraction,' Slick said.

Dunk and Cavre glanced at each other and then at Pegleg.

'What are you waiting for, lads?' the coach said pointing them off toward the west side of the hollow. 'Go, go, go! Head for the end zone! We'll keep them busy as long as we can!'

Dunk heard M'Grash say, 'End zone? Where?' as he and Cavre sprinted off through the darkness to the west. They curved around the edge of the hollow as they ran, and they soon came to the north side. Cavre cut to the right and raced up to the rim of the hollow.

Dunk caught up with the blitzer at the edge of the rim. Below in the hollow, the cultists seemed to be rallying. Most of them were clothed by this point, staring up into the darkness and pointing all around.

'What are they waiting for?' a balding man standing near the bonfire said. 'Why haven't they attacked?'

As if in answer, M'Grash and Edgar rose over the crest again. The treeman raised its branches tall and wide and let loose a horrible noise that seemed to shake every tree in the forest. At the same time, M'Grash hefted up a small boulder, a rock as large as a pirate's treasure chest, and flung it at the bonfire.

When the boulder hit the bonfire, burning bits of coal and wood exploded from it. These showered the hollow with glowing embers, some of which hung floating in the resultant smoke like angry stars in a murderous sky.

The cultists screamed like children and scattered like rats. The hollow's floor fell into total chaos as the cultists banged into and tried to climb over each other through the stinging smoke.

'Here,' Cavre said softly, handing Dunk a black bandana. The blitzer often wore one like this on the field, tied around his forehead or his biceps to absorb his sweat and keep his vision clear and his hands dry. He produced one for himself and tied it around his face, covering his nose and mouth.

Dunk followed Cavre's example and was happy to find the cloth dry and clean. He started to ask what it was for, but the blitzer raised a finger to cut him off.

Cavre signalled Dunk to follow him, and then plunged down the steep side of the hollow, toward the cultists' tent. As they reached it, Dunk saw that it bore strange symbols and patterns embroidered into the red fabric in black, green, and yellow threads. Dunk didn't look at them for long, but what little he did see made the inside of his head itch. After that, he avoided even glancing at them at all.

Cavre reached down and pulled up the tent's back wall and motioned Dunk inside. Before he could stop to wonder why it should be he who entered the place first, the thrower scrambled under the fabric and found himself inside the tent.

An awful stench stung Dunk's eyes and lungs and he tried to peer through the murky haze. At first, he thought that the flying embers in the chaos outside might have set the tent on fire. Or perhaps the noxious smell came from the too-sweet incense burning low in the brazier sitting in a far corner. Then he realised that the foul vapours in the air sprang not from any blaze but from the fleshy lump of a creature that sat in the centre of the place.

The sick thing that squatted there seemed like it might once have been a man, but it had long since left simple definitions of humanity behind. If it had any legs to stand on, it might have been taller than Dunk, judging by the size of its massive, flabby torso, but those limbs had been carved away, along with its arms. From the slick sheen of rot over an angry red rash on its pale, almost formless flesh, Dunk might have thought the once-man dead if it had not moved at the sound of their entrance.

As the creature rolled toward the intruders, gangrenous pus squished through the stitches where the limbs had once been, and the scent of rot grew stronger. Its blind eyes stared toward them through its red-rimmed, lidless sockets. Its nose had been removed, probably through some insane act of mercy, or perhaps to prevent it from constantly nauseating itself with its own stink. No stitches sealed that wound, though, which bore only the blistered marks of a cauterizing brand.

The thing's mouth was far wider than any human's could have been, its cheeks sliced wide with a jagged knife and stitched back to form ragged approximations of lips. As it smiled at him through its gaping mouth, Dunk could see that all of its teeth had been pulled and its tongue bifurcated neatly down the middle, almost to its root. The thing welcomed them softly in either gibberish or some ancient tongue long since lost to all but sorcerers and madmen. As it did, it thrust its groin at them, bursting a number of poorly laid stitches that finally managed to escape its putrescent flesh.

Dunk stepped forward in a daze, his first instinct to kill the thing with his bare hands. It would be a mercy killing, both for the creature and himself – and perhaps for the kind of world that could produce such an abomination.

Cavre's hand on Dunk's arm held him back. The thrower looked back at his team-mate and saw him shake his head. His eyes drawn away from the spectacle in the centre of the tent, Dunk realised the blitzer was right. They needed to find the cup first, before the cultists discovered them here.

Cavre pointed to the ceiling of the tent, right near the front flap. There, nestled in a thin bit of netting, hung a golden cup studded with emeralds and diamonds. Despite having been lost for over 500 years, the trophy – for that's what it was, no simple cup at all – gleamed as if freshly made.

Dunk drew his sword, and the creature jerked at the scraping noise, despite the fact that its ears had been removed. Steeling himself, the thrower skirted past it to cut the trophy free with a single slice of his well-honed blade. It dropped into his free hand, and for a moment he cradled it in his arm and gazed upon it.

He could see why people had killed for this cup. It wasn't just the money it was worth. Having seen it for just a moment, he couldn't conceive of ever giving it up. He'd share it with his friends, sure – the Hackers, Slick, people he trusted – but sell it? Never. He had to have it, or at least a part of it, forever.

'Amazing,' Cavre said as he reached out to take the cup from Dunk. The thrower hesitated for a moment before letting the blitzer take it.

Cavre never touched the cup itself. He had removed his shirt while Dunk stood captivated by the sight of the cup, and he'd draped it over his hands. As he took the cup from Dunk, Cavre wrapped his shirt around it, hiding it beneath the dark fabric.

With the cup out of sight, Dunk remembered where he was. Before he could turn to leave the tent though, he felt something strike him in the feet. He looked down to see the rot-infested creature trying to wrap itself around his boots. Disgusted, he raised his sword to hack the thing to pieces, but once again Cavre stopped him.

'This poor, damned soul is ill, but he is also infectious – catching. If you destroy it with your sword, you risk becoming ill as well. Believe me,' Carve said, looking down at the creature with pity, 'this is a fate you would not wish on your most hated foe.'

Dunk coughed once and nodded as he backed away from the creature. Then he strode to the glowing brazier and kicked it over with his boot. The coals lay on the rug for an instant before the carpet caught fire.

Dunk and Cavre watched as the fire licked along a trail of invisible slime the creature on the floor had left behind as it had squirmed across it. Soon, it caught up with the revolting sack of illness. It crept along its skin for a moment, and the creature stopped its insane, incomprehensible babbling and started to scream.

Cavre pulled Dunk to the back of the tent again and raised the flap for him to scoot under. Just before he went, Dunk looked back at the creature and saw its blistering flesh burst into flames.

'May Nurgle never find your soul,' Dunk whispered as he left the tent. Cavre, the covered cup tucked under his arm like a football, followed close on his heels.

CHAPTER THIRTEEN

'NOW WHAT?' DUNK asked, gathered with the rest of the Hackers around a table in the back yard of the nameless pub in which they'd first met Olsen.

'How about another round, lad?' Olsen said. The wizard had already downed more beer than Dunk thought he should have been able to hold in his frame, but he showed no signs of stopping. 'We'd like to toast the man who's finally given us the chance to end this cursed life of ours.'

'Again?' Dunk said, the contents of his stomach curdling at the thought.

'Again!' the red-faced Olsen roared. 'Aye! And again and again until there's no more toast – we mean, toasts! – to be made.'

Dunk tried to wave the gesture off, but a barmaid showed up with a fresh bottle of whiskey at that point. Olsen tried to grab the bottle to pour a fresh round of shots, but he knocked the bottle from the table instead. Cavre snatched the bottle from the air before it could smash against the ground, and he quickly poured the drinks himself.

Dunk noticed that Cavre had skipped over his own glass. 'Hey!' the thrower said. 'That's not fair! You're just as much to blame for getting that trophy as I am.'

Cavre grinned. 'Too true, Mr. Hoffnung, but someone has to stay sober enough to pour the drinks.'

Dunk turned to point at the barmaid, but his head swum around even faster. He had to reach back to clutch the table in front of him for fear of falling to the earth. 'Whoa!' he said, laughing. 'Are we back on the ship already?'

For some reason, the others at the table found his antics hysterical, especially Lästiges, who wrapped an arm around Dunk and leaned heavily against him.

'You're damned – damned – damned cute,' she said around her hiccups, smiling up at him with her dark eyes, ruby-red lips, and Cabalvision-perfect teeth. 'If I wasn't already with your brother –

Dunk became aware of Lästiges's breasts pressing against his shoulder, and he turned to gaze wobbily into her eyes. They seemed to be asking him – no, begging – to kiss those soft, red lips, the ones his brother–'

'My brother!' Dunk said, shrugging the reporter away. 'Wait until he hears about – whoa!'

Only intending to move a bit out of Lästiges's range, Dunk had overbalanced himself, and he tipped and fell backward off his seat. He landed flat on his back, which knocked the wind out of him for a moment, but the alcohol had numbed him so that the landing didn't hurt a bit.

The rest of the table went silent. Slick leaped up on the table, nearly slipping in a pool of spilled beer, and stared down at the young thrower. 'Dunk!' he said, his voice cracking with worry. 'Are you killed, son?'

When Dunk could breathe again, he started laughing harder than ever, and the others all joined in. After a moment, he stopped and clutched at the ground beneath him, dizzy enough to wonder whether he might spin out into the night sky should he let go. He closed his eyes and hoped that the vertigo would go away.

'So, wizard,' Edgar said, 'when will you end your life?'

That stopped the laughter dead.

Dunk pried his eyes open to see the treeman standing tall over him, his branches seeming farther away than the moon. Even from this angle, Dunk could see the creature wince, realising he had said something to spoil the mood.

'My apologies, mate,' he said. 'You seem like a good bloke, and I'm in no hurry to shove you off this mortal coil. I just – well, I haven't–' He stopped and mulled something over for a moment. 'Bollocks. Are you planning to die all at once – together, I mean – or in turns? And is this something I can bloody well lend a hand with?'

Dunk snorted at this but then realised no one else was laughing along. Embarrassed, he decided he had to do something to set this right. He sprang to his feet to launch himself into an impassioned speech about the sanctity of life, especially among friends, but he tipped over backward again before he could start.

Edgar caught him in his branches and set him upright. 'I'm sorry, mate,' he said. 'This is maybe a bit too human for me.'

'Not at all,' Dunk said. 'It's just, well, we're not all bent on killing ourselves – despite what it may look like on the gridiron. It's only Olsen here who's up for giving that a go, and only because we finally found the one thing that can kill him: the cup.'

'So you lot, as his friends, risked your lives to be able to help him kill himself?'

'Actually, we don't know him all that well. He paid us. With the cup.'

Edgar shook its upper branches. 'I don't suppose I might ever understand you lot.'

'This is a rare situation,' Olsen said to the treeman. 'Rare situations call for rare solutions.' He looked at the others around him. 'And this is about as rare a group of people as you'd ever want to find.'

A smile burst on the wizard's face. 'And we can't imagine wanting to leave such rare people behind tonight!'

A cheer rose, and many glasses clinked together at the announcement.

'A Blood Bowl team can always use a wizard on its side, Mr. Merlin,' Pegleg said with a grin. 'With your kind permission, I'd like to hire you as our full-time consultant on all matters sorcerous, magical, and otherwise unnatural.'

'Nothing could please us more, chappie, but we don't need your money.'

Pegleg's smile grew wider than ever. 'Better yet, Mr. Merlin. Better yet.'

The wizard leaned over the table and spoke directly into the coach's face before bursting into uncontrollable laughter. 'But I didn't say I wouldn't take it!'

The fact that Pegleg still kept his smile on his face indicated how drunk he must have been, Dunk thought. He knew that money was never a joking matter with the ex-pirate. Perhaps the smile wasn't as real or as strong now as it had been before, but maybe only because Pegleg knew better than to antagonise a drunken wizard.

'Now all we need are some more players to fill out our roster,' Slick said.

Olsen stopped laughing at this. 'How many players are you lot shy?'

'Eleven,' Cavre said. While the blitzer had been drinking with the rest of them, Dunk couldn't see that he'd suffered from it at all. He was as stoic as ever.

Dunk wished he could say the same for the team's other blitzer. M'Grash had washed down their celebratory feast with a personal keg of bitter ale, and now he lay sleeping like an elephant-sized baby curled up under the wide, round table.

M'Grash made for a friendly drunk at least. Dunk hated to think how bad it would be if strong drink turned the ogre surly instead. The last thing he needed was to spend his nights trying to keep M'Grash from picking a fight. As it was, he often just had to baby-sit as the ogre slept instead.

'Eleven?' Olsen said. 'Gods preserve us.' He looked around the table at the Hackers sitting there. 'We just assumed–' He stopped to count the players.

'Faith. Only five of you here?' The wizard gazed into the eyes of each of the Hackers. Dunk noticed the mirth had left the yard. 'You're all that's left then?'

Pegleg grimaced. 'The best of the lot too,' he said. 'The fittest survived.'

'Well,' Olsen said, 'there's only one thing for us to do then. We'll have to find another team to merge with in time for the Far Albion Cup tournament!'

'Wait.' Pegleg held up his hook to silence the wizard. 'We're in no shape to jump back into the game just like that. The Far Albion Cup tourney starts in less than a week.'

'Correct,' Cavre said. 'We're out of training, and even if we could manage to find enough players to fill out our roster, we'd never be able to work in enough practices to forge a team that could win a major cup.'

'But this isn't a major cup,' Slick said, nodding to Olsen and Simon. 'Apologies to our friends from Albion, but the competition here can't be anything like what we're used to back home. Even with just five players, we'd probably tear some of these local clubs apart.'

Simon pounded his glass on the table and spilled his beer as he pushed himself to his unsteady feet. His glassy eyes seemed like they might roll back into his head at any moment, but he still spoke, slurring out his words as best he could. 'Now, see here, Mr. Tiny Agent. We may not have the best football players in the world here in Old Blighty, but we're not nearly so bad as you... Wait... What was I on about?'

'Cheers!' Dunk shouted, raising his glass.

'Cheers!' everyone else replied, including Simon, who seemed pleased to be able to rid his mind of whatever it was that might have been bothering him.

After everyone had put their drinks back down, Olsen signalled the waitress for another round and said, 'Opinions of the relative strength of our local lads aside, you'll need to fill out the team with some warm bodies at least – or cold if you'd rather line up a willing necromancer. Not our area of expertise, we're afraid.'

'He's right,' said Slick. Even though the halfling stood less than half Dunk's height and had drunk at least as much as his client, he spoke in a steady voice, his eyes bright and strong. 'You have to start the game with at least eleven players. Otherwise, you forfeit automatically.'

'But where are you going to find any players willing to join a foreign team only days before the tournament starts?' Lästiges said. 'Who'd be so foolish?' She made a solid effort at a professional manner, but her hair rested cockeyed on her head from when she'd fallen asleep at the table during the dessert course. Dunk couldn't wait for her to see the Cabalvision images her camra was recording.

'I bloody well would!' Edgar said, waving about an empty wooden bowl. He'd been drinking a sweet, fragrant concoction made of warm, fermented maple syrup that Dunk could smell on his breath, even from half a table away.

'I'd be honoured to be a part of this team,' the tree-man said. 'I've never seen such a great bunch of mates before in my life. If you lot say you can win this bloody game of yours, then I believe you, and I'll play by your bloody side.'

Pegleg and Carve looked at each other for a moment. Cavre hesitated for a moment, and then nodded. The coach shot to his feet, then, and raised his glass for another toast.

'Well, lads, here's to Edgar!' Pegleg said. 'A finer team-mate you could never want.'

Those able to stand did so and joined the ex-pirate in his cheers. Dunk looked over at Edgar, who jumped for sheer joy, and smiled. He'd already come to like the treeman a lot, and he could see how he would be a huge asset for the team. Even if Edgar had never played a game of Blood Bowl in his life, size and speed like his had to be good for something.

Sticky tears of sap rolled out of Edgar's great, green eyes. 'I've never been so – Whoa!'

As the treeman leaped once more, he landed off-balance and tipped over backwards. He seemed to fall in slow motion, as if the leaves in his upper branches dragged through the air like it was water. He came down flat on his back with a resounding thud that Dunk felt all the way through to his teeth.

Dunk leapt up on to the table to get a better view of the treeman where he lay. He couldn't tell if Edgar was breathing or not. Nor, he realised, did he know if Edgar ever breathed.

'Are you all right, Edgar?' Dunk asked.

'All right?' the treeman said. 'I'm bloody better than "all right", mate! I'm a bloody Bad Bay Hacker!'

* * *

'RISE AND SHINE, son!'

Dunk wanted to pry open his eyes, but the pounding in his head told him that if he tried the sun would kill him by frying holes through his retinas that would burn through his brain and burst out the backside of his skull.

'Go away,' he murmured. He wanted to shout at the intruder, but he couldn't muster the energy to speak so loudly, sure that it would shatter his eardrums if he tried.

'Come now, Dunk. It's past noon. Time to get a move on.'

It was Slick's voice, but Dunk didn't believe the halfling could ever be so cruel to him. It had to be an impostor, an evil doppelganger who had taken Slick's place in order to alienate all of his friends with his inhuman deviltry. Either that, or Dunk was going to need another agent when he recovered from this, as such a horrible act of intrusion was unforgivable.

'Here, son,' Slick said, as he helped Dunk sit up. 'Drink this.' The halfling shoved a mug of something hot into his client's hands.

The room spun around Dunk as he struggled to keep his back to the wall behind him. He put out a hand, trying to keep himself from tumbling from the bed beneath him. As he veered to the left, a bit of the scalding liquid spilled from the cup and landed on his lap.

That woke him right up.

'Yowch!' Dunk shouted, flinging off the wet sheet over him as his eyes flew open. The pain from the light stabbing into his eyes made them flinch closed again, and only his newfound respect for whatever it was in his mug made him careful enough to keep it from spilling on him again.

'For Nuffle's sake, can you keep it down!'

The voice next to him belonged to a woman. It was close, perhaps sitting in a chair at the side of the bed. Dunk reached out his free hand to push the woman away, but she wasn't where he expected her to be. He let his hand fall, and it landed on her breast.

'Hey!' the voice said. Her voice, Dunk realised, recognising it at last: Lästiges's voice.

'Gah!' Dunk leapt from the bed, flinging his eyes open again, even as he held the burning mug of liquid in both hands out of respect for the damage he knew it could do. Once he was standing, he looked down past the mug and spotted Lästiges's form in the bed, huddled under the dry part of the sheet with only her head and her unkempt hair sticking out.

'No, no, no!' Dunk said, the shock at what he saw causing him to forget for a moment the pain pounding in his temples. 'How drunk can a man get?'

'Oh, you're no catch either, I'm sure,' Lästiges said as she wrested open her own bloodshot eyes. 'Don't you-' Her eyes caught Dunk's and locked there in sheer terror.

Lästiges screamed.

Dunk screamed.

Slick screamed too. Then he started to laugh.

'I don't see what's so damn funny,' Dunk said.

'Perhaps he got a good look at your-' Lästiges started. 'Wait. You're still in your clothes.' She pulled down the sheet covering her and looked at herself.

'So are you,' Dunk said. Relief washed over him, with a wave of nausea quick on its heels. He staggered backward, and Slick guided him into a nearby chair.

'So we didn't…' Lästiges said.

'No, no, no,' Dunk said, smiling despite the fact his shrivelled brain seemed to be trying to force itself out either of his ears.

'You don't have to be so relieved about it,' the reporter said. Her camra rose from its resting spot near the door and began to hover near her again.

'It seems not even your daemon-infested device there could bring itself to bear witness to that potential horror,' Slick said. Lästiges whipped a pillow at his face, but he neatly caught it.

'Drink that,' the halfling said to Dunk. 'It's from Olsen.'

The thrower sniffed at the steaming mug in his hands as he wondered how he could hope to swallow something so hot. It smelled like week-old pig vomit.

'Something to put me out of my misery?'

Slick grinned. 'One way or the other. It's safe. I had one earlier myself.'

Dunk blew out a long sigh, and then tossed the drink back, swallowing it in one huge gulp. The hot liquid scorched him straight down his gullet and into his belly, where it seemed to take on a life of its own. He could feel it growling around in his stomach like a trapped badger trying to figure out the best route by which to claw its way free.

Dunk leaned over and put his head between his knees. He thought if he could just let loose the contents of his stomach, he'd feel much better, but he couldn't make it happen. Instead, after a moment he got tired of trying and sat back up.

'Hey,' Dunk said, 'my head doesn't feel like an over-ripe melon any more. And I can feel my tongue again.'

'See,' Slick said.

Dunk rolled his tongue around in his mouth and then made a horrified face.

'Olsen tells me that the taste should go away in a day or three.' Slick shrugged up at the thrower.

'I need something to eat,' Dunk said. 'Anything.'

'It doesn't help,' Slick said, patting his bulging belly. 'Believe me, son, I've tried.'

'Do you have any more of that junk?' Lästiges said, rolling out of the bed.

Dunk noticed that she still had on every bit of her clothing from the night before, right down to her shoes. He breathed a silent sigh of relief. He couldn't imagine cheating on Spinne, as much as he loved her, but to do so with his brother's girlfriend would have been even worse.

'Olsen has a kettle of it in the main room,' Slick said. 'I'd have brought you a cup if I'd known you were – Ah, who am I kidding? I wouldn't have bothered.'

Lästiges spat a bitter 'Thanks' at the halfling, and then scurried from the room.

Dunk remained silent for a moment after watching her go. 'What happened last night?' he finally asked.

'We all had a little too much to drink last night, son,' Slick said. 'All right: a lot. The last I saw of you, you had offered to escort that girl back to her room in a valiant effort to protect the honour of your brother's girlfriend.' He chuckled. 'A fool's errand if ever there was.'

'Fortunately, nothing happened. We must have just passed out here together.'

'Sure,' Slick said. 'Unless, of course, you managed to get your clothes back on after drunkenly violating the trust of your respective lovers.'

Dunk gave the halfling a sidelong glance. 'You can't be serious.'

Slick shook his head. 'No, I'm not, but Pegleg is. He sent me to find you for the team meeting.'

'What team meeting?'

'The one to meet your new team-mates.'

Dunk stared at the bed in the corner of the room. It called like a siren, offering the one thing he still wanted after that foul drink: the oblivion of a good, long rest. 'I've already met Edgar,' he said.

Slick frowned. 'Not him, son. The others.'

'Others?'

The halfling beckoned for Dunk to follow him as he strode out the door. 'Come and see,' he said.

CHAPTER FOURTEEN

'You MUST BE Dunkel Hoffnung,' the man in the black clothes said as he extended his hand in greeting to the thrower when he entered the pub's courtyard. It looked far bleaker in the midday sun than it had the night before. 'A pleasure. I am Bavid Deckem.'

The sandy-haired Deckem stood an inch taller than Dunk, but massed a stone less. He moved with a dancer's grace, seeming to always be on the tips of his toes, every gesture a study in economy and grace. The thing that struck Dunk the most, though, was the shade of Deckem's eyes, which were the icy blue of an arctic sky.

'Mr. Deckem is the finest football player in all of Albion,' Olsen said.

'Ah, to be damned with such fulut praise,' Slick said, sliding around from behind Dunk to take his place at the great, round table in the centre of the courtyard. He immediately started in again on a plate filled with half-demolished fruits and pastries.

Dunk glanced around and saw that the rest of the Hackers were there. Guillermo and Simon chatted on one side of the table, while Cavre sat quietly with M'Grash on the other. Behind the table, in the far corner of the courtyard, Pegleg stood talking to a group of fit-looking men dressed in clothes identical to Deckem's. Dunk didn't see Lästiges anywhere, but that suited him fine.

'Permit me to introduce you to my compatriots,' Deckem said, ignoring Slick's comment. With Olsen at his side, he led Dunk over to the men standing around Pegleg. The circle of the group parted without a word to admit the three newcomers.

Deckem spoke, pointing to each of his doubles in turn as he did. 'Mr. Hoffnung, I'm pleased to present your new team-mates: Oliver Dickens, Lemuel Swift, Long John Stevenson, and Victor Shelley.'

Each of the men shook Dunk's hand without a word, just the same hint of a smile on their faces.

'Team-mates?' Dunk asked, puzzled.

'Mr. Deckem and his friends here have come to fill out our roster,' Pegleg said with an unreserved smile.

'Really?' Dunk raised his eyebrows. 'How did you know we needed anyone?'

'Word about such famous Blood Bowlers as yourself travels fast,' Deckem said, 'at least among Albion's own aspirants.'

Dunk nodded. They'd only been in Albion for just over a day, but plenty of people had seen them arrive in the *Sea Chariot*. He'd been surprised at the absolute lack of any kind of reception then, so he thought he should be pleased to know that someone had finally recognised them. When he looked into Deckem's eyes, though, he couldn't conjure that emotion.

'I understand your surprise,' Deckem said. 'Under normal circumstances, we would have waited, given you some time to acclimatise yourself to your new surroundings. Time, however, is a luxury we no longer have.'

'The Far Albion Cup tournament starts in Wallington in less than a week,' Pegleg said. 'If we're to take part, we need to start practising today.'

'You really think we can manage this, coach?' Dunk asked. 'Even with our new recruits here, we only have eleven players. Isn't that cutting it a little close?'

Deckem put a hand on Dunk's shoulder. 'Do not fret, Mr. Hoffnung. My friends and I have promised not to hurt you. If we need more players at game time, we can procure them.'

'Does that work for you, Dunk?' Pegleg asked.

Dunk shrugged. 'Do I have a choice in the matter, coach?'

A toothy smile on his face, the ex-pirate slapped Dunk on the back. 'None at all! See, you are learning.'

'Ah, my little boy is growing up,' Slick said around a mouthful of jam-slathered crumpet. 'A rookie no longer. I'm so proud.'

THE WEEK SAILED past before Dunk could get his bearings. Pegleg and Cavre worked the team from dusk till dawn, with only short breaks between. These were mostly for drinks of water. In the evening, the innkeepers stuffed them full of bland, starchy foods served alongside large slabs of steak.

Over one lunch, Dunk noticed that the newcomers all ate their steaks nearly raw. 'Is that where the term "bloody" comes from?' he asked Simon later while waiting for their turn on the makeshift obstacle course Cavre had set up at their impromptu training camp. This was held in an open park nearest to the nameless pub the Hackers had adopted as their Albion home.

'Nah. It's just that many chaps around these parts prefer their meat to still be mooing when served. "The rawer, the better" they say.'

Dunk shook his head. 'Do they eat other meats the same way? Like chicken? Or fish?'

Simon snorted. 'Blood Bowlers make enough money that they don't have to eat anything but steak. Raw fish? Around here we call that "bait"!'

'Mr. Sherwood! Mr. Hoffnung!'

The two snapped their heads around to see Pegleg glaring at them. 'Yes, coach?' they said in unison.

'This isn't a knitting circle for little old ladies. You can blather on to each other in your own time. Right now, I want to see five laps around the park from each of you.'

Simon rolled his eyes.

'Make it ten!'

'Right, coach!' Dunk said, grabbing Simon and pulling him along after him before Pegleg increased their punishment again.

'So THIS IS Kingsbury,' Dunk said, craning his neck around from the deck of the *Sea Chariot* as it docked at the city's largest pier, within throwing distance of the largest palace the young man had ever seen. 'Impressive.'

'Sure,' Slick said, wrinkling his nose in disgust. 'There's an impressive amount of sewage floating in the river. And an impressive haze of soot in the impressively rain-filled air. And an impressive smell wafting from farther inland.'

'The Mootland I'm sure it's not,' Slick said, 'but that's what happens when you get so many people packed together in a single place.'

'We suppose you'd prefer we Albionmen all lived in dirty, little warrens like you wee folk,' Olsen said.

'Only because it would make it easier to bury you all alive,' Slick retorted. 'This town is an abomination.'

'What about the palace?' Dunk said. 'Look at those towers stabbing into the sky. Have you ever seen anything that tall?'

'Seems to me the sign of a sovereign who's over-compensating for some other shortcoming, if you follow me, son.' Slick hacked on the thick air. 'How are you going to be able to play in this stuff without losing a lung?'

'Don't you fret about that, Mr. Fullbelly,' Cavre said. 'The Buckingham Bowl where the Far Albion Cup games are held is enchanted to provide clear air and good weather at all times.'

'How'd they manage that?' Slick said. 'You'd think if they could afford to clean up the area around the stadium they'd at least do the same for the King's own palace.'

'The BBC paid for it, of course,' Simon said.

'BBC?'

'Boring-Brilliant Cabalvision. They broadcast all the games. If the air around the stadium was like it is here in the Smoke, their subscribers wouldn't be able to see a thing.'

'They're both boring and brilliant?' Dunk asked.

Deckem arrived at the railing and slipped into the conversation. It struck Dunk that he was the only one of the new recruits he'd ever heard speak. 'Those were the names of the founders: Billy Boring and Bobby Brilliant.'

'You have to be kidding,' Lästiges said. The camra circled her head at high speed, trying to fan the stench away.

'You can't make stuff like this up, Miss Weibchen.'

THE CROWD ROARED as the Hackers took the field for their first game in the Far Albion Cup. By this time, Dunk's sense of smell had already gone dead. The night before, at dinner, he'd realised that this was why the Albionmen ate such bland food. With their noses so effectively deadened, what was the point in making flavourful meals? No one could taste them anyway.

Here in the Buckingham Bowl, though, under its protective enchantments, his senses came alive again. He inhaled the crisp, clean air through his nose, and a smile spread across his face.

'I love the smell of Astrogranite in the morning,' Guillermo said as he trotted out onto the gridiron beside Dunk, stripes of black painted under his eyes, in the way of all of Nuffle's faithful. 'It smells like – hey, I can smell again!'

Dunk grinned under his helmet. He wore the war paint too, although for him it was purely a practical matter. The black paint cut down on the glare of the sun under his eyes, which made it easier for him to look for a catcher downfield. He didn't believe in Nuffle or any of the dozens of other gods worshipped across the Old World and beyond. He wasn't above using their best tricks for himself though.

A voice echoed out over the stadium's Preternatural Announcement system. 'And, all the way in from the Empire, please give a warm, Albion welcome to the Bad Bay Hackers!'

An image of a man dressed in a sheepskin coat stared down at the stadium from the Jumboball on the north end of the field. Dunk shuddered as he looked at the thing, not from the man's wild grin but the memory of his last encounter with such a device. Fortunately, this Jumboball weighed in smaller than the one in the *Spike! Magazine* Tournament, and it sat on a large, round pedestal instead of the easily sabotaged legs that had held up the one in Magritta.

'That's Mon Jotson,' Simon said proudly. 'He's a living legend around here. He's been commenting on our games for hundreds of years.

Dunk looked carefully at the man and detected the telltale pointiness to his ears and other features that labelled him an elf. His brown hair looked like it had long ago formed into a helmet itself, as it stayed perfectly rigid in the winds that flapped the flags standing behind him. He wore a pair of wide, round spectacles with wooden rims that seemed to turn his face into that of an owl.

'Yessir,' Jotson said, 'it's not every day we get a visitor from out of town to play in the finest tournament in our land. The last one I remember was from just last year at this very event. The Evil Gitz, as they were called, only lasted a single round before our fine gentlemen from the Kent Kickers bought them a one-way ticket back home.'

Dunk laughed.

'That's no joke, Mr. Hoffnung,' Deckem said as he waved to the crowd. Even in a Hackers green-and-gold uniform, the man seemed to be dressed all in black. He exuded the colour in everything he did and said. 'The Kickers are the wealthiest team in the land. They paid off enough of the Gits that the visitors had to forfeit the game.'

'Aren't we playing them today?' Dunk asked.

Cavre nodded. 'They already tried to buy us off,' he said. 'Pegleg refused to talk with them unless they were willing to match the tournament's grand prize.'

'Why would they do that?' Dunk said.

Cavre slapped the thrower on his right shoulder pad. 'Now you're catching on, Mr. Hoffnung.'

As team captain, Cavre met the leader of the Kickers in the middle of the field for the coin toss. He called 'Eagles' and won. The Hackers swarmed down to the south end of the field to receive the kick-off.

The ball came sailing down the field toward Dunk, and he called for the catch. Before the ball reached him, though, Deckem dashed forward and plucked it from the air.

Dunk tried to protest, but Deckem sprinted up the field before Dunk could even open his mouth. All he could do was chase the new blitzer up the field and try to help.

As the first of the Kickers – dressed all in blue with a white helmet that featured a blue boot on each side – reached Deckem, the oncoming player launched himself into the air and aimed a vicious kick at the new Hacker's head. Deckem dodged the attack neatly, and drilled his opponent straight in the groin with a powerful jab of his free hand. The player dropped to the ground, writhing in pain.

Before the next Kicker could try to tackle Deckem, Swift and Dickens came at him from both sides, crushing him between them. Blood burst between the bars in the Kicker's face guard, and he fell to the Astrogranite and did not move again.

'Ouch!' Jotson's voice said. 'That sort of killing blow could really hurt someone!'

Another Kicker charged up and hurled a roundhouse kick at Deckem. Anticipating the attack, Deckem spun and pitched the ball backward to M'Grash, who bobbled it a few times before tucking it into the palm of his hand. Then he turned to block the Kicker still coming at him.

Deckem reached up and caught the Kicker's foot as it sailed through the air at him. In a single, smooth motion, he spun around, using the Kicker's momentum to slam him into the Astrogranite. Then he grabbed the Kicker's helmet and gave his neck a sharp, horrible twist.

At that point, Dunk lost track of the new Hacker. A trio of Kickers came straight at M'Grash, doing their level best to knock the ogre to the ground. M'Grash snarled at them, and Dunk noticed a dark, wet patch appear in the front of one player's pants.

'We don't see too many ogres in the Far Albion League,' said Jotson's voice. 'From the looks of Major's uniform, he may have just encountered his first!'

As they'd done in practice countless times, M'Grash swivelled back and handed the ball off to Dunk. The thrower tucked the ball under his arm and followed the ogre into the fray. There were few players as accomplished at blocking as M'Grash. He had a way of clearing a runner's path that none of the other Hackers could match.

While M'Grash made quick work of most of the Kickers who came his way, Dunk knew that one of them would eventually figure out how to get around the ogre and attack the ball carrier: him. He kept his eyes open downfield, hunting for a team-mate who was open for a pass.

To his surprise, a tree stood in the end zone. He'd seen a lot of strange things on the various fields on which the Hacker's had played, but most of them had gone to great lengths to remove large obstacles like that, especially in the end zone. The Athelorn Avengers' home field sat atop the Great Tree of the Greenwood, of course, but even that only had a few large branches that stuck through from below.

For a moment, Dunk wondered why someone had draped the tree in green and gold cloth. Perhaps a Hackers fan had gone to the trouble to decorate it. Then the tree waved its upper branches at Dunk, and the thrower realised he was looking straight at Edgar.

Dunk cocked back his arm to chuck the ball into Edgar's waiting branches. Just then, though, a Kicker dashed through between M'Grash's trunk-like legs and barrelled straight at him.

Dunk snarled at his challenger and tucked the ball under his left arm. With his right, he lashed out at the Kicker and smashed him in his exposed throat. The man collapsed, clutching his dented windpipe, and Dunk had to repress the strong urge to finish him off while he was down.

The feeling disturbed Dunk. He'd never been a dirty player. Sure, he knew the rules in Blood Bowl were more of a set of loosely followed suggestions, but he didn't believe he had to hurt people just to win games.

Right now, though, it was all he could do to pull himself away from murdering the hapless Kicker sprawled out before him. It would only take one, short move, and the Kickers would be down one more player. If that might help the Hackers win the game, wasn't it the right thing to do? If he really wanted to win, shouldn't he be willing to pull out all the stops?

Dunk pushed those thoughts aside and stepped back into the open area that M'Grash always left in his wake. He cocked his arm back and hurled the ball down the field. It spiralled smoothly through the air, arcing up into the sky like a shooting star and then landing square in Edgar's branches.

'Touchdown!' Jotson shouted. 'Our aggressive guests take the early lead from our proxy hosts, the Kickers. If things stay like this, there will be no stopping them!'

Somewhere, a referee blew a whistle and signalled the score. M'Grash scooped Dunk up in his arms and trotted back over to the Hacker bench, where he set the thrower down.

'Excellent work, men!' Pegleg said, almost crowing with delight. 'Perhaps it's true what they say about the team who owns the Far Albion Cup. You look unbeatable out there!'

'Oh, dear,' Jotson's voice said. 'A few of the Kickers would be more than just depressed about that last score if they weren't too dead to care. I count five casualties on the field, and a sixth – that's Clive Keegan, hometown favourite – being carted off the field with what looks like a crushed windpipe. We'll have to check in with the Kicker apothecary to see what his chances are for coming back into the game.'

Dunk's stomach sank at the news.

'Fantastic!' Pegleg said, happier than ever. 'Now they only have ten players left. The only thing better than taking the lead is doing it while crushing your foes' bodies and spirits!' The coach's face turned sharp. 'How are you all doing?'

Dunk knew what Pegleg was getting at. In games this bloody, it was rare for the damage to be one-sided. Once the initial victims figured out what kind of game they were in, they usually tossed all compunction out of the stadium and worked the bloodletting angle as hard as they could.

The thrower turned to see one of the new players, Shelley, cradling his left arm. When Dunk looked closer to see what was wrong, he noticed it was no longer attached at the elbow. Despite this, Shelley seemed able to ignore the pain.

'Are you okay?' Dunk asked.

Deckem answered. 'He'll be fine. Just give him a few minutes. He'll be set to play in time for the next kick-off.'

Dunk goggled at the new Hacker. 'You're kidding, right?'

'I never kid.'

CHAPTER FIFTEEN

Dunk said nothing to Pegleg, and no one else seemed to notice Shelley's injury. The thrower wanted to see how Shelley could possibly take the field again in this game. Despite what Deckem had promised, Dunk didn't think a player missing an arm would be much good to anyone.

By the time the Hackers were ready for the next kickoff, though, Shelley seemed fine. He even waved at Dunk with the arm that the thrower had seen detached just a moment before. He wondered if he could have been mistaken about the extent of Shelley's injuries. After all, Dunk always spent every Blood Bowl game pumped on adrenaline, and he guessed it might have made him see things that weren't there.

Then Cavre kicked the ball over the heads of most of the Kickers, and the game started up again.

The rest of the game was a blur for Dunk, who spent most of his time trying to avoid getting killed by the Kickers. The shock of losing so many of their players wore off fast, it seemed, and now they were determined to inflict even greater losses on the Hackers. Most of the players completely ignored the ball, setting out to break some bones instead.

'I'm going to tear off your arms!' a Kicker snarled at Dunk after planting a snap-kick straight into the thrower's gut. Laying on the Astrogranite, gasping for breath, Dunk realised there wasn't a damn thing he could do to stop the Kicker from making good on his pledge.

Then Shelley smashed into the Kicker from behind and laid him out flat. They landed next to Dunk, close enough so he could feel the ground shake from their impact. The Kicker's helmet came off and dribbled away across the field, exposing him as a thick-cut man with short-cropped, dark hair and a series of scars on his face that made his face look more like a treeman's than a human's.

The Kicker reached back, grabbed Shelley by the arm, and pulled. The limb separated at the elbow once again, and the Kicker found himself holding Shelley's forearm in his fist. He screamed at the sight of the amputated arm before he dropped it and tried to scramble away.

Dunk saw that the arm had torn stitches running all the way around its elbow end. Stranger yet, while he'd expected to see blood pouring from the end of it, there was not a single drop.

Shelley picked up his forearm in his other hand and smashed it down on the Kicker's helmet like a hammer.

The Kicker screamed in horror until Shelley smashed him with the loose arm again. It must have been like bringing a hammer down on the Kicker's skull. After the second blow, he fell silent, but Shelley kept beating the Kicker's face into a bloody mess. The whole time, he never said a word.

Jotson's voice kept up a steady commentary on the action, though it didn't seem to all be happening in front of Dunk.

'By all the stones in the henge, that's some serious killing going on down there. I haven't seen this kind of mayhem since – well, since last week, at least! Have you ever witnessed a tougher team than these Hackers? Shelley there is beating Percy to death with his own arm! That's one way to give a man a hand – into the grave!

'Of course, Stevenson's having his way with Silver on the other end of the field. He seems to be under the mistaken impression that Silver's head is the ball, as he's taken to spiking it in the end zone. Sorry, friend, but that's not going to score points with anyone but the fans!

'At midfield, it's Dickens and Swift having a go at Bantam, pulling his legs apart and cracking him like he was a wishbone. The Kickers can only wonder if the referee got a premium price for self-induced blindness during this game or if the Hackers robbed him as well!'

Something black and white and red all over came spinning through the air at Dunk. At first, he thought it might be the football, which he'd lost track of, and he threw up his hands to catch it. Then he noticed its strange colours, and he dodged out of the way instead. More than one Blood Bowl player had reflexively caught a bomb when he thought it was the game ball, and Dunk wasn't about to make the same mistake as Stumpy Kajowski.

The 'ball' sailed over Dunk's head and bounced three times before rolling to a rest on the Astrogranite behind him. When it came to a stop, he saw it for what it was: a human head wearing a black-and-white striped cap.

Dunk stared back down the field from where the head had come and spotted Simon standing over the referee's decapitated corpse, an insane grin on his face. The catcher's eyes flashed red at Dunk before he trotted away down the field.

'It looks like… It could be… Yes! He could… go… all… the… way!' Jotson's voice shouted. 'Touchdown, Hackers!'

The crowd roared, although whether with outrage or delight, Dunk couldn't tell. He was just thankful that the action had stopped for a moment and he could get his bearings again.

'Who scored that?' Dunk asked as he ran back over to the Hackers' bench.

'Deckem certainly hasn't lost any of his panache,' Jotson said. 'It's good to have him back out of retirement. I knew that fatal injury of his wouldn't keep him down!'

Dunk glanced back at the Jumboball to see an instant replay of the score. In the huge image, Deckem sprinted toward the goal line, the football tucked under his arm. As he neared the end zone, a large Kicker stepped between him and the goal. Deckem stuck out his arm and drove it into the Kicker's chest as he shoved him back over the plane of the goal line.

In the image, the crowd in the end zone seats behind Deckem went nuts. The new Hacker stood over the unconscious Kicker's form and hurled the ball up toward the cheap seats. Then he threw something else that landed even further up into the stands. A fight broke out in both locations as the fans trampled each other for a chance to claim Deckem's discarded prizes.

'Good work, Mr. Deckem!' Pegleg said. 'We're up two to nothing, and it's only halfway through the first half.'

Dunk turned to see Deckem trotting up behind him, still waving at the wild, adoring crowd. His hands were covered in blood, but not a drop of sweat marred his smooth, pale brow.

'Thanks, coach,' Deckem said with a smile. 'I don't believe in toying with my prey. It's an act of mercy to end things as soon as possible.'

'Great Nuffle's cooler of Hater-Aid!' Jotson said. 'Do you see what that second present Deckem sent to his fans is?'

The image on the Jumboball zoomed in tight on a tattooed dwarf with a bright-orange mohawk and more piercings than an archery target. He roared in triumph as he smashed aside the other treasure-hunters and thrust his prize aloft in a bloodied fist.

It was a battered human heart, still beating from the looks of it.

'Crikey! I have ten quid that says that ends up on B-BA tonight and fetches a princely sum!'

'Bee-bay?' M'Grash said, scratching his head.

'The Blood Bowl Auction network,' Slick said. The halfling stood on the end of the Hackers' bench, looking up at the Jumboball too.

'Yessir! Who wouldn't want to have that up on their mantel?' Jotson asked. 'But wait!'

The camra panned over to show a force of blue-uniformed knights in blood-spattered armour slashing their way through the crowd. Most of the fans parted before their wedge formation, and those that didn't tasted the knights' steel.

'It looks like the Kickers have sent their cheerleaders into the stands to get that vital part of Hartshorn's anatomy back. With luck, their team apothecary will be able to get it back into him in time!'

The dwarf clambered up on the shoulders of a nearby fan and held the heart aloft again, defying the armoured cheerleaders, daring them to take it from him. The crowd growled in anticipation of the coming fight, and the cheerleaders marched on undeterred by the dwarf's antics.

Just as the knights reached the dwarf, he tossed the heart back to a tall, thin, dark-haired man standing behind him, and then launched himself into the knights. Spreading his compact form out as much as he could, he bowled over the front two ranks of the knights. They might have all gone over if the crowd rushing in behind them hadn't been forced to hold them up for fear of being crushed themselves.

The man with the heart bobbled it for a moment, and then caught it tight. As he did, one of the cheerleaders broke free from the dwarf and pointed her sword straight at the man's neck. Terrified, the man pitched the heart farther up into the stands and then dived down over the gawkers standing below him.

The fans below caught the man and started to pass him toward the exit, overjoyed at the chance to foil the cheerleaders' efforts. At the same time, the fan who caught the slippery heart hurled it counter-clockwise along the stands, straight into another section. The crowd cheered, and the noise went up time and again as fan after fan who found himself holding the heart tossed it on again.

Dunk stared at Deckem in disgust as the man grinned up at the images on the Jumboball. 'You would rip out a man's heart just to score a touchdown?' Dunk asked. 'He couldn't have stopped you anyway. You didn't have to kill him. What kind of player would do that?'

Deckem turned and looked the thrower straight in the eyes. The smile had left his face. 'A winner,' he said before he turned and headed for the locker room.

'THOSE GUYS SCARE me,' Dunk said before he took another pull from his ale.

'You're not the only one,' Slick said, gazing around the cosy pub – a well-appointed place called the Cock and Bull – every inch of which seemed panelled in dark, rich woods. 'I've never seen so many people blow off a victory dinner as I did tonight. I poked my nose into the dining room at the inn, and the only ones there were Pegleg, Cavre, and Deckem and his four stooges.'

'Not even Simon?' Dunk rubbed his chin as he gazed around the room. One of the first things he'd noticed about the place was that it had no Cabalvision. That alone had been enough to recommend the place. Dunk didn't feel like sitting though endless replays and joking commentary about that afternoon's game – or "wholesale massacre", as one of the BBC anchors had called it. 'I thought for sure he'd be whooping it up with his fellow countrymen.'

'Maybe he has other friends in town, folks who aren't so murderous.'

'We won, didn't we?' Dunk said. He waved for another beer, even as he polished off the one in his hand. 'Isn't that what it's all about? Win the tournament, grab the prize? The wealth of kings and the adulation of the fans?'

Slick nodded slowly, as if trying to convince himself of Dunk's words. 'That's the standard story, son, the one we all try to sell ourselves. Sad thing, isn't it, that it so rarely turns out that way?'

Dunk narrowed his eyes at the halfling for a moment. 'What do you mean?'

'Well, it's all just a big fairy tale, isn't it?' Slick leaned back in his chair, which was much too large for him, forcing him to bring his legs up so that his feet hung out over the edge of the seat. 'I mean, how many Blood Bowl teams are there?'

Dunk shook his head. He had no idea. 'Dozens?'

'More like hundreds if you count all those local club teams full of amateurs who play for the "fun" of it.'

Dunk accepted his next beer from the barmaid, a pretty, blonde woman dressed in a farm girl's clothes.

'Thanks,' Dunk said. 'Cheers, I mean.'

The barmaid smiled. 'You're not from around these parts, are you, love?'

Dunk shook his head, his thoughts drawn to the people back home he missed most: Spinne and his brother Dirk.

'Business or pleasure?' she asked.

'A bit of both,' Dunk said. 'We're here for the tournament.'

'Cor blimey,' the woman said, her blue eyes sparkling. 'It's been a cracking good tourney so far, hasn't it? That game this afternoon? What a bleeding bloodbath.'

Dunk's face froze. 'You like that sort of thing?'

The barmaid stuck out her bottom lip as she considered the question. 'I dunno, really. I don't normally care much for Blood Bowl. Too much going on, if you ask me. I'm more of a *real* football fan myself.'

'But you watched that "bloodbath" this afternoon?'

'Not really,' she said. 'I caught the replay on the chryssy. Just the highlights.'

'That's all you care for?'

'Well, I know there's a lot more to the game than fighting and killing, but that's all over my head, innit? It's like when you watch the chariot races. The only part anyone cares about are the crashes.'

Dunk hoisted his beer to the woman and said, 'Cheers.' She wandered off to find others in need of drink.

What the woman had said crawled around in Dunk's guts like a long-tailed rat. He knew all that most of the fans cared about was action, but were people really that bloodthirsty? Could they ignore the fact that real people were killed in front of them? And that they cheered to see it?

'What were you saying?' Dunk said to Slick.

'There are hundreds of Blood Bowl teams out there. Thousands of players. How many of them can be winners?'

'About half of them, every week,' Dunk said.

'No, no, no, son. I'm talking about real winners. How many can win one of the four major tournaments? How many have any kind of a shot at playing in the Blood Bowl, much less winning the trophy? Just a handful of teams.'

Slick moved forward in the chair until his legs dangled over the edge. As he spoke, he gestured with his hands to punctuate his points, warming to his subject. 'Maybe a dozen teams have a shot at the title every year – probably less than that. But how many of those teams *think* they're in that top dozen?'

Dunk shrugged.

'Dozens more. Maybe even hundreds. Half of the teams out there, at least. They think they can win it all, and they're dead wrong. Just ask the Gobbo next time you see him. Ask him how many teams have odds to win the title that are in the single digits.'

'I don't know if I'll see him again if I keep hanging out with you.' Dunk thought back to how the halfling had tried to beat the bookie up back in

Magritta, and a smile flitted across his face. He washed it down with another swig of his beer.

Slick rolled his eyes. 'The *point* here – and I do have one, son – is that most Blood Bowl players spend their entire career chasing after a dream they have no real chance of achieving. They'd be better off shopping around for headstones instead. They're about ten times more likely to need one of those rather than a free spot on their hand for a championship ring.'

Dunk nodded, and Slick fell silent. They both worked at their beers for a moment, neither of them wanting to speak before the other. Finally, Dunk gave in.

'Are you telling me to quit?'

Slick looked across the table toward Dunk, a sad frown on his face. 'You're a big boy,' the halfling said. 'I can't tell you to do anything. Hell, I'm not sure what I want you to do myself. We've had a great ride with the Hackers over the past year. That bonus cheque we got at the end of the last season put quite a few good pies in me.'

Slick rubbed his belly at that thought. 'But money's no good to someone who's too dead to spend it.'

Dunk took another pull at his beer and considered this. After a while, he shook his head. 'I can't do it,' he said. 'I can't leave the team.'

'Why not?' The halfling asked the question as if he wanted to know what Dunk wanted for dinner.

'What would the team do without me?' Dunk said. 'They wouldn't have enough players to play. They'd have to forfeit.'

Slick snapped his fingers. 'You'd be replaced like that. There are always people desperate to get on to a decent Blood Bowl team. Just look at Deckem and his friends. Pegleg didn't even have to go looking for them. They came hunting for him.'

'But they're my friends,' Dunk said. 'What about Cavre or Simon or Guillermo or M'Grash? I can't leave them to fend for themselves.'

'Why not? They were there before you came around, and they'll manage well enough after you leave.'

'What's the first thing I told you about Blood Bowl?' Slick said.

Dunk had to think back about that one. 'When someone offers you a contract, get it in writing?'

'Yes! But that's not what I meant. What else?'

'Never shower with an orc?'

Slick nodded. 'That's a good one too, but it's not what I meant. What else?'

'It's only a foul if the ref sees it?'

'Wow, son. I am a positive fount of wisdom, but that's–' The halfling raised his hands to cut Dunk off. 'Here it is, the relevant secret: Never make friends with the other players.'

'What?' Dunk said.

'You never know when you might get traded or released. The people you're playing alongside this week could be your mortal foes the next. Don't get too attached to any particular team because you might find yourself having to play against them next week.'

'You never said that,' Dunk said.

Slick squinted at his client. 'Are you sure?'

'Yes.'

'Hm,' Slick said. 'Well it's good advice no matter when you get it. Sorry I skipped over it the first time around.'

'I think you're making things up as you go along.'

The halfling grinned up at the young man. 'You know, for a Blood Bowl player, you're pretty smart.'

'Such faint praise,' Dunk said.

'Hey, I can only work with what you give me. I'm an agent, not a miracle worker – your career rocketing toward the top aside.'

'I thought I was responsible for that.'

'See, son,' Slick said, reaching out a hand to pat Dunk's arm. 'That just goes to show how little it is you know.'

Dunk smirked. 'Thankfully I have you to watch out for me.'

'I think you could do better than that.' Deckem stepped around a pillar of polished wood. 'A player of your talents deserves a first-rate agent.'

Slick stood up on his chair. 'They don't get any better, pal!'

Deckem smiled at the halfling, and then pointedly ignored him. 'You are a fine player, Mr. Hoffnung. I admire your skills on the field. Even if they aren't as refined as my own, you have a great deal of natural talent for the game.'

'That's kind of you,' Dunk said, picking his words with care.

'I'd encourage you to stick around,' Deckem said. 'As Mr. Fullbelly points out, you could be replaced, but I don't think that would be in the best interests of the team. The more original Hackers on the team, the better. From a marketing point of view, at least. Otherwise, we become just another FA League team rather than the newest kids on the block. There is some mileage to be extracted from that if we are willing to squeeze hard enough.'

'I'll keep that in mind.'

'Of course, if you did leave, my friends might decide we were better off without the rest of the Hackers. I've done my best to convince them otherwise, but they are rather… single-minded.'

Dunk stood up at that. 'Are you saying you'll kill the others if I leave?'

Only Deckem's eyes smiled. 'I would never say that, Mr. Hoffnung,' he said as he turned to leave. 'But I would never say it couldn't happen either. You're a smart lad. Keep that in mind, would you?'

As Deckem left, Dunk slumped back into his seat, stunned. 'What? What should I do? What am I going to do?'

'Barmaid!' Slick said, motioning for the waitress to bring them another round. 'I think we're going to be here a while!'

CHAPTER SIXTEEN

THE KICK-OFF FOR the Hackers' next game went just as badly as the first – at least from Dunk's point of view.

'Cracking!' Mon Jotson's voice said over the PA system. 'Over the past week, fans, I've done some research on the new darlings of our little ball. The Far Albion Cup has been kind to the Hackers so far. Their Casualties Inflicted per Game has skyrocketed since they arrived in fair Albion. If that last play is any indication, they're on their way to bumping up their numbers once again!

'I see one, two, three – oh who can count them all? Some of them are in parts! There are at least five bodies in Mancaster Knighted uniforms scattered across the field. '

The news made Dunk feel sick. 'How many did we lose?' he asked.

'One of Deckem's men lost a leg,' Slick said. 'But he seems to be doing fine.'

Dunk followed the halfling's gaze over to where the team apothecary – a wizened old, woman with a swing-down monocle attached to a black band around her head – sat stitching Swift's leg back on at the knee. Even with it barely attached, the Hacker could still move the foot that had just been separated from him.

'Who are these guys?' Dunk asked. 'Could you learn anything about them?'

Slick shook his head. 'The whole country knows Deckem, but the rest of his contingent is a real mystery. Despite the fact they play great ball, no one's ever heard of them before.'

Dunk spotted Lästiges standing in the corner of the Hacker's dugout, behind Slick. He hadn't seen her since the morning she'd raced from her bed, almost a week ago. For his part, that had been fine. He knew he hadn't done anything wrong, but skating that close to the edge had upset him. If he hadn't seen anything of the reporter until the trip back to the Old World – or even later than that – he would not have minded.

She nodded at him tentatively, her usual aggressive bravado put aside, at least for the moment. He knew he should go over and talk to her, clear the air between them, but now wasn't the right time.

'How much longer do we have to put up with them?' Dunk asked.

'As long as we keep winning games, Mr. Hoffnung,' Pegleg said, slapping his starting thrower on the back. Dunk had never seen the ex-pirate happier.

'Coach,' Dunk said. 'Some of us are worried about our new team-mates. They're a little – well, violent.' As the words spilled out of Dunk's mouth, he regretted them. They sounded feeble even to his ears.

Pegleg laughed. 'It's a violent game,' he said. 'People die. Or don't you remember our last match in Magritta?'

Dunk nodded. He didn't think he'd ever forget it.

'It's a kill or be killed game, Dunk.' Pegleg's manner had turned softer now. 'If you're going to play, it's best to be on the side of the killers.'

'But it doesn't have to be that way,' Dunk said. 'We could just play the game – outscore the other team.'

'A win is a win. I spent enough years with nothing but losses. I'll take a win any way I can get it.'

'That's the kind of attitude I like to hear, coach,' Deckem said, strolling up to where Pegleg stood over Dunk on the bench. The new blitzer wiped his blood-stained hands off on his jersey as he spoke. 'A winning attitude.'

Dunk leapt to his feet and glared right into Deckem's eyes. 'If you're such a winner, why'd you ever leave the game in the first place?' he asked. 'Why'd you retire?'

Dark amusement danced in Deckem's ice-blue eyes as he smirked at Dunk. 'Strictly speaking, Mr. Hoffnung, I never did retire. I was killed.'

Dunk mulled that over. He'd long suspected that Deckem and his friends had long since felt the last beats of their own hearts. That wasn't too unusual in Blood Bowl players though. The Champions of Death, the Erengrad Undertakers, the Zilargan Zombies, the

Crimson Vampires – all of those teams featured all-undead rosters.

But they all had necromancers – sorcerers of death – as either coaches or owners too. Pegleg was many things – most of which he refused to share with his players – but he was no necromancer.

'Who brought you back?' Dunk asked. 'Or did you manage that all by your lonesome?'

'Now, now, Mr. Hoffnung,' Deckem said as he jammed his bright yellow helmet back on to his head. 'We all have our secrets. Let me keep mine, and I won't pry too hard into yours.'

The new Hacker turned and sprinted back out on to the field, and the crowd went wild. Dunk looked up and saw Deckem's grinning face on the Jumboball. The undead player spat something thick and black through the bars of his helmet, then winked right at the camra.

'What's this?' Jotson's voice said. 'I think we may have a new record for the shortest game ever in the Far Albion Cup! Four of the remaining Knighted players are refusing to take the field!'

Dunk glanced across the gridiron to see the Knighted coach screaming at his reluctant players, but they were already on their way to the locker room. The fans booed and hurled full steins of beer at the players, which bounced off one Knighted's helmet, but this only made the players who were left decide to join them.

'I've never seen anything like this,' Jotson said. 'What cowards! This will forever be a blight on the unimpeachable honour of the great city of Mancaster and its much-vaunted Knighted. But wait! What's this?'

Dunk stared off across the field at the Knighted coach as he tackled one of his own players. The crowd roared in delight as the coach tore the player's helmet off and started to strip him of his uniform.

'Feefa's spotted balls!' Jotson said. 'It looks like Coach Fergus Alexson has decided to take out all his frustration on Team Captain Neville Rooney, and poor Rooney's getting the worst of that match-up. Perhaps you'd have been safer on the pitch, Neville.'

'What is he doing, Dunkel?' M'Grash asked from over the thrower's shoulder.

Dunk shook his head, amazed. He looked back and saw that all of the living Hackers were lined up behind him, staring out at the spectacle too. Deckem and his crew still stood down near the Hacker's end zone, ready to kick the ball off again. None of the others had joined them yet.

'It looks like he's stripping his own player down to his briefs.'

'He's taking his uniform,' Carve said. 'For himself.'

'What?' Guillermo said. 'Why would he do something as insane as that?'

'The game's not over yet,' Simon said. 'Fergie hasn't forfeited yet, and the ref hasn't called it.'

'What ref?' Slick asked sarcastically.

Edgar remained silent, but Dunk thought he detected a guilty look on his wooden face.

'Dear Nuffle,' Pegleg said, his voice heavy with awe. 'He's going out there himself.'

The living Hackers all turned to goggle at their coach, and then went back to watching Coach Alexson kick his battered player away from him and start to put on the stripped uniform, starting with the pads. The crowd fell silent for a moment, unable to understand what it was that Alexson had in mind. When Alexson slammed Rooney's helmet onto his head and trotted out onto the gridiron though, they went nuts.

The Jumboball showed the Knighted coach charging onto the field and getting ready to receive the kick-off. When the roar of the crowd died down enough that Dunk could hear again, Jotson's voice spoke. 'This is inconceivable, yet not entirely unexpected. If you could ever expect any coach to stand up for the honour of his team, it would be Fergie. Even with all of his players abandoning him, he stands unwilling to surrender. He prefers death to dishonour.'

The image on the Jumboball switched to that of Deckem glaring down the field at Fergie and cracking his knuckles. The other Hackers on the field mirrored his actions.

'And if Deckem has his way, Fergie will get his wish. Oh, the drama! The Knighted coach – one of Albion's favourite sons – faces five of the killer Hackers – invaders from the Old World! While you have to admire such gumption, you can't imagine that old Alexson has a chance here. Farewell, Fergie, it is then! We'll remember you well!'

'No,' M'Grash said, frowning and shaking his head.

Dunk knew just what the ogre meant. 'We can't let them do this.'

'What's that, mate?' Simon said. No one but Slick and M'Grash had been able to hear Dunk over the roar of the crowd.

'We can't let them do this!' Dunk shouted. 'We have to stop it.' He looked to the others for support.

M'Grash bore a grin into which he could have stuffed a pig. The more restrained Slick nodded in approval. Guillermo and Simon goggled at Dunk as if he'd suddenly sprouted another head that had begun reciting epic poetry in a long-forgotten tongue. Edgar looked aghast. The unreadable Cavre's face remained impassive, betraying no thoughts at all.

In stark contrast, Pegleg was livid. His fiery glare forbade Dunk to do anything unusual here. 'Belay that, Mr. Hoffnung,' he snarled. 'If you take one step on to that field, you'll be warming the bench for the rest of the game.'

Dunk locked eyes with the ex-pirate. There was no doubt that Pegleg meant to threaten much worse than that. The game would be over here in minutes anyway, one way or the other. Then Dunk looked up at the Jumboball.

There, framed in the giant crystal, crouched Fergus Alexson. Dunk had never seen the man play before, but he'd heard about the man's reputation as a coach. Despite his greying hair, he had the fit and ready body of an athlete, someone who trained alongside his players. But there was no doubt in Dunk's mind that Deckem and his pals would tear Fergie apart in a matter of seconds.

Dunk strode out onto the gridiron and walked straight toward Deckem. The crowd – thinking that Dunk was going to help his team-mates annihilate Fergie – booed.

'Hello, Mr. Hoffnung!' Deckem said over the noise. 'Come to take your place with the winners?'

'You can't do this,' Dunk said. 'This is pointless. That man doesn't need to die.'

'But he does,' Deckem said. 'Killing him sends a message to everyone that there's nothing the Hackers aren't willing to do to win.'

'You're not a Hacker,' Dunk said. 'I don't care if you wear the uniform. You're a disgrace to it.'

'I think that's up to Coach Pegleg,' Deckem said, 'not you. He seems to appreciate my efforts, no matter how crude my methods may be.'

'He's not here right now. *I'm* telling you to stop it.'

Half amused, Deckem raised an eyebrow at this. 'No. Now get out of my way, or I'll kill you too.'

Dunk had learned a lot of things in his misspent youth. As two sons of nobility, he and his brother Dirk had wandered through many of the slums of Altdorf, looking for trouble, for some excitement in their safe and placid lives. They'd found plenty of it, and sometimes a brawl came arm in arm with it.

Many times, Dirk had thrown the first punch, starting the whole fight – or so it seemed. This irritated Dunk for a long time, as he didn't care for fighting like Dirk did, so one day he confronted him about it.

'Why do you always start all these fights?' Dunk asked him one night over a bottle of Bugman's Best Ale in their favourite hole in the wall, a dive called the Skinned Cat.

Dirk just smiled. 'I don't start any of the fights. I finish them.'

'You know what I mean. You always hit the other guy first.'

Dirk sipped his beer and smiled. 'When I'm standing nose to nose with a guy like that, do you think there's going to be a fight?'

'There always is.'

'And who do you think is going to win that fight?'

'Usually it's you.'

'Always,' Dirk said, raising a finger. 'I always win. You know why? *Because* I hit first.'

'But you could just walk away.'

'You think that guy's just going to let me walk away? What about that orc in the Full Moon the other night. Think he'd have just let me traipse out of the pub?'

'But–'

'But, nothing. He'd have clocked me from behind, and you'd have ended up carrying me home that night.'

'I did.'

'Those victory celebrations do sometimes get out of hand.' Dirk smiled at the memory. Then he turned serious again. 'Instead, I hit him first. He starts the fight wounded, one good hit behind me. I may not be the biggest dog on the block. I may not be the best fighter. But give me an edge like that, and I'll come out on top every time.'

These thoughts shot through Dunk's head as Deckem stood nose to nose with him, daring him to try to stop him. Dunk reached out and put his hands on Deckem's shoulders. The new player glanced down at his arms and said, 'I'm really not in the mood for a hug.'

Dunk pulled the man to him and drove his head forward at the same time. His head-butt smashed

Deckem's nose flat and cracked his head back so hard Dunk thought he felt the man' neck break. When he let go of Deckem's shoulders, the man collapsed to the Astrogranite.

The crowd cheered louder than ever.

As Dunk stepped back from where Deckem sat, the man's four friends started toward the thrower. Dunk knew he had no hope to take them all on at once. While he'd been able to surprise Deckem, these four were alert, ready, and not going to wait for him to attack.

'Now, guys, can't we talk about this?' he said, getting ready to turn and run. He thought he might be able to outdistance them in a short sprint to the Hackers' dugout. As undead, though, they wouldn't tire and would catch him if the chase went on for long.

Then Dunk felt the earth move beneath his feet, a low, thrumming he felt through his boots. He recognised it from dozens of games, and he grinned. He glanced over his shoulder to see M'Grash and Edgar stampeding toward him, rushing to his aid. Cavre, Guillermo, and Simon raced along behind them, unable to match their long-legged pace.

'Do not hurt Dunkel!' the ogre roared. 'He's my friend!'

'Incredible!' Jotson's voice said. 'Now it's the Hackers against the Hackers! Perhaps Fergie has a chance after all.'

The crowd cheered the thought, and Dunk saw an image of himself grinning, gazing out from the Jumboball. For a moment, seeing his head forty feet tall stunned him, but then Dickens lunged at him.

Dunk dived to the side. He refused to get into a fair fight with Dickens or any of the rest of Deckem's cronies. He'd seen them take apart nearly a dozen players already, and he had no desire to be the next notch on their collective belt.

Dickens flew past him and skidded along the ground. Before he came to a stop, M'Grash picked him up and hauled him into the air. The ogre held the man so that their noses almost touched. Dickens's feet kicked out wildly, hitting nothing, as he dangled in the air.

'Don't!' M'Grash shouted into Dickens's face.

Dickens twisted about like a hanged man trying to wriggle out of his noose. Then something popped loose, and he fell to the ground, leaving his helmet in M'Grash's meaty hand.

It took Dunk a moment to realise that Dickens's head was still in his helmet.

'Well,' Jotson said. 'Would you look at that? That's going to leave a mark.'

The crowd roared its approval.

M'Grash peered into the helmet through its face-guard and screamed in surprise. Without thinking – something the ogre rarely did – M'Grash flung the helmet away, and it went sailing into the stands.

Dunk stared in horror, but even before Dickens's occupied helmet landed something hit the thrower from behind. He spun around in the green-armed grasp to find Swift tackling him to the ground.

They hit the Astrogranite hard, and Dunk felt Swift's fingers reaching for his throat. He turned and smashed a spiked elbow pad into the man's forehead, and there it stuck for a moment before he could wrestle it back out.

'Crikey! You don't see a brawl like that every day,' Jotson said. 'Well, not between team-mates, at least. Ur, on the field.'

'Still, it's one cracking good fight! And wait! One of the Hackers has broken loose from the brawl and is racing toward Fergie!'

Dunk glanced up at the Jumboball and saw Deckem sprinting away down the field. The hapless Fergie stood there in his ill-fitting gear, fists balled, chin out, and ready to face his foe.

'No!' Dunk shouted. He was too far away, though, and Swift's death grip around his middle meant he couldn't even stand. The other living Hackers were too busy fighting with the dead ones to be able to stop Deckem either.

'This is it, blokes,' Jotson said. 'When – I mean, if – Deckem knackers Fergie, that's it for the game. If Mancaster can't field a single player for its team, the game is over!'

'No!' Dunk twisted Swift's head around hard enough that he was looking the other way. This didn't slow the undead player down at all, but it kept him from seeing what he was doing. Dunk pried himself loose from the effectively blinded Swift's fingers and scrambled to his feet. He launched himself down Deckem's path. He'd be too late to stop the new Hacker, of course, but maybe he could still avenge a good man's death.

In the Jumboball, Dunk saw Deckem stalking toward the Mancaster coach, who stood his ground, unwilling to run although he faced certain death. Deckem smiled so broadly that, even by way of the Jumboball, Dunk could see his too-white teeth behind his helmet.

As the undead Hacker came within reach, Fergie leapt at him, swinging both of his spiked gauntlets up at Deckem's face. It was a desperate ploy, for sure, but Dunk couldn't see the coach had any options left to him.

'No!' Dunk shouted, stretching out his hands to stop the massacre, even though dozens of yards separated him from the two combatants.

A flash of light blinded Dunk then, and a peal of thunder louder than even the noise of the crowd followed closer after. When Dunk's vision cleared, he saw Fergie's smoking body stretched out flat on the Astrogranite.

Deckem stood over the Mancaster coach's fallen form and spat something black at him through his faceguard.

'Feefa's blessed fife! What was that?' Jotson said. 'Fergie is down! He's down! Hackers win!'

The crowd booed louder than ever and started throwing things on to the field: empty beer steins, half-eaten rat-on-a-stick treats, hapless snotlings, even the remains of the missing referee. Dunk and the other Hackers had to sprint for their dugout, dodging flying debris every step of the way.

As Dunk ran, he spun about, his eyes searching the field and the stands, hunting for whoever or whatever had struck the Mancaster coach down. Anything that could strike out of the blue like that could attack anyone else as well, and there was no telling who or what its next target might be.

Of course, Dunk couldn't ignore the fact that the bolt had taken out Mancaster's last hope – however unlikely – just as Deckem had been about to kill him. Who would have bothered to kill a man already doomed to die?

✦ CHAPTER SEVENTEEN

WHEN DUNK REACHED the Hackers' dugout, Pegleg stomped over toward him, smacking the tip of his wooden leg angrily on the concrete as he did. 'What in the name of Nuffle's dirty jockstrap were you thinking, Mr. Hoffnung?'

Dunk glanced about and saw all of the other players – both living and undead – staring at him, seeming as eager for an answer as the Hacker coach. Slick stood off to one side, watching his client from a safe corner but not stepping forward to help. Lästiges stood next to him, her camra zipping about the dugout, switching back and forth between focusing on Dunk and his coach.

When Dunk had sprinted across the gridiron to confront Deckem, he hadn't given much thought to the issue at all, but that wasn't going to be good enough for the ex-pirate, he could tell.

'I couldn't just let Deckem and his goons – or should I say 'ghouls' – kill that man. He didn't deserve to die.'

'No one deserves to die, Mr. Hoffnung,' Pegleg said. 'Yet our lives are littered with corpses. He was as deserving as anyone else.'

'More so,' Deckem said. 'He dared to stand against us.'

Dunk started toward Deckem, but Pegleg stepped between them.

'What if I *dare* to stand against you?' Dunk said to Deckem. 'Will you try to kill me too?'

Deckem smirked. 'I won't just "try".'

'No one hurts Dunkel!' M'Grash lashed out with one hand and shoved Deckem up against the back wall of the dugout. The blow might have killed a living man, but it just held Deckem in place. He stared up at the ogre with an odd smile on his face that sent a lance of ice up Dunk's spine.

'Belay that, Mr. K'Thragsh,' Pegleg snarled. 'Both of you back to your corners. This is a conversation between Mr. Hoffnung and me.'

'I don't have anything else to say,' Dunk said. 'I saw what the right thing to do was, and I did it.'

'Well, I'm not finished,' Pegleg said. 'You're fired!'

'What?' Dunk had been prepared for many punishments from his coach, up to and including death, but the thought that he might lose his position with the Hackers had never crossed his mind. To him, the Hackers weren't just a team. In many ways, they'd become his family, and you couldn't just kick someone out of a family.

Then Dunk remembered how his father had disowned Dirk when he'd run off to play Blood Bowl. He had no doubt the same fate would await him if he ever saw his father again, no matter how unlikely that may be. He had no intentions of ever running into his parents again.

'You can't do that,' Slick said, stepping forward. 'We have a contract!'

'Had!' Pegleg said. 'Mr. Cavre, cashier Mr. Hoffnung immediately. Give him his sentence, strip him of his uniform, and send him on his way.'

Dunk gaped at the star blitzer, the captain's first mate. Would he really do it? He couldn't imagine that Cavre would defy the coach as Dunk had.

'Captain Haken,' Cavre said, 'I believe Mr. Fullbelly has a point. According to the terms of the contract he negotiated with you, we must give six weeks' notice before cutting him loose.'

'Or else what?' Pegleg never took his eyes off Dunk.

'Or we're in breach, and he can sue. Given the fact he has Mr. Fullbelly as an agent, I assume that's a foregone conclusion. They would clearly be in the right and–'

'I don't care!' Pegleg said, frothing at the mouth. 'I will not stand for this. Disobedience! Mutiny!' He pointed his hook straight at Dunk's heart. 'It's either unemployment for you – or death!'

'Captain Haken,' Cavre said calmly. 'There's also the matter of the Far Albion Cup Final. Our victory puts us in the game, which is only a week from today. If we release Mr. Hoffnung, we will have to replace him or be forced to forfeit the game.'

'Then replace him! Use any warm body! Take Mr. Fullbelly! Or Miss Weibchen! Or maybe I'll take the field myself. Apparently, in this blasted country, other coaches do!'

'No,' M'Grash said. 'If Dunkel goes, I go too.' He let Deckem fall to the floor and then strode over to stand next to his friend.

'Aye,' Edgar said, stepping in behind the ogre. 'That bloody well goes for me as well. And next time I won't do you the bloody favour of taking out the referee by pretending to be a tree standing outside of his quarters, will I?'

Simon and Guillermo looked at each other, then shrugged and walked over to stand next to Dunk. They didn't say a word, just glared at Deckem and his compatriots, right along with the others.

'You can't replace us all,' Dunk said. 'You need us.'

Pegleg's eyes looked as if they might burst from their sockets. 'You cannot do this. You will not get away with this. This is my team! Mine!'

Deckem stepped up next to the coach. 'He can't replace you, but I can.' He tossed a thumb over his shoulder at the four undead players behind him. Dunk noticed that Swift had his head back on his shoulders, but he needed to hold it in place with both hands.

'You see those fellows?' Deckem said. 'I can come up with another dozen just like them in the space of that week. They'll be just as tough, strong, and unbeatable as me. And they won't question a single order.'

'Not one?' Pegleg raised an eyebrow beneath his yellow tricorn hat, still keeping his eyes locked on Dunk.

'They can't.'

Pegleg turned to shake Deckem's hand. 'You, sir,' he said, 'have a deal.'

Then the coach turned on his living players – all except Carve who stood off to one side of the argument still – and said, 'You bastards. You traitorous bastards. You're *all* fired.'

With that, he pivoted on his wooden leg and left the dugout through the underground passageway that led to the Hackers' locker room. After shooting Dunk a sympathetic look, Cavre followed close on the captain's heel.

Dunk and the others stared after them for a moment. As they did, Deckem snorted. 'Well done, my *former* team-mates.' He sneered as he spoke. 'I couldn't have planned this better if I tried. Within the course of a few weeks, I've gone from dead to complete control of an entire Blood Bowl team. You have my *undying* thanks.'

Before Dunk could reply, Deckem followed after Pegleg and Cavre. His four compatriots strode after him, Swift still balancing his head on his shoulders.

'He's right, you know,' Olsen said as he stepped into the dugout from the field. 'You've totally cocked this up.'

'Where have you been?' Lästiges asked. 'Isn't a team wizard supposed to stay in the dugout at all times?'

'Of course, our fair lass, unless said wizard wants to do something for which we wouldn't care to be fired.'

'It was you,' Dunk said. 'Wasn't it? You blasted the Mancaster coach with your wand.'

Outside the dugout, the crowd loosed a massive cheer followed by a long, loud ovation. 'I don't believe it!' Jotson's voice said. 'He's up!'

Dunk peered out over the lip of the dugout and saw Fergus Alexson getting to his feet on his own power, shaking off the outstretched hands of the Mancaster team apothecary as he did. A bit of smoke still rose from his body, particularly his hair, which now stood up on end and was scorched black at the tips. Still, he was alive and leaving the field without assistance.

'Amazing!' Jotson said. 'I've never seen such determination from a fellow who is not dead. Except for the *un*dead, of course. They always play like they have so little to lose!'

'If you mean, "Did we save the life of that fool-hardy man?" then, yes, we did. The only way to do that seemed clear. We just had to win the game before he died.' He took his wand out and blew a bit of smoke off the tip of it. 'So we did just that. Notice that by our discreet measures, we never risked the wrath of our coach. Nor did we get fired.'

'Couldn't you have lit that thing off a few minutes earlier?' Slick said. 'You could have saved these boys here a whole lot of trouble.'

Olsen shrugged. 'Their antics provided us with the distraction we needed, wee one. Without that, we might not have taken the chance at all.'

'So thanks for bloody nothing, mate,' Edgar said. 'Only my second game as a Blood Bowler – as a part of a team – and I don't even make it out of the first half! I haven't played in a full game yet!'

'I'll bet you always got picked last for games as a sapling, too, didn't you?' Slick said, patting a sympathetic hand on Edgar's bark.

'How in the bloody Fire-Breathing Forest did you know that?' Edgar said, sap-like tears welling up in his glowing green eyes.

Slick looked toward Dunk and rolled his eyes. 'Just a lucky guess,' he said.

Dunk felt his heart slip down into his boots. He looked at the halfling – his agent, his friend – and slowly shook his head.

'What do we do now?' he asked. 'We're five Blood Bowl players without a team.'

'Six!' Edgar said.

'Six,' Dunk said. 'Slick, you're my agent. You're the one who directs my career. What should we do next?'

Slick came over and put an arm around Dunk's leg. 'Don't worry about it, son. Sometimes getting fired is the best thing that can happen to you. It gives you a chance to renegotiate your contract, which is great if you're in a position of strength.'

'And we are?' Guillermo asked, his voice filled with desperate hope.

Slick snorted. 'Not even close,' he said with a laugh. 'But that doesn't mean we can't get there from here.'

'What do we do next then?' Simon asked.

'I recommend we grab some grub, shoot around some ideas over a few beers, and then – as the Albionmen say – get "knock-down pissed".'

No one argued with that.

* * *

'HERE'S TO UNEMPLOYMENT!' Dunk said, raising the latest in a countless series of ales to his fellow ex-Hackers sitting at the table with him and Slick in the Cock and Bull.

A roar went up throughout the pub. As the Hackers had bought the first few rounds for themselves, they'd picked up drinks for everyone else in the place as well. They had soon found themselves surrounded by dozens of brand-new friends.

When the locals realised who their benefactors were, they'd cheered even louder. Their defence of the everpopular Coach Alexson had made them national heroes, and the fact they'd lost their jobs over it only cemented the admiration the average Albion football fans felt for them. The bartender had refused to let them pay for another drink.

'Here's to sleeping in!' Simon said.

'Here's to getting soft!' Guillermo said.

'Here's to beer!' M'Grash said. That got the loudest cheer of all, and he grinned wide and sheepish at the applause.

'Here's to the Hackers,' Edgar said from his spot outside an open window.

While M'Grash had been just able to squeeze through the pub's door, it had proved too much of a hardship for the treeman. 'It's all right, mates,' he'd said. 'I can't bloody well sit down anyway.'

Dunk had felt bad for Edgar, but the treeman had kept his spirits up and joined in the fun by peering in a wide window in the front of the pub and occasionally reaching in for the bartender to refill his bowl of fermented maple syrup. Every now and then, someone on the street would remark on the fact that a tree had sprouted right there in the middle of a Kingsbury street, and Edgar would spin about and spit out a drunken, 'Sod off!'

This never failed to set off waves of laughter through the pub. When Edgar toasted the Hackers, though, the crowd fell quiet, as did the players at Dunk's table.

'Bollocks!' Slick said, jumping up on the table. 'Bollocks to the Hackers!'

Everyone in the bar roared at this, and Slick pranced proudly around the table at how well he'd sensed the mood of the place. When he slipped in a small pool of spilled beer, the roar changed to a sound of concern, but Dunk reached out and caught the halfling before he could crash to the floor. The patrons raised their glasses and cheered again.

'I don't like you talking about the team like that,' Simon said. 'It's not proper.'

'I guess you missed the part where we were fired,' Guillermo said. 'Hackers we are no more.'

'No more Hackers?' M'Grash said. He looked as if a tear might roll from his eye and plop into his barrel-sized tankard of ale.

'Don't you worry about it, big guy,' Dunk said. 'We're not done with the Hackers yet.'

'You dead sure about that?' Simon asked. 'I didn't see a doubt in Pegleg's mind.'

'He'll be fine once he calms down a bit,' Slick said. 'Cavre will talk some sense into him. Or we'll hit him with a big enough wrongful-termination lawsuit that *we'll* own the Hackers.'

'Now who'd want a washed-up team of losers like that?' Lästiges said as she strode into the pub, her camra zipping along behind her.

'They're only washed up because they no longer have us,' Guillermo said. 'We can repair that.'

'Don't kid yourself,' the reporter said. 'Your team has always got along more on luck and a prayer than any real talent. Your big run last year was nothing but a fluke.' She looked at Dunk as she said this. To avoid blushing at her, he turned away.

'Where have you been?' Slick asked, narrowing his eyes at the reporter.

'Following your former manager and team-mates around, of course,' she said. 'Captain Haken is still furious – mostly at you, Dunk.'

'Will coach be happy again soon?' M'Grash asked.

Lästiges gave the ogre a condescending smile and patted the back of his hand. 'Not today, I'm afraid. Cavre tells me that he thinks Pegleg will be in a better mood tomorrow – but that he'll still be willing to hire a fistful of snotlings to replace you rather than have you back.'

'He wouldn't,' Simon said in horror.

'He won't have to,' Lästiges said. 'Deckem has already offered to fill out the team's ranks with more of his clammy "friends".'

'Can he do that?' Guillermo said.

'He claims he can.'

'Where in all of bloody Albion did he come up with those creatures anyway?' Edgar shouted in from the window. 'They should be fertilising my bloody roots!'

'He doesn't know,' Lästiges said smugly.

'Wait,' Dunk said. 'You asked him?'

'See, that's why I like you,' she said, batting her eyes at him. 'You're one of the smart ones. Of course, I asked him. It's my job to ask questions.'

'Well?'

'Well what?'

Dunk choked back an urge to throttle Lästiges. 'What did he say?'

'He didn't know. After his retirement, he decided to travel the world a bit. The last thing he remembers is running into a crowd of irate fans of his former opponents. Then he wakes up in a shallow grave somewhere in the Sure Wood a couple of weeks back.'

'You're kidding.'

'He said that Wee Johnson almost keeled over from a heart attack when Wee and his friends heard Deckem trying to dig himself out of the ground. Brother Puck ran screaming off into the night. When they got over their terror, they started in helping with their bare hands and pulled him out.'

'That was right after we, um…' Dunk's voice trailed off as he realised that the other patrons in the bar might be able to hear him.

'Yes,' Lästiges said. 'It is.'

'They have to be connected,' Slick said.

'It could be a coincidence,' Guillermo said, visibly shaken. 'I mean, just because we happen to come upon an artefact of unearthly power and bodies of football superstars suddenly start pulling themselves up out of the dirt doesn't mean – oh, dear Nuffle…'

'What about the others, though?' Dunk asked. 'Where do they come from? They know how to play

Blood Bowl, but – does anyone recognise them as retired players too?'

Everyone else at the table gave Dunk a blank look.

'I've followed Far Albion football ever since I was a lad,' Simon said. 'I used to be able to quote you every player's personal stats and on-field numbers for five years back. They don't look familiar to me. They sure do play like the greats of old though.'

'Did you ask Deckem about that?' Dunk said to Lästiges.

'Of course.'

'And…?'

'"No comment".' She scowled. 'I can't tell you how much I *hate* those two words.'

'He'll bloody well blab to me,' Edgar said, turning to leave. 'I'll strip the leaves from his limbs!'

'Hold it!' Dunk said before the treeman could stride away. 'I think I have a better idea.'

# CHAPTER EIGHTEEN

'WHY DON'T WE try the door, again?' Simon asked.

Dunk rolled his eyes as Slick shushed the Albion-man for the third time. 'It'll be trapped,' Dunk whispered.

'And the window won't?'

Dunk looked down from where he, Simon, Guillermo, and Slick stood in Edgar's upper branches. M'Grash waved up at him with a smile from where the moonlit pavement beckoned far below. The window the treeman held them in front of sat in a sheer, plas-tered, whitewashed wall, with nothing to grasp onto nearby but the brown-painted frame itself.

'Would you expect an assault from this angle?'

'Why would anyone want to assault me?'

'I can think of a half-dozen reasons off the top of my head,' Slick said. 'Now shut up.'

'You're noisier than a scurry of bloody squirrels in heat,' Edgar said. 'It's a wonder he's not awake already.'

The treeman staggered a bit to the right, and all four of the people in its branches yelled out. M'Grash reached out and caught Edgar before he went over like a felled oak.

'Whoa!' said Dunk. 'How much of that maple juice did you have?'

'Not enough,' the treeman said, righting itself as it shook free from M'Grash, and licking its lips with a tongue the colour of heartwood. 'You don't get hooch that bloody good in the Sure Wood, I can tell you that.'

'For Nuffle's sake,' Simon said. 'You're noisier than the lot of us. Can't you keep it down.'

Dunk glanced up and down the darkened street in which they'd found themselves. It was late, and all the lights in the inn before them were out. In their target room, nothing seemed to stir.

'He must sleep like the dead,' Dunk said.

'I don't think Deckem sleeps very well,' Guillermo said. 'Or at all.'

'That's because he's *un*dead,' Slick said. 'He *un*sleeps.'

That sent Edgar into a titter, and the treeman nearly dropped all of its friends. 'Whoops!' it said. 'My apologies, mates, but that was bloody funny!'

'How are we going to get in there?' Guillermo said. 'It's closed.'

'We just open it,' Dunk said.

'And if it's locked?' asked Simon.

'Don't take your eye off the ball,' Slick said. 'One thing at a time.'

Edgar extended one of his branches forward, and Dunk crept along it until he could reach the window. There were two of them, actually, hung side by side on hinges so you could pull them into the room. Dunk pushed against them, hoping they would just give. They held firm.

'They're locked,' Dunk said.

'Here's your next thing,' said Simon.

'Let's just break the bloody things,' Edgar said. 'Then we drag him out of his bed and haul him into some dark corner of that wooded park we passed. No one will hear us – or him – there.'

'You don't think that this will wake him up?' Guillermo said. 'This breaking of glass?'

'Just throw the halfling through,' Simon said. 'We can follow right after.'

Slick gaped at the Albionman. 'First, no! Second, don't you think something like that would wake even the dead?'

'So what if it does?' Edgar said.

At that, the windows opened into the darkened room, and Olsen stepped forward, the moonlight catching him in the frame.

'Aye,' the wizard said. He looked older than Dunk had ever seen him, worn and on the verge of exhaustion – and not in a good mood. 'Whatever will you do?'

'Run?' Edgar squeaked in a tiny voice.

Olsen snorted, and a weary smile crept across his lips, leaving his tired eyes undisturbed. 'Come on in, lads,' he said, stepping back into the darkness. 'We think it's time we talked.'

Leaving M'Grash and Edgar out on the street to keep watch, Dunk, Simon, Guillermo, and Slick climbed into the wizard's room through the open window. By the time they all made it in, Olsen had lit a pair of lamps on either side of his bed and carried one of them over to a table on the opposite side of the room.

'Sit, lads, sit,' the wizard said, pointing to the four chairs arranged around the table. Dunk took one of them – the one nearest the door – and Guillermo and Simon each sat down too. Slick leaned up against the windowsill instead.

'So,' Olsen said, 'what can we help you with at this unusual hour?'

'You know why we're here,' Dunk said.

The wizard stared at the thrower in silence for a moment, a frown of regret on his face. 'Yes, we suppose we do. You want to know more about the Far Albion Cup.'

Simon, looking confused, said, 'We're here about Deckem and his deadboys, aren't we?'

'They're the same topic,' Olsen said. 'You can't talk about Deckem's lot without bringing the cup into it too.'

'What's going on?' Dunk asked.

'Ah,' Olsen said, settling back to sit on the end of his bed, 'now that's a simple question, but with a complicated answer.'

'We're unemployed,' Dunk said. 'We have plenty of time.'

'Right,' Olsen said. 'A long time ago, centuries before any of you were born, I was a great wizard.'

'Aren't you still a great wizard?' Guillermo asked.

'Perhaps. But back then, in the days of my youth, I *knew* I was a great wizard. I told everyone I knew that I was, and I set out to prove it. This was back before football of any kind had found our secluded isle, and fair Albion was sadly ignorant of such great discoveries. Without such a sport to play, I set out to make my mark by leading the effort to destroy the most dangerous and evil sorcerers of the day.

'My friends – compatriots, really – and I met with some successes. We ran off the Lizard-fiend of Loch Morrah, the Mole-master of Drogan Glen, and even the Black Oak of the Sure Wood.'

Dunk heard leaves rustle at this last name and glanced out the window to see Edgar shivering not in the breeze but stark fear.

'Then we set our sight on the greatest, most powerful evil in the land in those dark days: Tharg Retmatcher. That ancient crone ruled over most of Albion then, with the exception of the last bastion that was Kingsbury, and the king – King William I, in those days – bade us to take her down by any means necessary.'

Olsen bowed his head. For a moment, Dunk feared the old elf had nodded off. Then he raised his eyes again, red and puffy though they were.

'We were so sure of ourselves. We rode right out to Downing Castle and challenged her to show herself. Well, she did, and she destroyed us to a man. When – when I saw how the battle would go, I used my magic not to launch yet another futile attack, but to flee.

'I was the only one of us to survive.'

'What happened to Tharg?' Guillermo said.

'Hush,' Simon said, transfixed, never taking his eyes from the wizard. 'He's getting to that.'

Olsen nodded. 'I went into hiding after that, and Retmatcher's forces scoured the land for me. I was no longer here, though, having gone to hide in the Old World, in the majestic city of Altdorf.

'While in my exile there, I plotted for my return, for my chance to redeem myself and bring down Retmatcher once and for all. To that end, I constructed the ultimate weapon, an enchanted device so powerful that not even the dreaded Retmatcher could resist its power.

'When it was ready, I smuggled it and myself back to Albion aboard a pirate ship. I brought it to King William III, who now sat on the throne, and gave it to him to give to Retmatcher.'

'And she just accepted this 'gift' from her mortal enemy?' Slick asked.

Olsen raised finger to tell the halfling to be patient. 'William III had come to a sort of peace with this dictator. She let him remain on his throne, mostly as an impotent figurehead. In exchange, he retained control of Kingsbury and the surrounding area and paid her a regular tribute.'

'And he gave this weapon to her as part of his next tribute,' said Simon.

'Who's telling this story?' Olsen asked. The wizard waited in silence for an answer.

'My apologies,' Simon said. 'Please, continue.'

Olsen rolled his eyes but started talking again. 'William included the weapon in his next payment of tribute to Retmatcher.' The wizard ignored Simon's self-satisfied smile. 'When she saw it, she knew straightaway that she had to use it at once. I'd tailored it to fit her vanities and her taste. This might have made her suspicious, but she knew that King William had tried to do the same many times over the years, hoping to mollify her tempestuous nature.

'So, at dinner that night, she filled the cup with wine and drank deep from it.'

'The weapon was the Far Albion Cup?' Simon said, aghast.

'Not so clever as you think, eh?' Olsen said. 'Retmatcher was fooled as well.'

'So the cup killed her?' Dunk asked.

Olsen shook his head. 'Retmatcher was far too powerful for my magics to be able to kill her. Even though I invested a part of my own soul in the cup, the best I could hope for was to trap her. And that I did.

'The very night her tribute arrived from Kingsbury, Retmatcher hosted a feast in her own honour. At the height of the feast, she raised a toast to herself with my jewel-studded cup in her hands. As the sweet, red wine touched her lips, she fell over, dead to the world.'

'I thought you said you that it was not in your power to murder her,' Guillermo said.

'Despite appearances, she wasn't truly dead. Instead, the cup stole her soul as she drained that wine.'

Dunk narrowed his eyes at the wizard. 'Where did it go? Her soul, I mean?'

Olsen laid a hand on his own chest. In the wan light of the lamps, dressed only in his nightgown, the weary wizard looked older than ever. 'We have it,' he said.

Simon, Guillermo, and Dunk all gasped. Slick squinted at the wizard instead. 'You've been carrying this necromancer's soul around inside of you for all this time?'

'Nature – even magic – detests a vacuum. That's why I put a part of my soul in the cup. It created a conduit to the vacancy within me. That's how the cup could pull Retmatcher's soul from her flesh.'

Dunk considered this strange tale for a moment. 'How did that cup become Albion's national Blood Bowl trophy?'

Olsen nodded at the young thrower, impressed. 'Like all spells my magnum opus is not unbreakable. As you might have guessed by now, if we drink our own blood from the cup, the spell ends.'

'It would try to take your own soul from you and give it back to you.'

'Magic must follow its own rules – the internal logic that defies traditional logic. If it fails that test, it falls apart, and the spell ends.'

'But,' Simon said, 'isn't that what you wanted to do? You told us this would let you end your life.'

Olsen bowed his head and grimaced, then spoke. 'The spell had an unintended side-effect. The combining of my soul with Retmatcher's made me immortal. Her power is such that she refuses to let her soul's earthly vessel die – even if that vessel is her worst enemy: me.'

'So,' Slick said, 'you want to die and let this woman loose upon Albion again?'

The wizard's face sagged, emphasising the lines the centuries had graven there. 'We tire of this life. We have outlived everyone we ever knew. We long for the sweet oblivion of death. We are ready to pass into the great beyond and discover what awaits us in that mysterious country.'

'By "we",' Dunk asked, uncertain how to phrase his question, 'do you speak for both of you?'

Olsen nodded softly. 'We believe we do.'

The room fell silent for a moment as the Hackers considered the wizard's tale. When Dunk could take it no longer, he spoke. 'You still haven't answered my question – about how the cup became part of the Far Albion League.'

Rue filled the wizard's face. 'Just because Retmatcher was "dead" didn't mean she was defeated. We knew it would only be a matter of time before someone figured out what I'd done and tried to break the spell. Too many powerful people depended on her reign as ruler of Albion to let it end like that.'

Slick smiled his approval. 'You hid it in plain sight.'

'Exactly. When we learned of the founding of the new Far Albion Blood Bowl League, we made a gift of the cup to Bo Berobsson to serve as the travelling trophy for the league's annual champions. Who would suspect such a high-profile cup to be the same one as that which had been found near Retmatcher's hand as she lay sprawled dead on the floor of her dining hall?'

'And if anyone did, who better to protect it than a team of Blood Bowl players?' Guillermo said. 'What kind of thieves would be crazy enough to try to steal something that valuable?'

'Good question,' Dunk said, remembering how the cup had gone missing for five hundred years. 'So what happened?'

'We underestimated the greed of some Blood Bowl teams. Once word got out that the Far Albion League had such a handsome trophy, teams from the Old World swept into the tournament and tried to win it. We spent a few, harrowing years volunteering as the team wizard for any Albion team who would have us, doing our best to keep the trophy in the country, where we could keep an eye on it.'

'But one day your luck ran out,' Slick said.

'Aye. The Orcland Raiders joined the tournament and won, despite our best efforts to sabotage the bastards. They took the Far Albion Cup back with them to the Old World – they insisted on calling it "the Fah Cup" – and we never saw it again. Until now, that is. They said it was stolen, but we later learned they'd sold it soon after returning home.'

'They're orcs,' Slick said. 'What did you expect?'

'We spent some time trying to track it down and then gave up. If we couldn't find it, what were the chances that anyone else could? As long as it was well and truly lost, we were happy.'

'But that didn't last, did it?' Simon said.

'Not so much. As the years wore on into centuries, we decided that it was time to finally break the spell. But by then the cup was well and truly lost. It took us decades to determine it had somehow found its way into the Sure Wood. Then fortune finally smiled upon us when it brought you to help us recover the cup.'

'So what does all this have to do with Deckem?' Dunk said.

Olsen rolled his head back and looked up at the ceiling for a moment before loosing a deep sigh.

'Everything. It turns out we were wrong. We didn't get all of Retmatcher's soul. She was just too powerful. When the cup's magic tried to drag her soul through the cup to me, a good chunk of her soul stayed in the cup, along with the part of myself we'd stashed there.

'Over the years, the part of Retmatcher in the Far Albion Cup overwhelmed the part of me there. The cup slowly turned as evil as it could be, and it started to affect the world around it as best it could. It was likely the cup's influence that foiled our efforts and let the Raiders win that fateful tournament so many years ago, removing it from our influence so its evil could fester quietly on its own.'

'The cup brought Deckem back to life?' Dunk said, his eyes wide with horror.

'Aye, lad. He and all his friends. We suspect the others are ex-footballers too, but ones that Deckem, er, assembled from many bodies. Notably, he replaced each one's head with that of some random victim exhumed from any nearby grave, making it nearly impossible to identify them.

'Deckem and his cronies are nearly immortal, products of Retmatcher's enormous powers and her centuries of festering hate. If we destroy them, the cup will only create more of them. In fact, if what Deckem said after the last game is accurate, the cup may already be conjuring up more such creatures to replace you lot on your team.'

'No!' a voice outside the window hollered. Then the building shook with the force of three mighty blows.

'Bloody hell!' Edgar said, sticking his face in the window. 'You bastards have upset our wee ogre! Can someone have a bloody word with him before he shakes the building down and turns yours truly into so many toothpicks?'

Dunk dashed to the window and called down to the ogre, who sat in the gutter below, pounding his fist into the side of the building as he sobbed loudly. 'Hold it, M'Grash! I'm coming!'

The thrower leapt out of the window and slid down Edgar to land next to the weeping ogre. 'It's all right, big guy,' Dunk said. 'Don't cry. We can fix this.'

M'Grash raised his head as Dunk came over and wrapped an arm around one of the ogre's biceps as if he were trying to comfort a tiny child. 'How?' M'Grash said, wiping the tremendous tears from his face and tusks. 'How can we save the team, Dunkel? How?'

Dunk patted the ogre on the back as he watched flickering lights start to fill the windows all around them. They had overstayed their welcome here and had to leave right away.

'I don't know, buddy,' Dunk said to the ogre as he helped him to his feet. 'I don't know, but I promise you this: we won't let the Hackers go without a fight.'

 # CHAPTER NINETEEN

'THE HACKERS SCORE again!' Mon Jotson's voice called out over the PA system, which echoed throughout the stadium and beyond, even into the depths of the visiting team's locker room. 'That makes five unanswered touchdowns against the scoreless Kingsbury Royals. If the Hackers can keep this up this pace, there will be no stopping them!'

The crowd booed and hissed at the news. Jotson and the rest of the press had spent the whole of the last week vilifying the Hackers – or what was left of them, anyway – every chance they'd had. Even Lästiges had chipped in, appearing on several Cabalvision shows on all five of the Albion stations to slag Deckem and his 'deadmen,' as they'd taken to called the undead linemen.

'They only have five stations?' Slick had said, stunned. 'How do they sell anything around here?'

'And two of them are owned by the King: BBC 1 and BBC 2. Then there's also the Itinerant Telepathic Visionaries network, and the innovatively named channels Four and Five. I've been on each of them twice already, and I'll go back for another round just before game time.'

'How many of them will show the game?' Dunk had asked.

'All of them?'

'*All* of them?'

'You think there's anything better to watch on a Sunday afternoon around here?'

At the time, Dunk had felt some strange sense of pride that the entire nation would tune in at once to watch the Hackers play in the Far Albion Cup final, even if he wouldn't be on the field. Now, the idea of an entire nation so fully focused on the game that there weren't any other activities scheduled for the day bothered him – especially given what he and his fellow ex-Hackers had planned.

Security around the game had been tight, but the guards – stuffy looking men in red uniforms and tall, furry, black hats – had recognised Dunk and the others as members of the team and waved them on through the gates. At Slick's insistence, they'd waited until just after the opening kick-off to get to the stadium, ensuring that Pegleg and his new-version Hackers would be out on the field when they arrived.

As predicted, the locker room lay empty, not even a straggling reporter poking through the team's gear skulking about. Everyone knew the big story was out on the field. Everyone but Dunk and his friends.

Slick strode into the room first, scouting ahead. When he signalled the all-clear, the rest tumbled in after him: first Dunk, then M'Grash, Simon, and Guillermo, with Edgar – bowing over the best he could to fit through the doorway – shuffling in at the rear.

'So,' Dunk said, 'where is it?'

Slick scurried about the place, peering into every nook and cranny he could find. 'Olsen said he'd leave the cup in his locker, but it's not there.' The halfling pointed over at a red door left flung open in the far corner of the room.

Indecipherable runes etched in gold, silver, and other, nameless inks glowed softly on the inside of the door and throughout the interior of the locker. Even in the dim light from the sigils, Dunk could see the locker stood empty. There wasn't even a bit of dust inside the thing.

'Isn't that just the way of things, lads?' Simon said, shaking his head.

Guillermo frowned, and Dunk noticed the man shiver. 'Then where bloody is it?' he snapped.

Edgar snorted. 'You can't use "bloody" like that,' he said. 'It's an adjective, not an adverb, except in some unique circumstances.'

'You can bloody well shut your mouth,' Simon said.

'Ah,' Edgar said with a laugh, 'like that.'

'Olsen must not have been able to leave the cup behind,' Slick said. 'Maybe Pegleg guessed what he might be up to and decided to put it under lock and key instead.'

'Would that work?' Dunk asked. 'Doesn't it have to be with Pegleg for the Hackers to always win?'

'Do I look like a wizard?' the halfling said. 'It's magic, son. It works like it wants to work.'

'Besides which,' Edgar said, 'with the way Deckem and his bloody deadmen are playing, who needs the bloody cup to assure a win?'

'Maybe that's how the legend manifests itself every time,' Dunk said. 'We don't know. We should have asked Olsen more questions.'

'What would you like to know?' the wizard said as he entered through the tunnel that led underground to the Hackers' dugout.

'Where did Merlin put the shiny cup?' M'Grash said, looming over the wizard. The ogre looked ready to hunt through Olsen's entrails for whatever clues he could find.

The wizard put a hand to mollify the ogre, but M'Grash took this as a threat. His meaty hand lashed out and wrapped around Olsen's neck. As the wizard clawed at the ogre's fingers, trying to pry them from his throat, M'Grash hauled the wizard up to his level so he could talk straight into his face.

'Where is the cup?' M'Grash demanded.

Olsen's feet kicked in the air below him as he struggled to maintain consciousness. He gurgled out a few syllables, but words were beyond him.

'Put him down, M'Grash,' Dunk said carefully. 'He can't talk like that, and he's no good to anyone dead.'

Dunk caught Olsen in his arms as the ogre dropped him. 'I'm sorry about that,' the thrower said as the wizard gasped fresh air into his lungs. 'He's a little on edge about stealing the cup from Pegleg.'

'That's bloody true of us all,' Edgar said, his leaves trembling as he spoke. 'Crikey, betraying your bloody coach isn't something any footballer should do lightly.'

'We're not betraying him,' Dunk said, setting Olsen down to sit on a nearby bench. 'We're saving the team – for him.'

'You think Pegleg would see it that way, son?' Slick asked. Olsen bent over double and sounded as if he meant to hack up a lung or two.

Dunk frowned as he checked to make sure that the wizard would survive M'Grash's interrogation. 'He will – eventually.'

Finished clearing his throat, Olsen sat back up with a wry smile on his face. 'You may get your chance to find out, lad. Your good coach stripped me of the responsibility of keeping watch over the cup. Apparently he feels I'll be far more useful to his cause if I spend my time zapping some of those poor, damn Royals off the pitch.'

'The deadmen haven't killed them yet?' Slick asked.

Olsen shook his head. 'They watched the DVDs of the last two games. Those Daemonic Visual Displays are bloody amazing, and they come out so fast these days. Anyways, their coach came up with a strategy to beat savage murderers like the deadmen.'

'And this strategy, it works?' Guillermo asked.

'So far. They haven't scored yet, but they're not dead either. They just flee whenever any of the deadmen get close to them, and they throw the ball forward as best they can.

'Sadly, the Royals aren't well known for their passing game. They tend to drop as many balls as they catch.'

'So,' Dunk said, trying to steer the conversation back to what they needed to know, 'where's the cup?'

'Pegleg has it sitting next to him in the Hackers' dugout.' The wizard sighed. 'He's planning to give it back to the Far Albion League at halftime.'

'What?' the others in the room all said.

'He believes that the team that controls the cup can't be beaten, right?'

The others nodded.

'Well, if the cup goes back to being the Far Albion Cup's travelling trophy, the Hackers get it right back. Legitimately too. And once that happens, the Hackers will never lose. They'll always get the cup back every year.'

'That's insane,' Dunk said. 'The legend can't be true then. Otherwise, how would the Orland Raiders ever have been able to win the trophy? Whoever had it before them would never have lost it.'

'Ah,' Olsen said ruefully. 'Here's where Pegleg's plan breaks down, just at it did for the Royals, who had it before the Raiders took it. You can only win the tournament if you show up to play. The Raiders made sure that the Royals never made it to the final game. Those damned orcs won the game by forfeit.

'It's hard to stop a team full of deadmen, though. If someone kills most of your team, you just conjure up a fistful more, and you're ready to go. They don't even have to be good players, right? You've got the cup, you don't really care about skills any more.'

'We have to get that cup,' Dunk said. 'How much time do we have?'

'And there's the two-minute warning!' Mon Jotson's voice said. 'This is the first time the Hackers have made it to one of these in a Far Albion Cup game!'

The crowd booed louder than ever.

'No time, son,' Slick said. 'No time at all.'

Dunk raced down the tunnel to the Hackers' dugout. He had no sort of plan in his head. He only knew that he needed to act, and now. He heard the others hot on his heels, including the thumping tromps of M'Grash and the scraping branches of Edgar as they forced their way through the too-small space. He hoped that the noise of the crowd's disapproval would be enough to mask their approach from Pegleg and Deckem, but he had little choice but to proceed either way.

When Dunk reached the end of the tunnel, he held up a hand to signal the others to stop, and he peered around the corner of the portal. To Dunk's relief, only Pegleg stood there in the dugout. The ex-pirate glared out across the gridiron, leaning on his wooden leg and tapping his booted toes against the cut-stone floor. Something sat on the bench behind him, wrapped in a burlap sack. From the size and shape of the thing, Dunk knew it could only be the Far Albion Cup.

'I'll get it,' Slick whispered.

Dunk glanced down to see the halfling peering around his leg, staring hard at the cup.

'Are you nuts?' Dunk asked. 'If he sees you, he'll gut you on the spot.'

'Shh,' Slick said. 'I'm a halfling. This is the kind of thing we do.' With that, the agent slipped past Dunk before the thrower could reach out to stop him.

Slick padded toward Pegleg, silent and smooth, and Dunk briefly wondered if Slogo Fullbelly had earned his nickname from his reputation as an agent or a thief.

For a moment, Dunk turned his attention to the field. Out there, he saw Deckem with his arms out, palms up, raising them up and down, exhorting the fans to be louder than ever. They obliged him by hissing and booing with insane fervour and tossing larger and larger things on to the field. A large chunk of a wooden bleacher seat – half of a long log cut lengthwise – bounced off the top of the dugout and rolled into the field in front of Pegleg, but the coach ignored it, steadfast as a sea captain sailing into a coming storm.

Dunk tensed for a moment, fearful that Pegleg might turn and see him in the darkened rear of the dugout, but the ex-pirate's gaze never wavered from the gridiron. Out there, Deckem continued to incite the crowd to an insane pitch as his deadmen trotted in circles around him. Some of them picked up the detritus the fans had thrown at them and hurled them back into the stands, where the tight packing of the fans guaranteed the junk would hit somebody.

Meanwhile, the Hackers' apothecary stood amid it all, stitching one of the deadmen – Dunk recognised him as Swift – back together. He'd somehow lost an arm, but it didn't bother him at all as the healer darned it back on to him with a thick, black thread.

Dunk understood Deckem's intentions. He wanted the field to be such a terrifying place that the Royals would refuse to go back on to it. No living creature in its right mind would want to dive into such a mael-strom, but few would accuse any Blood Bowl player of being entirely sane under even the best of circum-stances. In his heart, Dunk rooted for the Royals to stand up to Deckem's attempt to intimidate them, no matter how foolhardy it might seem.

The crouched-over Slick reached out and put his hand on the sack-covered cup. He followed it with another. Then he wrapped his arms around the cup, cradling it from underneath its bowl and slowly stood up to his full height.

Despite the roaring noise outside the dugout, when Pegleg spoke, his voice seemed to cut through it all. 'What, Mr. Fullbelly, do you think you are doing?'

Slick looked up at the coach, who still hadn't torn his gaze away from the field. He shivered, but he did not drop the cup. Instead, he took one step backward, carrying the big burlap sack in his arms.

'Just thought she needed a little polishing, Pegleg,' the halfling said. 'You can't give it back to the league officials with it all dirty like this.'

'Your concern is touching, Mr. Fullbelly.' Pegleg's hook lashed out and pierced the top of the sack. Once the canvas was securely snarled in the hook, the ex-pirate turned about to stare into the halfling's eyes. 'But that won't be necessary.'

'Listen, my old friend,' Slick said. 'We're here to help you. This cup of yours, it's evil through and through.'

'Winning is never evil,' Pegleg said. 'Not in Blood Bowl. Not in life.'

'You see?' Slick said. 'That's just what I'm talking about. It's already got its hooks in you. You're a tough coach and a good one, one of the best I've ever had the pleasure of working with. I've known you for years, and I consider you not just a patriarch of the game but a good friend. Winning might have always been important to you *on the field*, but you've always been able to leave it there, on the field, when the game was over.'

Pegleg scowled. 'So you say. I was raised to be a gentleman, but this is not a gentleman's game. Still, I deported myself as best I could given my current vocation. And what did I get for my troubles?'

Slick shook his head, his mouth open but silent as he gaped up at the coach.

'Nothing. Unless you count poverty, hardship, and a bleeding ulcer. But I coached the way I wanted to, the way I thought I should, no matter how horrible the insults visited upon my team, no matter how many of them were *murdered* as I sat on the sidelines here and watched, helpless to do anything to stop it.

'And what did I get for that? The admiration of my peers? The accolades of the fans? The respect of our so-called reporters?'

Pegleg sneered down at the speechless halfling. 'No. None of that. Not one whit. Instead, we – me and my team – were branded losers. *Losers!* They *laughed* at us.'

Slick glanced out at the field, and Pegleg followed his gaze. 'Well,' the halfling said, having to shout to be heard over the noise, 'no one's laughing now.'

Pegleg nodded at this. 'I know. And, Mr. Fullbelly, it's about damned time.' Then he pulled the cup from the halfling's arms and set it down on the floor next to him. Once it was safely down, he freed his hook and brought it around to bear on Slick, who cowered from it as it glinted in the light.

'You can't do this,' the halfling said. 'We only came here to help!'

'We?' The coach turned toward the entrance to the tunnel toward the Hackers' locker room and spied Dunk peering around the corner. He coughed out a bitter laugh and beckoned toward the thrower with his hook.

'Come, Mr. Hoffnung,' Pegleg said. 'Why don't you join our conversation? I confess I'm learning a great deal about my so-called friends.'

Dunk stepped forward out of the tunnel, and the others emerged one by one behind him. Edgar stopped only halfway into the dugout, and even then his top branches nearly jutted out past the shelter's protective roof.

'So this is how it is,' said Pegleg as he watched his former players join Dunk and stand behind him. 'This is gratitude for you. After everything I've done for you.'

'Like fire us?' Dunk said. 'All of us? Come on, coach. Can't you see this is not like you? When have you ever fired a player before?'

Simon nodded. 'You always said firing was too good for me. It was worse punishment to keep me on the team.'

Pegleg smirked at this. 'That way you might actually get the beating you deserved, Mr. Sherwood.' He scowled again. 'But I grew tired of waiting for that. Better to cut you loose – to cut you *all* loose – and start over again.'

'Not all of us, coach,' a voice shouted out.

Everyone's head turned to see Cavre step into the dugout from the end nearest Pegleg. The star blitzer doffed his helmet and tossed it down on the bench with practiced ease. He wore a look of raw determination on his face. Dunk had seen this on the field many times, but never off, where Cavre's natural stoicism had become the stuff of legend. The fires in this man's soul burned hot, but he had kept them focused on the game – until now.

'I'm still here,' Cavre said, struggling to keep the anger from his voice. 'I've always been here. I've been with this team since I first played the game, and I'd always hoped they would bury me in my Hackers uniform. But not anymore.'

'Hold your tongue, Mr. Cavre!' Pegleg snarled at the blitzer, but Dunk could tell his heart wasn't in it. Here was a 'betrayal' from the one corner he'd never allowed himself to consider.

Pegleg's eyes flitted from Cavre to the others, then back again. Dunk felt he could read the coach's thoughts, so clearly did he wear them on his troubled face. If Cavre stood against him with the others, then perhaps he'd been wrong. Perhaps there was something to all this balderdash about the cup.

'No!' Pegleg growled. 'I won't let this happen! I'm so close! I'm about to win the whole damn thing!'

'There's no "I" in "team", coach,' M'Grash said hopefully.

'Arrgh!' the ex-pirate said. 'Who's been filling your empty head with such banalities, Mr. K'Thragsh? There's no "we" in "team", either! In fact, the damned word lacks an entire twenty-two letters from the alphabet, and none of them matter one damned bit!'

'There's no 'we' in this team any longer,' Cavre said, pulling off his jersey. He wadded it up into a ball and threw it at Pegleg's feet. 'Good luck with your new players, Captain Haken.'

Cavre shouldered his way past Pegleg and made for the exit tunnel. As he reached its portal, the coach called out after him.

'Wait!' Pegleg said. As a man who'd cultivated the image of a pirate legend he'd always taken great care with his grooming. Dunk had rarely seen him with a hair out of place. Now, though, the man looked dishevelled, rumpled even, and a dozen years older.

The coach looked down at the cup, which had somehow managed to find itself in Slick's arms again. The halfling flashed his most innocent smile up at the ex-pirate, fooling no one for even an instant. Pegleg ignored the gesture and reached down and tapped the cup with the curve of his hook.

'Get rid of it,' he whispered, his voice hoarse with raw emotion.

'What, coach?' M'Grash asked, cupping his massive ear in an effort to hear Pegleg over the still-roaring crowd.

'Take the cup,' the coach said, louder and more forcefully now. 'Take it and dispose of it. Do what you must.'

'What's going to happen to the game?' Simon said. 'It's the Far Albion Cup Final.'

Pegleg stared at each of his ex-players in turn and said. 'I don't care. The game and my new players can be damned.'

'What a stroke of luck for you, then,' Deckem shouted down into the dugout, his deadmen assembled behind him. 'We already are!'

CHAPTER TWENTY

DECKEM'S EYES GLOWED red as the undead player glared down at his coach and former team-mates. 'Look!' he said. 'A reunion of everyone I haven't got around to killing yet.'

Dunk looked to Slick, who hefted the sack-covered cup up in his arms and tossed it to the thrower. 'Run!' the halfling shouted before diving under the bench.

Without stopping to think, Dunk snatched the cup from the air and tucked it under his arm. He glanced up at the field and saw the deadmen had fanned out to block the way onto the gridiron. He dashed over to his right and hesitated as he stood before the grinning Deckem.

'Go on, mate,' Deckem said with an amused sneer. 'Give it a go.'

Dunk feinted a lunge up the steps that led out of the dugout, then spun on his toes and sprinted out through the locker room tunnel, ducking around Edgar, who still knelt there. As he went, Dunk heard Deckem snarl after him and then cry out, 'Get him!'

Then Dunk heard a horrible crack from the dugout, and a roar of frustration from Deckem.

'Would you look at that?' Jotson's voice said. 'Now they're throwing benches at the Hackers from *inside* their own dugout! I haven't seen that kind of team discord since the last time Khorne's Killers played here. Worshipping a god of Chaos can wreak havoc with team unity, it seems!'

Dunk just put his head down and ran. He knew it wouldn't be long until Deckem and his fellow deadmen came after him. While he might be able to outrun them all for a while, he would eventually tire. The living dead like Deckem had no such limitations. They'd just keep coming after him until they wore him down into the dirt.

When Dunk reached the Hackers' locker room, he skidded to a halt. There, right in front of him, stood Merlin Olsen, his wand at the ready.

'That the cup you have with yourself there, lad?' the wizard said.

Dunk nodded. Somewhere behind him, there was another loud crack, and an inhuman wail chased after it.

'That Deckem and his blokes pounding along after you like a herd of headless orcs?'

Dunk nodded again.

'Then get out of the way, lad.' The wizard snapped his wrist, and his wand began to crackle with bright arcs of golden power. 'This is about to get ugly.'

Deckem darted into the locker room then, a long, leafy branch in his arms. From down the tunnel, Dunk could hear Edgar wailing in pain. Seeing the power coursing through the wizard's wand, though, pried his attention away from that, and he dived to one side, flinging himself along the open floor.

'You old fool!' Deckem said. 'What do you think you can—?'

Every hair on Dunk's body stood on end all at once as the crackling sound from Olsen's wand zoomed to a quick crescendo. The sound reminded Dunk of when his brother Dirk had once thrown a hive full of bees at him while they'd been staying at the family's country home. As the enraged insects chased him over and into the lake, they'd made a noise something like that, except it had ended with a splash into the cool, protective waters rather than an eardrum-bursting peal of thunder.

When Dunk managed to scrape himself back up off the floor, blood trickling from his ears, he looked back and saw a long line of crispy corpses starting at the entrance and flowing back into the tunnel as far as he could see. They each stood flash-baked into the positions in which they'd been at the moment Olsen's spell had gone off, like some grisly queue of grotesque sculptures still smoking with the heat of their creation.

Olsen reached out with the end of his wand and gently tipped the lead corpse backward. It fell into the

one behind it, knocking it back into the others in a
horrible domino effect. As each of the bodies tumbled
backward, it fell apart to ashes, leaving only fragments
of charred skeletons behind.

As Dunk staggered to his feet, the wizard came over
and mouthed something at him. The thrower couldn't
make it out over the ringing in his head. After another
attempt, the wizard realised what was wrong and
stopped trying to talk. Instead, he clapped Dunk on
the back and gave him a big thumb's up.

Dazed, Dunk wandered over to a nearby bench and
sat down on it, still clutching the cup to his chest. The
last thing he remembered was telling himself not to
let go of it, not for any reason, not even death.

DUNK AWAKENED IN darkness with the distinct feeling
that the world was swimming underneath him. He
squeezed his eyes closed tight and fought against the
vertigo for a moment, but it refused to go away. After
a moment, he gave up and tried to open his eyes, but
he discovered that something lay bound over them,
keeping the light out.

For a moment, Dunk panicked, thinking to find
himself bound, gagged, and blindfolded, but his
hands, he found, were free, his mouth uncovered. He
brought his fingers up and removed the eyeless mask
of black silk.

He saw that he lay in a bed on one side of a low,
cramped room lit only by a single candle that burned
softly on a desk along the opposite wall. Dark, hand-
polished wood panelled the walls, floor, and ceiling. A
couch in crimson velvet sat against the wall nearest

Dunk's feet, along which hung long, heavy, black curtains. Only the slightest hint of daylight peeked around them, but it was enough to show the outline of the man sitting at the desk across the room, staring at the flickering light before him.

Shelves filled with books and scrolls lined every available inch of open wall. Most of these were tucked neatly away, except for a set of navigational charts sprawled across a low table that squatted in front of the couch. A capped pot of ink and a pilot's compass served as paperweights for these on one side, ensuring they didn't slide or slip off the table with the slow movement of the room. A full set of silver tea service, along with a pair of fine, ceramic cups and saucers, perched on the table's far end.

As Dunk slipped out of the bed, he realised he wore only his breeches. He wondered where his clothes had gone, but at the moment that didn't seem as important as figuring out where he had landed. He stole over to where the man sat at the table, watching – as it turned out – a crystal ball. In its glowing depths, images of a Blood Bowl game flashed by.

The players stood in a familiar stadium – the one in Kingsbury, Dunk remembered after a moment's reflection – and they wore the purple and gold uniforms of the Royals. The man in the middle – the coach perhaps? – thrust a cup into the air in a gesture of victory.

The camra panned out over the cheering fans, then returned to a close-up of the Royals' coach kissing the cup. It was a cheap replica of the original Far Albion Cup, a battered piece of tin that wouldn't be used for more than catching spit in any but the toughest pubs in Albion.

'Welcome back to the land of the living, Dunk,' Pegleg said, never taking his eyes from the image. 'I'm glad to see that rather expensive apothecary's efforts weren't all for naught.'

Dunk tried to think of something to say, but his tongue caught in his mouth. He stared down at the back of his former coach's head and coughed.

Pegleg turned slowly to face the thrower, a faint smile on his lips warring with concern in his eyes. 'You can hear me, can't you? That scurvy dog swore up and down that your ears would be fine.' When Dunk didn't answer, Pegleg raised his voice to a shout. 'CAN YOU HEAR ME?'

'Yes!' Dunk said, covering his ears at the noise. 'I heard you fine the first time. I'm just a little... Where am I?'

'My quarters, Dunk, aboard the *Sea Chariot*.'

Dunk blinked, confused. 'We're... What happened? Where are we going?'

'One thing at a time,' Pegleg said, taking Dunk by the arm and moving him over to sit on the couch.

As the coach poured them each a steaming cup of tea, Dunk gazed over at the crystal ball on Pegleg's writing desk. 'We lost,' he said. 'I'm – I'm sorry, coach. I mean, captain.'

Pegleg frowned as he handed Dunk his tea. 'Don't concern yourself with it. It's all over with now.'

'What happened?'

Pegleg chuckled at this. 'Didn't you see what Olsen's spell did to Deckem and his crew? Incinerated every last one of them. We're just lucky the rest of us had stopped to help Edgar up before following them.'

'All of you?'

Pegleg blushed a bit, which shocked Dunk. He didn't think the captain had the capacity for embarrassment. 'Not all. Some were busy keeping me from chasing after you and ripping out your eyes.'

Dunk's gaze flickered to the captain's hook then back to his tired, resigned eyes. 'Don't worry yourself, Dunk. I've given up those plans.'

'For good?' Dunk worked up a little laugh that sounded weak even to his ears.

'For now, at least,' Pegleg said with a mischievous grin.

'So what happened after the big boom?' Dunk asked, eager to get off this topic of conversation. 'It looks like the Royals won.'

'By default.' Pegleg grimaced, the pain showing all the way through to his eyes. 'We didn't have any players left – except Mr. Cavre, that is.'

Dunk gaped. 'What about the other guys? The living ones, I mean. Weren't they willing to play?'

Pegleg chuckled again. 'They all volunteered to go back on to the field, just as I'm sure you would have, had you been conscious. But the rules on these things are clear. You can only field the players you start the game with. Otherwise, a coach could just keep flooding a game with fresh players, right? And where would the sport be in that?'

Dunk shook his head. 'I thought you'd already taken care of the referee. Who would have stopped you?'

Pegleg smiled again, this time wider than Dunk could remember seeing since they had first procured the cup. 'It's not always a matter of getting caught by the officials. If we had tried to send on anyone but Cavre, the Game Wizards would have been on us like carbuncles.'

Dunk had dealt with two such GWs during the last season, a paired dwarf and elf by the names of Blaque and Whyte. He knew from experience how tenacious they could be. The Cabalvision networks hired them to keep the game in line and give it some semblance of fairness. It was one thing to cheat – in the sense of trying to gain a small edge or get away with a cheap shot – and something else entirely to flaunt the rules in front of a game's entire audience.

'Some of the men wanted to suit up in the deadmen's uniforms, but these had been burnt to cinders along with their bodies. The GWs aren't always the sharpest blades in the body, but even they can read those great numbers on the backs of the players' jerseys.

'Cavre insisted on going out there alone of course.'

Dunk nearly choked on his tea. 'And you let him?' If any one of the Hackers could take on a team by himself, it would be Carve – or perhaps M'Grash. Cavre would employ his experience and finesse to stay alive, though, while the ogre would rely purely on brute force.

'No, no, no,' Pegleg said. 'It would have been a fool's errand, Dunk, and I'd already played the fool far too often that day. I wasn't about to let my best and most loyal player risk almost certain death on the off-chance that he could manage to make up for a ten-player deficit on the gridiron. He's good, but not that good.'

'So you say,' Cavre said as he entered the room, 'but I would have liked a chance to test that theory.' The bright light of the day spilled in behind him, blinding Dunk until his eyes adjusted to its intensity.

'Where are we?' he asked. 'Have we left Albion behind?'

Cavre smiled wide, his white teeth almost as blinding to Dunk as the sunlight. 'You might say that, Mr. Hoffnung. We left land behind two days ago, and the people of Albion were happy to see us go, as the scorch marks along our stern testify.'

'Is everyone okay?' Dunk pushed himself to his feet, which wobbled under him, and not just from the rolling of the sea.

Cavre nodded. 'You got the worst of it. We didn't want to have to move you, but if we'd have left you there the Albion fans would have torn you to pieces.'

'So that means we're back down to six players again: you, Simon, Guillermo, M'Grash, Edgar, and me.' Dunk rubbed his eyes. 'Barely better off than when we left for Albion. At least we don't have to worry about the Far Albion Cup anymore.'

Cavre and Pegleg traded a guilty glance.

Dunk's eyes flew wide. 'I said, "At least we don't have to worry about the–" Ah, damn it! You still have it don't you.' He glowered at Pegleg.

The coach put up his hands to placate his thrower. 'We went through a lot to get our hands on that bit of hardware. It would have been a waste to leave it behind.'

'Also,' Cavre said, 'Olsen warned there could be dire consequences if we left the cup behind. He wanted the time to deal with it himself.'

Dunk did a double-take. 'He's still here? On this ship? With us?'

'All three,' Pegleg said. 'There's no better expert on the subject of the cup than Mr. Merlin. If we want to crack how to best use it without repeating the events in Albion, he's our best hope.'

Dunk gaped. 'Here's our best hope: throw the cup overboard.'

'Now, Mr. Hoffnung,' Pegleg said. 'That would condemn that poor soul to wander this damned world until the end of time. That hardly seems fair.'

'Oh, no,' Dunk said, 'to be condemned to live forever? I can think of worse fates – like getting killed, which that wizard almost managed to do to me.'

'Now, don't get upset–'

'Why not?' Dunk asked. 'If there's ever been something for me to get upset about, I think this is it. Do we even know if Olsen's telling the truth? Maybe that was just some sob story to get us to help him find the cup. Maybe he knew what would happen when we did. Maybe we should try tossing him overboard and see what happens.'

'Mr. K'Thragsh already did.' Cavre smiled softly. 'When he found out who'd hurt you, it took three of us, including Edgar, to keep him from ripping Mr. Merlin's head from his shoulders. Once he calmed down, we thought things were fine until Mr. Merlin somehow offended Mr. K'Thragsh.'

'M'Grash threw him into the ocean?' Dunk fought the impulse to laugh. 'How'd Olsen get back on the ship?'

'Edgar went in after him,' Pegleg said. 'Did you know that treemen float, Mr. Hoffnung? They might have drifted all the way back to Albion if we'd not gone back for them.'

'You should have let them.'

'Mr. K'Thragsh was willing to give it another try. Edgar stopped him, but the treeman wasn't fast enough to keep the ogre from trying to rip off the wizard's head instead.'

'And he's still here?'

'Not through any lack of effort on Mr. K'Thragsh's part, I assure you. Had he been able to murder Mr. Merlin, we'd have had a lovely funeral at sea by now.'

Dunk frowned and sat back down on the bed, his head in his hands. After a moment, he looked up at Pegleg and Cavre. 'That cup,' he said, 'it's poison. You know that. Why do you keep it around?'

Cavre started to answer, but Pegleg stopped him. He leaned forward and stared into Dunk's eyes. 'The cup is but a tool, Dunk, albeit a very powerful one. If we can master it, think of what we could do with it.'

'Think of what could happen to us – what almost did.' He scowled. 'Is this one of those "sharp, pointy bits of metal don't kill people – people kill people" arguments?'

Pegleg smiled. 'Something like that, but there's more. If we can figure out how to harness the cup's power, imagine what it would mean for the team. We'd win every game. We'd never lose a player again.'

Cavre nodded. 'You have seen many of your team-mates die, Mr. Hoffnung, but you have not been with the Hackers for long. Of those we have left, only Mr. K'Thragsh and myself have managed to complete more than a single season.' He sat on the couch across from Dunk and reached out to him with his dark eyes. 'I've lost many a friend over the years, Mr. Hoffnung. In one sense, I'm used to it. I've been around long enough to know it's all part of this game. But if we could stop that – if there's even a chance to do so – then I can't imagine why we wouldn't take it.'

'There's a better way to avoid getting killed on the gridiron,' Dunk said. He got to his feet and staggered toward the door. When he reached it, he turned back to Pegleg and Carve and said. 'Just don't play.'

# CHAPTER TWENTY-ONE

'I DON'T LIKE this,' Dunk said as he gazed out over the Hackers' practice field in Bad Bay. 'Not one bit.'

'I know, son,' Slick said, fanning himself. 'I've never liked tryouts much. It wears me out just watching these things.'

'Don't you have a chance to sign new players though?' Dunk asked.

Slick shook his head. 'I'm a one-player kind of agent. Unless I can get two or more players on the same team, it's too hard to follow them around and give them the kind of help they need. Even I can't be in two places at once.'

Dunk looked down at the halfling. 'Have you tried to recruit anyone else on the Hackers?'

Slick rubbed his hands together. 'Most of them already have adequate if lesser representation.

However, as a complete novice to the game, I generously took Edgar under my wing and helped him negotiate his contract with the Hackers.'

'You didn't let Pegleg pay him in maple syrup, did you?'

Slick scoffed. 'And what would I do with my fifteen percent of that? I love syrup as much as the next halfling, but that's a lot of pancakes.'

'I thought you got ten percent,' Dunk said. 'That's what I pay you.'

Slick shrugged. 'Edgar's a treeman. He doesn't under-stand money at all and has little use for it – or so he thinks. He was happy to pay me a bit extra to work as his financial advisor as well.' He looked up at Dunk, a glint in his eye.

'I can handle that myself.'

'Of course, of course.'

'But I didn't mean adding new players to the team,' Dunk said. 'That's not what I don't like. We need new players – about ten of them – but I'd rather not do it while Pegleg still has his hands on that cup. I mean, have you seen some of the hopefuls?'

Dunk pointed out at the gridiron, where Cavre ran the latest round of prospects through a set of drills. Most of them were built like bulls, and some featured thick coats of fur and savage claws or tusks. They came in various shades of green, brown, pink, and grey, and they bore tattoos, piercings, and filings. One and all, they seemed barely more than savages, ready to disembowel their foes and then strangle them with their own intestines. In fact, two players had already been cut from the tryouts for doing just that to their nearest competitors.

'I admit they look like the rejects from the Chaos All-Stars training camp, but what do you expect? After Lästiges's Far Albion Cup special aired on Wolf Sports last week, just as many people think the Hackers are cursed as blessed. After all, we've lost twenty-one players already this year, cup or no. You'd have to be a pretty desperate sort to want to join up with such an outfit.'

'Or to stay with one.'

'You're not thinking of leaving the Hackers, are you, son? I could probably get you signed with another team, but not until the season's over. Peg-leg's contracts are rock solid about that.'

Dunk shook his head. 'I don't give up that easily. It's just...'

'There are places you'd rather be.'

Dunk hung his head and nodded.

'Have you heard from Spinne again?'

'Not since we got back.' Dunk frowned. He could feel her letter in his pocket. He'd taken it out and read it at least three times a day since he'd got it. 'I can't believe they used that footage of me waking up in Lästiges's bed. You'd have thought she'd have more control over things like that.'

'The camra followed her around every second of that trip, son. Sadly, the little daemon inside doesn't have a discriminating memory. But if you had to be with that reporter woman every moment of your life, you'd probably be eager to ruin her life too.'

Dunk shrugged. Out on the field, one of the hopefuls snapped another prospect's arm in two with a sickening crack. The injured player kept right on running, though, leaping past another assailant and spinning his way into the end zone.

'Have you heard from your brother?'

Dunk frowned. 'Not at all.'

'I hear he broke it off with Lästiges too.'

'That's what ESPNN said on its *Best Damn Blood Bowl Show Period*. The Gobbo laughed so hard at the news I thought he'd choke on his own rancid spit.'

'We should be so lucky.'

Dunk sighed. 'I'm not looking forward to seeing him again.'

'I guess you're lucky we were still at sea when they announced the Blood Bowl would be in Kislev this year. There's something rotten about that though.'

'If Pegleg could have made the *Sea Chariot* grow wings, he would have flown us there in a heartbeat.'

'I heard he asked Olsen to try.' Slick laughed.

'And we would have done it too, given a bit more time.'

Dunk and Slick turned around to see the wizard standing behind them. Dunk felt his anger at the wizard start to rise, but he shoved it back down and bottled it up.

'So we could get there without enough players?' Slick asked. 'Or would you have just let the cup recruit them for us so we could duplicate our experiences in Albion?'

'We'd have worked it out,' the wizard said. 'Where there's a wand, there's a way.'

'You don't think sorcery's done enough harm to your life?' Dunk asked. 'Such as it is?'

'We lay in a bed of our own making, all of us, laddie. Don't think you're any exception.'

Dunk shot a hard look at the wizard. 'I'm just wondering why you're still here. Didn't you have a date with a cup of your own blood? For someone so weary of life, you seem to have taken a shine to it again.'

Olsen smiled as he bent over to pick a tiny white flower from the ground. 'There's nothing like staring the abyss in the face to make you long for the light.' He brought the bloom to his nose and sniffed it deeply. 'Aye. Everything suddenly seems much brighter than before.'

'If you like them so much, perhaps you'd like to gather a bouquet for yourself,' Slick said. 'I understand there's a real demand for ex-Blood Bowl players who know their way around a floral arrangement.'

Olsen smiled down at the halfling, then reached over and tucked the flower behind Slick's ear. 'Perhaps we will at that, my wee friend. The world has seen stranger things.'

With that, the wizard turned on his heel and strode off, smiling as he raised his face to the gentle rays of the sun.

'You know,' Slick said, 'that guy's really starting to get on my nerves.' He snatched the flower from his ear and threw it down to grind it into the dirt with his heel.

'WHAT'S WRONG?' DUNK said as he opened the door to his modest room above the FIB Tavern, which took its name for the opinion the owner held of the particular variety of Imperial Bastards ruling the Empire from distant Altdorf.

'Simon, he is sick,' Guillermo said. 'I think it is serious.'

Dunk rubbed his eyes. 'It's the middle of the night,' he said. 'Why bother me? Shouldn't someone get an apothecary?'

The Estalian nodded. 'Slick, he is already on his way, but I thought you might want to see this.'

Dunk paused for a moment, and then nodded. 'Let me get my boots and my blade.'

Moments later, Dunk and Guillermo stood outside Simon's room in the Hacker Hotel, the finest such establishment for at least fifty miles around. Most of the Hackers stayed here. In fact, at the moment only Dunk and M'Grash did not.

While the ogre didn't feel welcome at the Hacker Hotel – and rightfully so, given the way the staff always treated him like a lit bomb during his infrequent visits – Dunk had spent too much time worrying about money to patronise such a place. The FIB had everything he needed, and at a quarter of the price. As the son of a nobleman, Dunk had known great wealth in his youth, but his family had lost all that years ago. Having tasted both fortune and poverty, Dunk had the respect for gold that many of the other players lacked.

'His room is next door to mine,' Guillermo said. 'Tonight, we drank in the great hall downstairs with some of the new recruits. I had enough, so I excused myself and went to sleep. Later, I heard horrible moans coming from Simon's place, loud enough to wake me up. I got up to check on him, but the door was locked.'

Dunk saw where the frame around the lock's bolt had been shattered. 'You didn't let that stop you.'

'How could I? If you'd have heard the noises, you'd have–'

A plaintive groan interrupted the Estalian, emphasising the point he'd been about to make. It sounded like it could only have come from an animal that had lain dying for a long, pitiless time.

Dunk gave the door a push, and it swung wide on well-oiled hinges. Inside, a large, canopied bed with an airy mattress stood near the window in the far wall. A lamp flickered on the bedside table, showing something – someone, Dunk corrected – writhing in the once-crisp sheets now soaked with sweat.

As Dunk followed Guillermo into the room, the first thing that hit him was the sweet stench of decay. For a moment, he wondered if Simon had left a meal out in his room before they'd left for Albion. Only so much time with old meat left to rot could explain such a horrible smell, or so Dunk thought.

Then he saw Simon.

The catcher looked like he'd caught something horrible. An oily, grey sheen covered his skin and seemed to have stained through his breeches and soiled the bedclothes. He shivered as if adrift on an artic plain, although the night wind that breezed in through the open window was warm and humid.

Guillermo reached out to pull a cover over Simon. That was when Dunk saw the red rash crawling over Simon's skin. He snatched Guillermo's hand back before he could touch the soiled sheets.

'You see that?' Dunk asked the scowling Estalian. The rash seemed to be moving like a horde of insects along Simon's skin. 'I've seen that before – although it wasn't moving like that then.'

'Where?'

Dunk's mind flashed back to the horrible, maimed creature in the cultists' tent in that damned hollow in the heart of the Sure Wood. The rash on his skin had looked similar to this, although it hadn't crawled in the same way. Dunk wondered, though, if that was because it had already done as much damage as it could have to that poor soul.

'Just don't touch him,' Dunk said, giving Guillermo's hand back to him. Then a horrible thought struck him. 'Or have you already?'

'No,' Guillermo said. 'So I swear. When I first came in, he was thrashing about so much that it terrified me. I went for help right away. I found Slick in the hall, and he told me to watch over Simon while he went for help.'

'But you came to get me instead?'

Guillermo hesitated, and then seemed to make a decision. 'What you have not yet told me, that is what I feared.' He glanced down at his suffering friend as he loosed another pathetic moan for mercy. 'I had hoped this would not be.'

'Why didn't you just wake up Cavre? He's right here in the building.'

Guillermo grimaced. 'I know where his loyalties lie: with the captain. If Captain Haken had found out about this before I did, I am sure we would have only found an empty bed in the morning, with no explanation ever.'

Dunk put a hand on Guillermo's shoulder. 'I have more faith in Cavre than that, but I understand.' He looked over at Simon and winced. 'So, what should we do?'

'I had hoped that you might have an answer to that.'

Dunk knew immediately that the right answer was to kill Simon on the spot, to burn his body the way he'd immolated the creature back in the Sure Wood. That way, he could make sure no one else contracted the disease as well. But if he did that, he might never learn how Simon got sick.

'An illness like this doesn't come from nowhere,' Dunk said. 'We need to find out what happened to him.'

'But how?' Guillermo asked, terror creeping into his voice.

'Have you tried talking to him?'

The Estalian shook his head, his eyes bulging wide.

Dunk turned toward where Simon writhed on the bed and called his name once, softly, then again, louder.

Simon screamed as he sat bolt upright in his bed.

Dunk jumped back a step. He heard Guillermo let out a little squeak behind him, and when he glanced over his shoulder he saw the lineman back out in the hallway, peering around the frame of the door.

'Simon,' Dunk said. 'Listen to me. You're sick. Very sick. Do you know what happened to you? Can you tell me?'

Simon's eyes were wide but seemed to be watching something outside the room's four walls. Unfocused and bloodshot, they darted back and forth, searching for creatures that existed only in the fevered corners of the catcher's mind. Dunk called his name again. 'Simon? Simon Sherwood?'

The catcher screamed again. This time, he did not stop.

'You cannot do it like that,' Cavre said as he strode into the room in only a pair of long flowing pants, naked to the waist. 'You must be more forceful. Observe.' He stood at the end of the bed and glared down at the shivering Simon sitting there in his soiled sheets, stopping screaming only to take another breath before starting again.

'Mr. Sherwood!' Cavre said.

Simon's head whipped up, and his eyes snapped into focus on Cavre. His scream caught in his throat. For a moment, the only sound in the room was the Albionman's still-panicked panting.

'You are sick, Mr. Sherwood. If you do not listen to me and follow my instructions, you will die before sunrise.'

The catcher stared at Cavre with eyes as wide around as saucers. He said not a word, but his breathing slowed its pace, and he nodded at the star blitzer's words.

'Who did this to you?'

Simon shook his head as if not one word of the question made a bit of sense.

'You slept with someone tonight.'

Simon nodded.

'Who was it?'

'Ragretta,' the catcher croaked. 'She said her name was Ragretta.'

Guillermo moved a bit further into the room from where he'd been cowering behind the door. 'I saw him with a girl with long, curly hair,' he said. 'He disappeared with her about a half hour before I went to bed.' He stared down at his friend. 'I thought he'd got lucky.'

'He's lucky he's not already dead,' Cavre said. 'Have you sent for an apothecary yet?'

Dunk heard the patter of little feet out in the hallway, along with longer, steadier strides. Slick burst into the room, a lit lantern swinging in his hand and a bowl-shouldered old woman wrapped in a black shawl right behind him. The woman took one look at Simon and gasped.

'I – there is nothing–' she looked at the blade hanging at Dunk's side. 'Kill him,' she said, her eyes wild with fear. 'Cut off his head and burn his body. There is no other way.'

Dunk balked at this. 'There must be!'

The woman snatched at his sword, but Cavre caught her fragile wrist in his hand. 'He is not too far gone yet,' the blitzer said. 'I know something of this sickness. Work with me to save him.'

The woman shuddered for a moment, looking up at Cavre with wide, watery eyes. Then she lowered her head and nodded. 'It will be pointless, but I will try.'

'We could use you on our cheerleading team,' Slick said.

'What can we do to help?' Dunk asked, feeling as helpless as a child.

'Find this Ragretta,' Cavre said.

'And bring her back so you can force her to cure Simon?' Guillermo said hopefully.

Cavre shook his head gravely. 'Kill her and burn her body, but be careful not to touch her yourself. I'm afraid that for what Simon has there may be no cure.'

CHAPTER TWENTY-TWO

Dunk thought Guillermo might fall to his knees right there and weep. Before that could happen, he grabbed the lineman by his shoulder and dragged him out of the room. Slick followed after them, closing the door behind them.

Dunk trotted down to the great hall, the others keeping up as best they could. When they got there, though, the place was dark but for the dying embers of what had once been a roaring fire in the main hearth.

'How will we find her now?' Guillermo said, his voice cracking with despair. 'She could be anywhere.'

'Well,' Slick said, 'if I were a wanton, Nurgle-worshipping harlot who passed on her dread lord's diseases through sex, where would I go?'

'Hush,' Dunk said, raising a hand as he cocked an ear. The hotel stood quiet at this hour of the night. The staff had all turned in for the night, and most of the guests were likely asleep in their rooms. If the cultist was still awake, they might be able to–

Dunk's head snapped up, and he beckoned for the others to follow him. He strode through the hall until he reached the door to the kitchen, under which a faint light flickered. A series of soft grunts and groans emanated from the room beyond. He drew his sword as silently as he could and motioned for Guillermo to quietly push open the swinging door.

Back in the Sure Wood, he'd seen the orgy from a distance, and he'd done his best to ignore it. Recovering the cup had been at the top of his agenda, and he'd refused to let prurient curiosity jeopardise his chances at that. Here, though, now, with the three participants right in front of him – lost in the throes of their disease-tainted ecstasy – he could not avoid it.

What the woman was doing with the men – who Dunk recognised as two of the more bestial prospects in the training camp that week – wasn't unbelievable, but her bare skin crawled with the same mobile, crimson rash that Simon had borne. As he watched, the rash slipped from body to body, transferring between the woman and the men where bare bits of flesh rubbed against each other, and then coming back again.

The trio turned at the sound of the opening of the kitchen door. The two prospects leaped away from the woman, surprised at having been caught with her. The woman, on the other hand, showed no sign of shame.

She flashed Dunk a sly wink and licked her lascivious lips, beckoning for him to join them in their twisted tryst.

There was a moment – just a brief one, a fraction of a second – when Dunk considered joining the woman, knocking the others aside and taking her for himself. Her seductive eyes begged him to do so.

Instead, he brandished his sword at her. 'I know what you are,' he said. 'Plaguebearer.'

The prospects looked at the woman, as if for the first time, and gasped as they saw the rash writhing along her skin. Then they saw the same marks moving through their own flesh, and they screamed in horror.

The sound startled Dunk, and the woman took the opportunity to leap at him. He stumbled as he tried to avoid her, tripping backward through the door and dropping his blade. She leapt after him as he landed on his rump and tried to scramble away in a desperate crabwalk.

'Join us,' the woman hissed, her breath the sweet, fetid odor of a fresh corpse. She gathered up his sword in her hands and caressed its blade.

Before Dunk could respond, Slick threw his lit lantern at the woman. When it smashed into her, the lamp's oil burst and its flame set her ablaze. She howled, although whether in agony or fury, Dunk could not tell. Guillermo cut the horrible noise short when he stepped forward and brained her with a cast-iron frying pan.

Later – after Dunk had carted off the woman's burnt remains, and Slick and Guillermo had carefully brought the two prospects to see Cavre – the three sat around the glowing embers in the hearth, drinking from a flask of wine Slick had appropriated from the kitchen.

'Did anyone touch them?' Dunk asked.

'Just my frying pan,' Guillermo said, pointing at the weapon he'd tossed into the crackling fire, along with another log. 'They did not put a finger on me.'

Slick nodded along with the lineman. 'Careful you don't let Pegleg know you're that good with a frying pan,' he said. 'The next time we're on the *Sea Chariot*, he'll make you the ship's cook.'

'Leave it in the hearth,' Dunk said, jerking his chin at the pan. 'The fire should have cleaned it well enough, but why take the risk?'

'What about your sword?' Guillermo said. Dunk had left it wrapped in the same tarp they'd used to haul away the woman's charred body. 'It is a handsome blade to throw away.'

'It's just a thing,' Dunk said. 'I can always get another sword.'

'That's a good attitude, Mr. Hoffnung,' Cavre said as he walked into the great hall. 'It is far better to be cautious than cauterised.'

'How is Simon?' Guillermo asked. Dunk could hear a bit of guilt mixed in the worry lacing the lineman's words. 'And the others?'

'Simon will live,' Cavre said, 'although only Nuffle knows for how long. The two prospects killed themselves when they saw him and realised what lay in store for them.'

Dunk, Slick, and Guillermo gasped. 'Does he suffer so?' asked the lineman.

Cavre grimaced. 'Not as much as before. The old woman and I had to wrap him in strips of linen from head to toe and soak the wrappings in beer.' The blitzer stopped when he saw the others goggling at him. 'The alcohol helps to sterilise his skin. He has also consumed enough of it for it to have a sedative and anesthetic effect.'

'How long will he have to be like that?' Dunk asked.

Cavre shook his head. 'It is impossible to say. For now, the disease is under control, although I wouldn't share a bottle with him.'

Slick looked wall-eyed at the flask of wine now in his hands, then set it gingerly on the table before him. No one else reached out for it.

'It could take him at any time,' Cavre continued. 'Or he could live for years.'

'Can't you do anything about it?' Guillermo said.

Cavre shook his head. 'In my homeland, deep in the Southlands, such an illness is considered untreatable. The old woman knew it not at all.'

'What about Olsen?' Dunk asked.

'We're afraid not, lads,' the wizard said as he entered the great hall. 'Our skills go more to harming things than healing them. The best we could offer that poor sod is a quick release.'

'Will he ever play ball again?' Guillermo asked.

Cavre nodded. 'As long as he stays covered in his wrappings and keeps them wet, I do not see why not.'

Dunk looked over at Slick and saw that the halfling had his head down and his shoulders shaking. The thrower reached out and tried to comfort his friend with a hand on his shoulder.

Slick threw back his head, his face shining with tears. Dunk had never seen the halfling show such emotion before, and he felt his own grief over Simon's fate rising in his chest, threatening to break through as terrible sobs. He heard Guillermo already sniffling beside him.

'I'm sorry,' Slick said, wiping the tears from his face with the palms of his little hands. 'I'm so sorry!'

'No,' Dunk said. 'It's not your fault. You had nothing to do with it.'

'Or did you?' Olsen asked. 'Is there something you'd care to share with us, wee one? Secrets you need to slough from your soul?'

'No,' Slick said, his body shaking again. 'Not that. I'm sorry for laughing so damn hard.'

With that, the halfling doubled over, gasping for air.

Dunk stared at his agent for a moment, then at the others, all of whom goggled at the callous creature.

'What's so damn funny?' Dunk asked, pulling Slick back up to sit straight in his chair. 'What?'

'I know it's horrible,' Slick said. 'But all I can see in my head is Simon charging down the field in his wet wrappings, smelling of yeast and barley.' He put his hands out in front of him as if to frame a picture, then thrust his arms forward, his hands formed into claws.

'Imagine a drunk, diseased, living mummy staggering down the field at you like a walking bar rag.'

Olsen started to snicker. 'He'd be almost too drunk to stand, but everyone would be afraid to tackle him.'

'Talk about a mummy's curse,' Guillermo said, a wry smile on his face. 'He'll be fine – as long as stays away from the toilets. M'Grash might mistake him for an ogre-sized roll of toilet paper.'

Dunk had to laugh at this, despite himself, and even Cavre joined in.

'Thirsty ogres might be a hazard too. Jim Johnson might try to wring him out so he can drink all the beer.'

'Oh,' Slick said, 'if he did that in the announcer's booth in front of that bloodsucker Bob Bifford – now there's a cage match I'd *pay* to see.'

This set the entire group off, giggling like children until they were finally too tired to go on.

Dunk felt better about Simon for a moment, but he felt guilty too. 'I can't believe we're joking about a dying team-mate,' he said softly. That capped the laughter, and everyone fell silent.

Slick, solemn as the rest of them now, reached over and clapped Dunk on the knee. 'Laugh or cry, son,' he said. 'Laugh or cry.'

'The Hackers sure have made a comeback since their devastating loss in the *Spike! Magazine* tournament, Jim. They look like a whole new team!'

'They practically are, Bob! As chronicled in the Wolf Sports' Cabalvision special *The Hackers Far Albion Cup*, they picked up a treeman known only as Edgar during their time in Albion, the only survivor of the slate of rookies who joined the team while on that distant isle. Isn't that right, Lästiges?'

Dunk saw the lady reporter's smiling image appear in the monstrous Jumboball squatting over the east end zone of Emperor Stadium. This crystal ball was, if anything, larger than the one in Magritta, and just looking at it filled Dunk's head with thoughts of rolling, shattering balls again.

'It's anchored down tight, son,' Slick said, standing next to him on the edge of the Hackers' dugout. 'Don't give it another thought.'

'The Hackers are one of the most resilient teams I've had the pleasure to follow,' Lästiges said in a chipper tone. Dunk thought he could see something sad around her ten-foot tall eyes, though, and he wondered about his brother.

Dirk would be somewhere in Altdorf today too, along with Spinne and the rest of the Reavers. They were supposed to be playing a game later today in the Altdorf Oldbowl, their home stadium, against Da Deff Skwadd, a team of orcs, trolls, and goblins hailing from the distant Badlands, just west of the furthest end of the Worlds Edge Mountains. The oddsmakers – including the Gobbo – heavily favoured the Reavers, which comforted Dunk a bit. He didn't really care who won the game, though, as long as Dirk and Spinne came out of it all right.

'What else can you say about a team that only has two of the same players from two seasons ago?' Lästiges continued. 'They lost another fifteen players in the Far Albion Cup finals too in a tragic magical accident involving their own team wizard, the legendary – at least in the small media market of Albion – Olsen Merlin.

'Amazingly, the Hackers still have Merlin in their employ. This reporter can only speculate that this has something to do with the wizard's long history with the Hackers' new lucky charm: the original Far Albion Cup itself. The question in most fans' minds today, though, has to be: can a trophy, however pretty it might be, be enough to boost the Hackers out of the basement?'

'Now, Lästiges,' Bob said, 'the Hackers did make it to the finals of the Blood Bowl Open last year. What makes things so different this time around?'

Lästiges laughed. 'I suppose you must have been napping during the last game the Hackers played in the Old World. In the *Spike! Magazine* Tournament, the Chaos All-Stars handed the Hackers their heads – literally, in some cases. There's been rampant speculation since then that the Hackers might have somehow benefited – knowingly or not – from the machinations behind last year's Black Jerseys scandal.'

'Did you just use the word 'machinations' in a Blood Bowl broadcast?' Jim asked with a rude cackle. 'I think most of our viewers' eyes just rolled back into their heads. Let's get down to the action!'

Dunk tried to ignore the announcers for the rest of the game. The Jumboball made that hard though, and every time he heard Lästiges's voice he glanced up there and wondered if she'd managed to reconcile with Dirk yet. If there was hope for those two, then there might be some for Dunk and Spinne too.

Dunk hadn't allowed himself to think too much about Spinne since he'd got her letter. He'd written back to her three times, explaining himself, but he'd never received any response. He'd wanted to go to Altdorf to find her, but Slick had talked him out of it. Both the Hackers and the Reavers were in training for the Blood Bowl. His team needed him here.

More of a problem was the fact that, as this year's favourites, the Reavers had hidden themselves away in a secret camp for the entire month before the game. Their coach wanted no distractions, and he'd gone to great lengths to make sure that even people as dedicated as jilted lovers wouldn't be able to bother his players.

The Hackers lost the toss and set up down at the west end of the field to kick-off the ball. The Darkside Cowboys, a team composed entirely of dark elves dressed in black and blue uniforms, jogged down to the east end to receive.

'These Cowboys are mean bastards,' Pegleg had said in his pre-game talk to the entire team. 'They may not have the raw power of a team like the Oldheim Ogres, but they make up for it by playing the most vicious and ruthlessly efficient football I've ever seen. Their star blitzer – Raghib 'the White Rocket' Ishmael – once tore out two players' hearts and stuffed them into each others' chests, right in the middle of the game. And they played for the Cowboys!'

'Why do they call him 'the White Rocket'?' Dunk had asked Slick later.

'He's an albino, son,' Slick said. 'Skin whiter than the silver hair you see on most dark elves. And he's faster than just about anything else on two legs. He's got an amazing arm too. Used to be a whaler on a ship called the *Ahab*, and he hurls that ball like a harpoon.'

Dunk gritted his teeth as he waited for Cavre to kick the ball to the waiting Cowboys. He gazed around at the others players on the field and realised he didn't know but half of them well. He'd practiced with the new players, but they mostly kept to themselves. With all the death that had surrounded the team lately, Dunk hadn't felt like getting to know them. He didn't want to make more friends just to lose them too.

Besides which, they were a surly lot. Something about the new recruits put Dunk's teeth on edge. He had to admit they were good players, if not spectacular, but he wished they were all on someone else's team. They might be his team-mates but never his friends.

He told himself he was overreacting. The whole debacle with Deckem and his deadmen had left him with a foul taste in his mouth when it came to Blood Bowl. This was his first game since the Far Albion Cup Final. Once he got back into the zone, it would all be fun again.

Right?

The roar of the crowd rose as Cavre put up his hand, signalling to the others that he was about to kick the ball. As he ran forward, the noise reached a blistering crescendo, and then fell off as the ball sailed through the air toward the Cowboys.

Dunk raced straight down the field, following in M'Grash's wake as the ogre charged along the north side. Edgar cleared out the south side as he strode into and through the oncoming Cowboys, forcing the ball carrier back into the centre. Peering around the ogre's shoulder, Dunk saw that Ishmael, who stood taller than all of the other dark elves, had the ball.

'Oh, my, Bob! Did you see that move?'

'Barely, Jim, barely. The White Rocket is zooming along so fast I almost missed it. Too bad for the Hackers' rookie lineman Karfheim that Ishmael didn't miss him.'

'I wonder how the White Rocket gets out blood-stains when they fountain all over him like that. Perhaps Lästiges would know?'

'Just because I'm a woman doesn't mean I know one end of a laundry tub from another, girls,' Lästiges said. 'You're a vampire, Bob. Don't you know?'

'I know better than to get blood on my clothes,' Bob said. 'Oh! And there goes another player, the Cowboys' Meion Sanders. It's always sad to see a future Hall of Famer take a fall like that.'

'The only future Meion has is with an undead team now,' Jim said, 'if they can piece together enough of his corpse.'

Dunk spotted Ishmael jinking his way, and he spun out from behind M'Grash to launch himself at the Cowboy's star blitzer. Ishmael was ready for him and tried to stiff-arm him out of the way, but Dunk just grabbed the albino's white-skinned arm and spun him to the ground.

The ball tumbled free, and Dunk scrambled after it. Before he could reach it though, he felt a pair of wiry arms wrap around his lower legs and bring him to the Astrogranite.

'You dare to stand before the White Rocket, Hoff-nung?' a voice rasped into his helmet. 'You should expect to pay.'

CHAPTER TWENTY-THREE

Dunk FELT A blade cut across the back of his thigh, trying to hamstring him, but as the edge pierced his flesh, he wriggled away. The razor secreted in the edge of Ishmael's gauntlet missed its mark.

Dunk reached back and grabbed Ishmael's helmet by the face guard. The albino pulled away, slipping out of the helmet before Dunk could twist his head off. 'Well played, Hoff-Nung,' the not-so-dark elf hissed, 'but no one can stop a rocket.'

Dunk spun about, looking for the ball, and saw that Simon had scooped it up. As he ran for the end zone, many of the Cowboys seemed to be avoiding him, shoving their team-mates toward the diseased Hacker instead.

'Would you look at that?' Bob said. 'First the Hackers have an ogre on their team. Then a treeman. And now it's a mummy! Now that's diversity for you. Never let anyone tell you the dead and the living don't mix!'

'As we can testify ourselves, old friend,' said Jim. 'But according to the lovely Lästiges, that's no mummy!'

'Has anyone told the kids?'

'Ha, ha,' Lästiges said mirthlessly. 'That's none other than Simon Sherwood, the Albion native who joined the Hackers at the start of last season. Simon had a bit of a run-in with a ladyfriend who should have been playing groupie for Nurgle's Rotters instead. Now he's the poster child for safe sex.'

'And just how do you have safe sex with a Nurgle cultist?' Jim asked. 'An all-over body wrap like that? It seems Sherwood's trying to seal up the dungeon after the daemons are already out.'

'That's right,' Bob said. 'It seems like the secret to safe sex is the same as it is for comedy.'

'Is that so? Then tell us, what is–'

'Timing!'

Dunk felt a burning sensation across his back and turned around to see Ishmael standing behind him, his gauntlet running with blood. The albino grinned at him, showing a set of jet-black teeth behind his pale, white lips.

'You must be the sensitive sort, Hoff-Nung,' the albino said. 'Most people never feel the White Rocket's cuts until they're dead.'

'It's because your blade's just like you,' Dunk said, smashing the Cowboy over his unprotected head with his own helmet. 'Dull.'

The albino went down, crimson blood spurting from his shattered nose. Against Ishmael's white skin, the fluid looked redder than Dunk thought possible. As he watched it flow, he had to fight back a terrible urge to keep pounding at the helpless dark elf with his helmet until his head was only a bloody smear on the Astrogranite.

'Touchdown, Hackers!' Bob said. 'Simply amazing. Have you ever seen a score like that, Jim?'

'Not since the last time the Hackers played in the Old World, back in Magritta, but they were on the other side of the equation then. It seems they've learned how to play that kind of game. It's not often you see a body count that high on a team's first possession.'

Dunk looked back toward the Cowboys' end zone, where Simon was still letting loose with a complicated victory dance that threatened to unwind his wrappings. Between the thrower and the end zone, bodies in black and blue uniforms littered the field. In fact, by Dunk's count, not one of the Cowboys who had started the game still stood.

'Damn,' he swore, dropping Ishmael's helmet next to the albino's unconscious form. 'Not again.'

'IT'S THE CUP,' Dunk said to Pegleg. The coach's office attached to the Hackers' locker room was a cramped place made even more so by the large crystal ball mounted on the lone desk. It made the ex-pirate seem more dangerous than usual, perhaps because with the door shut behind him Dunk knew there was no place in the room that was out of the coach's reach. He wondered if the room had been built with that in mind.

'What, Mr. Hoffnung, is your point?'

'Coach, we can't go around killing off every team we face.'

'And why not?' Pegleg leaned back in his chair and ran a hand back through his long curls. Far more grey streaked them than had when they first met, Dunk noticed. 'Blood Bowl is a violent game. People get killed in it all the time.'

'We've already had this conversation,' Dunk said. 'You gave the cup up once before.'

'That was in a moment of weakness,' Pegleg said, leaning forward, his fingers splayed across the desk. 'I should never have given in. What did that do for us? We lost the Far Albion Cup tournament – including the purse, which would have helped defray the exorbitant expenses of the trip.

'A Blood Bowl team is not a charity. You expect to be paid, don't you? Your agent certainly expects you to, and the rest of the team would like to take their sacks of gold home, too, twice a month whether I have the cash or not.'

'Money isn't everything,' Dunk said.

'Spoken like a nobleman's son,' the coach said, scowling. 'You're right!' he continued as he leapt to his feet and stabbed his hook into the desk's mahogany surface. 'It's the *only* thing!'

'Coach.'

'Mr. Hoffnung. As long as I *am* the coach and you are the *player*, you will respect my decisions!'

Dunk noticed that Pegleg's hook was caught where he'd embedded it in the top of the desk. The ex-pirate tried to twist it free, but he was stuck. This took the wind from his sails, and he sat back down in his chair, the hook still jammed into the wood between them.

'Dunk,' Pegleg said, his manner softer, more reasonable. 'This isn't like the last time. Mr. Merlin has assured me of that. He believes he can control the cup and its effects.'

'But can he control our new players?'

'That is *my* responsibility, although he seemed to do a fine job of it last time.' He narrowed his eyes at Dunk. 'You might recall how it went.'

The door to the office swung open, and Dunk had to step aside to avoid it hitting him. There, framed in the entrance, stood the two Game Wizards who had stalked Dunk through much of the previous season: Blaque and Whyte.

Despite the fact that Whyte was an elf and Blaque was a dwarf, the two stood equally tall. As pale as Ishmael, but with white teeth and blue eyes, Whyte had never smiled that Dunk had seen. He didn't know if the elf even could.

Blaque, on the other hand, smiled all the time but in a wry, sarcastic way. He looked like he'd been carved from a mountain and covered with hair the colour of the coal mined from the range's roots. Like Whyte, he wore a crisp-pressed GW uniform: a dark robe sashed with a crimson rope, a frothing wolf's head embroidered across the chest.

'What a happy reunion this is, don't you agree, Whyte?' the dwarf said with a smarmy grin. 'All of us back together again. It's just like old times.'

'I can't say I care for old times,' the elf said solemnly. 'They weren't all that good either.'

'What can I do for you, gentle wizards?' Pegleg said. He gave one last tug on his hook, subtly enough that the GWs might not notice, but Dunk saw that he was still stuck.

'The Far Albion Cup,' Blaque said. 'We're here to take it.'

'I'm afraid that's not possible.' The ex-pirate showed a savage smile that exposed his golden teeth.

'What do you think?' Blaque asked Whyte. 'Does he have much of an imagination?'

'I'd hazard not,' Whyte said. 'People with an imagination know that all sorts of things are possible.'

'It's not going to happen,' Pegleg said, the smile fading from his face.

'See, now this is where my imagination starts to kick in,' Blaque said. 'I can imagine all sorts of ways that this can happen.'

He stuck out one stubby finger. 'First, you can give it to us peacefully, and we'll quietly take it away.'

He stuck out another finger. 'Second, we can take it from your bloody corpse.'

The dwarf looked at the elf, concerned. 'Actually, that's it for me. I'm all out. You have any other notions?'

'You're the one with the imagination. Those sound like fine options to me.'

'You're not taking the cup, and you will not lay a finger on me.' The coach looked a lot more confident about his pronouncement than Dunk felt.

'Interesting,' Blaque said, chewing a chubby lip. 'Seems he does have a wild imagination after all.'

'That cup is the property of the Hackers, and its use falls within the rules as laid down by Sacred Commissioner Roze-El, directly from Nuffle's Book. If you take it from me – or lay a hand on me or any of my players to try it – I'll report you directly to Ruprecht Murdark himself.'

'Murdark's not here this time, is he?' Blaque said. 'By the time he asks us what happened, they'll be laying flowers on your grave. What kind do you think we should send?'

'Lilies,' Whyte said. 'I always like lilies.'

A wide grin grew on Pegleg's face as he looked past the Game Wizards and into the locker room beyond. 'Welcome, Mr. Merlin,' he said. 'Do you happen to know these two? Allow me to introduce–'

As the two GWs turned to see who Pegleg was talking to, the Albionish wizard bared his teeth at them in an unfriendly way. 'Only by reputation, laddie, but that's enough for us.' He glared at the two shorter wizards in turn, fingering the wand in his hand as he spoke. 'Listen to us, you two charlatans. Blackguards like you may be able to intimidate the ignorant with your parlour tricks, but we are not impressed. If we catch you talking with our employer again, we're going to assume you're up to no good and fry you on the spot.'

He paused for a moment to measure the looks on the other wizards' faces. 'Is that clear?'

Blaque jerked his head toward the door, and Whyte headed for it. Olsen stepped aside to let him pass, and the dwarf followed after him. Once he was out of the office, Blaque turned back and said, 'We're not through with this yet.'

Olsen barked a sharp, short laugh. 'Faith! Of course not, laddie. It won't end until you force our hand.' He stuffed his wand back into his robes. 'Then it'll be over before you know it.'

'HE SAID HE'D meet you here?' Slick asked, gazing around the Skinned Cat.

Dunk nodded, as he nursed his pint of Bugman's XXXXXX. It looked the same as ever: rough-hewn tables and chairs that looked like they'd been used more often as weapons than furniture, sawdust on the floor to soak up the spilled beer and vomit and blood.

It was the kind of seedy joint in which the patrons kept to themselves and minded their own business. The tourists in town for the Blood Bowl mostly stayed clear of this part of town, as it had a deserved reputation for being deadly dangerous. When Dunk had lived as a boy here in Altdorf, he would never have considered entering such a place, except in his most adventurous daydreams.

If anyone recognised Dunk as a Blood Bowl player here, they refused to admit it, and that was just what he wanted: a measure of anonymity. When the Blood Bowl Open came to town, a kind of madness invaded the city, carried in the hearts of the hundreds of thousands of fans in town for the games. Not all of them could manage to get tickets, but that deterred no one. Just being close to the stadiums when the games were being played was enough. That's why the Skinned Cat had become such a precious place to Dunk, a haven in which he could escape – at least for a little while – the insanity running rampant through Altdorf.

'There he is now,' Dunk said as he got to his feet. There, framed in the lamplight streaming in through the open doorway, stood Dirk

Dunk hadn't always got along well with his younger brother Dirk. They hadn't spoken much after Dirk left home to join the Reavers. That had only changed in the past year, when Dunk had followed in his prodigal brother's footsteps. Around this time last year, during the previous Blood Bowl Open, Dunk had felt like they really were *brothers*, in every sense of the word, for the first time since he could remember.

Now, looking at his brother's solemn face, he feared all that had been lost, perhaps forever.

'Dunk,' the younger man said as he approached. He looked well but worn, which was no surprise, as he'd played in a Blood Bowl game with the Reavers just hours before. A shallow cut under his left eye had been expertly stitched and looked to already be healing well. Still, he neither stuck out his hand nor opened his arms wide in greeting. He just took one of the open chairs at the table and sat down.

Dunk nodded and sat down as well, signalling for the barmaid's attention as he did. 'What'll you have?'

'Got any Hogshead in this hellhole?'

'Sorry,' the barmaid said without a trace of remorse. She was a hard-bitten woman who looked tough enough to play for the Hackers herself. 'They went out of business.'

'Really?' Dirk said. 'I thought they made the official beer of the GWs.'

'Used to be. They drink Green Ronin nowadays.'

Dirk nodded at that, and the barmaid sauntered off.

'So,' Dunk said.

'So,' said Dirk.

'Can we cut the chit-chat, boys?' Slick said. 'This is painful enough to just watch. You're brothers, for pity's sake. This is over a *woman* – *Lästiges*, for the love of Nuffle.'

'Hey!' Dirk said.

The halfling threw up his hands in surrender and then looked at both of the men in turn. 'Can't you just shake hands and make up.'

Dirk scrutinised Dunk. 'Can we do that?'

'I'd like that,' Dunk said.

'After what you did…' Dirk shook his head ruefully.

Dunk protested. 'This is all just a horrible misunder– '

Dirk cut off his older brother with a sweep of his hand. 'Oh,' he said, a grin spreading across his face, 'I know.'

Dunk paused in the middle of running through the explanation he'd been preparing ever since he'd got Dirk's message asking for this meeting. He cocked his head at his brother, looking deep into his so-familiar eyes, and said, 'What?'

'I know,' Dirk said, sitting back with a smirk on his face. 'Lästiges broke into my room earlier this week and forced me to watch the unedited footage of the night you ended up in bed together.' He shook his head and cackled. 'You weren't a threat to anyone's honour that night – not even your own.'

Dunk sat back in his chair, stunned.

The barmaid shoved a tall, greenish beer in front of Dirk. As opaque as a stout, it carried a thick, full head. Dirk grabbed the beer and took a huge slug of it into his mouth.

Dirk's eyes bulged out of his head, and for a moment Dunk thought he might spray the table with whatever swam around in his mouth. Dirk managed to keep it down, though, swallowing hard, and then gasping for air.

'This is *less* bitter?' he said, his eyes watering.

'You want me to get you something else?' Dunk asked, already looking for the barmaid again.

Dirk stared at the top of the beer for a moment, and then took another tentative sip. 'No,' he said. 'I actually like it. It grows on you fast.'

'I'll take your word for it.' Then he glared at his brother. 'But if you're okay with all this, why did you make me suffer for so long?'

Dirk made a face at his beer before taking another drink. He shook his head like a wet dog drying itself, then smiled at Dunk. 'Hey, just because nothing happened doesn't mean it couldn't have. You still needed to pay for it – if only just a little.'

'You son of a–'

'Yes, my brother?' Dirk said innocently.

Dunk tried to come up with something horrible to say, but as the words rolled around in his mouth, struggling to come out in the right order, a shout pierced the background noise of the tavern and drove itself straight into his brain.

'Dunkel Hoffnung!' the voice said. 'You've got a lot of nerve showing your face around here!'

CHAPTER TWENTY- FOUR

DUNK'S HEAD SNAPPED around to see Spinne standing just inside the doorway, glaring at him with the intensity of an angry valkyrie sent down to haul his sorry carcass back up to the heavens for judgment. She had her long, strawberry-blonde hair pulled back in a warrior's braid, and her blue-grey eyes burned with a hellish intensity. She stomped over to him on her long, athletic legs and parted her wide, full lips to snarl down at him.

'What do you have to say for yourself?'

Dunk stood up in her face, took her into his arms, and planted a long, loving kiss square on her mouth. Her arms came up and wrapped around his neck, and to his delight they held him in a gentle, non-strangling way. For those precious seconds, the months they'd been apart seemed to melt away.

When they finally parted, moments later, she wore a wild, happy smile. 'What was that–?' Then she glared down at Dirk. 'You told him, didn't you?'

'I couldn't help it,' Dirk said, pointing at the greenish glass in front of him. 'It was the beer.'

Spinne narrowed her eyes at him and then at Dunk. 'I want you to know, I'm still mad at you. You never should have put yourself in that kind of position.'

'What kind of position?'

'The kind that lands you in bed with another woman so that it can be broadcast on a Cabalvision special.'

Dunk grinned. 'So, as long as there aren't any camras…?'

She cut him off with another kiss. 'Don't press your luck.' She broke free from their embrace then, and they sat down next to each other, with Spinne between Dunk and Dirk.

'So,' Slick said, 'one big happy family again, eh? That calls for another round.' He signalled the barmaid again.

'Add a Black Widow to the order if you don't mind,' Lästiges said, as she appeared from a darkened booth in a distant corner of the tavern's main room. She winked at Dunk, and he realised she'd been watching him the whole time.

'I spoke too soon,' Slick said with a wince. Despite this, he relayed Lästiges's request to the barmaid too.

'I'm so glad you're all here,' Dunk said, looking Spinne and Dirk in the eyes, measuring them up. 'I have a special favour to ask of you, and I don't know exactly how to put it.'

'Go ahead,' Spinne said, holding his hand. 'After this debacle, I think we can take it.'

Dirk nodded eagerly.

Dunk screwed up his courage and said, 'The Reavers need to drop out of the tournament.'

Everyone at the table froze, staring at Dunk. Only Slick seemed to understand what Dunk meant, and he hid behind his empty stein of beer rather than stand between Dunk and his friends.

'You're insane,' Dirk said. He turned to Slick. 'Did he get his bell rung in the game today? He's not making any sense.'

Lästiges didn't say a word. She just frowned at Dunk and drummed the long, red fingernails of one hand on the battle-scarred tabletop.

'What are you talking about?' Spinne said, her brow furrowed with concern.

Dunk took a deep breath. He knew this wouldn't be an easy sell, but he had to try. 'You two saw Lästiges's documentary.' Both Spinne and Dirk scowled at this.

'The whole thing,' Dunk added quickly. 'You know about the Far Albion Cup, right? Well, we – the Hackers – still have it. And it's just as dangerous here as it ever was in Albion, maybe more so.'

'What's your point?' Dirk said. 'With that fancy goblet, the Hackers are unbeatable, so we shouldn't even try?'

Dunk nodded. 'Yes! But that's not all. It's not just that we can't be defeated. It's that we'll kill most of the other players who make it on to the field. If the Reavers end up playing us in the finals like last year, you might both be killed.'

Spinne looked at Dirk, who scoffed with a bitter laugh. 'This is really pathetic,' he said to Dunk. 'Did Pegleg put you up to this? Or Slick?'

The halfling gave a too-innocent shrug. The drinks arrived just then, and he snatched up his fresh stein and hid his face in it. The others left their orders untouched.

'You can't expect us to quit our team because of some ancient legend,' Spinne said. 'We're Blood Bowl players. If we left the game every time there was some kind of threat, we'd never be able to take the field. Just being out there on the gridiron is one of the most dangerous things you can do.'

'But this isn't a legend,' Dunk said. 'It's real. I've seen it in action, both in Albion and during the game today. If you play against us, you'll be killed, and I don't want to see that happen.'

'So why don't you quit?' Dirk said. 'Or steal the cup? Or destroy it? Or sabotage the Hackers? Why should we have to forfeit our shot at the championship?'

Dunk frowned. He could feel the conversation slipping away from him. 'Don't you think I've thought of that? Pegleg has hidden the cup away, and he's got our team wizard, Olsen Merlin, guarding it for him. I've tried talking to them both, but it's no use. They want the championship, and they don't much care how many people have to die for them to get it.'

'You could say the same thing about any Blood Bowl coach,' Spinne said, unimpressed. 'Dunk, I wanted this to be a happy moment for us. Why do you have to ruin it like this?'

Dunk saw the disturbed look on her beautiful face, and he knew she wanted him to stop, to ignore the threat to her life and let her handle it herself, just like she always did. She was a Blood Bowl player. She lived with mortal danger every day, and they never talked about it. They preferred to ignore the threat of death that always hung over their heads, sticking to the moment instead, enjoying it for what it was, not what it might represent. To her, this threat of the Far Albion Cup was no different than any other – and a poor excuse for shattering the good mood.

But Dunk couldn't help himself. He couldn't sit here, finally reunited with her after so many months, and forget about the fact that the Far Albion Cup might make his team murder hers on the field. There was no way around it.

'You have to quit,' he said. 'Both of you. Or, if you care about your team-mates, you have to lose a game. Not right away, of course, but before the Hackers meet you in the playoffs.'

'What makes you think you scruffy bastards will make it to the playoffs again?' Dirk said.

Dunk snarled at him. 'Pay attention, would you? This isn't some joke. This is your life I'm talking about, and yours,' he said to Spinne.

She got to her feet. 'I've had enough of this,' she said. 'I thought you'd be glad to see me, to know that I'd decided to give you a second chance, but this…' Dunk thought he saw tears welling up in her eyes. 'I trusted you. I loved you, but this…'

He saw her reach down inside herself and clamp down on whatever it was that produced emotions in her. In an instant, she turned cold and distant. The woman he loved – correction, the woman who loved him – was gone.

'Let's go,' Spinne said to Dirk.

He stood up, shaking his head at his brother as if at a small child who hadn't learned to curb an insolent tongue. 'What are you thinking?' he spat.

Spinne frowned down at Dunk. 'We'll see you on the field,' she said, 'if you're lucky.'

With that, the two Reavers turned and left.

As they walked out of the Skinned Cat, Lästiges rolled her eyes at Dunk. 'Well played,' she said. 'To get back the girl and lose her in the space of minutes, I'm impressed.'

'You know what I'm talking about here,' Dunk said. 'You have to talk to them.'

'We've seen just how much good that's done.'

'You can't just let the Hackers kill them.' Dunk strove to keep his desperation out of his voice.

Lästiges raised her perfectly sculpted eyebrows at Dunk. 'We're a long way from that point yet. We're still in the opening round, and there's no chance the two teams will meet yet. Wolf Sports is counting on a match-up at some point in the playoffs. If – *if* – that hits the schedule, I'll say something then, but not before.' Her eyes wandered toward the door, which Spinne had long since slammed behind her. 'Not before.'

'By then, it might be too late. The closer they get to the finals, the less the chance they'll listen to reason. The chance at being the repeating champions will be too much for them.' Dunk buried his face in his hands and growled in frustration. 'Why will nobody help me?'

'Well, kid, just tell me what it is you need,' a greasy voice said, slithering into Dunk's ear. 'Maybe we can cut some kind of a deal.'

The thrower groaned, leaving his face in his hands. 'Leave me alone, Gunther.'

'Hey,' the slimy bookie said, 'would a good friend abandon another in his time of need?'

Dunk uncovered his eyes and shot the Gobbo an ironic look. The nauseating creature looked a shade greener than ever.

'Oh, whoops!' the bookie said dramatically. 'I guess that's what just happened here, isn't it? Well, when your friends abandon you, then who's left?'

Dunk glared at the Gobbo. 'What do you want?'

'What everyone wants: gold. To get that, I want to ask you the same question: What do you want?'

'I'll tell you what,' Dunk said. He regretted the words even as they left his mouth, but he didn't stop talking. 'If you can help me, I'll help you.'

'That's what I do,' the Gobbo said, phlegm flying from his rubbery lips as he chortled. He let loose a loud belch that smelled of old, fried meat. ''Scuse me,' he said. 'I'm a bit off my feed today. I think that last rat-on-a-stick at the game tried biting me back.' He tried to suppress another noisy burp and failed. 'Anyway, how can I help you?'

'Get the Reavers to lose a game so they don't meet the Hackers in the playoffs.'

The Gobbo rubbed his greasy chin. 'That's a tall order, kid. Last year, if you'd asked, I could have mobilised the Black Jerseys to make something happen, but someone,' he glared at Dunk here, 'caused me to fumble that little operation.'

Dunk nodded knowingly. 'What would you want in return?'

The Gobbo grinned. 'You don't like being on this side of it now, do you?' he said. 'Needing me? What I can offer? How does it feel?'

Dunk made a fist. 'Do you want to make a deal or not?'

'Sheesh!' the Gobbo said. 'Can you let a guy gloat a little?' Then he turned serious. 'I want you as the captain of my new version of the Black Jerseys.'

'Never,' Dunk said instantly.

The Gobbo showed even more of his teeth. 'You sure you don't want a bit more time to think that over, kid? What if I'm your only chance to keep your brother and your girlfriend alive?'

'There has to be a better way, son,' Slick said softly, his stein now on the table in front of him.

Dunk thought about this for a long moment, and then shook his head. 'All right,' he said to the Gobbo. 'If you can pull that off, I'll throw one game for you.'

'Just one?' the bookie looked distressed. For a moment, Dunk worried he might belch again – or worse. 'Aren't the lives of the two people closest in the world to you worth more than a single game?'

'That's the deal. And if you take it, I'll throw in a bit of advice about the Hackers for free.'

The Gobbo rubbed his chin until Dunk thought he might crack it wide open. 'All right,' he finally said. 'It's a deal.' He offered his clammy hand, but Dunk ignored it.

'How do I know I can trust you?' the Gobbo asked.

Dunk rolled his eyes. 'Of the two of us, who would you – even *you* – trust most?'

'Good point, kid.' the Gobbo said. 'So what's my "free" advice?'

'Consider it a down payment on the deal,' Slick said. 'If you don't produce, then you might owe us.'

The bookie sneered at the halfling, but before he could respond, Dunk spoke up. 'As long as the Hackers have the Far Albion Cup, don't bet against us.'

'That's it?' the Gobbo said. 'You're just going to repeat that tired legend from the lady's Cabalvision special?' He leered at her, and Lästiges squirmed away from him in her seat.

'It's no legend,' Dunk said. 'Didn't you pay attention? Everything in that show was real.'

'Everything?' the Gobbo said, trying to peer down Lästiges's shirt. She clasped a hand to her chest and scooted her chair farther away. Then his eyes snapped open and he sat bolt upright, a look of surprise on his face.

'It's a deal. Gotta go!' With that, he slid off his chair and waddled his way in the direction of the nearest latrine, holding his thighs together the entire time.

'WHAT A NIGHT!' Lästiges said, as she stumbled on a loose paving stone, nearly taking a spill in the dimly lit street. Dunk reached out and steadied her with an arm attached to a body only slightly less intoxicated than hers.

'You got that right,' Slick said as he scurried out of her way. 'You make up with your lovers, you run them out of the bar, and then you cut a deal with the slimiest creature this side of Nurgle himself.'

'By "you," I think he meansh *you*,' Lästiges said, wrapping an arm over Dunk's shoulder for support. Drunk, she'd developed a lateral lisp. '*I* wouldn't have done any of that. Well, maybe the firsht part – making up with our loversh – which was all my fault, thank you very much. But not the other two thingsh.'

'And thank you for that, by the way,' Dunk said. 'I'm just sorry I had to go and throw a wrench into that.' He hesitated for a moment, then continued.

'But loving someone doesn't mean much if you're willing to let them get killed, does it? It just frustrates me that they refused to listen. Isn't life more important than Blood Bowl?'

'Damned loser.'

Dunk spun about, nearly spilling Lästiges to the pavement as he did. They stood, he noticed, on the darkest stretch of street he'd yet seen on their stagger home. The voice – a low growl, really – seemed to have come from nowhere, as if the darkness itself had spat out the words.

'Slick?' Dunk said. 'Did you have something you wanted to get off your chest?'

The halfling, white as a sheet, shook his head. 'That wasn't me, son, not with my worst cold ever.'

A low, rumbling laugh emanated from the darkness overhead. Dunk snapped his neck back to glare into the clear night sky, but he saw nothing there, not even a wisp of a cloud scudding between the tops of the buildings on either side of the street.

Then Dunk felt a tap on his shoulder. He turned about and came face to chest with a huge person dressed all in black. He craned his neck backward and found himself nose to nose with a monstrous, pale orc staring down into his eyes.

'Boo,' Skragger said.

Lästiges unleashed a scream that Dunk thought might make his ears bleed. As she did, the orc grabbed her around her cheeks with a rough, hairy paw. His long, claw-like nails dug into her flesh as he forced her to stare into his glowing red eyes.

Lästiges stopped screaming.

'Sleep,' Skragger said, and the woman collapsed into Dunk's arms.

'You're dead,' Slick said, his voice constricting with terror. 'We saw you die.'

The massive orc stepped back from Dunk and Lästiges and snickered. 'I am dead.' He drew a long nail across his chest, pulling back his heavy, black cloak and revealing a white logo embroidered on his black shirt: a winner's cup made of human bones and a human skull.

'You're with the Champions of Death,' Dunk said. As the words left him, he realised their significance and recoiled in horror.

Skragger bared his jagged, broken teeth and tusks in a cold approximation of a smile. 'Von Irongrad found me. Made me this.' He opened his mouth wider, and a pair of fangs sank down from behind his thick upper lip.

'Tomolandry has the Impaler working as a vampire recruiter?' Slick breathed. 'Ingenious. How is the Champions' pay scale?'

'Sucks,' Skragger said, baring his fangs. 'But so do I.'

Dunk hefted Lästiges in his arms, wondering if he could outrun the vampire orc if he tossed the woman over his shoulder. When Skragger was alive, it would have been a close race, but give him the unending stamina of the undead, and Dunk didn't see how he had much of a chance. He couldn't just drop Lästiges and leave her to the merciless Skragger, although maybe the orc *would* just chase him instead. After all, he wanted to kill Dunk, right? But what about Slick too?

Skragger leaned forward into Dunk's face. 'Not here for revenge,' he said. 'Not for me. For Guterfiends.'

Dunk's jaw fell, and he nearly dropped Lästiges to the pavement. The Guterfiend family had been behind his family's downfall. They lived in the old Hoffnung estate now, here in Altdorf. Dunk had thought he'd be beneath their notice now. They'd beaten his father so thoroughly that the man had fled town without even bidding his son good-bye. What could they want with him?

'Guterfiends got gold,' Skragger said. 'Lotta gold.' He reached up and used a long fingernail to scratch a small cut in Dunk's forehead.

Dunk held still, terrified and trapped. He felt a rivulet of blood start to trickle down between his eyebrows and along the side of his nose. Skragger watched it as it went, and he licked his lips, catching his tongue for a moment on each of his fangs.

Dunk lunged forward and drove his forehead into the vampire orc's face. The impact stunned him as well, and he fell backward to land on the pavement, Lästiges still in his arms. Skragger looked down at Dunk and laughed, then used a pale finger to wipe the thrower's blood from his forehead. He stuck the finger in his mouth and licked it clean.

'Tasty,' Skragger said. 'Get it all tomorrow.'

Dunk stared up at the orc, his voice catching in his throat. 'What?' was all he could croak out.

'See you on the gridiron,' Skragger said, his eyes burning red as his too-pale form faded into insubstantial mist that blew away on an unfelt breeze. 'We got a game.'

CHAPTER TWENTY-FIVE

'NUFFLE'S BALLS!' BOB's voice rang out over the PA system at Emperor Stadium, barely piercing the crowd's roar. 'Did you see that hit?'

Dunk hadn't seen a thing, but he'd sure felt it. Something the size and speed of a stampeding bull had smashed into him and sent him skittering across the Astrogranite. Only his armour had kept him from being crushed.

'Skragger's really giving it to Hoffnung today,' Jim said. 'You'd almost think it was personal. Oh, wait! It is!'

'Sure enough, Jim. This isn't just the first round of the Blood Bowl playoffs. It's a grudge match! Besides the fatal encounter Skragger had with Hoffnung last year, Coach Tomolandry's team is itching for a chance to avenge that bone-rattling loss at the Hackers' hands in last year's Dungeonbowl.'

'Another hit like that, Bob, and they might find themselves recruiting Hoffnung next! Maybe they can use him to replace Ramen-Tut, who turned to dust in that same game last year, in a pile-up beneath Hoffnung and the late Kur Ritternacht.'

Dunk scrambled to his feet and looked up, the ball still in his hands. He clenched his teeth, fighting through the pain, and wondered how many steps he could make before he got hit again. Then a sight rarer than an ogre with an education greeted him, and he froze in astonishment.

There, right in front of the thrower, stood a goblin dressed in a black cap and a shirt with black-and-white, vertical stripes. He had something silvery in one hand and something bright yellow in the other. As he threw the yellow thing – some kind of weighted handkerchief that sailed through the air – he brought the silvery thing up to his lips and blew a shrill blast.

'Penalty!' the goblin shouted.

Taken aback by this vision, Dunk stumbled backwards, a goofy grin on his face. Here, right in front of him, not only was there a referee but he had called a penalty on that cheap shot he'd just taken.

Then Dunk realised the ref was pointing at him.

'Unnecessary roughness!' the ref said.

'Can you believe it?' Jim said. 'The call is *against* Hoffnung. Talk about adding insult to injury.'

The crowd booed and hissed at the call. Dunk drew some small comfort from this, even though he knew it was only because Blood Bowl fans hated anything that slowed the pace of the bloodshed on the field.

'I don't know,' Bob said. 'I think Hoffnung had it coming. After all, he did get right in Skragger's way there. The all-star player almost tripped right over him.'

'But to get kicked out of the game for that?' Jim said. 'That seems more than a bit much.' The crowed booed in agreement.

Frustrated, Dunk dropped the ball on the ground and glanced back at Skragger. The snarling vampire orc drew his hand across his own throat in a cutting gesture. A sense of relief washed over the thrower.

'Ha!' he said to Skragger. 'This guy just cheated you of your revenge. You can't kill me in front of all these people if–'

The referee scurried past Dunk then, almost knocking him over. The thrower realised then that Skragger hadn't been making the signal at him but the referee.

'What's this?' Bob said. 'The ref is picking up his flag and waving off the call. There is no penalty!'

The crowd roared its approval.

'I don't know how much the Champions are paying that referee,' said Bob, 'but he sure seems intent on earning it!'

'No 'scape,' Skragger said, pointing a pale finger at Dunk. 'Not this time.'

Dunk scooped the ball back up, turned, and ran.

The Hackers hadn't had much of a game so far. The strategy that Pegleg pursued these days, under the auspices of the Far Albion Cup – killing enough of the opposing players to force them to forfeit the game – crashed against the shoals when it came to the Champions of Death. The Champions were already dead, which made them impossible to kill. To get them out of the game, you had to tear them apart instead, a much more involved process.

For once, Dunk wished his new team-mates were *more* destructive. As it was, he needed to do something fast or Skragger would be collecting his fee from the Guterfiends before halftime.

There was no way for him to stand up to Skragger toe to toe. When the orc had been breathing, he'd been more than enough to handle Dunk. Now that he had the hellish powers of a vampire as well, he'd be able to pound the thrower into a sponge, and then use him to soak up the spilled blood and wring that out into a nice brandy snifter to enjoy later with a good book.

Of course, vampires had their weaknesses as well: sunlight, running water, holy water, and wood. But where could Dunk find any of those? The sun shone brightly overhead, and it didn't seem to bother Skragger at all. Dunk suspected the vampire orc had one of those Sun Protection Fetishes that von Irongrad was known to use. Dunk didn't know what an SPF looked like, though, or if he'd be able to destroy it if he found it.

Could Dunk find an aqueduct somewhere and route the water onto the field? He might as well ask for one of those spiked steamrollers the dwarf teams used to magically show up with in the end zone. He didn't know if crushing Skragger with a machine like that would put an end to him, but Dunk would have been happy to give it a shot.

Maybe there was a priest in the crowd?

Dunk spotted an open Hacker downfield – Edgar, who was busy stomping the stuffing out of 'Rotting' Rick Bupkiss while Matt 'Bones' Klimesh tried to chew through the treeman's bark – and he had his answer. In mid-stride, he cocked back his arm and rifled the ball toward Simon, who had just broken free from Gilda 'the Girly Ghoul' Fleshsplitter.

The ball sailed high, but this presented no problem for the treeman, who reached up and snagged the ball with his upper branches. Dunk looked back to see Skragger still dogging his heels, not caring at all if the thrower still had the ball or not. This wasn't about the game anymore. At least, it wouldn't be until one of them had to be carried off the field in pieces.

'Edgar!' Dunk yelled as he sprinted toward the treeman. 'I need a hand – a branch, actually.'

'Sure thing, mate!' Edgar said. 'Just as soon as I get rid of these bloody bits of walking fertiliser!'

With the zombie under his feet pounded into paste, Edgar swung a mighty branch at the skeleton gnawing at him and scattered the creature's bones across the field. Then he turned to face Dunk and the vampire orc steaming up his wake.

'Literally,' Dunk said as he neared the treeman, 'can you break me off a branch?'

Edgar recoiled in horror. 'You're a bleeding loon! Give up one of me own limbs? What would you say if I asked that of you?'

Dunk dashed around Edgar, putting the treeman between himself and the angry, undead orc. 'I'd say, "How badly do you need it?"'

'Move!' Skragger bellowed as he circled around the treeman, trying to catch Dunk, the thrower always two steps ahead of him. 'Move, or I'll crush you to toothpicks!'

'Just you bloody well try it!' Edgar said. It swatted the vampire orc back with a swing of a long, solid branch. The effort laid open Skragger's cheek.

Skragger reached up and felt the hole in his face, then gazed up at the treeman, his eyes wide with terror.

'Tackle him!' Dunk shouted.

'I'm not really built for such things, mate,' Edgar said, 'not being able to bend at the – Whoa!'

Knowing he only had split seconds to act, Dunk barrelled into Edgar from behind. Already overbalanced from leaning forward to smack Skragger, the treeman toppled on top of the vampire orc and pinned him to the ground.

The scream Skragger let loose would have been enough to curdle Dunk's blood, but the roar of the crowd drowned it out. The thrower knew he didn't have much time to act. In moments, the orc might figure out he could turn to mist if he wanted to. Maybe he couldn't when he was pinned under a fallen tree. Maybe he could. But Dunk didn't want to find out the hard way.

Dunk leaped over Edgar and found himself face to face with Skragger. Blood surged from the orc's pale lips as he tried to find enough air in his lungs to curse each and every one of the Hackers to their last dying days.

Dunk reached down and grabbed the vampire by his helmet. He tried to pull it off, but the damned thing was strapped on tight enough to be like an extension of Skragger's skull.

Skragger finally cleared his throat enough to spit a mouthful of someone else's blood into Dunk's face. The thrower nearly gagged, but instead he gritted his teeth, grabbed Skragger's helmet by the face guard and started to twist.

'Think you're tough?' Skragger howled. 'Think you can kill me? I'm already dead!'

Dunk ignored the vampire orc's ramblings and kept twisting the helmet as hard as he could to one side. Skragger fought him every inch of the way, but Dunk had the position and the leverage he needed. He put one last burst of strength into his effort, and the report of a loud crack from Skragger's neck rewarded him.

'Won't stop me!' Skragger growled as Dunk continued to twist. 'Can't kill the dead!'

Dunk knew Skragger was right, that what he did here would only be a temporary measure, but he didn't care. As long as he stopped Skragger from killing him today – and collecting his fee from the Guterfiends – he didn't mind a bit.

Dunk twisted the head around until Skragger faced him again. The vampire orc spit blood at him again. Dunk gave the vampire orc's head another twist, then another, and more, until the inevitable happened. With a final wrench of Skragger's black helmet, Dunk felt the creature's torn and shattered neck finally give. The helmeted head snapped free of Skragger's body.

Dunk bobbled the head and almost lost it. When he came up with it again, Skragger still stared back at him. 'Think this stop me?' he said. 'Nothing can stop me!'

'Not from talking, at least,' Dunk said. He got to his feet and thrust Skragger's head aloft.

The crowd loved it.

'Sensational!' Jim's voice said. 'So rarely do you get to see such a powerful rivalry end so badly for the vampire.'

'It's horrible!' Bob said, his voice heavy with emotion. 'The orc had barely been blooded. To see eternity cut so savagely short… I… I…' He sobbed for a moment, and then shouted, 'Just what is immortality for if you can't enjoy it?'

'Uh, right,' Jim said as Bob's microphone went dead. 'I think this one might have hit a little too close to home for our old friend here, folks.'

Dunk didn't care. The crowd kept roaring for him, sounding like a never-ending peal of thunder. When the noise finally started to ebb, Dunk heard a high-pitched noise piercing through it. He glanced around to find it and saw the referee standing next to a flag thrown on the Astrogranite, his face a bright red from blowing his whistle so hard.

When the ref caught Dunk's eye, he pointed a thin, green finger at the thrower, then threw his thumb back over his shoulder, toward the cheap seats in the stadium. Dunk was being tossed out of the game. This time, though, he didn't mind. He tucked the still-cursing head of Skragger under his arm – the face guard keeping the vampire orc from being able to bite him, no matter how hard he tried – and trotted over to the Hackers' dugout, smiling the whole way.

'So, son, how do you feel about your new team-mates now?' Slick asked.

Dunk sighed, and then took a sip of his Killer Lite – after all of the blood in his face today, he wanted something smooth and easy – before he answered. After the Hackers' victory, they'd run off to the Skinned Cat again, where Dunk had rented a private room in which he and Slick could watch that night's game, a match-up between the Reavers and the Evil Gits. While there may not have been any crystal balls in the main room, the Skinned Cat's management was savvy enough to keep a few on hand for their customers with the heaviest purses.

'It's hard for me to feel bad about anyone putting down the kind of monsters you find in the Champions of Death,' Dunk said. 'Most of them will be up and running about again the next day anyway.'

'Too true,' Slick said. 'And, hey, the Hackers made it to the Blood Bowl finals for the second year in a row. Not too shabby!'

'Only with the help of the Far Albion Cup. I can't feel much pride in that.'

Slick sighed. 'It's part of the game, son. Every team does everything it can to tip the scales in its favour. You think the Champions of Death would do any different? Or the Gits? Or the Reavers?'

Dunk frowned. 'I don't object to the cup helping us win so much as how it does it. It turns us into a team of merciless killers. I feel it when I'm out there on the field too: a whispering in the back of my head urging me to kill any foe in my path.'

'Is that so bad?'

'It's a game, not a battle. According to the teachings of Commissioner Roze-El, Nuffle sent us the rules for

Blood Bowl to end the eternal series of wars that once wracked this world. Now, instead, of fighting those wars, we play Blood Bowl, and the people who would have been the foot soldiers in those battles cheer us on.'

'I thought you didn't believe in any of that stuff.'

Dunk raised his eyebrows and glanced down at the table. 'I don't. But whether I believe the godly bits about the story or not, it's true, isn't it? We don't send thousands of troops to war against each other any more. We just watch Blood Bowl on Cabalvision. Maybe it satisfies some deep need for violent conflict we all have. Maybe it just distracts us so we can't be bothered with other things like border skirmishes or invasions. Either way, it works out the same in the end.'

He rubbed his chin a moment before he continued. 'But the Far Albion Cup, it doesn't want that. It digs into your head and screams for total annihilation. If it could, it would find a way to lead us all into war instead, leading an undefeatable army to conquer the entire world.'

'Seriously?' Slick said, his eyes wide.

Dunk took another sip of his beer.

'Well then, son,' Slick said. 'Maybe getting the Reavers to lose a game isn't really enough, is it?'

Dunk drank deeply this time. 'No,' he said, 'not really.'

'What did you end up doing with Skragger's head, anyway?' The halfling shuddered as he tried to change the subject. 'I'd rather he never reported in for the Champions' line-up again.'

'I know what you mean,' Dunk said, grateful to talk about anything but the Far Albion Cup for the moment. 'Even decapitated, the cruel bastard just wouldn't shut up. He kept threatening me. "Just wait till I heal.", "Put me down so I can bite you.", "Scratch my nose".'

'So, did you?'

Dunk grinned. 'I gave him to Cavre.'

'You thought he wanted a talking trophy to put on his mantel?'

'I don't know. He came to me and asked for it.' Dunk shrugged. 'Why not?'

'Why not, indeed!' the Gobbo said as he slid into the room.

Slick scowled. 'The sign on the door says, "Private".'

'Does it now?' the Gobbo grinned as he pulled up a chair next to the halfling and sat down. 'I never did learn how to read or write. Nasty habits that waste your time and tend to leave evidence lying around all over the place.'

'What do you want?' Dunk asked.

'A woman who truly understands me.' The Gobbo's grin told Dunk this was far down on his list of desires. 'Or at least one who could suck the fire out of a dragon's belly through its nose.' He cackled at his own joke.

'Really, though, I came here so I could brief you on your mission.'

'What mission?' Slick asked, standing up in his chair so he could stare the Gobbo straight in the eyes.

'The game the kid's going to throw after the Reavers lose this match.' The Gobbo laughed in Slick's face. 'I always collect my winnings.'

The halfling started to protest, but Dunk cut him off. 'He's right. If he manages to pull it off, I'll keep my end of the bargain.'

The Gobbo grinned at Slick as he sat back in his chair. 'It's always a pleasure to do business with such a gentlemen. With some of the others, I have to resort to blackmail to get them to hold up their side of a deal. I can see I won't have to do that with your client.'

'Right,' Slick said sarcastically, giving Dunk a disappointed look the young thrower managed to ignore. 'I'm so proud.'

'So who's your plant?' Dunk asked, keeping his eyes on the crystal ball. 'I'd guess Breitzel from the way he's been playing.'

'And you'd be right, kid.' The Gobbo clapped Dunk on the back. 'I've been grooming him for years. When the GWs cleaned house at the end of the last season, they only got about half of my guys. Breitzel hadn't done much of anything for me up till then, and he slipped right through their fingers.'

'How fortunate for you,' Slick said.

'Hey,' the Gobbo said, 'joke all you want, but that little scandal almost put me out of business. I considered going back into defence contracting for the Empire instead, but hey, I gotta have some sense of decency left.'

Dunk stared at the bookie for a moment before he realised he wasn't kidding. He decided to ignore the implications. 'You really think Breitzel can sway the game? He's not exactly the Reavers' star player.'

The Gobbo snorted. 'It doesn't take much to tip a game one way or the other, kid. All he has to do is fumble the ball at the right moment. Just like that!'

Dunk looked at the crystal ball and saw Breitzel drop the ball deep in the Reavers' own territory. An ogre with the nickname 'Kill! Kill! Kill!' emblazoned across his back scooped it up and zoomed into the end zone. Breitzel made a feeble attempt to tackle the creature but got knocked flat on his rear for his trouble.

'Don't you guys have the sound up on this thing?' the Gobbo said. 'I want to hear the play-by-play.' He reached out for the ball, but Dunk intercepted his warty hand and pushed it away.

'I hear enough of Jim and Bob while I'm on the field,' he said. 'I don't need more of them while I'm off it.'

The Gobbo gloated as the score flashed up on the ball. 'It doesn't matter. That's the only stat that counts. Gits: 3, Reavers: 1.'

'It's only the first half,' Slick said. Dunk couldn't believe it, but he found part of himself rooting for the Reavers too. Even though he knew it would destroy his plan to save Dirk and Spinne from death at the Hackers' hands, he hated the thought that he would owe the Gobbo a favour – and he shuddered to think what he might have to do to pay it off.

'Look, kid,' the Gobbo said to Dunk as the thrower stared into the crystal ball. 'This is your last chance. If the Reavers win this one, they'll face the Hackers in the finals. What will you do then?'

Dunk groaned, and then buried his face in his hands. 'It looks like I'm going to get the chance to find out.'

'How's that, kid?' the Gobbo said. 'This game's in the bag. And once it's over and official, you and me will need to talk.'

Dunk reached out and tapped the crystal ball's base. Sound burst out of it then, carrying Jim and Bob's voices over the crazed roar of the crowd.

'Did you see that, Jim? Absolutely amazing!'

'How could I miss it? I haven't seen that much blood since – well, since we had lunch!'

'If I was a Reaver, I think I'd be careful about how hard I played from now on – nothing but a hundred and ten percent! Otherwise, just look what could happen.'

'Too true, Bob. We've heard reports from the Reavers' camp that team captain Dirk Heldmann was struggling with some discipline problems, but it looks like those might be over.'

'What happened?' the Gobbo said, elbowing Slick out of the way so he could get a better view of the crystal ball.

'Let's see that again, Jim! This is one for the highlights tonight!'

As Dunk, Slick, and the Gobbo watched, the camra panned from Kill! Kill! Kill! celebrating his touchdown in the end zone to just a few feet away where Spinne stood beating the tar out of Breitzel. Then the traitorous Reaver stripped off his helmet and started using it as a weapon to bash Spinne over the head.

Spinne went down trying to defend herself from the helmet with her arms, but Breitzel kept hammering at her. Then, just as the traitor was about to start kicking in Spinne's ribs, Dirk came out of nowhere and smashed Breitzel into the Astrogranite. Then he crawled on top of the traitor's back and used both hands to smash the man's unprotected head into the ground until the fight left him for good.

'I think,' Slick said, turning to the Gobbo, whose face looked greener than ever, 'you just saw a flaw develop in your master plan.'

CHAPTER TWENTY-SIX

'HERE'S TO THE Hackers!' Pegleg said, raising a glass to the team assembled around the long table he stood at the head of. 'And here's to the Blood Bowl championship!'

Dunk joined the others in clinking their glasses together, but he remained silent as the others cheered. Looking around, he knew that some of his friends felt the way he did, but they all somehow managed to put up a better front. Normally, everyone enjoyed a Monday-evening feast after a victory. Even the players nursing injuries wore irremovable smiles. Tonight, though, the grins pasted on the faces of the new players were savage ones, and the old guard – which Dunk thought ironic to find himself in – wore their smiles as masks.

'So, mate,' Simon said, clapping Dunk on the back, 'how about those Reavers? What do you think about going up against your brother and your girlfriend again, just like last year?' The Albionman still wore the bandages that kept the disease he'd contracted from advancing any further. So far, they seemed to be doing all right, even though Simon's eyes looked like he'd been drinking almost constantly since the game had ended the night before.

'Not much,' Dunk said, not bothering to keep his voice down. 'I don't care to see strangers get killed, much less family and friends.'

Simon grinned, and his breath stank of liquor and rot. 'Well, that's what it's all about, though, in'nit? Beating down the other team? By *any means necessary!*' He staggered forward, and Dunk put out a hand to steady him. 'In'nit that what happened to me? It's all part of Nuffle's damned game.'

'Maybe,' Dunk said. He glared around the room at the new players, and then at Pegleg and Olsen, who sat chatting at the far corner of the table, enjoying their goblets of wine. Dunk noticed that Pegleg didn't seem to want to be anywhere near him at the moment, and given the sourness of his mood he could understand why. 'Maybe. But I don't have to like it.'

Simon put a wet-wrapped hand on Dunk's shoulder. 'You don't have to like it, though, do you? You just have to get the job done. Make the money for the team. For our investors. Earn that pay cheque. And we're paid well indeed, aren't we?'

'I suppose so.'

'Don't you think that'd take the sting off it? You know, dull the edge of the knife a bit as they keep digging it into you week after week? I used to think it would. I did.'

The catcher sat back and hugged his arms across his chest. 'But look at me now. A prettier picture you'll never find, eh? All my money, and what good does it do me now. If I get killed out there…' Fat, hot tears rolled out of Simon's eyes, but the wrappings on his face instantly soaked them up. He choked back the raw emotion in his voice. 'Well, what good will all that gold do me then?'

Dunk put a hand on Simon's shoulder to steady him, to lend his friend some strength. Before he could say a word, though, a voice rang out in what Dunk realised was a silent room, but for Simon's soft, muffled sobs.

'Mr. Hoffnung,' Pegleg said. 'I wonder if I might have a word with you before our first course arrives.'

'Please,' Dunk said, gesturing for the coach to talk.

'In private, if you don't mind,' Pegleg said, an uneven smile on his face.

'Can't we speak openly in front of my team-mates?' Dunk asked. 'Let's be honest as we can about this. I have nothing to hide.'

Pegleg shot a glance at the wizard sitting next to him. Olsen nodded at him grimly, and the ex-pirate grimaced at the thrower. 'All right,' he said, but he hesitated to continue.

'What is it?' Dunk asked.

'Can I ask what it is you've said to turn Mr. Sherwood into a sobbing mess?'

Dunk started to respond, but Simon put a gauze-swaddled hand on his arm. The Albionman gawked at the coach for a long, painful moment, then spoke. 'He said nothing to me. Nothing. What would anyone have to say to a creature like myself to set me off, whimpering like a battered schoolgirl?' He sprang to his feet so fast Dunk feared he might burst through his wrappings. 'Look at me!' he screeched. *'Look at me!'*

Guillermo came up behind Simon then and grabbed him by the shoulders. The catcher spun into his friend's arms and let him lead him out of the room, his sobs still wracking his frame, his feet squishing along the floor as he walked out.

Dunk glared across the table at the ex-pirate and the wizard hunched over next to him, whispering something in his ear. Edgar and M'Grash stared back and forth at them both, waiting for something to happen. Cavre gave Dunk an appraising look, his face betraying nothing.

The others – the new players who'd joined the team in Bad Bay – all looked to Pegleg for direction. Dunk knew that they'd turn on him and tear him to pieces at a word from their coach.

Olsen refused to meet Dunk's glare.

'Can you explain that, Mr. Hoffnung?'

'Explain what, coach?'

Pegleg leaned forward in his chair. 'Just why a game-hardened veteran like Mr. Sherwood might dissolve into tears like that in your presence.'

A dozen snappy answers rolled through Dunk's brain: the body odour of the new team-mates; the fact that the bar was out of Killer Lite; the godlike presence Dunk exuded that made all lesser men reconsider their manhood; the fact that M'Grash had asked Simon if he could borrow a tissue. But he cast all those aside. It was time to tackle the truth.

'It's the Far Albion Cup,' Dunk said. 'We need to get rid of it.'

Pegleg rolled his eyes theatrically, and the new players all began to mutter murderous somethings under their breath. 'Are we on to that again, Mr. Hoffnung? Honestly, it's become tiresome. The cup is staying with us, and that is that.'

Dunk got to his feet. 'Coach, you can't tell me that you don't see what that thing has done to us. Maybe you don't feel it when we're in the middle of a game – you're in the dugout, not on the field – but it's turned us into a pack of killers, a bunch of murderous thugs.'

Pegleg laughed maliciously at this. 'And how am I supposed to tell the difference between that and a regular Blood Bowl team?' he asked. Then realisation spread across his face. 'Oh, yes! I know now. It's that we've finally started *playing* like a regular Blood Bowl team.'

The new players and Olsen all laughed along with Pegleg's mirthless joke. Only M'Grash, Edgar, and Cavre did not join in.

'The cup was behind Simon's disease too,' Dunk said. 'He has the same illness as those cultists we took it from.'

'Mr. Sherwood should consider that an abject lesson in taking care in picking his flings – and his friends.'

Dunk shook his head. 'Don't you remember Deckem and his crew? The cup brought us those recruits. What makes you think this lot here isn't just as tainted?'

The new players all scowled at Dunk then, and a shudder ran through him as he realised just how outnumbered he was. This wasn't a time for him to think about his personal safety though. He had to convince Pegleg to give up the cup.

'This is about your brother, isn't it?' Pegleg said. 'Him and that Schönheit woman you've been seeing.' He shook his head. 'Were we in the navy, I'd have you flogged for consorting with the enemy.'

'They're players on another team.'

Pegleg smashed his hook into the table at that. 'They are the *enemy!*' he thundered. 'We must do everything we can to *crush* the enemy. That's the difference between winners and *losers!*'

'You didn't have a problem with that before,' Dunk said.

'We lost before, didn't we, Mr. Hoffnung? I let my urge to be a good coach – a friend to my players – blind me. I don't want to be a *good* coach any more.'

'Congratulations,' Dunk started. 'You're well on your–'

'I want to be a *great* coach! I want to lead my team to win *championships!* The Bad Bay Hackers have been losers for the *last* time! And I will kill anyone who stands in my way!' Pegleg snarled at his star thrower before he lowered his voice to a menacing whisper. 'Including you.'

'Ah, gee,' Blaque said as he strode through the door, Whyte walking alongside him. 'What's the chance of him being named coach of the year with an attitude like that?'

Whyte shook his head as they stood next to each other at the foot of the table, just to Dunk's right. 'Not good,' the pale-skinned elf said. 'Not good at all.'

'Faith!' Olsen said, standing up at the other end of the table, a little rickety from too much drink. 'We don't believe anyone invited you two blackguards to this party. Leave, or we'll throw you bastards out ourselves.'

'We're here for the cup,' Blaque said. 'And we're not leaving until we get it.'

The sound of chairs scraping backward as every player in the room rose to his feet filled the otherwise silent air. The two Game Wizards stared down the table at the assembled Hackers, and Dunk wished, not for the first time tonight, that he was someplace else.

'Stand down, men,' Pegleg said to the players and to Olsen as well. 'Stand down. It's far too late for the GWs to do anything about the cup at this point – or for anyone else.' He glared directly at Dunk and just down behind him.

Dunk turned to see Slick peeking in around the edge of the dining hall's doorway. He waved a little hand at the thrower, than disappeared before Pegleg could snarl at him again.

Pegleg looked at the Game Wizards, his gaze flicking back and forth between the two. Then he gestured for the players to all sit. The new ones sat without further comment. Edgar and M'Grash waited to see what Dunk would do. When he sat down too, they complied as well. Cavre was the last to take his seat.

Olsen remained standing. When Pegleg nodded at him, he turned to the GWs and said, 'Once a team has taken full possession of the cup, there is nothing that can be done to break it, short of disbanding the entire team.'

'You think that can be arranged, Mr. Whyte?'

'Certainly, Mr. Blaque. Mr. Murdark tells me he's behind us a thousand percent. Something about how killing off one team after another could be construed as harmful to the long-term prospects of the sport.'

'You wouldn't dare,' Pegleg said. 'We're just about to play in the Blood Bowl finals. You'd rob us of that? The fans would scream foul for decades to come. Anyway, you can't do it. It's not your choice.'

Blaque grimaced. 'True enough, but we don't have to disband the team to stop you. We just have to refuse to let you play in the game.'

'Or else what?'

'Or else Wolf Sports won't broadcast it.'

Pegleg snorted at this. 'Blood Bowl has a dozen networks lined up to take your place.'

'Just give us the cup, Captain Haken,' Blaque said. 'It doesn't have to go down this way.'

'It won't do you any good,' Pegleg said. 'It's been *attuned* to us – to me. And it can only be destroyed if Olsen here drinks his own blood from it.'

It was Blaque's turn to snort as he drew his wand. 'We'd be happy to make that happen. What would you think about that, Mr. Whyte?'

'Icing on the cake,' the pale elf said, pulling his wand from his robes as well.

'We'll fight you lot to our dying breath,' Olsen said, his wand appearing his in hand. 'Destroying the cup would kill us dead. You two only have your jobs on the line. For us, it's our life.'

'Sounds like more icing to me,' Blaque said.

'Hold it,' Dunk said, surprising even himself. 'Wait. It doesn't have to happen like this.'

'We don't mind,' said Blaque. 'Really.'

'Belay that,' Pegleg said. His soft words carried throughout the room. 'If you destroy the cup, you'll seal my fate as well.'

'Come on, coach,' Dunk said. 'It won't be that bad. We made it to the finals last year on our own, without the cup. We can do it again, and we can *win*.'

The ex-pirate shook his head sadly. 'Aye. Maybe we could at that, Mr. Hoffnung, but I've made my choice and bound myself to the cup in every way possible.'

A shiver ran down Dunk's spine. 'What are you talking about, coach?' He knew he didn't want to hear the answer. He didn't want to, but he had to anyway.

Pegleg held up his hook and used his good hand to pull back that sleeve, baring the maimed arm. There, in the crook of his arm, he wore a large, white bandage, a few dark spots on it where the blood had seeped through.

'With Mr. Merlin's help, I bled myself into that damned cup of his, and then I drank my fill.'

'Bloody, bleeding hell,' Edgar said. 'That's not like someone tapping a tree, mate. You could have lost your life.'

Pegleg wore a sad smirk on his lips. 'It wasn't my life I lost, Edgar, but a part of my soul. That special piece of me now resides in the cup, right alongside the spirits of Mr. Merlin and Miss Retmatcher.'

Dunk wanted to vomit. 'Why, coach? Why would you do that?'

Pegleg arched his eyebrows. 'A cup – even one as magnificent as that one – is a thing. As such, it can be lost, stolen, or otherwise go missing, just as it once did for over five hundred years.' He bowed his head for a second before continuing on. 'I – I couldn't let it just leave me. I couldn't take the chance it might be taken from me. It's been a long, hard road to find myself standing just outside the winner's circle, waiting for you mates to pour the cooler full of Haterade over me. I just couldn't let it get away.'

'You are terrified of water, coach,' Cavre said quietly.

'For that, Mr. Cavre, I think I might have been able to make an exception. Just once.'

'So, if the cup is destroyed?' Blaque said.

'I'll die, along with Mr. Merlin here,' Pegleg said. 'And you'll have our deaths on both of your heads.'

'What do you think about that, Mr. Whyte?' Blaque said.

'Sounds like cherries on top.'

The two wizards levelled their wands at Pegleg and Merlin.

Without a word, the players all got back on their feet. The threat was clear. If the GWs made a move, the Hackers would make sure they'd pay.

Dunk's mind flashed back to his last up-close encounter with battle magic, when Olsen had flung that lightning bolt down the tunnel and fried all those deadmen. He didn't know what it would be like to be in a room with three powerful wizards letting loose their worst on each other, but he didn't want to find out.

Dunk smashed Blaque in the face with his elbow, and then spun past him to drive his fist into Whyte's gut. Both wizards went down hard, and before they could realise what – or who – had hit them, he snatched their wands from their hands.

'You'll regret that,' Blaque said, his nose bleeding freely. Whyte sat on the ground, still struggling to catch his breath.

'The only thing I regret,' Dunk said, 'is not doing it sooner. This doesn't have anything to do with you two or Wolf Sports. It's a Hacker matter, and the Hackers will handle it – alone.'

Blaque's fists started to crackle with raw power. 'We don't need the wands, you know. They only help us to focus our spells. We could still bring the roof of this place down around your – urk!'

With the GW still in mid-threat, M'Grash plucked him from his feet and held him dangling in the air. Edgar did the same with Whyte, who struggled not at all, still trying to get air back into his lungs. The tree-man held him out at arm's length, dangling him there in his smaller branches as if the wizard might some-how be toxic.

'Listen to Dunkel,' M'Grash said directly into the dwarf's face. 'Dunkel, Dunkel, Dunkel smart!'

Blaque nodded, then spat in the ogre's face. 'You and your barking mad friend there had better put us both down, or I'll–'

M'Grash dropped the dwarf, who landed with a hard thud. Edgar did the same with Whyte.

'Toss them out of here,' Dunk said. 'If they come back, toss them farther – like into the Reik.'

'I hear they have forty-foot-long, carnivorous, mutant eels that glow in the dark living in that river,' Slick said, poking his head back in the room.

'They'd be lucky to have those find them first,' said Dunk as M'Grash and Edgar stormed out of the room, toting the GWs under their arms like a couple of footballs come to squirming life.

'So, Dunk,' Pegleg called out from the far end of the table, 'are we good then?'

Dunk glanced back over his shoulder at the ex-pirate standing there next to Olsen. 'Not by a million yards,' he said. 'I'm trying to make sure we don't all get killed, because you know that's what it'll come to next, right? As soon as word gets out that we have some kind of magic goblet that keeps us from losing, someone else is going to want it. Even if they can't get it, they'll settle for killing us, just so their team can have a fighting chance.'

'How can you be so sure?' Olsen asked.

'It's what we would do.' With that, Dunk strode out of the room, leaving Pegleg alone with Olsen, Cavre, and their murderous new recruits.

CHAPTER TWENTY-SEVEN

'WHAT IN ALL the hells did you do?' Lästiges said as she stormed into the Hackers' practice.

Dunk held up his hands, both as a gesture of innocence and so he could defend himself if the reporter decided to attack him. She looked angry enough to chew through both M'Grash and Edgar to get to him, and Dunk noticed that his two gigantic friends had scurried out of the way when they had seen the woman coming.

'I'm not sure what you mean,' Dunk said slowly, trying to calm Lästiges down.

'With Dirk and Spinne!' she said. 'Are you out of your walnut of a mind?'

Dunk winced and glanced up at the golden camra hovering over the reporter's head. 'Is this on the record or deep background?'

'What were you thinking, talking to the Gobbo?' A vein in her normally flawless forehead pulsed so hard and fast that Dunk feared it might burst.

'Ah, that,' Dunk said, putting an arm around the woman and gathering her to him as he walked her off the field. None of the Hackers knew about Dunk's attempt to cut a deal with the bookie, and he wanted to keep it that way. 'Let's talk somewhere more private.'

Lästiges let the thrower escort her from the practice field. He waved at the other players, and said, 'I'll be right back,' to Cavre. Pegleg and Olsen, who'd been chatting at the other end of the field stopped to watch the two leave, but they said nothing to stop them.

Dunk steered Lästiges through an open doorway in the high, stone wall that surrounded the place, which Pegleg had paid an exorbitant fee to rent. Most of the money went not for the field itself, which was fine enough, but to pay for the strict security surrounding the place. With the Blood Bowl finals looming ahead, Pegleg wanted to make sure his players didn't have to worry about angry rivals or overexcited fans. Dunk wondered for a moment how Lästiges had got through, but he realised that other reporters wandered in and out of the place all the time. Her press pass must have been enough.

As they strode into the empty locker room, Lästiges jabbed an elbow into Dunk's ribs and strode away from him while he rubbed his injured side.

'What was that for?' he asked.

'You deserve a lot worse,' she said, spinning to wag a long, crimson-nailed finger at him. 'Making a pact with the Gobbo to get Breitzel to ruin the Reavers' game? You might as well have cut a deal with Khorne himself!'

Dunk put his hands up in front of him again, just in case. 'I only meant–'

'It doesn't – that doesn't – I don't *care* what you *meant* to do. "I just wanted to save my little brother and my little girlfriend". Well, you screwed that up and everything else too!'

'Hey, at least I tried. I did *something*. You were with us when we found the cup. You know how it works. You know what's going to happen in the finals. We're going to systematically *murder* the Reavers on the gridiron.'

'I know,' Lästiges said, putting a hand to her forehead, perhaps trying to hold that pulsing vein back from bursting. 'I tried to tell them that. I know you did too, but what you did…'

'It didn't work anyway,' Dunk said, surprised at his own bitterness. A part of him had been relieved to not end up beholden to the Gobbo, but he would have gladly been so if it would have saved Spinne and Dirk's lives. 'It doesn't matter.'

'So you think,' Lästiges said. 'They know all about it.'

Dunk felt a chill in his gut. 'Who?'

'Spinne and Dirk! Once Breitzel came to in the infirmary, they really put the screws to him. He gave them the Gobbo's name.'

Dunk closed his eyes and shook his head.

'They found the Gobbo in the Skinned Cat, and he skavened you out. Then they came looking for me.'

Dunk opened his eyes again and stared at Lästiges. 'Why? You had nothing to do with that.'

'I *know!*' she said, frustration marring her picture-perfect face. 'But do you think they believed that? They thought I was in on it with you from the beginning.'

Dunk frowned. 'I'll talk to them,' he said, more to himself than Lästiges. 'I'll set this right.'

'How?' she asked. 'How? They told me they never want to talk to you again. If it weren't for the finals, they'd never want to *see* you. Or me either!'

'I just wanted to keep them safe.'

'Then you should have quit the game and got them to do the same! Do you know what the average life expectancy of a Blood Bowl player is? Two and a half seasons. And all the immortals who have been playing for hundreds of years throw off that curve! Most players never make it past their first season, either from injury or death or post-traumatic stress.'

'What's your point?' Dunk didn't like where this was going.

'It's a dangerous game. Lethal.' She was screaming now, tears flowing, and makeup running down her face. 'If you were so damned worried about living forever, you should have stuck to something easier – like fighting dragons!'

Neither of them said anything for a moment, letting the heavy silence hang between them. The only sound came from Lästiges's sniffles.

'Are you through?' Dunk asked.

Lästiges nodded, wiping her face and nose with a handkerchief she pulled from her pocket.

'I will make this right,' he said. 'I will make sure Dirk knows you had nothing to do with it. I don't know how to make up for what I did – best intentions aside – but there's no reason for him to be mad at you. I'll set him straight.'

'You'd damn well better,' she said. She'd stopped crying now, but her voice was still raw. She opened her mouth to add something else, but it seemed – for the first time since Dunk had met her – she had nothing to say. She gave him a wan smile, then turned and left through the locker room's back door.

Dunk rubbed his face with his hands and turned around to get back to practice. Cavre stood in the doorway, watching him, an easy smile on his face.

'You are having a difficult time, Mr. Hoffnung.'

Dunk started to say something flippant, then just nodded and said, 'Too true.'

'This is a hard time for us all. The captain isn't himself these days. The grip of the cup on him is strong. It gets stronger all the time. If we do not break this grip before the end of our season, I fear it may have him for all time.'

'You don't think it's already too late? Didn't he give the cup part of his soul?'

Cavre nodded. 'But the cup has yet to live up to its end of the bargain: to give the captain a Blood Bowl championship. There is still a chance, although it is small.'

Dunk looked into Cavre's deep, brown eyes. For a man as tough as the veteran was, they were soft and filled with hard-won wisdom.

'I wondered which side you'd come down on,' Dunk said. 'Pegleg's or mine.'

Cavre smiled at that, his teeth glaring white against his dark skin. 'I'm on our side, Mr. Hoffnung, the Hackers. That includes us all.'

'Does that mean I can count on your help.'

The blitzer reached up under the right spaulder on his practice armour – the Hackers only used the spiked variety during official games – and withdrew a small pouch made of finely worked links of steel. He tossed it to Dunk, who snatched it from the air.

'I thought you might find this entertaining if not useful,' he said. Then, before Dunk could open the pouch, he turned and trotted back onto the practice field.

Dunk hefted the pouch in his hand. It felt heavier than he thought it should. He opened it and dumped the contents into his other hand.

Out tumbled a miniature Hacker helmet, green and gold with the crossed blades forming the well-known Hacker H. Dunk smiled, thinking the team captain had made him a souvenir, a symbol that showed he would always be part of the team, a handy charm for good luck.

Then the helmet moved in his hand.

Dunk bobbled the helmet for a moment, but he managed to fight his first instinct: to drop the helmet on the floor and stomp it flat. If it had come from anyone other than Cavre, he might well have, but he trusted the veteran as much as he did anyone.

He held the helmet carefully between his index finger and thumb to inspect it. Other than its size, it seemed an exact replica of a Bad Bay Hacker helmet, right down to the chinstrap, which was fastened and seemed to be holding something inside.

Dunk turned the helmet around so he could peer in through the faceguard, and he saw a pair of tiny, eyes staring back at him out of a pale green face. The level of detail on the face stunned the thrower. How could anyone make something look so real? The face looked so lifelike, so real, so… familiar?

Then Dunk placed the face. 'Skragger?' he said.

The face opened its mouth and snarled, in a squeaky, high-pitched voice, 'You're dead, Hoffnung! Dead!'

Dunk froze, staring into the tiny eyes that shot daggers of hatred at him.

'You hear me? Get my hands on you, you're dead!' Even in a voice strung higher than that of a tiny child, the bile in the tone could not be mistaken.

Dunk blinked at the shrunken face in his hand and then threw back his head and laughed. He laughed loud and long and in a way he didn't think he had since he'd first laid eyes on the Far Albion Cup back in that damned camp in the cursed Sure Wood. Fat, happy tears rolled down his reddening cheeks until he realised he could barely breathe and had to sit down on the locker room floor. He coughed and hacked some air back into his lungs until he could start to laugh again, and he did.

'Ah, Cavre,' he said as he stuffed the little helmet back into its pouch, which muffled the tiny voice until it fell silent. 'I don't know how anyone could top that.' He wiped his face dry as he pulled himself to his feet, and then shook his head as he trotted back out onto the practice field. "Hands," he chuckled. 'That's priceless.'

'I'M SO GLAD you agreed to talk with me,' Dunk said.

Spinne shut the door to her suite of rooms behind him as he entered. 'A little voice in the back of my head tells me this is a bad idea, but I never did listen to that when it came to you.'

Dunk smiled his thanks at her. She gestured for him to take an overstuffed chair in a sitting area near the room's bay window, and he did. She sat down on a matching couch opposite him, a low, empty table between them.

'Lästiges came to see me,' Dunk said. 'She was pretty upset.'

'So was I.' Spinne looked out the window. The sun shone bright over the rooftops of Altdorf, glinting off the spires of the Emperor's castle in the distance.

'But you're not anymore?' Dunk tried to keep the hope in his heart from creeping into his voice.

'I've had some time to reflect.'

'I'm sorry,' Dunk said. 'I just wanted to say that. I really am. I didn't mean to – I don't know. I just wanted to keep you safe.'

Spinne nodded. 'I get it. I understand what you were trying to do.' She shook her head. 'You just picked one of the worst possible ways to do it.'

Dunk started to speak, and then snorted softly. 'I don't want you to die on me. Every other team we've faced while we've had the Far Albion Cup has suffered seventy-five percent or more casualties. I couldn't bear to watch that.'

'Then don't. Quit the Hackers. Leave it all behind.'

'That's not much of a solution – unless you leave the game too.'

Spinne gave Dunk a thin-lipped smile. 'I like playing Blood Bowl. How many other women do you know who can say that? I'm a bit of a freak, I'm afraid.' She looked out the window again. 'It's the only thing I'm really good at.'

'Aren't you going to ask me why I did it?'

Spinne looked confused. 'What do you mean?'

'Why I made the deal with Gobbo? Why I tried to rig your game against you? Or don't you care about any of that?'

She smirked in a not unkind way. 'Go ahead. Tell me.'

'I love you,' he said. 'I don't want to lose you.'

'Is that right?'

'You don't believe me?'

Spinne lowered her head. 'Oh, I believe you, Dunk. I love you too. But for two people who love each other so much, we haven't seen much of each other lately.'

The conversation had taken a right angle from where Dunk had thought it was headed.

'I – I guess you're right about that, but after the massacre in that game in Magritta, Pegleg decided to take the team to Albion.'

'And you decided to go along.'

'Yes.'

'Even though you knew it would mean we might not see each other for months on end.'

Dunk sighed. 'Spinne, we often go for weeks at a time without seeing each other. We live in different cities. We play games in different parts of the world. About the only time we can guarantee we'll see each other is during one of the four major tournaments.'

'Two of which, you missed this year.'

'I couldn't do anything about that,' Dunk said. 'I was in Albion. We got stuck there longer than I'd hoped. I – I almost died trying to get us out of there.'

'That's your excuse? "I almost died". That's supposed to make me feel better.'

Dunk groaned inwardly. 'I'm just trying to tell you what happened and why.'

Spinne nodded. Dunk could tell she was getting reading to say something big, so he kept quiet. When she spoke, she held her voice even and calm. When she looked at him, though, he could see her eyes were red and swollen from struggling to dam the flood of tears behind them.

'I don't know if we should be together anymore.'

Dunk sat back in his chair, stunned. 'What?'

'I don't know if we should be together anymore.'

'I heard what you said. I meant, why?'

'We're not really together as it is, are we? We've seen each other only a handful of times in the past nine months.'

'I write to you all the time.'

'And I love your letters,' she said. 'I really do, but they are cold comfort on a lonely night. I can't curl up next to your letters.'

'But–' For a moment, Dunk couldn't think of anything with which to follow that up. 'Are you just trying to get back at me for what happened in your last game?'

Dunk hoped the answer would be yes. If so, maybe Spinne would change her mind when the season was over and she'd had a chance to calm down. Maybe all he needed to do was to stall, to get her to wait breaking it off with him a week or so more, until she had time to forgive him in her heart.

'No,' she said, and Dunk's heart cracked.

'I've had some time to think about this,' she said. 'At first, I wasn't sure. I mean, I was angry with you, really angry, and that was hard to separate out from how I feel about you.

'But I've been having these thoughts for a long time. When you didn't make it to the Dungeonbowl, I understood. After all, the Grey Wizards went with the Reavers again, so your slot was gone. And you were still stuck in Albion.'

'I heard about what happened in the Far Albion Cup Final just as we were getting ready to leave for the Chaos Cup. I thought maybe I'd finally see you then, but when you got back to Bad Bay, you just stayed there. Then I saw that Cabalvision special with you in bed with Lästiges, and I had all these horrible feelings toward you. I hated you then – at least as much as I could.'

'But that was all innocent,' Dunk said. 'You know that.'

'Sure,' Spinne said, 'but it didn't change how I felt. In the end, I realised I wasn't jealous of Lästiges so much because she'd been found in bed with you but because of how much time she'd got to spend with you. She was with your team throughout that entire trip of yours to Albion, and I didn't get to see you once. Not once.'

'But, Spinne,' Dunk said, 'I'm back now – for good. All that stuff – going to Albion, disappearing for months at a time – that's all over with now. It won't happen again.'

'You can't know that,' Spinne said. 'You could have said the same thing to me this time last year. Would it have made a difference in what you did?'

Dunk swallowed hard as he considered the question. He knew, just looking at Spinne, that he had to be as honest as possible. She'd see straight through any lie he might tell, and not giving enough thought to the issue would be just as bad.

'I don't know,' he finally said. 'I'd like to think that I might have done things differently, but I didn't expect things to work out that badly back then. I don't suppose I would if the same situation came up again either.'

Spinne gazed at him solemnly, and all Dunk could think about was how much he just wanted to lose himself in her blue-grey eyes and leave the rest of the world behind.

'Thank you,' she said. 'If you had lied or dissembled or…' She put her hand to her mouth to cut off a sob.

'I think you should leave now,' she said.

'Oh. Okay.' Dunk got up to go, unsure what he should do. He wanted nothing more than to put his arms around her, to comfort her, to tell her everything would be all right, but he couldn't tell if that was what she would want. He took a tentative step toward her, and she turned away.

'Just go,' she said, pointing at the door as she gazed out the window at the wide world beyond. Outside, a flock of white birds caught the rays of the evening sun flaring through their feathers.

'Can I come to see you again?' he asked. 'There's a team dinner tonight, but I could—'

'No. Never.'

Dunk gaped at her as his heart crumbled into bright, sharp shards in his chest.

'Good-bye, Dunk,' she said. She never took her eyes from the window.

Dunk started to reach out to touch her strawberry-blonde hair, but then pulled his hand back. Without a word, he turned and left. He heard her begin to sob as he closed the door behind him.

CHAPTER TWENTY-EIGHT

'NUFFLE'S CODPIECE,' SLICK said as he poked Dunk in the shoulder. 'I was afraid I'd find you like this.'

Dunk tried to raise his head to respond to the halfling, but he only succeeded in turning his face to the side instead. He spotted his agent standing there, a stern look on his face, but sideways – and more than a little blurry – and the image made him laugh.

'Hi, Slick!' Dunk said. 'Glad you could make it! I'm a…' He fumbled for the right word for a moment, and then held up his hand with his thumb and index finger just a little bit apart. He tried to adjust them to the right distance apart, but they just kept moving about. Or were they? He decided to not worry about it any longer. 'Weeeee bit drunk.'

'Uh, really, son?' Slick said. 'Is that why M'Grash here sent word for me in the middle of the night? I thought perhaps you might be hosting a surprise birthday party for me.'

Dunk sat back in his chair and grinned as the world swam around him. 'It's your birthday? Why didn't you say so? Hey, bartender!' He swung his arm up to signal for another drink, but he lost track of it somewhere between where it started and where he wanted it to end. He looked down and saw Slick's hand holding his arm down.

'It's not my–' Slick shook his head. 'Never mind. I hear you've had a rough night.'

'What do you mean?' Dunk said. 'I'm having a *great* time. I'm just out here celebrating the Hackers' success with my biggest friend and my smallest one.' He put his arm around M'Grash here.

The ogre looked down at the halfling and shrugged as innocently as he could. 'Dunkel drunkel.'

'You got that right, big guy!' Dunk said, chucking M'Grash in the shoulder. 'Living large and loving it!'

'You're breaking training, son,' Slick said. 'If we get you back to your room soon, Pegleg might be none the wiser. I know an apothecary who has a hangover remedy that will keep you from wanting to commit ritual suicide tomorrow morning to end the pain. It's expensive, but you can afford it.'

'What do I care about Pegleg?' Dunk asked. 'He's gonna fire me right before the big game? His star thrower? Ha!'

'Dunkel not happy,' M'Grash said, with a frown big enough to bring down the entire room. 'He very sad.'

'I can see that,' Slick said. 'What in the Emperor's name has he been drinking?' The halfling peered over the rim of Dunk's stein.

'Tastes great!' M'Grash said.

'Less filling!' Dunk answered.

'Now, you two, don't start up with that!'

Dunk and M'Grash laughed so hard they had to hold each other up for fear of falling off their stools. Then M'Grash started to tip over backward, and there was nothing that Dunk could do about it. They toppled over and landed hard in an area behind them that mysteriously had no tables in it.

'All that's holy!' Slick said, climbing up on the table so he could look down at the two friends tangled on the floor. 'You two better be more careful. You're going to kill someone.'

'Don't worry about that,' the barmaid said as she righted the steins that had fallen over along with Dunk and M'Grash. 'After the first time, we got smart and moved the other tables away to give them some space.'

Slick looked aghast. 'How long have you two been at this?'

Dunk glanced at M'Grash, the crash to the floor seeming to have sobered him up just a bit. 'What day is this?' he asked.

'Beerday!' M'Grash shouted in reply.

'Beerday?' Slick said. 'When's beerday?'

Dunk grinned at M'Grash, and the two answered in unison. 'Every day is beerday!'

Slick slapped a hand over his face and groaned.

Dunk continued on. 'A wise man once said... he...' The thrower stopped and turned about, looking all around him. 'Hey,' he said, a note of true concern in his voice. 'Where'd my little friend go?'

'I'm right *here*,' Slick said, exasperated.

'No.' Dunk stopped hunting for a moment to look at the halfling and giggle. 'Not you. The *little* guy. M'Grash? Have you seen him?'

'Uh-uh, Dunkel.' The ogre set his heavy stool – more of an ironbound bench, really – back into position and recovered what was left of his drink. He threw back the dregs in one clean move, and smiled wide, showing his tusks all the way down to his teeth.

Then he started to gag.

M'Grash's hands went to his neck as he coughed and hacked, searching for some way to clear his throat. Dunk swept around behind him and started to beat him on the back with a barstool. Thunk! Thunk! Thunk!

On the fourth or fifth thunk, the ogre hacked hard, and something small and slimy came flying out of his throat to land on the table in front of him. Dunk scooted around from behind his friend to see what it was.

There, lying in the centre of the table, lay Skragger's shrunken head.

'You bastards!' Skragger's squeaky voice railed at Dunk and M'Grash. 'Good thing I don't breath, or I'd be dead! Stuck in a beer and can't damn drink!' He howled in despair.

M'Grash kept coughing through it all. The barmaid brought him another keg-sized stein on a wheeled cart, and he snatched it up, draining half of it in a single draught.

'Ha!' Skragger said. 'Almost killed you, didn't I? *That* woulda been worth it!'

Dunk picked the shrunken head up by the sides of its helmet and peered into its eyes. 'So,' he said, 'what was it you said before, wise man?'

'Beer is proof the gods love us and want us to be happy!'

'Right,' a new voice said, 'and hangovers are proof they hate us and want us to wish we were dead.'

Dunk's head snapped around, and his eyes struggled to focus on the speaker. 'Funny,' he said, dropping Skragger's head in the middle of the table, 'that sounded just like my old teacher.'

The man standing before Dunk was shorter than him and slighter of frame. He wore his silver hair cropped short over sparkling, grey eyes. His cloak was the same drab colour as the stone walls of the buildings in Altdorf's ancient quarters. He shook his head as he looked at Dunk, a mixture of disapproval and understanding blended in his face.

'Lehrer?' Dunk said, unsure his drunkenness wasn't leading him astray.

'Hey, kid.' The man's raspy voice made Dunk feel like a child again, and he felt aware of how silly he'd been acting. 'I'd ask you how you're doing, but it seems pretty clear.'

'Sit down,' Dunk said, signalling the barmaid to bring them each a drink. 'Stay a while.'

'I don't have long,' Lehrer said, even as he took the offered seat. 'The Guterfiends will miss me if I'm gone for too long.'

'Who?' Slick asked. 'What's this all about?'

Dunk, far more sober now, pointed at Lehrer and said. 'This man was in·charge of security at my family's estates since before I can remember. He taught me everything I know about fighting, with weapons and without.'

Dunk put a hand on Slick's shoulder and his other on M'Grash's arm. 'This is Slick Fullbelly – my agent – and M'Grash K'Thragsh, one of my best friends. And that,' he pointed to the miniature helmet in the centre of the table, 'I believe you may already know.'

'Is that…?' Lehrer leaned over to peer in through the tiny helmet's faceplate. 'Skragger?'

'Help me, you bastard!' Skragger squeaked.

Lehrer gaped at Dunk and his friends. 'How? Did one of you manage this?'

Dunk shook his head. 'It was Cavre. Something he learned how to do during his childhood in the South-lands. He says his father was some kind of witch doctor.'

'You lead an interesting life,' Lehrer said, staring at the thing inside the little helmet.

'You don't know the half of it,' said Slick.

Lehrer grunted at this. 'Sadly, I don't have the time to sit here and catch up the way I probably should. The Guterfiends – who now occupy Dunk's family home *and* who cover my wages each week – have apparently decided to give up on their little vendetta against Dunk here. At least, for now.'

'Why's that?' Dunk asked, hoping he didn't sound as drunk as he still was.

'After you knocked Skragger's head off, they went nuts. Would have been ready to burn down half the town if they could've guaranteed you'd be in it. They hadn't said anything to me or anyone else on the old staff up till that point, but they were hopping mad and started screaming how much they wanted you dead.'

'So why don't I have a dozen assassins chasing me through town?'

'Wiser heads prevailed. Someone who knows you well convinced them that targeting a Blood Bowl player during the week before the final game wasn't such a bright idea. Said you would all be on high alert, and there was no way a killer could get through such tight security.' He looked around the Skinned Cat and then back at the drunk Dunk. 'Sorry to see I was so wrong.'

'What happens after the game?' Slick asked.

Lehrer nodded at Dunk. 'The Guterfiends declare open season on him. This time around, they might just put a price on his head and let all comers take a shot at it. Hiring the best guy for the job didn't work out so well for them last time.' He looked down at Skragger's head. 'Did it?'

Skragger cut loose with a string of curses so evocative that they made Dunk blush. Unperturbed, Lehrer reached over and picked up the head, then dropped it into his beer, where it sank to the bottom, the liquid instantly muffling the creature's complaints.

Then Dirk walked in. He strode through the front door of the bar as if he owned the place. The regulars in the crowd hailed him, shouting, 'Dirk!' in unison. He waved back at them all, not cracking a smile, despite the adoration in the room. When his roving eyes found Dunk, though, he made straight for him.

'Spinne told me she broke it off with you. I thought I might find you here,' Dirk said, looking around the room and then down at Dunk with a hint of disgust. 'And maybe like this.'

Dunk waved at his brothers – all three of them.

Dirk scanned the faces of the others at the table. When his gaze lighted on Lehrer, who sat looking straight ahead, stone-faced as ever, his face fell into a sneer. 'But I never thought I'd find you with *him*.'

'Hey,' Dunk said, his head clearing again as he picked up on the implied threat of violence in his brother's voice. 'Aren't you happy to see an old friend?'

'Friend?' Dirk said, his eyes wide in disbelief. He looked down at Lehrer and bared his teeth as he took a half a step back. 'You can't be that drunk, can you?'

'Hey,' Dunk said, getting a little offended himself now. 'What's the matter with you? Don't you know who this is? He's one of the good guys.' Then he pointed at Dirk. 'You, I'm not so sure about. I try to save your life– '

'By trying to arrange for my team to lose in the semi-finals!'

'–and do I see any gratitude? A word of thanks? Maybe my methods were bad– '

'Try "the worst ever".'

'–but my heart was in the right place.' He shook his head which started to swim again at the movement. 'All I wanted was to keep you and Spinne safe, and what do I get for that? My girlfriend dumps me, and my brother won't talk to me!'

'I'm talking to you now,' Dirk said, barely containing his anger. For a moment, Dunk wondered if his brother might launch himself across the table at him.

'So,' Dunk said, mustering every ounce of seriousness he had in him, 'what do you have to say?'

Dirk glanced down at Lehrer and edged away from him again before stabbing a finger at Dunk. 'You are an idiot! This is the same kind of crap you used to pull when we were growing up. "Dirk's too young. I need to protect him".'

Dunk started to protest, but Dirk cut him off.

'I'm not finished.' He grimaced and took a deep breath before starting again.

'I'm not a kid any more. I was never that much younger than you. I'm a Blood Bowl star with more seasons under my helmet than you.' He leaned over the table and stabbed his finger into its surface to punctuate every word. 'I don't need your help.'

Dunk looked into his brother's eyes and saw how badly he'd hurt him. The two had grown closer over the past two years than they had been since they were children racing around the ramparts of the family keep. Until then, Dunk hadn't realised how much he'd missed that, the connection, and the sense of brotherhood that nothing could sever.

And now he'd done something that seemed like it might cut that bond forever.

'Look,' Dunk said. 'I was only trying to help. I tried to warn you and Spinne about the Far Albion Cup. Damn it, I've been trying to warn Pegleg too, and nobody seems to want to listen. But this isn't some kind of game. We're not playing knights and orcs back in the keep anymore. It's deadly and real.

'If you had just listened to me–'

'Maybe if you'd stop telling me what to do–'

'Maybe if you didn't need it so badly–'

'That's it!' Dirk roared, stepping back. 'It's bad enough that you colluded with the Gobbo to harm my team. That I can forgive. Other teams do it all the damn time. Why shouldn't you, no matter how "noble" your reasons?'

'See,' Dunk said, 'that's all I was trying to say.'

'But to come in here and see you sitting at a table with *him*…' Dirk glared over at Lehrer, who still stared off into space, ignoring him. 'That's just beyond the pale.'

Dunk narrowed his eyes at Dirk. 'What are you talking about?' He glanced at Lehrer, then back at Dirk. 'That's our teacher, our mentor. One of our oldest friends. He was best friends with our parents since before we were born.'

'And now he works for our family's most hated enemies, the Guterfiends,' Dirk said. 'Doesn't that tell you something?'

Dunk stared at his brother. 'So do most of the old staff. What else could they do? In case you don't recall, our parents abandoned the place. All those people needed to eat, Lehrer included.'

Dirk cocked his head at Dunk. 'You don't find it the least bit odd that the Guterfiends would keep on our "loyal family friend" in any capacity? Much less putting him in charge of their security?'

Dunk couldn't believe what he was hearing. 'He just came here to warn me about how the Guterfiends plan to put a price on my head after the Blood Bowl finals. They paid Skragger to try to kill me in the semis.'

Dirk stared at Dunk. 'And who do you think hired Skragger in the first place?'

Dunk's eyes snapped toward Lehrer, but the man had already bolted from his seat and started sprinting for the door.

'Stop him!' Dirk shouted.

Dunk stood up to take after Lehrer. He wanted an explanation for all of this as much as anyone. His legs wobbled beneath him as he did, but he refused to let that stop him.

M'Grash overturned the table as he stood up and started after Lehrer. Only a step later, though, he tripped over the chair that Dirk had left behind as he raced ahead of them.

As the ogre stumbled toward the door, he flailed his arms wildly to try to regain his balance. When it became clear this wouldn't work, M'Grash leaped for the door instead.

Getting in and out of the Skinned Cat had always been a challenge for M'Grash. Despite how much he liked the place, which always surprised Dunk, it wasn't built for ogres. The chairs were too small – he'd broken three before the innkeeper had supplied him with a wide bench instead – the tables too fragile, and the steins too small. He'd taken to ordering his drinks by the cask and prying one end off with a battered nail.

So, when M'Grash's off-balance bulk smashed into the door that he'd had to so carefully navigate in the past, he didn't fit through it smoothly. In fact, he didn't fit through it at all. He only got his head and shoulders through the frame before he became stuck.

As the ogre howled in pain and frustration, Dunk clambered over his back to see what had happened to Lehrer and Dirk. When he reached the street, though, by sliding down over M'Grash's massive head, they had already disappeared.

Dunk cursed as he peered down both directions on the long street, which wound like a snake through the worst part of Altdorf. He couldn't even tell which way they'd gone.

In his frustration, Dunk roared up at the distant sky. 'How can this day get any worse?'

Then a small strange voice came from behind. 'Dunkel help?'

Dunk turned to see M'Grash struggling to free himself from the doorway. The ogre had landed hard enough to wedge himself in good, though, and at such angle that he couldn't find the kind of leverage he needed to force himself free.

'Don't worry!' Slick called from inside the tavern. Dunk could just see his eyes peering over the top of the fallen ogre. 'I've already got an order placed for every bit of butter they have in the place.'

The halfling cocked his head and grimaced as he evaluated M'Grash's plight once again. 'I might have to ask for every bit of cooking oil and rendered fat too.'

Dunk groaned, then reached out and patted the whimpering M'Grash on the top of his head.

CHAPTER TWENTY-NINE

'AND THERE'S THE kick-off to start the championship final in this year's Blood Bowl Open!' Bob's voice echoed out over the stadium, barely audible over the cheers of the crowd.

Dunk raced down the field with three goals in mind. Winning the game came last, he realised, which he felt odd about. Before that, he wanted to survive the game. He'd never been one of those 'team first' players, and if there was ever a sport meant for people to watch out for themselves Blood Bowl was it.

In last year's game, he hadn't felt that way at all. Back then, he'd cared about everyone on the team, with one exception: Kur Ritternacht. Given that Kur had wanted to kill him, Dunk couldn't see how he should feel bad about that.

This time around, though, he only gave a damn about M'Grash, Edgar, Simon, Guillermo, and Cavre. The rest could all go back to rotting in whatever hell they'd come from, as far as Dunk was concerned. He was pretty sure the new players felt the same about him, if they gave him any thought at all.

Dunk slammed into the first Reaver he saw, knocking him to the ground. The thrower had learned a lot in the two seasons he'd been playing the game. Things like, 'Hit lower than the other guy,' stuck with you once you'd been trampled a few dozen times.

'The Hackers are in rare form tonight!' Jim said. 'They've become a truly brutal team. Most of the credit has to go to team coach Captain Pegleg Haken. Can this really be the same team the Chaos All-Stars tore to pieces nine months ago?'

'Not really,' Bob said. 'Only five players survived that rout. Even though they all started the game tonight, there's more fresh blood on the Hackers' side of the field than old.'

'That, and their new team wizard, of course. He's been in the Hackers' dugout since day one of their return. His wand and a little item known as the Far Albion Cup seem to have turned the Hackers' fortunes right around. Perhaps our roving reporter can tell us something more about it. Lästiges?'

Dunk spun out of the grasp of one Reaver and straight into another. He hammered at his foe twice with his fists, and then rammed the crown of his spiked helmet at the man. The Reaver let go of Dunk's spaulder then, and the thrower ran back into the thick of the game again. As he did, he saw Lästiges's face appear on the Jumboball. She stood next to Pegleg and Olsen in the Hackers' dugout, the Far Albion Cup itself on display behind them.

'Thanks, Jim! I'm down here with Captain Haken and his team wizard, the legendary Olsen Merlin. What can you gentlemen tell us about the Far Albion Cup and the effect it's had on the team?'

'Bugger off,' Olsen said. 'We're working here.'

Pegleg stepped between the wizard and the camra, a nervous yet charming smile on his face. 'What my esteemed colleague means to say, Miss Weibchen, is that the cup is more of a symbol of what our team has gone through over the past season rather than any kind of an object of raw, magical power. Our players have become fond of it and look on it as a mascot more than anything else.'

'So this cup is your team mascot?'

'Well, yes, I suppose it is.' Pegleg's smile widened, becoming both more charming and more nervous.

'I think that says more about their off-field antics than I ever could.' Lästiges gave the camra a savage smile, while Pegleg blustered in the background. 'Back to you, Jim!'

Dunk smiled behind his faceguard as he jinked to the right, dodging past a Reaver intent on slamming him into the Astrogranite. He spotted Dirk upfield from him, the ball tucked under his arm as he scrambled away from M'Grash.

Dunk hadn't talked to Dirk since his younger brother had chased Lehrer from the Skinned Cat. When Bob had called Dirk's name out while introducing the Reavers before the start of the game, Dunk had sighed with relief. At least Dirk was all right, although Dunk still wondered about Lehrer. Was he really the traitor Dirk said he was? After the game ended, he knew that he had to find out, even if it meant digging through the darker parts of his family's history.

Dunk charged towards where he thought Dirk would end up if he managed to elude M'Grash. Sure enough, his brother burst out of the pile-up in the middle of the field and swung right, looking downfield for a target. As Dunk closed in on him, he cocked his arm back to throw.

Dunk lowered his shoulder and smashed into Dirk's middle. As he did, he knew that Dirk would get the pass off, but Dunk wanted to make him pay. Also, he thought if he tackled Dirk that might get the new Hackers to leave him alone and go after other prey.

'What an amazing throw!' Jim said. 'As Hoffnung takes him down, Heldmann hurls the ball downfield in a perfect spiral. Schönheit reaches out for it under double coverage and pulls it down! She stiff-arms Schmidt and races into the end zone. Touchdown, Reavers!'

'First blood,' Dirk shouted over the roar of the crowd. 'So much for your damned cup.'

'What an amazing play!' Bob said. 'The Reavers state their case to be crowned champions by picking up a quick score.'

'But they seem to have bought their point with blood,' Jim said. 'I count one, two, three Reaver casualties on the field already, and they don't look like they're getting up.'

'What about Hoffnung and Heldmann? The two brothers seem to have taken each other out. If so, that would be an anticlimactic end to their sibling rivalry!'

'Dunk?'

'Yeah, Dirk.'

'You can get off me now.'

'Oh, right!'

Dunk scrambled to his feet, and the crowd saw that he and Dirk were all right. He stuck out his hand at Dirk, and his brother took it.

'Brothers forever,' Dunk said.

Dirk grinned despite himself.

The fans roared in approval.

Some of those roars, though, soon turned to screams.

'It seems something's happening in the cheap seats on the south side of the stadium,' Jim said. 'Most times the fans are happy to watch the action unfold on the field, but it looks like that might not have been enough for that crew. But, wow, I don't think I've seen that much blood spilled in the bleachers since, well, when was your last birthday party, Bob?'

'I stopped celebrating them decades ago, but even in my youngest years the festivities never looked much like that. What's going on over there?'

As Dunk trotted back to the Hackers' end of the field, he looked up at the Jumboball, which showed the view from a camra focused on the top of the stadium's south side. Dozens of people had stripped off their clothes and were going at each other in an amorous way. Each person's skin had a greyish cast, except for the red rash that seemed to crawl along under the flesh.

In the centre of it all stood a rat-on-a-stick vendor with a particularly bad rash and a wild look in his yellowing eyes. He stood flinging his product into the stands, yelling for people to eat the free grub, despite the fact that – other than his food harness – he was buck naked and, from all appearances, thrilled about it.

'You know, Bob, I don't think those are your standard rats-on-sticks there.'

Dunk raced back down the field to the Reavers' side. A few of the players getting into position there tried to slow him down, but he slipped past them until he reached Dirk, who was preparing to kick off the ball.

'Hey,' Dirk said. 'How long have you been playing this game? You're not allowed back – Hey!'

Dunk snatched up the football and then raced back toward the middle of the field. When he reached it, he slung his arm back and then unleashed a powerful throw that sailed through the air and caught the rat-on-a-stick vendor square in the chest. The spike on the tip of the ball pierced the vendor's heart, but he stood there for a moment, shocked at his imminent death and raging against it. Then his heart burst from his chest, showering all those around him in bloody gore.

'That's one way to handle an unruly fan,' Bob said. 'Remind me to never get Hoffnung angry at me – or to have ball-proof glass installed in the announcers' booth.'

'Maybe our new friend Olsen Merlin could tell us something about what's happening here. Lästiges?'

'Yes, Jim, I'm here in the Hackers' dugout with–' The reporter cut herself off with a horrified scream.

Dunk looked over at the dugout and saw that all of the new Hackers had dashed into it. One of them dashed out of the place with the Far Albion Cup tucked under his arm. A few others chased after him, Lästiges stretched out among them, struggling to free herself with all her might.

Then something in the dugout exploded, and the other new Hackers came flying out of the place, some in more pieces than they'd been in while entering.

The fans in the stands behind the Hackers' dugout started to scream. Then they stampeded away from the field, trying to escape whatever horrible thing they expected to issue forth from the dugout. Their path took them up and south, directly toward the fans in the higher stands, whose skin writhed faster and redder now than ever. Most of them had stripped off their clothes, and either set to scratching at their rashes, heedless of the amount of blood they drew, or started to copulate with any vaguely compatible person they could find, whether infected or willing or neither.

'Lästiges!' Dirk shouted. 'Lästiges!'

Dunk watched his brother call for his fellow Reavers to follow him and then chase after his woman, who the new Hackers were dragging into the stands.

Dunk did not see how this could end well. All he knew was he had to put an end to it – now. He sprinted toward his team's dugout. As he did, he bumped into a Reaver he almost ran over. When he turned to snarl at the Reaver, he recognised her instantly.

Spinne.

'Come with me,' he said as he grabbed her hand.

'Let me go!' she shouted, pulling her arm free. 'I need to help Dirk.'

'He doesn't stand a chance!' Dunk spun back and held Spinne by her spaulders. 'You can't fight a sickness like that. You have to kill it at its cause.'

'And where do you think we could find something like that, Dunk?' Spinne's tone told Dunk she'd lost all patience with him. Despite that, he needed her to trust him just a minute more.

'Follow me!' he said, offering her his hand once again. To his amazement, she took it.

When they reached the dugout, Dunk planned to skirt around it and take off into the stands after the traitor Hackers carrying away the Far Albion Cup. Instead, Slick charged up the stairs at them, a Hacker helmet on his head.

'We need to get the cup!' Slick shouted at Dunk. 'Olsen says it's the only way.'

'Figures,' Dunk said, glaring up into the stands. The players absconding with the cup were already a few rows into the seats. If they reached the exit only a handful of rows ahead of them, they could disappear in the tunnels beneath the stadium and beneath Altdorf itself. If so, Dunk might never be able to find them.

Simon and Guillermo sprinted for the stands, hoping to catch the other Hackers on foot. The crowd parted before the diseased Simon, seeming to identify him as a mummy and fearing such a creature's legendary rotting touch. Dunk could tell, though, that the two would never catch up with the other Hackers in time.

'M'Grash, Edgar!' Dunk shouted, pointing up to where the cup moved through the stands. 'I need to get up there fast!'

'How the bloody hell do you propose we manage that, mate?'

'Throw me?'

Edgar looked at Dunk. 'I don't think I could. You're a bit bloody large for a trick like that. The wee one here,' he pointed at Slick, 'sure, but you're full grown.'

'Not you alone,' Dunk said, gesturing to Edgar and M'Grash with open hands. 'Both of you. Pick me up and swing me up there – together.'

'That's a bloody long way, mate. Could kill you dead.'

Dunk glanced up at the cup as it neared the exit. 'No other way,' he said, putting out his arms for the two giant creatures to grab. 'Let's do it!'

'On three,' Edgar said as it picked up Dunk's left arm and leg and M'Grash got the right.

'Three?' the ogre said. He nearly dropped Dunk as he tried to scratch his head, but he recovered in time to keep the thrower from hitting the dirt.

'You know: one, two, three?' The treeman narrowed its glowing green eyes at M'Grash. 'Oh, bollocks. Just throw him when I say "Go". Ready?'

The two swung Dunk back and forth.

'Set?'

Back and forth.

'Go!'

Back and gone.

Dunk held his breath, waiting for something horrible to happen, for Edgar to let him loose and M'Grash to keep his hold, for someone to pull his arm from its socket. Instead, he zoomed off, arcing high into the air over the stands.

When he reached the apex of his flight, Dunk realised he had no way to steer himself. The best he could do was keep his arms out and his legs together, like a diver reaching for the water of a pool. At that moment, far too late to do himself any good, he questioned how desperate he must have been to get the cup that he not only let someone throw him through the air like a stone from a catapult but had actually asked for it.

Fortunately, M'Grash and Edgar had excellent aim.

As Dunk came soaring in at the Hackers with the Far Albion Cup, he brought his armoured arms and knees to his front and bore down hard on his targets. He slammed into the back of the bestial Hacker holding the cup, a black-furred man-shaped thing with crimson horns shaped like those of a ram. His helmet had been carved back to expose these horns while still offering some protection to the back and sides of his head. His face, however, stood unguarded.

The ram-horned Hacker never saw Dunk hit him. One moment, he was dashing for the exit, gloating at how easy it had been to wrest the cup away from Pegleg and that old wizard. The next, he'd been knocked unconscious as Dunk's full, armoured weight slammed into him from behind and drove his face into the last of the cut-stone steps he'd been about to top. The impact cracked his horns off near their bases and forced the jewel-encrusted cup to go flying from his hands.

While Dunk's target absorbed most of the momentum from his fall, Dunk still had to roll past the ram-horned one, tumbling end over end like a football dribbling along the gridiron after a kick-off. He came to a halt in the frame of the exit, the cup there next to him, within arm's reach. His every bone aching, he snatched up the trophy and scrambled to his feet.

Dunk stared down the stairs behind him and saw five of the new Hackers gaping up at him. 'Hi, guys,' he said, hefting the cup in his hands.

He glanced around and saw that the fans in this part of the stadium had all fallen silent in shock. While the stands to the south were filled with people screaming for their lives – images of Dirk and the Reavers closing in on Lästiges and her kidnappers flashed across the Jumboball – here everyone stood in shock at how Dunk had taken out his ram-horned team-mate, staring with open mouths at him and his bejewelled cup.

Dunk pointed down at his five team-mates and shouted to the crowd, 'Are we going to let those cowards get out of here alive?'

The fans roared in glee and converged on the bestial Hackers like a school of sharks on bloodied prey. One of them, a wolf-faced man with a snout full of vicious teeth that he'd somehow already bloodied, squirted free from the crowd and charged Dunk.

The thrower considered throwing the cup back toward the field, but he doubted he'd be able to manage it with its unwieldy shape. Instead, he grasped the cup's neck with both hands and brought it down on his attacker's green and gold helmet with all his might.

The cup dented the crown of the wolf-faced Hacker's helmet, knocking him to the ground. When Dunk brought the cup back up to strike again, though, only the cup's base and neck came back. The bowl of the cup had snapped off its mooring with the impact.

Dunk winced and held his breath as he waited for the sky to open up and for the magical energy stored in the cup to strike him down for destroying it, but nothing happened. It seemed it would take more to break the cup – and its curse – than that.

The wolf-faced Hacker staggered to its feet and snarled at Dunk with a sound that wasn't human, its reddish eyes glowing with evil and hate. The thrower pulled back his arm, the cup's neck still in it, hoping he could use it to bash the Hacker's helmet in even farther.

Instead of charging, though, the wolf-faced Hacker reached down and scooped up the rest of the cup. It glittered in his hands as he let loose a jackal's mad cackle of triumph.

Dunk steeled himself for the creature's attack. The wolf-faced creature lowered itself on its powerful haunches and launched himself straight at the thrower. Dunk went low, hoping to knock the creature back, just as he would have on the field. As he did, he saw his attacker sail straight over his head.

At first, Dunk felt relieved that he'd avoided the assault, but he wondered how he'd been able to do that so easily. Then he realised that the wolf-faced Hacker hadn't been coming at him at all. The cup in his hands, he'd been trying to escape, and Dunk had let him.

Dunk spun around and saw the Hacker sprinting for the exit, about to reach the tunnel that led through the stands to open daylight beyond. Then something green, yellow, and white burst out of the crowd and tackled the creature, knocking the both of them tumbling down into the tunnel.

CHAPTER THIRTY

DUNK RECOGNISED THE new assailant right away: Simon Sherwood. The diseased catcher had made good time through the crowd and caught up with the bestial Hackers and the cup at just the right moment.

Forging his way through the fans had been rough on Simon. He bled from a dozen cuts, and his beer-soaked wrapping had begun to unravel, exposing his greyish skin. The red rash there seemed worse than ever, red as blood and thrashing about under his flesh like a wild animal trapped in a bag of skin. His eyes were wild with madness, far worse than those of his wolf-faced foe.

As Simon tore at the bestial Hacker with his bare hands, the creature's jaws snapped at his face and throat. An unintelligible roar sprang from his lips, and Dunk knew that the illness now had him entirely, body and soul. He moved only on instinct and the final coherent thoughts that had driven him to pursue the cup and bring down anyone who held it.

Dunk wondered if Simon would have attacked him if the catcher had arrived a moment earlier and found the thrower with the cup still in his hands. Such thoughts didn't bear more consideration at the moment. He sprinted down the tunnel after the two, but before he could catch up with them, the wolf-faced man clamped his teeth around Simon's throat and tore it out.

Simon's blood exploded from his neck as if every ounce in his veins had been under pressure. The wolf-faced Hacker choked on it and tried to sputter it away, as the rush of fluid nearly drowned him.

Dunk pulled Simon's corpse off the blood-soaked Hacker and stabbed the creature in the chest with the jagged stem of the Far Albion Cup still in his hand. The wolf-faced man clawed at Dunk as he shoved the makeshift weapon further in through the creature's ribcage, its tip hunting for his heart.

When Dunk found the pulsating muscle, he gave the broken stem a hard shove and burst the creature's organ. As the wolf-faced Hacker's life spilled out of him, Dunk snatched the bowl of the cup from under his arm and shoved him back to the ground.

When Dunk turned around, he saw Simon's corpse lying there in the tunnel, its throat somewhere else. The pallor of its skin contrasted sharply with the quarts of blood that had covered it and soaked through the wrappings and splashed across the pavement around it. Still, the skin was clear now and rashless, and Dunk could see a savage, satisfied smile poking through the unwrapped parts of Simon's face.

Dunk tucked the cup's bowl under his arm and raced back up the tunnel and into the stadium. The fans around the entrance cheered as he held up the bit of the Far Albion Cup he'd recovered. Dunk didn't see any of the other bestial Hackers, as if the crowd had simply and permanently swallowed them up. He spotted an official Hackers helmet on one fan's head, and a couple of fresh jerseys on some others, and he wondered whether or not they'd been there just minutes ago.

'I need to get down to the Hackers' dugout!' Dunk shouted.

The fans nearby roared their approval and held their hands high over their heads, chanting something Dunk didn't understand. He cocked his head to the side and listened, and it became clear: 'Jump! Jump! Jump!'

Dunk remembered all too well what had happened the first time he'd been given up to the tender mercies of the crowd. At last year's *Spike! Magazine* Tournament, he'd been chucked into the stands after scoring his first touchdown, and the fans had body-passed him up to and over the top edge of the stadium in Magritta. He'd survived the fall but been beaten half to death by the owner of the food cart on top of which he'd crashed.

'Jump! Jump! Jump!' The fans kept chanting at him, and the words took on a hypnotic beat, encouraging him to discard caution and experience and trust them, to comply.

'Jump! Jump! Jump!'

Dunk peered down at the field and wondered if he could hurl the Far Albion Cup all the way down to the gridiron, where perhaps Edgar or M'Grash could catch it, but he couldn't spot them anywhere. When he looked over to where the Reavers had leaped into the stands to save Lästiges, though, he saw the two gigantic players forging their way through the sea of people to lend Dirk and his fellows a hand – or branch. Someone rode on the ogre's back, beating away infected fans with what looked like a long, thin fragment of a bench. It was Spinne.

Dunk stared back down the aisle that led through the bleachers to the field below, and fans crammed it from one end to the other. If he wanted to get down to the dugout before the entire stadium succumbed to the threat of the Sure Wood cultists, he had only one choice, only one chance.

'Jump! Jump! Jump!'

Dunk wrapped both arms around the bowl of the Far Albion Cup and made a mad dash for the fans standing right in front of him, chanting and stomping their feet so hard he could feel the vibrations through the ground around him. When he reached them, he launched himself into the air and gave himself over to their will.

Half-a-dozen sets of hands snatched Dunk from the apex of his jump and hoisted him farther into the air. Once he lay level upon them, or nearly so, the fans started to pass him around, from one set of outstretched hands to another.

Dunk closed his eyes rather than succumb to the vertigo that threatened to overcome him as he spun about over the heads of the crowd at terrifying speed. He clutched the cup to himself as hard as he could, keeping it from the occasional hand that grabbed at it and tried to tear it from his grasp. Then he felt the hands near his feet disappear, and he felt as if he were sliding off a cliff of ice, and into the great, wide unknown.

Unable to restrain himself any longer, Dunk opened his eyes, which gave him just enough time to bend his knees before he hit the ground. To his astonishment, he knelt crouched on the Astrogranite of Emperor Stadium instead of lying crushed and dying on the pavement just outside. He leapt to his feet, holding the cup over his head, and raced toward the dugout.

The crowd cheered.

'Can you believe it?' Bob's voice said. 'Hoffnung has the cup!'

'That's what I called dogged determination,' Jim said. 'Here the Reavers – including his brother – and two of his team-mates are fighting to the death to rescue our roving reporter from a breakout of a lethal disease that causes madness in all it touches, and Hoffnung's busy making sure the Hackers still have the magic artefact they need to ensure victory.'

'Too true! You just don't see many competitors that cold-hearted these days!'

Dunk dashed into the dugout and saw Cavre and Slick talking with Pegleg as Olsen railed at them all.

'This is *not* going to happen, laddies,' Olsen said. 'Not as long as we–' The wizard cut himself off as

Dunk entered. 'Ah, and here's the grand prize now, come to us in the arms of the reluctant hero. We're impressed you managed to recover it.'

'What can we do to stop this?' Dunk said, holding what was left of the Far Albion Cup before him. 'There are hundreds of people dying out there!'

'Faith, lad!' the wizard said, a strange cross between a smile and a scowl on his face. 'More like thousands. Soon, the entire stadium will succumb, we're sure.'

'You're the great wizard around here. Can't you do something about it?'

'Aye, lad, we could,' Olsen said, deadly serious now. 'But we won't.'

'What?' Dunk nearly dropped the cup.

'We could stop all this in an instant, cure the disease in even the worst of the cultists, and make everyone sing camp songs together all night long – if we wanted to. But we'd have to drink our own blood from that cup you're carrying.'

Dunk's jaw dropped. 'You're too much of a coward to face death to save thousands of people?'

'More like we don't give enough of a damn about them. If it comes down to us or them, well, it looks like it's us.'

Dunk goggled at the wizard. 'When we found you, you were ready to kill yourself as soon as you could.'

'Aye, we were. Ironic, isn't it? We suppose it's one thing to talk tough about it when it seems it could never happen.'

Olsen's wand appeared in his hand. 'And don't you go getting any bright ideas about making us change our mind. You're a good lad, Dunk, and we'd hate to see you get incinerated.'

Dunk held the cup between him and the wizard. 'You wouldn't dare. You might destroy the cup.'

Olsen snorted at this. 'That wee cup is far tougher than you give it credit for. You can bust off the base like you've already done, and still it works. You can try to break the bowl, but it can't be done, not by man nor god.'

The wizard nodded proudly at the aghast Dunk. 'When we work magic, lad, it's built to last.'

Dunk glared at the wizard. He only saw one option left, but he couldn't imagine how he might pull it off, and with each tick of the clock more and more people died – including, maybe, Dirk, Lästiges, M'Grash, Edgar, Guillermo, and even Spinne.

Then Slick hurled himself at the wizard. 'Get him, son!' the halfling said as he wrapped his arms around Olsen's leg. 'We'll force him to drink his own blood!'

The wizard swung his fist down and smacked Slick in the nose. The halfling spun backward and landed in a corner of the dugout. When he looked back, Dunk saw blood dripping from his face.

Dunk stepped toward Olsen, bringing up the cup to brain the wizard, but Olsen raised his wand and pointed it straight at him. 'Ah-ah-ah, lad. Don't think you can catch me out so–'

A helmet smashed into the side of Olsen's head, one of the spikes on the crest catching him in the temple. He slid to the floor, dead before his skull cracked against it. Cavre stood over him, the helmet's face-guard still in his hand.

'Sadly, that will not be permanent,' the catcher said, examining his handiwork. 'Unless we manage to destroy the cup before he rises again.'

'Oh, the humanity!' Jim's voice rang out.

'Don't forget the dwarves, elves, orcs, ogres, goblins, skaven – oh, hell with it! It's a bloodbath out there!' Bob said in a voice raw with emotion. Then, quieter: 'Makes me miss the old days that much more.'

'So how can we destroy it?' Dunk said. 'Any ideas?'

Slick shrugged. Cavre grimaced. Pegleg whistled innocently.

'What, coach?' Dunk said suspiciously. 'What is it?'

'Well,' Pegleg said, wincing, 'I hate to even mention it, but Olsen did suggest that, if someone whose soul was attached to the cup drank his own blood from it, well, that would destroy the cup.'

'I think we're clear on that, Pegleg,' Slick said.

'By 'someone,' I think he may have meant 'anyone,'' Pegleg said. 'Including me.'

Dunk's eyes flew wide. 'You can do that? Stop all this? What's the hold up?'

Cavre spoke low and serious. 'But, captain, won't that kill you?'

'I don't believe so,' Pegleg said, shaking his head. 'I won't live forever anymore, I suppose, but I'm not yet on borrowed time like Mr. Merlin here. He may crumble to dust, but I think I'd be just fine.'

Dunk stared at the ex-pirate. 'So what's stopping you?'

Pegleg sucked at his teeth before he spoke. 'The answer to your dreams doesn't come along every day, does it? Immortality *and* an unbeatable team? That's a dynasty built on a winning streak that could last forever.'

Cavre put a hand on Pegleg's shoulder. 'Captain,' he said, 'where's the challenge in all that?'

Pegleg bowed his head for a moment, then doffed his yellow tricorn and came back up with a rueful smile. 'Mr. Cavre, I can always count on you to set my sails in the right direction.'

With that, Pegleg drew the cutlass he always kept at his side. At a nod of his head, Carve pulled back the man's sleeve on his maimed arm, exposing the skin beneath. In a swift, sharp move, Pegleg drew the blade across his arm, and then held it over the bowl of the cup, which Dunk held under his wound.

The coach's blood dripped from his arm and pooled in the bottom of the cup. When it seemed like there was enough, Cavre used some gauze from the kit of the missing apothecary to bind the cut and stop the bleeding. Meanwhile, Dunk raised up the cup and helped Pegleg bring it to his lips.

'Prepare yourself, my friends,' the coach said. 'This could be one hell of a squall.'

Dunk tipped the cup up, and Pegleg drank deep from it, swallowing every last drop.

Dunk lowered the cup, and the ex-pirate licked the blood from his lips. For a moment, nothing happened. Then Pegleg opened his mouth and belched.

'I beg your pardon,' the coach started to say, but before the word 'beg' had left his tongue, the cup began to glow.

Pegleg stared at it and said, 'I think, Dunk, you might want to get rid of that as quickly as possible.'

Dunk leapt up the dugout's steps and looked for some place to put the cup where it had the least chance of hurting someone. Since the centre of the field was empty, he hurled it there. It bounced once on the midfield line, then rolled a short way before coming to a rest. With each passing second, it glowed brighter and brighter, until it became difficult to look at directly.

'Well, that's one way to get rid of a cursed trophy,' Bob said. 'In most parts of the stadium, leaving something like that on the ground wouldn't last–'

The cup exploded, and the noise drowned out everything else in the stadium. The force of the blast knocked Dunk to the back wall of the dugout, and for a moment everything went black.

When Dunk's vision cleared, he saw that everyone else had been knocked down but was unharmed. He stood up to peer out onto the field and saw a massive crater where the cup had last been. Out in the stands, the fans seemed mostly unhurt, slowly picking themselves up and dusting themselves off.

'Congratulations, Mr. Merlin,' Pegleg said solemnly. Dunk turned to see him poking the tip of his cutlass through the wizard's robes, which lay in a pile of ancient dust. 'You finally got your wish.'

'Nuffle's leathery balls!' Jim said. 'Have you ever seen anything so appalling in your life? Bob? Bob, where are you?'

Dunk poked his head out of the dugout to gaze up at the Jumboball looming over the stadium. The image in it panned over the higher sections of the south side of the stadium.

Only a few people stood there: a handful of Reavers, a few more fans, all of them drenched in blood. Dunk saw Edgar and M'Grash towering over the others. The camera pulled in tight on one particular Reaver who carried someone in his arms: Dirk and Lästiges for sure. But where was Spinne?

Dunk dashed out of the dugout and leapt on top of it so he could get a clear view at the stands above. 'Spinne!' he shouted. 'Spinne!' But he was too far away for anyone in that area to hear.

Then M'Grash turned around, and Dunk spotted Spinne still hanging from his back. His heart jumped back up out of the bottom of his boots and lodged itself in his throat. He vaulted over the restraining wall that kept the fans off the field and charged straight up to her, taking care not to slip in the gore as he went.

'We have some good news, Blood Bowl fans! Our roving reporter not only survived her kidnapping but is in the centre of that amazing mess down there. Lästiges, what can you tell us about what happened up there?'

The image in the Jumboball switched to show Lästiges and Dirk locked in a deep, probing kiss. It took her a moment to realise she was on camra, but when she did she pulled back from Dirk and flashed the viewers a winning grin. 'Hi, Jim!' she said. 'It's good to be back on the air.'

Dirk set Lästiges down gently, and the camra pulled back. 'It seems that the incident here in the stands was started by a cult of Nurgle related to the one in Albion's Sure Wood, to provide a distraction so that their agents on the Hackers could steal the legendary

Far Albion Cup. Little did we know how tightly their fate was tied to that of the trophy itself. When the cup exploded, so did every one of the cultists infected with the dread disease they passed among themselves. Sadly, they managed to infect a number of the fans during the game, too, along with a few of the Reavers who gallantly came to my rescue. Those brave souls were lost as well.'

'Thanks for that update, Lästiges. Um, you haven't seen Bob anywhere down there, have you?'

The camra panned to the right and focused on a vampire with thick sunglasses and slicked-back hair, dressed in a Wolf Sports jacket. He knelt in the bleachers, scooping the blood from the benches and into his mouth in wild handfuls. When he noticed the camra was on him, he turned toward it and smiled, showing his vicious fangs, and said, 'It just doesn't get any better than this!'

When Dunk reached Spinne, she slid down from M'Grash's back and landed in his arms. He started to say something to her – he wasn't sure what – but she kissed him long and hard instead. He responded in kind, and it was a long time before anyone dared to interrupt.

'IT'S LIKE KISSING your sister,' Slick said.

Dunk chuckled loud and long as he sat at the same, familiar table in the Skinned Cat again. It had been a long time since he'd felt free enough to enjoy a laugh like that. He put his arm around Spinne, who giggled too, and leaned over to the halfling and said, 'Like kissing *your* sister, maybe.'

'You leave Loretta out of this,' Slick said. 'You know what I'm saying. A draw! A tie! In the blasted Blood Bowl finals!'

'Well, we only had five players left,' said Dunk. 'And so did the Reavers.'

'So? You keep playing. Neither of those numbers are zero.'

'And there was that huge crater in the middle of the field.'

'That just makes the game more interesting.'

'And all those dead people in the stands.' Dunk peered into his friend's eyes, looking for a hint of compassion. He knew it was there, just as he also knew that Slick didn't want to show it.

'Professionals never let what happens in the stands–' The halfling scowled. 'Ah, forget it. It's over and done with, I suppose.'

'We'll get you next year,' Dirk said around Lästiges, who sat curled up in his lap. 'You were just lucky this time.'

'Lucky?' Dunk gaped. 'You call ending up in possession of a cursed trophy that nearly gets you killed time and time again "lucky"?'

'It got you into the championship game, didn't it?' Lästiges said with a grin.

Dunk sighed. 'Hey,' he said to Dirk, 'you never told me what happened with Lehrer.'

'Got away,' Dirk said around a sip of his beer. 'He's like a ghost when it comes to hiding in this city.'

'Think he's serious about the Guterfiends putting a price on my head now?'

'Do you really have to ask?'

Dunk rolled his eyes.

'Well,' Slick said, 'it's a good thing we're headed back to Bad Bay tomorrow then. We're ten players short of a full squad again, and the *Spike! Magazine* tournament is coming up just around the corner.'

'Ten?' Dunk said. 'There's only M'Grash, Carve, Guillermo, Edgar, and me left. That's five. We need eleven?'

Slick arched his eyebrows at Dunk and then at Spinne. 'You haven't told him yet?'

Dunk's heart stopped. 'Told me what?'

'Meet my newest client,' the halfling said. 'I just got her a new contract with–'

'I'm playing with the Hackers!' Spinne said, her eyes sparkling.

Dunk's jaw fell open, and he stared at Spinne as if she'd just sprouted horns from her head.

'What?' she said. 'You're not happy?'

'No,' Dunk said, shaking his head. 'To say it like Edgar would, I'm bloody ecstatic!' He leapt to his feet and dipped Spinne back in his arms for a long, lingering kiss.

All of the pain and horrors of the year melted away from Dunk in that moment. Thoughts of Deckem and his deadmen, of diseased cultists, of vampire orcs out for revenge, and even of the Guterfiends and their unknown plots all faded from his mind. As his lips parted from Spinne's, he looked deep into her eyes and said, 'This is going to be the best year ever.'

A GUIDE TO BLOOD BOWL

Being a volume of instruction for rookies and beginners of Nuffle's sacred game.

(Translated by Andreas Halle of Middenheim)

NUFFLE'S SACRED NUMBER

Let's start with the basics. To play Blood Bowl you need two warrior sects each led by a priest. In the more commonly used Blood Bowl terminology this means you need two teams of fearless psychotics (we also call them 'players') led by a coach, who is quite often a hoary old ex-player more psychotic than all of his players put together.

The teams face each other on a ritualised battlefield known as a pitch or field. The field is marked out in white chalk lines into several different areas. One line separates the pitch in two through the middle dividing the field into each team's 'half'. The line itself is known as the 'line of scrimmage' and is often the scene of some brutal fighting, especially at the beginning and halfway points of the game. At the back of each team's half of the field is a further dividing line that separates the backfield from the end zone. The end zone is where an opposing team can score a 'touchdown' – more on that later.

Teams generally consist of between twelve to sixteen players. However, as first extolled by Roze-el, Nuffle's sacred number is eleven, which means only a maximum of eleven players from each team may be on the field at the same time. It's worth noting that many teams have tried to break this sacred convention in the past, particularly goblin teams (orcs too, but that's usually because they can't count rather than any malevolent intent), but Nuffle has always seen fit to punish those who do.

TOUCHDOWNS AND ALL THAT MALARKEY

The aim of the game is to carry, throw, kick and generally move an inflated animal bladder coated in leather and – quite often – spikes, across the field into the opposing team's end zone. Of course, the other team is trying to do the same thing. Once the inflated bladder, also known as the ball, has been carried into or caught in the opposing team's end zone, a 'touchdown' has been scored. Traditionally the crowd then goes wild, though the reactions of the fans vary from celebration if it was their team that just scored to anger if their team have conceded. The player who has scored will also have his moment of jubilation and much celebratory hugging with fellow team mates will ensue, although a bear hug from an Ogre, even if his intention is that of mutual happiness, is best avoided! The team that scores the most touchdowns within the allotted timeframe is deemed the winner.

The game lasts about two hours and is split into two segments unsurprisingly called 'the first half' and 'the second half'. The first half starts after both teams have walked onto the pitch and taken their positions, usually accompanied by much fanfare and cheering from the fans. The team captains meet in the centre of the pitch with the 'ref' (more on him later) to perform the start-of-the-game ritual known as 'the toss'. A coin is flipped in the air and one of the captains will call 'orcs' or 'eagles'. Whoever wins the toss gets the choice of 'kicking' or 'receiving'. Kicking teams will kick the ball to the receiving teams. Once the ball has been kicked the whistle is blown and the first half will begin. The second half begins in much the same way except that the kicking team at the beginning of the first half will now become the receiving team and vice-versa.

Violence is encouraged to gain possession, keep and move the ball, although different races and teams will try different methods and varying degrees of hostility. The fey elves, for instance, will often try pure speed to collect the ball and avoid the other team's players. Orc and Chaos teams will take a more direct route of overpowering the opposing team and trundling down the centre of the field almost daring their opponents to stop them.

Rookies reading this may be confused as to why I haven't mentioned the use of weapons yet. This is because in Blood Bowl Nuffle decreed that one's own body is the only weapon one needs to play the game. Over the years this hasn't stopped teams using this admittedly rather loose wording to maximum effect and is the reason why a player's armour is more likely than not covered in sharp protruding spikes with blades and large knuckle-dusters attached to gauntlets. Other races and teams often 'forget' about this basic principle and just ignore Roze-el's teachings on the matter. Dwarfs and goblins (yes, them again) are the usual suspects, although this is not exclusively their domain. The history of Blood Bowl is littered with the illegal use of weapons and the many devious contraptions brought forward by the dwarfs and goblins, ranging from monstrous machines such as the dwarf death-roller to the no-less-dangerous chainsaw.

THE PSYCHOS... I MEAN PLAYERS

As I've already mentioned, there are many ways to get the ball from one end of the field to the other. Equally, there are as many ways to stop the ball from moving towards a team's end zone. A Blood Bowl player, to an extent, needs to be a jack-of-all-trades – as equally quick on the offensive as well as being able to defend. This doesn't mean that there aren't any specialists in the sport, far from it – a Blood Bowl player needs to specialise in one of the many positions if he wishes to rise above the humble lineman. Let's look at the more common positions:

Blitzers: These highly-skilled players are usually the stars of the game, combining strength and skill with great speed and flexibility. All the most glamorous Blood Bowl players are blitzers, since they are always at the heart of the action and doing very impressive things! Their usual job is to burst a hole through their opponents' lines, and then run with the ball to score. Team captains are usually blitzers, and all of them, without exception, have egos the size of a halfling's appetite.

Throwers: There is more to Blood Bowl than just grabbing the ball and charging full tilt at the other side (though this has worked for most teams at one time or another). If you can get a player on the other side of your opponents' line, why not simply toss the ball to him and cut out all that unnecessary bloodshed? This, of course, is where the special thrower comes in! These guys are usually lightly armoured (preferring to dodge a tackle rather than be flattened by it).

Throwers of certain races have also been known to launch other things than just the ball. For decades now, an accepted tactic of orc, goblin and even halfling teams is to throw their team-mates downfield.

This is usually done by the larger members of said teams such as ogres, trolls and in the case of the halflings, treemen. Of course this tactic is not without risk. Whilst the bigger players are strong it doesn't necessarily mean they are accurate. As regular fans know, goblins make a reassuring 'splat' sound as they hit the ground or stadium wall head-first – much to the joy of the crowd! Trolls are notoriously stupid with memory spans that would shame a goldfish. So a goblin or snotling about to be hurtled across the pitch by his trollish team mate will often find itself heading for the troll's gaping maw instead as the monster forgets what he's holding and decides to have a snack!

Catchers: And of course if you are throwing the ball, it would be nice if there was someone at the other end to catch it! This is where the specialist catcher comes in. Lightly armoured for speed, they are adept at dodging around slower opponents and heading for the open field ready for a long pass to arrive. The best catcher of all time is generally reckoned to be the legendary Tarsh Surehands of the otherwise fairly repulsive skaven team, the Skavenblight Scramblers. With his two heads and four arms, the mutant rat-man plainly had something of an advantage.

Blockers: If one side is trying to bash its way through the opposing team's lines, you will often see the latter's blockers come into action to stop them. These lumbering giants are often slow and dim-witted, but they have the size and power to stop show-off blitzers from getting any further up the field! Black orcs, ogres and trolls make especially good blockers, but this fact has hampered the chances of teams like the Oldheim Ogres, who, with nothing but blockers and linemen in their team, have great trouble actually scoring a touchdown!

Linemen: While a good deal of attention is paid to the various specialist players, every true Blood Bowl fan would agree that the players who do most of the hard work are the ordinary linemen. These are the guys who get bashed out of the way while trying to stop a hulking great ogre from sacking their thrower, who are pushed out of the way when their flashy blitzer sets his sights on the end zone, or who get beaten and bruised by the linemen of the opposite side while the more gifted players skip about scoring touchdowns. 'Moaning like a lineman' is a common phrase in Blood Bowl circles for a bad complainer, but if it wasn't for the linemen whingeing about their flashier team-mates, the newspapers would often have nothing to fill their sports pages with!

DA REFS

Blood Bowl has often been described, as 'nearly-organised chaos' by its many critics. Blood Bowl's admirers emphatically agree with the critics then again they don't like to play up the 'nearly-organised' bit, in fact some quite happily just describe it as 'chaos'. However, it is widely accepted that you do need someone in charge of the game's proceedings and to enforce the games rules or else it wouldn't be Blood Bowl at all. Again, this point is often lost on some fans who would quite happily just come and spectate/participate in a big fight. In any case, the person and/or creature in charge of a game is known as 'the ref'. The ref, in his traditional kit of zebra furs, has a very difficult job to do. You have to ask yourself what kind of mind accepts this sort of responsibility especially when the general Blood Bowl viewing public rate refs far below tax collectors, traffic wardens and sewer inspectors in their estimation.

Of course some refs revile in the notoriety and are as psychopathic as the players themselves. Max 'Kneecap' Mittleman would never issue a yellow or red card but simply disembowel the offending player. It is also fair to say that most (if not all) refs are not the bastions of honesty and independence they would have you believe. In fact the Referees and Allied Rulekeepers Guild has strict bribery procedures and union established rates. Although teams may not always want to bribe a ref – especially when sheer intimidation can be far cheaper.

THAT'S THE BASICS

Now I've covered the rudimentary points of how to play Blood Bowl it's worth going over some of the basic plays you'll see in most games of one variation or another. Remember, it's not just about the fighting; you have to score at some point as well!

The Cage: Probably the most basic play in the game yet it's the one halfling teams still can't get right. This involves surrounding the ball carrier with bodyguards and then moving the whole possession up field. Once within yards of the team's end zone the ball carrier will explode from his protective cocoon and sprint across the line. Not always good against elf teams who have an annoying knack of dodging into the cage and stealing the ball away, still you should see the crowd's rapture when an elf missteps and he's clothes-lined to the floor by a sneering orc.

The Chuck: The second most basic play, although it does require the use of a semi-competent thrower, which rules a large proportion of teams out from the start. Blockers on the 'line of scrimmage' will open a gap for the team's receivers to run through, and once they are in the opposing team's back field the thrower will lob the ball to them. Provided one of the catchers can catch it, all that remains is a short run into the opposing end zone for a touchdown. The survival rate of a lone catcher in the enemy's half is obviously not great so it's important to get as many catchers up field as possible. The more catchers a team employs, the more chances at least one of them will remain standing to complete the pass.